PRAISE
A DREAM TO

"Susan Ritz's debut novel, *A Dream to Die For*, is an intriguing, original mystery that had me turning pages late into the night. Ritz does a brilliant job of making us care about what happens to her characters and is a master of detail. Impossible to put down!"
> —**MICHELLE COX**, author of the award-winning Henrietta and Inspector Howard series

"Oh, what a wonderful book! It's everything I want in a mystery! A wild imagination that made me believe every word."
> —**ABIGAIL THOMAS**, author of *A Three Dog Life* and *Talking About Memoir*

"A small-town crime caper with plenty of action and a cast of quirky, unforgettable characters. Ritz's comic timing is flawless, and her rollicking plot is expertly balanced against a sobering premise: That last bastion of personal privacy—our own dreams—may no longer be secure. The idea has an alarming ring of plausibility, adding a shivery edge to this entertaining mystery.
> —**KATHRYN GUARE**, award-winning author of The Conor McBride suspense series

"Susan Ritz's *Stolen Dreams* exposes our universal human need to identify "us" and "them," and the confusion that can come when group dogma no longer lines up with experience. Her dialogue rings true, and her lively small-town characters make sore subjects fun. Her mystery embodies crises we all face in a new world of techno fake news and resulting divisions.

What's real? What truly matters? Who can you trust? There's nothing like a murder or two to clarify purpose, community, and one's deepest identity as a blood-pounding, passionate woman with a brain."

—**RICKEY GARD DIAMOND**, author of *Screwnomics*: *Making Economics Sexy* and *Second Sight*

"A gripping Gothic whodunit featuring obscure clues muttered by a dying man, strange encounters in foggy cemeteries, car chases on lonely roads, and clairvoyant dreams."

—**BERNIE LAMBEK**, author of *Uncivil Liberties*

"With intrigue and humor, Susan Ritz has created an arresting novel that strikes at a core fear: what if your dreams were not safe? This psychologically compelling mystery about the murder of a therapist-cum-cult leader proves Ritz a natural storyteller. Her descriptions of the characters who people one small New England community expose both the best and the worst of human nature: the desire to pull together in difficult times, the terrible impulse to betray one another under pressure. Fortunately for us, Ritz is masterful at leading readers through a small city's best and worst instincts with finesse and wit. Hold your own dreams close, but be sure to share *Stolen Dreams*, a most tangible tale of virtual reality that stays with you long after every secret is revealed."

—**SHELAGH SHAPIRO**, Vermont author and host of "Write the Book" podcast

A
DREAM
TO DIE
FOR

A
DREAM
TO DIE
FOR

A NOVEL

SUSAN Z. RITZ

SHE WRITES PRESS

Published July 2019
Printed in the United States of America
Print ISBN: 978-1-63152-557-5
E-ISBN: 978-1-63152-558-2
Library of Congress Control Number: 9781631525575

For information, address:
She Writes Press
1569 Solano Ave #546
Berkeley, CA 94707

Interior design by Tabitha Lahr

She Writes Press is a division of SparkPoint Studio, LLC.

This is a work of fiction. Names, characters, places, and incidents either are the product of the author's imagination or are used fictitiously. Any resemblance to actual persons, living or dead, is entirely coincidental.

This book is dedicated to the women
who helped bring it to life

Shelagh, Coleen,
Kathryn G, Tamar,
Kathryn D, and Eliza

and to Ethan, the best man I know.

The world is under no obligation
to make sense to us.
—Eric Zencey, *Panama*

CHAPTER ONE

MORNING IN RIVERTON FALLS

Celeste reached for the remnants of last night's dream. She'd woken, gasping for breath, throat raw and sore as if she'd been screaming in her sleep. *A woman at a window, bushes blowing in a soft breeze. A shadow coming at her from behind.* She'd scribbled down the disjointed images in her journal before she'd even opened her eyes, but now the morning had whisked the rest away. Still, she couldn't shake the feelings of panic and guilt. She tried again to find a thread that would lead her back in, but it was too late.

Battered old Mr. Coffee burped and spluttered the last drops of java into the carafe. Celeste poured herself an oversize mug and stumbled back to bed to see what she could figure out. Propped against a pile of pillows, she opened the black leather notebook and sipped her coffee. Nothing in the trio of lines she'd scratched out in black ink explained why the dream left her feeling both frightened and ashamed. At least nothing she could figure out on her own. She wondered what Larry would make of this dream—the last she would share with him after four years of therapy.

All that time, Celeste had tracked her dreams, learning to decipher the letters and words she'd jotted down, often with eyes still closed, on the unlined pages of her journal. She'd poured out hundreds of dreams—some just scraps or a single startling image, others pages long, like surreal short stories. But now, if she could stick to her plan, she was done. Today was the day she was going to tell him she was quitting, and there was no way he was going to talk her out of it again. She'd had enough of Larry Blatsky, his Dreamers, and this thing he called the "Dreamscape," the thing Jake called a cult.

Celeste tossed the journal onto the heap of library books, magazines, and last Sunday's *New York Times* that littered the floor next to her side of the bed. Jake's side was as neat and uncluttered as it had been since he'd moved out six weeks earlier. She rolled over onto the smooth, cool sheets. There was no trace of Jake there, no scent on the pillow she hugged to herself. She wanted to touch his body, then run her hand through the tangle of dark curls on his chest, pat his beer belly. She wanted to feel his legs stretched long against hers and play footsie under the comforter. She'd allowed Larry to take it all away.

"Larry will destroy you," she remembered Jake saying the night he left, as he jammed his clothes into his duffel bag. "This isn't a game, Celeste. He'll turn you into someone you don't know or even recognize. That's what he does. Believe me, I've seen it. I can't stay and watch that happen to you."

She shook her head, trying to dislodge the memory. If Jake were still there, lying where he'd been the whole six whirlwind months of their engagement, she knew she could go through with her plan.

"Get down there and tell him it's over," he'd say, the calloused fingertips of his guitar strummer's hands on her cheeks, pulling her face to his for a good-luck kiss. He'd say, "You're tough. Larry's no match against you in a fight! Go get it over with."

Without Jake to back her up, though, Celeste wondered if she had it in her. She'd tried to stand up to Larry before, but she'd always left her therapy session feeling defeated and hopelessly mired in what he called her "Demon Mind," the labyrinth of self-loathing and doubt Larry had unearthed and then used to control her.

Not this time, she thought, getting up to raise the shade to the wan November light. Larry wasn't going to win while she still had a chance at happiness. She'd waited too long for the enlightenment he'd promised. Now all she wanted was love. She was going to get Jake back in her bed where he belonged.

Celeste shuffled through the pile of clothes she'd left thrown over the back of the folding chair the night before. With Jake gone, she had no reason to fold her sweaters, or hang up her skirts, or even clean the apartment. Not like she had much to control anyway. Some yard sale furniture, pots and pans from Salvation Army, a functional but minimal wardrobe from New To You—all things she could put out with the trash or recycle if she needed to make a quick getaway, like she had from the last couple of towns where she'd lived before landing in Riverton Falls. She could still fit everything that mattered into two suitcases in the back of her trusty old red Jetta and hightail it out of town.

"Not this time," she said out loud to herself. "This time you're going to stay. But not with Larry."

Celeste pulled on a pair of crumpled brown cords, then gave her russet sweater a quick sniff to make sure it was relatively free of sweat and booze.

You're wearing that? Right on cue, her mother's voice rang through her head.

Better hurry! You're going to be late again, her father added.

Even Larry hadn't been able to silence her parents' critical comments, though they'd both been dead for years. She combed back her mop of wiry blonde hair into a ponytail. As usual she struggled to get up and organized for these early morning appointments, even if early morning for Celeste was actually noon. Sometimes she thought about giving up tending bar and getting a serious day job, but she liked having her mornings and afternoons wide open. Besides, with Jake out of the picture, the bar at least kept her from some lonely evenings. For now.

Teeth, face, juice, another cup of coffee. She ran back into the bedroom and from her dresser she grabbed the tiny verdigris mermaid, one of the few possessions that had traveled the world with her. Her good-luck charm. A present from her mother one long-ago birthday. Celeste shoved her journal in her pack and banged out through the doorway into the damp, late autumn morning, zipped up her ratty down vest, and took off at a brisk pace for Larry's house, fifteen minutes across town.

It was the kind of morning that made her dread winter's arrival—dark and damp, with the threat of sleet hanging in the low gray clouds. The big Victorian houses along the way looked as dreary as the day, their porches emptied of summer's wicker furniture, tired perennial gardens cut down to spiky stems, front stoops dotted with wrinkled, worn-out jack-o'-lanterns. Dry brown leaves scuttled across the sidewalks in the raw wind, and a raucous murder of crows wheeled above the bare trees on the hills overlooking the town. Once winter actually arrived, Celeste would feel better, but the anticipation of the increasingly dark weeks ahead made this transition hard to take. Everyone seemed depressed and cranky between Halloween and the first week in December when the Christmas lights went up at last and, with some luck, an early snow brightened the rolling New England landscape.

Celeste hugged her journal to her chest as she walked through town, head down, trying to figure out the dream. Maybe it was one of those "big" dreams Larry had always hoped she'd have. Like the one about the whale bones she discovered with the Indian elders. Or the one with the tall, African man in his sky-blue caftan holding her hand as they gazed out to sea from atop a grassy bluff. Maybe she'd finally broken through into the Third Level dreams Larry promised would emerge when she joined the Dreamers, Larry's hand-picked group of advanced clients. Great. Right when she was about to jump ship and leave all that craziness behind, she may have finally crashed through the barrier that had kept her on the fringes for almost a year.

No. One dream was not going to crumble her resolve. Celeste began to practice her lines.

"Larry, I'm done. Larry, I'm leaving you," she chanted under her breath right up to the walkway leading through an overgrown lilac hedge, across the patchy brown lawn to his little brick Cape. It stood out in this town of wooden clapboard homes, always reminding her of the third little pig's house— too sturdy to be blown over by the big, bad wolf.

She hesitated before stepping onto the flagstones, stuffing the journal into her pack. She could still skip the appointment. She didn't need to tell Larry she was quitting. The old Celeste, the one she'd been before Larry, wouldn't have had any trouble just walking away; but Larry had huffed and puffed until her defiance finally crumbled into compliance. Besides, she was curious about that dream. She felt for the mermaid in her pocket. Squaring her shoulders, she marched up the walk, past the weed-choked flower beds, through the front door, and into Larry Blatsky's waiting room.

CHAPTER TWO

THE END

In Larry's overheated reception area, Celeste squirmed on the lumpy couch, rearranging the heart-shaped silk pillows nestled in its corners. She'd never been good at sitting with her thoughts, and today she was so nervous she couldn't stop fidgeting. To distract herself, she perused the few paintings that hung on the walls—a half dozen small watercolors of starry nights and blue skies filled with diaphanous angels. In the beginning, Celeste had thought all the art must have been done by children, but she learned via the local bar gossip that these were the only traces left of Larry's wife. She'd disappeared, whispered the group of Larry's loyal insiders. Ran off with some hippie guy, they'd heard, and Larry had never mentioned her since. Strange. Why hadn't he tried to erase these reminders of their life together? Perhaps he'd just never gotten around to it, like she still hadn't managed to throw out Jake's can of shaving cream in her medicine cabinet. As long as it remained, there was still hope he'd be back.

Still restless, Celeste picked through the faded back-pack she used as a purse, looking for something to read. She pulled out her journal and began thumbing through the last few months of dreams. When she'd first begun therapy, Celeste had filled up one of these notebooks in a matter of weeks. Lately, though, her dreams had seemed mundane: no more handsome leading men, Larry's so-called Golden Princes, no more villainous "Dark Mother" figures to puzzle over or gestalt in her visits to Larry. In fact, her dreams had shrunk down to snippets, mostly truncated reruns of the events of her day, either too boring to even bother recording or dreams about Jake she knew would cause trouble. The dreams had lost their potency as the pain of losing Jake had replaced the pain Larry kept trying to get her to dredge up from her past.

She was still flipping through the pages when the door to Larry's office opened. Out came an unfamiliar man, tall and gaunt, wearing mirrored Ray-Bans, clutching his own dream journal, a flimsy composition notebook. New client, she guessed, or at least one she'd never seen before. Larry was right behind him. The man turned in the doorway and the much shorter, much stouter Larry reached up and threw his arms around the man's concave chest in his ritual good-bye hug. The man pulled back and stiffened.

Larry's hugs were something Celeste also tried unsuccessfully to avoid. At five foot ten she towered over him, and too often he ended up with his head pressed against her admittedly small breasts. She never liked hugs from anyone, but from the beginning Larry had forced them on her, telling her that she needed to surrender to his love.

"Open your heart to me, Cel," he'd say as he came in for the clinch. "Drop the armor and let me in."

She'd done exactly that for Jake and discovered that his hugs were warm and comforting, while Larry's continued to feel cold and forced. Larry had managed to convince her that her unwillingness to melt on contact was her own fault. It had taken her far too long to understand that Larry's game wasn't actually about opening her heart. It was about opening her wallet, over and over until there was nothing left. At any rate, she doubted he'd be hugging her today.

"Okay, man, you know the plan, right?" said Larry, thumping the man on the back so hard his whole bony frame shook and a shock of white hair tumbled across his forehead. "See you in a few."

The man nodded, then walked by Celeste, looking down at his feet and smiling to himself. He looked familiar. Maybe the new pharmacist over at Downtown Drugs? Or perhaps she'd seen him in the meditation room at the Buddhist laundry.

Other therapists, she'd heard, had separate entrances and exits for clients or would at least space their appointments to avoid any embarrassing encounters. That would have made sense in this small town where Larry seemed to be ministering to almost everyone. Larry, however, didn't believe in confidentiality.

"Privacy is overrated," he'd said after telling her all about the erotic, almost pornographic, dreams one of the Dreamers had had about her.

In fact, Larry made a point of sharing intimate details of his clients' lives and dreams because, he'd once explained, it deepened the Dreamscape for all. "My wish," he'd told her years ago, "is to have all my clients sharing their dreams, caught up in the big web of the Dreamscape. We could be the collective unconscious of Riverton Falls!" That sounded great at the time, very spiritual and deep, until she realized Larry's real need was to be the Dream Master himself, in charge of not only his clients' dream lives but their waking lives, too.

"Come on in, Cel," Larry said, waving her through the door.

"It's Celeste, actually." Larry and the Dreamers were the only people who ever called her Cel, and until now she'd never had the confidence to correct them. Today would be different.

She slid by him, looking down. Larry's head barely reached her shoulders, allowing her to take measure of the growing bald spot that he tried to cover by teasing back his thinning blond hair into a feathery pompadour.

Larry's office was as drab as his waiting room, plain old brown office furniture she guessed he'd salvaged from a bankruptcy sale, though Celeste figured with the rates he charged, he could afford better. She sometimes wondered just what exactly he did with all the money he hauled in from his clients. Probably stashed it in some overseas tax-dodge account. The fancy-looking computer on his desk was the only thing in the office that didn't look tired and worn.

No diplomas or certificates hung on the walls, something Celeste should have paid attention to the first time she'd entered his office. Never having been to a therapist before, maybe, she'd naively thought, dream therapists didn't display their credentials like doctors or massage therapists. It never occurred to her that Larry had no certificates.

Celeste sat in one of the two mismatched, straight-backed chairs in front of Larry's desk, crossing her legs and folding her arms tightly against her chest. Suddenly from behind her came a loud command: "Feel the pain! Feel the pain!"

Celeste grabbed both sides of her seat and turned her head to glare at the talker. In the corner, pacing freely along a thin bamboo perch, Larry's blue and green parrot bobbed his head up and down. Pete never failed to alarm her, especially when he landed on her head and pecked at her ears, as he had on more than one occasion. Sometimes when she was deep in a gestalt of some particularly scary or disconcerting dream, he would fly in frantic circles around the office. Larry refused to clip the bird's wings. Something about leaving him wild and free.

"Shut up, Pete!" Larry yelled. "Tea?" He wiggled the mug Celeste was certain the pharmacist had just finished drinking from and walked to the closet where he kept his electric kettle, along with some Lipton tea bags and powdered creamer.

"No thanks."

They went through this same ritual every week, but Larry never noticed how she cringed just imagining drinking from the crusty mug.

"Cookie?" Larry asked, returning to his rolling chair and pushing a plate of hard chocolate discs toward her. His own half-eaten baloney sandwich rested on a paper napkin on his desk. Celeste remembered when his cookies had always been so deliciously gooey and homemade and his grade-school-style sandwiches had seemed charming. In the beginning, she'd felt like she'd been invited to tea with a friend who was there just for her, ready and willing to listen to her darkest secrets and deepest fears.

Back then, Larry had seemed eccentric, so even though he'd often been overly tough on her, she'd forgiven what seemed his necessary ass-kicking. He just wanted her to dive into her dreams and crack open her psyche, which he claimed had grown calloused and cold after all those years she'd turned her back on what he called her "Vital Self." For years, she had completely trusted his guidance, believing he could see more of her than she could see of herself. Larry could drop inside her like a spelunker into a deep, dank cave and hunt down every last lie she'd ever told herself or anyone else. Even now, she believed he'd transformed her life by opening the door to her heart. Once that door was flung wide, however, and Jake had walked in, everything changed.

She looked at the plate of cookies on the desk. The time

for tea and sympathy was long past. "No thanks. Larry, I . . ." She now realized she should tell him right off the bat this was her last session, before she lost her nerve and succumbed once again to his offerings. But that dream—she had to know what it was. Maybe this plan to leave Larry wasn't about Jake at all, but another attempt to sabotage her own progress, as Larry had made her believe when she'd tried to get away before. No, she scolded herself, Larry's not dragging me back in. Not this time.

"Done your homework?" Larry continued, shoving the last crust of sandwich into his mouth then leaning back in his chair. Celeste watched him chew, little crumbs gathering at the corners of his mouth.

Homework. She hadn't even thought about it since her last session. When she'd first started coming to Larry, the homework had consumed her.

"Feel your pain, your abandonment, how deeply afraid you are," Larry had urged. "*Be* the little orphan girl of your dreams. See how hungry she is, how hard she is trying to keep help from getting in the door? Stay with her." Back then he'd seemed an insistent but not unkind guide, challenging her to uncover what he called her "Shadow," the parts of herself she'd hidden away long ago to protect herself from the chaos her drunken parents created around her. He'd explained how, with his help and her dedication to the homework, she would be reunited with the "Magical Child" she had once been, the child who still huddled somewhere inside her.

For the first couple of years, she'd immersed herself in the dream images. She'd walked and walked, spending hours on the twisting paths of Hutchins Park, feeling the sadness and utter hopelessness of her dream children, looking down so no one would notice that her eyes were perpetually red from crying. She had nursed the little nub of pain until it blossomed into a hardy vine, twisting through her thoughts, strangling the seedling of self-confidence she'd tried so long to cultivate. The pain had made her life feel significant. So what if she spent most of her time alone, weeping and wailing in the woods or huddled in the corner of her living room couch conjuring up images of starving babies and misshapen children hidden in the dungeons and attics of her dreams? She was growing into her authenticity, Larry had said, into her Vital Self.

Every time any niggling doubts about his methods or insights crept into her sessions, Larry pounced, reeling her right back into the Dreamscape. "Cel, Cel, that's your false pride, your Demon Mind talking. It's scared. It's fighting back. It knows you're trying to kill it." Over and over, Larry had managed to convince her that she was on the verge of a breakthrough, dangling the reward of a new life just out of her reach. All she had to do, he whispered, was let go, surrender, and let herself drown in the streams, the ponds, the waves always flooding her dreams.

"Come on! Stop being afraid of the water! Ya gotta let yourself sink, dive into the waves. You gotta die to be reborn. Then you'll be ready to become a Dreamer." Still, she kept struggling to stay afloat. Dream after dream, she fought the pull of the tide. Until Jake.

Now she forgot her homework assignments the moment she walked out the door. Looking back, she couldn't believe she'd actually fallen for Larry's promise of a life free from the self-doubt and anxiety that still plagued her. Here she sat, older and in many ways wiser, and Larry still hadn't delivered. In fact, when she'd made the big leap and fallen in love at last, he'd ripped all the happiness she'd found right out from under her. No, she'd had enough of the Dreamscape.

She wasn't only leaving Larry, though. She'd also have to say good-bye to the Dreamers, the group that had become her family. Maybe this was finally the dream that would make her a full-fledged member at last, part of the inner circle, the members who claimed they dreamed each other's dreams. How could she know unless Larry told her? After these years with Larry, she'd almost forgotten how to think for herself or trust her own intuition.

"So, ya didn't do your homework, did ya?" Larry leaned back in his chair. The buttons on his flowered Hawaiian shirt strained over his big belly. "What's your problem? You're looking a little uneasy today, nervous. Letting your shame take over? Again?"

Celeste looked down at her lap, struggling to hold on to her determination as Larry described exactly the feelings that had swallowed her a few hours earlier. How did he know she'd woken up feeling like she'd done something she needed to hide?

"You're letting the Demon Mind swamp you even after all the work we've done together. Don't you understand you're paralyzed with fear—that you're getting older, that your life is getting smaller and more meaningless by the day? Instead of reaching inside, like I've told you and told you, you're just letting it happen. And I thought we were actually getting somewhere with you."

She tried to push her hurt feelings back down where they belonged, angry at herself for the tears gathering along her lower eyelids.

"There's some tissues on the table if ya need 'em."

Celeste shook her head no, stifling her little snuffling whimpers, and screwed up her resolve. She would not let Larry make her cry today. He would not bully her into anything ever again.

Larry pushed the Kleenex box toward her anyway, then leaned forward in his swivel chair, waiting to type up her words. "Let's get to work on your dream. I presume you brought a dream even if you didn't do your homework." He sounded fed up with her. "Let's get in there and find out what those tears are all about so you can work on them for next time."

"But I'm not—"

Larry talked right over her. "I'm serious here, Cel. If ya wanna keep working with me, then ya gotta keep up. How many times do I gotta say it? You go right back to the same old defensive patterns. Look at how you're sitting, all locked up around yourself, keeping that heart suited up for battle, but afraid to make a move. Am I right?"

Celeste shook her head, staring down. She watched as a fat tear from each eye fell into her lap, and then she hugged herself tighter. How could he still have this much power over her? Do it, goddamn it, she yelled inside her head. Tell him!

"I'm not—"

"Feel the pain!" Pete squawked, drowning out her whispered words.

Larry wasn't listening to her anyway. "Like how you still got that ring on."

Celeste protectively covered the engagement ring with her right hand. Jake had designed it for her before he'd even asked her to marry him—a sapphire, her birthstone, a sky-blue Ceylon surrounded by diamond chips in an antique white-gold setting—the most beautiful thing she'd ever owned, better than anything she'd ever imagined—though engagement rings had never been something she'd thought much about.

"Jesus, Cel, when are you going to let go and move on in your life? Don't you know it's over with Jake? We've gone around and around on this. Your dreams are crystal clear, even if you refuse to believe them. Jake's no good for you; he's holding you back, keeping you from surrendering to the Dreamscape, to Dreamland. Let go of him. The choice is clear. You can't keep living this double life." Larry shook his head, puckering his lips as if he wanted to spit. "Jeez, just make up your mind once and for all."

Celeste felt her face flush red. "Jake's none of your business, Larry. In fact, I'm . . . this is . . ." She drew in her breath, trying to summon her earlier resolve, but just as she was about to get the practiced words out, Larry exploded from his chair, arms outstretched, hands waving like signals in the air. He suddenly looked like a furious dwarf out of some Grimms' fairytale, bellowing and snorting at her as he shot out from behind his desk on his stumpy, little legs.

"No, I'm just your therapist! Are you fucking kidding me? Everything's my business! When are you going to finally get that?"

She shrank back as he barreled toward her. "I guess never, since this is my last appointment." There, she did it. Triumph and relief.

But Larry kept coming at her until he stopped abruptly in front of her, looking down at her sitting there and squinting through his tiny washed-out blue eyes. "So we're going to play that game again, are we?" His voice softened, but she could still hear the cold steel under his words. "You know you're not ready to leave, Cel. We've been through this how many times?" He bent toward her, his face just inches from hers, the baloney and onion fumes on his breath making her wince. "Can't you hear yourself? Can't you hear that pride, that stubborn resistance to any help anyone wants to offer you? Sometimes I have to wonder what you've even gotten out of all these years of work."

"Me too." Celeste could feel the rising sob finally overwhelming her. Larry hadn't always been such a bully. She stared at her boots to avoid his eyes and his breath as he hovered over her. She could almost feel the heat drain from him, replaced by the sharp, cold edge of anger that scared her once again into submission. Her courage was slipping away like water down the drain, leaving a dirty ring of fear and resentment.

Larry walked to the window and stared out at the bare branches of the lilac hedge that surrounded the house, and she watched him breathe deeply, almost visibly reining in his anger. "You're letting your Demon Mind run ya, Cel. It's the same poisonous voice that tells ya to go back to Jake, to do the thing that undermines your true strength. Look at the timing." He drummed his stubby fingers on the window sill, striking them one at a time as he made his points. "You've been making big breakthroughs. You're starting to make an impact on the Dreamscape. You're moving at last into Upper Level dreams, exactly what we've been trying to get to all this time. Any day now, you're going to start entering the Collective Dreams. I can feel it, this close." He turned back toward her, holding his two hands barely an inch apart, as if saying all she had to do was take that last little leap. As if telling her she stood a hair's breadth from Nirvana. "Now you're scared, ready to run off to some hidey-hole instead of reaching out one more time, when everything you've wanted is almost in your grasp. Jake's an excuse, Cel. A way to avoid facing yourself once and for all."

Maybe he was right. Running away just when things got interesting was her specialty. She was an expert at pulling up stakes, moving on whenever anyone got too close or wanted anything more than a superficial smile. Give her a promotion or an engagement ring and she was out the door. Sure, Jake had been the one to move out, but her lies had sent him away. Now here she was with this dream, maybe *the* dream, and she was ready to jump ship once again.

Larry turned back to the window and sighed. "Anyway, you know Jake and Nicole are seeing each other again, don't you?"

Celeste grabbed the arms of the chair. He had to be lying.

Jake had barely spoken to Nicole since their divorce. "I don't believe you," she said. "You don't know that."

"Yes, I do, Cel. Nicole told me yesterday. That she was thinking of moving back in with him."

Now she knew he was messing with her. Even if Jake had wanted Nicole in his life again, there was no way Nicole— with her perfect hair and her fashionista wardrobe—would be going back to live with Jake in his off-the-grid cabin out in the woods. And, after all the crap Jake had given Celeste about becoming a Dreamer, she knew he'd never want the woman in charge of the group to move in. Even if that woman was Nicole, his own ex-wife. Celeste smiled to herself with relief, but Larry just shrugged and continued to gaze out the window, looking forlorn as he always did when he talked about Nicole, his Dreamscape queen and, as far as Celeste could tell, unrequited love.

Finally, Larry turned back toward Celeste, his lower lip trembling, his gaze both plaintive and sympathetic. "Believe me, I know how much that hurts to hear. But here's the proof." Larry walked back behind his desk, fiddled with the keyboard. He swung the monitor toward Celeste, revealing a full-screen shot of Jake and Nicole, sitting on a bench, heads inclined toward each other, looking into each other's eyes.

Celeste turned her head away and shrugged. "So?" she said. "What were you doing? Stalking them?" She thought Larry could be trying to trick her, but he'd already popped a big hole in the hope she'd felt that morning.

"So admit it's over and begin the healing. To be happy, it's the Dreamscape you need, Cel. Not Jake." Larry held out his hand to her. "Jake is moving on, and you need to do the same. I'm here to help. Time to give me that ring."

Celeste looked at his open palm. No way, she screamed inside, no way I'm trading in this ring for you and the

Dreamscape. She didn't want to follow this absurd request. She didn't want to turn over the most important thing in her life. But Larry always knew how to find her most vulnerable spot and drive the knife in. The anger and hurt the photo had unleashed poured through her as she wriggled the ring up her finger and eased it over her knuckle.

There was his hand—cupped fingers ready to take the last hope of Jake from her, and she was letting it happen. She couldn't stop herself. Jake was right. She still couldn't stand up to Larry, and until she could, Jake would never take her back. But maybe it was too late anyway. Maybe Jake really was going back to Nicole. Maybe surrendering to Larry was the only way Celeste would find happiness. Still screaming inside—*no, no, no*—she watched her ring fall like a shiny tear into Larry's waiting hand.

"Now, you see, you'll be able to give Bruce a chance."

"I don't think that's going to happen," Celeste said, keeping her eyes on Larry's closed fist. Larry loved playing matchmaker, and she'd seen him rearrange couples because of a handful of dream images. Those long-time Dreamers fell for it, switching partners as if they were at a contra dance. But not her, even if she did give up her ring. "I still love Jake. I don't even like Bruce."

"His dreams, Cel, they say all I need to know. He's the one for you."

"*His* dreams? What about *my* dreams?"

"Your dreams? They're still full of mud. How can I know what you want?"

"But you just said I was so close." She held up her hands, palms nearly touching, just as he had done a few minutes earlier.

Shaking his head, he mumbled something she couldn't quite catch and walked back behind his desk. He dropped her ring into the inlaid wooden box next to his mouse pad. The lid fell shut with a snap.

"Speaking of dreams, we've got a few more minutes. You did at least bring a dream, right?" Larry pushed a craggy crystal as big as a baby's head toward her—the jagged five-pound chunk of smoky quartz he had often handed her, and no doubt his other clients, to clear their minds and empty their hearts of fear and anger and recall the depth of the dreams he claimed were the pathway to the "Shining Spirit."

Celeste nodded. She clutched the sharp-edged rock, thinking how much it looked like a frozen pile of snow at the end of a long winter, its surface a dirty gray, somehow still glinting in the light from the window. Larry sat down and swiveled his chair toward the computer, arching his hands over the keyboard, ready to type like a pianist about to play.

"I can't remember much of it. I woke up feeling like I'd done something terribly wrong. Like I'd gotten really angry and hurt someone. And at the same time, I felt like I was the one who'd been hurt. Only *I* didn't seem to be in the dream," Celeste said. "More like it was someone else's dream. Does any of that make sense?" She ran her fingers along the crystal's rough edges, trying to believe it could actually suck the shame from her. There was something creepy about that crystal— charged with the negative emotions of half the town, the same way Larry's computer held onto all their dreams.

"Everything in the dream is *you*. You know that. Why don't you read it to me, then close your eyes and see if anything comes back. That works sometimes."

Balancing the ungainly rock on her lap, Celeste bent over and pulled her journal from her backpack, trying to hide the tears she wished weren't gathering again in her eyes. Once more she'd been defeated, and now she was following directions as if nothing had happened. She wondered how she would ever get away from this man.

She read what she'd written down that morning, then

closed her eyes and leaned back in the chair, edging back into the dream, trying again to remember. Larry was right. An image swam up behind her closed eyelids. "A kitchen," she whispered. "A woman, apron tied around her neck, rocking forward and back, like she's kneading bread." Just then everything went black, the image disappearing from Celeste. Her eyes flew open and she gagged, gulping for air, suddenly terrified. Biting down hard on her lower lip, she tried to bring herself back into the room where she expected Larry to be waiting for her.

Instead she found a man she hardly recognized, his face sheet-white, shoulders hunched, hands clutching the left side of his chest. "Larry?"

He looked up. "Is this a joke? Who gave you that dream? Did Jake put you up to this?" His voice sounded thick, as if he had a hard time forcing out the words.

"Jake? Why?"

"What kind of game are you playing? Who told you to come here with this?"

She could hardly hear him now, and he seemed to be shrinking into his chair. "Told me? Are you okay?" Celeste wondered if she should help him. He looked like he was having a heart attack.

Gradually, he leaned forward and pulled himself to his feet. "Get out," he hissed, the words like a hot wind blowing across the desk. "Leave."

Fear bolted through Celeste. She jumped to her feet. The crystal crashed to the floor. Larry stumbled from behind his desk. Instead of coming at her, he went to the door and yanked it open. Celeste scooped up her pack and her vest, caught herself from tripping over the chair legs, and backed toward the exit.

"Awk!" screeched Pete, launching from his perch, his unclipped wings whipping the air in front of her face. She covered her head and took off.

CHAPTER THREE

TAROT TRICKS

Hurrying from the office, Celeste zipped her vest against a blast of November wind. Behind her, she could hear a door slamming over and over and Larry bellowing, his voice following her across the yard and out through the lilac hedge as she picked up speed. Her pack banged against her hip as she headed down Maple Street, muttering to herself, trying to figure out what had happened. She'd thrown back the curtain on the Wizard of Riverton Falls and found a half-crazed little man, as fearful as all the people he counseled. The dream had scared Larry enough to chase her away. She was free. That's what she'd wanted. Only he wasn't supposed to throw her out! She was supposed to leave him!

Slowing, she tried to catch her breath. A rising sense of relief calmed her confusion as she neared the center of town. The streets of Riverton were almost empty on this blustery day, except for the meter maid in her green uniform, pacing the curb, tapping her pen on her ticket book, counting the minutes for the next poor soul's meter to expire.

Celeste stopped outside the Corner Cup Café. Any other day, she would have gone straight in and joined the group of Dreamers who usually gathered around the diner's big center table, all inhaling their amaretto-flavored cappuccinos, Larry's drink of choice. She imagined them there now, the women in tunics and leggings, the men in loose pants and flowing shirts, discussing one dream or another someone had had the night before. It would be so easy to go in, pull up a chair on the outside of the circle, next to those two annoying newbies, Sarabande and Arun, and listen in. Everyone would welcome her with nods and smiles, still unaware of what had happened in Larry's office, unaware that her days as a Dreamer were over.

Instead, she headed for the bench on the Rialto Bridge down the block where, on sunny days, nomadic anarchists in their black leather jackets hung out, cigarettes dangling from pierced lips, and white Rasta wannabes kicked around Hacky Sacks and beat on African drums. In this weather, though, she had the bench to herself.

She dropped her pack on the wooden seat and plunked down next to it. The icy slats stung her thighs. Yes, she'd wanted out, but now she was really alone, just like she'd been when she went to Larry in the first place—older and wiser than when she'd started, maybe, but definitely a whole lot poorer. Not only had she lost her tiny savings and her fiancé, she'd also given up some essential sense of who she had always been—the tough, wisecracking, courageous Celeste who could take on the world one-handed. Until Larry got hold of her. He'd turned her into this whimpering woman she hardly recognized. She wished she could ask for a refund.

Getting up from the bench, Celeste leaned over the bridge railing, pushing one knee between the carved pillars of the granite balustrade. The West Branch, swollen with November rain, frothed and surged as it plunged beneath the street before spilling into the Pelletier River two blocks away. In the summer, she'd noticed kids in kayaks paddle beneath the bridge and disappear into a watery tunnel under the block of buildings on the other side of Maple Street. She admired their daring as they entered the darkness, not sure what they'd encounter. Now she wondered what the hell they thought they were getting themselves into, diving into danger that way, as she'd so heedlessly dived into the Dreamscape.

She watched the swirling eddies in the current below her on the bridge. The river wound and unwound itself, pulling in bits of twigs and trash and then spitting them out over and over again. Maybe it was too late to get her old life back. Not that she wanted all of it. That's why she'd gone to Larry in the first place: she was finally worn out from running, country to country, man to man. Until Riverton, until Jake. She had to thank the Dreamscape for that. If Larry hadn't ripped off her armor, she'd never have let herself open her heart. But if he hadn't torn the guts out of her at the same time, she would have been able to get away once Jake proposed. It was all such a contradiction. Shaking her head, she scolded herself. Get it together, girl! This is what you've been fighting for, a chance to retrieve your life!

"Tarot, lady? Futures for free!" Celeste spun around at the sound of the raspy voice that seemed to rise from the ground next to the bench. She looked down. A squirming bundle of rags on a moth-eaten blanket propped up a cardboard sign that read "Tarot Trickster—Readings by Donation" in smeared red Sharpie. Oh, *this* guy. The heap of rags, she realized, was actually a filthy Army-surplus-type greatcoat draped over a small man with a tower of dreadlocks that made his head look twice as tall as the rest of him. He reeked of stale tobacco and old sweat. Celeste wrinkled her nose. Over the past week, she'd noticed him huddled outside the Corner Cup Café, like a small grungy garden gnome, inviting every passer-by to sit down for a tarot reading.

"Hey, lady, come find out where you're going in such a hurry!" he'd plead in his cracked, reedy voice whenever she stormed by at her usual frantic pace. She wondered why he'd picked this cold time of year to wander into Riverton, anyway. He'd missed foliage season and all the tourists that blew in with it, if that's what he'd been looking for.

Celeste turned back to face the river, trying to block out his pleas. She'd just gotten away from one crazy man; she didn't need another. Still, right now, with everything sliding out from under her, she wanted someone to tell her what was around the bend. She pivoted.

"You did say free, right?"

The man pointed to his sign and held out a dirt-creased palm. Celeste sighed, pulled a dollar bill from her vest pocket and handed it over, pinching it at the edge so she wouldn't have to touch the man. She wasn't usually this wary; she'd seen people far worse off, but not in this part of the world. "There you go."

He looked at the dollar, then up at Celeste, and that's when she got her first good look at his face. She'd expected a weather-beaten Charles Manson type, eyes wild and deranged. Now that she looked at him more closely, she realized the Manson effect was a projection, as Larry would have warned—a scrim she had pulled over his actual face. His gaze was far from wild; in fact, it was strangely calming, and as she looked into those chocolate-brown eyes, she felt the raging tension of the last couple of hours begin to subside.

"I know it's not much, but it's what I have on me," she lied.

The man shrugged and nodded, seemingly unconcerned, then patted a spot on the blanket next to him. "Down here by me, by me, if you please, Lady Celeste, I guess?"

"How did you know my name?"

"Small town, big ears."

"Right. And you are?"

"Today I call me Adam." He giggled.

"All righty, Adam Today, but I can see the cards fine from over here." She sat back down on the bench.

"No bedbugs to bug you, lady." Adam's voice was high-pitched, kind of scratchy.

"No, not bedbugs," Celeste lied again.

He stared up at her with those eyes. Celeste could see herself floating in their pools of sorrow and compassion, and then she found herself, for the second time that day, being pulled to do something she didn't want to do. Once again, she couldn't help herself. She slid off the bench and knelt just outside the hem of rags. The cold of the sidewalk sent goose bumps up her spine. She pulled the collar of her vest around her face for warmth and as a buffer against the man's unpleasant odor. Now that she was closer, though, she was surprised to notice a spicy undertone. Aftershave? Whatever the scent, it somehow actually made it more bearable.

"All dust, all ashes, all one," Adam said as he shuffled the cards, quick and smooth as any card shark she'd ever gambled with in Singapore. "Open your heart, lady, to tarot's truth," he said. "Hearts believe, no matter the mind, no matter the song of the skeptic."

This little guy had figured her out fast. She thought Larry was the only one who could see right through her, but maybe she was easier to read than she thought.

"Yours to question, the cards to answer. Some sadness? Some hope? Your need, my command."

Celeste thought for a split second and then blurted out, "Now what?"

"Now the question." Adam watched her face, still sliding the cards between his hands.

"That *is* the question. What's next for me?"

He gazed up again, tilting his pile of dreadlocks from side to side as if sizing her up, getting her full measure. "Yesterday and today hide seeds of tomorrow."

"What's that about?" She sighed, shifting over on her freezing knees to huddle on a tiny corner of the blanket. Adam handed her the pack of cards, which she took gingerly, noticing their oily sheen. "Little donation, little reading," he told Celeste. Then he asked her to divide the cards into three piles and turn over the top card on each stack. When she was done, he let his gaze linger over the row, nodding and scratching at his patchy beard.

"What do you see?" Celeste asked.

"Angels and archetypes, fluttering, fluttering," he mumbled, still staring at the cards.

Archetypes? That was part of Larry's jargon. Larry thought he had the archetypal realm all locked up in this town, yet here was this street bum doing the same work, asking for dollar donations instead of a check for $150.

Pointing to the first pile with his dirt-encrusted, ragged fingernail, Adam began, "Your past brings you here, to this moment, this day." He handed her the card and she studied the colorful picture—a shining, golden-haired youth in flowered brocade appeared to march along blithely, completely unaware that he was about to plunge over a cliff into a roiling sea. A terrier mutt yapped at his heels, as if warning him to stop and look around before it was too late. At the bottom of the card she read two words: "The Fool."

"Unheeding, uncaring, the Fool rushes in, danger at your feet. Time to fly? Time to fall?" Adam fixed his brown eyes on her face, searching, it seemed, for some clue to her past.

She stared at the card wondering what to do next.

"Ask him your question, find your response." Again, the guy was using Larry's tricks. And Larry thought he was so special! "What part of my past are you?" she asked, looking the hapless Fool in his minuscule eye. Then, as if switching chairs for the gestalt in Larry's office, she shifted her weight from her right hip to her left and began to answer in a high voice she thought sounded like the sprightly voice of her younger, more foolish self. "I'm the girl who left home to wander the world, gaily unaware of danger, of the abyss. I am the girl who always looked out, never within."

"Yes, yes." Adam rubbed his filthy palms back and forth across his knees. "You be the sun-blind Fool. But ahead? Look down!" His finger traveled from the face of the boy down to the cliff at his feet. "Watch out! Stumble and bumble and over you go, into the pit of pain."

Whoa. That's right on the mark, Celeste thought. Larry had torn her open before pitching her into that pit of pain she'd been teetering above for years. Too bad he hadn't known how to pull her out again.

"Now is present," said Adam, tapping the middle stack.

Celeste picked up the second card and pored over the picture of a crumbling tower, a bolt of lightning striking and exploding its golden dome. Smoke poured from its windows, and two men in tights and jerkins leapt from the building headlong, escaping the blaze. "The Tower," she read.

"Flames and destruction!" Adam wailed, placing his little paw-like hands on either side of his eyes, like blinders framing his face, contorted into a silent open-mouthed scream. "Tumbling down all around you, lady!" He reached out and grabbed her arm, pulling her in closer. His grip tightened as Celeste tried to draw back, suddenly afraid of what she'd unleashed. But Adam was strong, and he pulled her face close to his.

"There is danger, lady, pulling you in, sucking you under!" He glanced around, making sure no one could overhear the warning, but the sidewalk was unusually empty.

Celeste jerked back. She didn't need to be swept up in this crazy guy's space. Not now. "Well, I think there might be some big changes, but danger? In Riverton? That might be an exaggeration." As she said this, Larry's panicked face sprang into her mind, but she brushed the image away.

Adam shook his head, clumps of matted hair flopping from his topknot. "Lady, I feel it here." He thumped his chest with his fist. "This moment is full of fire!"

"Okay, we'll see," she sighed, glancing at her watch, wondering how much longer this would take. He made her nervous. She took a breath and then asked what she'd wanted to all along: "What about the last one, the future? What about love? That's what I really want to know." She picked up the third card and flipped it over.

"Future grows from present seeds," he grumbled. "Pay heed!" Adam wagged his head from side to side, looking down at the card held in Celeste's outstretched hand—a blond woman by a stream—"The Star," he read. "In its own time, in its own way, love comes when you're ready, not when you plan," the raspy gnome answered, his tone flat, a deflated balloon.

Celeste wished he'd had the same enthusiasm for her future as he'd had for the clear and present danger he claimed was engulfing her right now.

Then he reached out and grabbed her hands again so quickly she didn't have time to maneuver away. "Please listen, the Star is far, but trouble is near. Take care, Lady Celeste. Darkness all around you."

"Great. Very comforting. On that note, I think I'm done for today."

She tried to pull her hands from his grasp, but he shook his head and said, "Time to jump in, not out," before finally letting go. Then he put the deck back into the pocket of his coat and pulled out a fat red pack of cigarettes.

"Kreteks! I haven't seen those since Indonesia." So that was the spicy undertone to Adam's stale odor: ground cloves mixed into the tobacco of his cigarettes. Oh, how she wanted one right now! If she was running too late for that beer, a kretek might hit the same spot. After Larry's freaky behavior and this guy's dire warning, her anxiety level was moving off the charts. She cleared her throat preparing to ask for one, maybe offer another dollar. "Adam?"

But Adam wasn't looking at her. He was staring, all jumpy-eyed, over her left shoulder into the distance. Across the street, behind her, she could hear footsteps running down the pavement. She turned to see what had disturbed him: Jake, pounding down the empty sidewalk in his paint-splattered Carhartt jacket and jeans and his heavy leather boots—not exactly jogging gear. He looked terrible, his usually placid face drawn and pained. At a solid six foot two, with thighs as thick and strong as tree trunks, Jake almost seemed too big a man for jogging. Always looking way more agile on back-country skis, even plowing through waist-high drifts, than he seemed right now, running through town, probably to Winzer's Hardware for some construction job he was on. Or perhaps to Nicole's.

Celeste pushed herself to her feet, ready to chase him down. "Jake!" she called, but a passing car drowned out her voice. He ran on past, rounding the corner at Jolly Jewels, without even glancing in Celeste's and Adam's direction. If she hurried, she could catch him. Just as she turned back toward Adam, she caught sight of him scuttling away beneath the awning of the Corner Cup, almost completely hidden in the thick folds of his drooping greatcoat, the crown of his piled hair just visible, bobbing above his upturned collar. She reached to retrieve her backpack from the bench. On top of it lay a single kretek.

"Thanks!" Celeste called after Adam, as he shuffled away, back up Maple, in the direction Jake had come from. She thought about trying to catch him to give him that dollar for the cigarette, but then she thought back to Jake, the guy she was really after today.

CHAPTER FOUR

REUNION

A bell jangled as Celeste walked into Winzer's, trying to find Jake among the jumble of crook-handled snow shovels, flimsy plastic sleds, and bags of dog food that lined the walls. She made her way to the back. No sign of him in the paint section, amid the pyramids of gallon cans. Or in the front among the dozens of drawers filled with every size screw and galvanized nail. Winzer's was the kind of place that probably didn't exist in too many towns anymore. The kind of place that once had lent her a drill—no deposit, no ID—when all she'd bought were two 10-cent screws. At Winzer's, Burt would always give her a 5 percent discount, even if she was only picking up shoe polish and a spray bottle of Simple Green. She breathed in the smell of rough lumber and paint, looking around each high-stacked shelf for a glimpse of Jake's mustard-yellow jacket. He wasn't in Winzer's.

There was only one other place he could have been going in this direction. Celeste turned around, running her hand over a toy Tonka truck that reminded her of Jake's green pickup as she passed by. She shouldered open the door, jingling its bell again, and back out into the cold, gray day. She turned right. She couldn't help herself. She had to know. Her feet moved on their own, dragging her across the street, up the hill straight to Nicole's driveway where Jake's Tundra stood parked, the driver's side door ajar, an overhead light faintly illuminating the empty cab. She walked over, shut the door, and then started toward the pub, wondering if Jake and Nicole were watching her from the window.

Larry might have been right. She didn't know Jake. The Jake she knew loved her. He couldn't love her and betray her at the same time. But here was his truck, and there'd been that photo . . . And Jake had never actually told her he loved her. Sure, he said he loved parts of her: her sense of adventure, her toughness, her independence, her ticklish earlobes. All of the things Larry had said were signs of her Demon Mind (except the earlobes!). But Jake had never actually said "I love *you*." She kicked at the gravel driveway and looked over her shoulder one more time. Maybe because Nicole still took up too much of his heart.

Faint gray light slanted through the large picture window at the front of the pub, leaving the rest of the long, narrow bar in shadow. Seamus, the bearded bartender, stood polishing a glass, murmuring "Come on, come on" to the players in the soccer game on the TV mounted over the tiers of booze. Three o'clock—the place looked empty and still smelled of lemon furniture polish and dishwashing detergent, the way most bars she knew smelled before the happy hour crowds arrived.

The Castaway Pub was the place Celeste came to on her days off. It reminded her of her grandmother's cottage on Cape Cod, with its nautical accents and battered cast-off furniture

Seamus had hauled from the recycling center. Faded armchairs, driftwood mobiles, and glass table tops set on pedestals made of lobster traps—you could almost smell the far-off sea breeze. She was glad she had the place to herself for at least a few minutes.

But as Celeste's eyes adjusted in the dimly lit pub, she saw him. There at the far end of the bar, on a rickety old kitchen stool, sat Jake, hunched over his drink, absorbed in his own thoughts, fingers drumming a nervous rhythm on the bar. Exactly where he'd been two years earlier, the first time they'd met.

The Castaway had been as empty then as it was today. That first day, she'd come in after a tough session with Larry that had left her feeling raw and scraped, as if he'd run over her with a lawnmower.

"Looks like you need a drink."

The deep voice caught her off guard. Celeste peered down the bar at the big man half-hidden in the shadows. She recognized him immediately. Though she'd never seen him before, she knew. Here was the man she was supposed to marry! She'd never been so sure of anything, even though the thought was completely ridiculous. Like something she would have dreamed up back in high school. She shook her head, trying to clear the crazy notion.

"That bad?" Her voice came out too loud. "Well, actually, why the hell not?"

"On me," he said, stroking his salt-and-pepper beard with a large, square hand. He looked like Sean Connery. Not in the James Bond years, but later, with his fuller face and graying beard.

She looked away, embarrassed, pretending to survey the day's beer on the chalkboard menu nestled in the fishing net above the bar. In her head, she could hear Etta James belting out "At Last" and it was all she could do to keep from singing along out loud.

"One of those local IPAs, please!" she said, trying to keep her voice steady. "Thanks!"

Seamus pulled the beer lever and passed her a tall glass, foam perfectly set on the amber brew. More shyly now, she turned back to the man and held up the beer. "Cheers!"

"Why don't you come on down here and drink that with me?" His voice was deep and smooth as bourbon. He pushed another distressed wooden stool out from under the bar, inviting her to slide in next to him.

Celeste picked up her glass and sauntered toward him, trying to look cool and casual. Until she tripped over the leg of the stool. In an instant she'd crashed into him, spilling beer down his shirt front. But he grabbed her arms, stopping her fall.

"Whoa! You all right?"

He smelled of mown grass, sawdust, coffee—and the warmth he emanated should have made her skittish. Instead she found herself clinging to his broad chest, and, completely unself-conscious, actually asking, "Where have you been all my life?"

He threw back his head and laughed, a rumbling laugh. "Waiting for you!"

Now, like that first day, Jake sat alone, staring into his glass, head in his hands. On his right arm, Celeste glimpsed the red flannel heart she'd used to patch a growing hole in his jacket.

"Heart on your sleeve," she'd joked when she'd given it back to him.

"All for you, my love," he'd said, kissing her on the neck. Three weeks later he'd moved out.

Now Celeste hesitated at the pub door, trying to rein in her longing and confusion. If only she could sneak up behind Jake, throw her arms around him, and nuzzle her face in his neck, drink in his familiar scent, tangle her fingers in the dark hair that now grazed the edge of his collar. Instead, she stood in the doorway, wondering what to do next. He might push her away, make a fool of her, like so many men she'd known before. Like her father. At least Jake wasn't with Nicole.

She walked over and slid onto the wobbly seat beside him. "Buy a lady a drink?" she asked, tapping her fingers lightly on the heart-shaped patch.

Startled, Jake looked up. His face was tight, brows knit low over anxious eyes. At first he didn't seem to recognize her, but then a slow smile gathered up at the right corner of his mouth, bringing out the dimple that seemed to appear only for her. Through the rough texture of his coat, she could feel his familiar heat.

"What are you doing here?" he asked.

"Sorry! Didn't mean to scare you. But I had to tell you."

"What?" Jake's smile disappeared and the wariness was back.

Celeste put her hand on his, shyly, as if they were strangers, and said, "I did it. I've left Larry! Now we can—"

Before she could go any further, he flinched. He looked her up and down. His eyebrows drew together. "When?" he asked. "What time?"

"What time? I don't know, a couple of hours ago?" Puzzled by the question, she looked at her watch. "Around one, I guess. Why? Don't you believe me?"

He looked away, then tossed back the whiskey.

Seamus passed by, flipped his dish towel over his shoulder. "Another shot, Jake?"

"Yeah. And keep 'em coming." Jake cleared his throat and turned his stool toward Celeste. "I believe you. Wasn't sure I heard you right, that's all." He reached out and patted her hand, sending a flicker of the same electric energy she'd felt the first time he'd touched her, only now his hand felt cold and clammy.

"I thought you'd be a lot more excited," she said, as Seamus plunked the shot glass down and slid a pint of Celeste's usual across the counter toward her.

"I am. Excited." Jake raised his glass to her without looking at her.

"You don't sound excited." She took a deep breath. "Because of Nicole, right?"

Now Jake's gaze jerked toward her. "Nicole? Did you see her?"

"No, no. I just . . ." Something was definitely going on. "Larry said you and Nicole were together again. He showed me a photo. And I saw your truck." There, she'd blurted it out.

"You believed that? Guy's a liar." Jake looked like he wanted to throw his shot glass across the room.

"Hey! Don't worry!" She reached out and put her hand on his cheek, stealing a quick stroke across the stubble above his salt-and-pepper beard. She noted for the first time how tired he looked, his deep-set gray eyes bloodshot, lids tinged pink and swollen. "It's over. Actually . . ." She hesitated. "Larry tossed me out. I had a dream about some woman in a kitchen, and it scared him to death. No idea why. Said you put me up to it. But I was going to quit today anyway," she finished with a rush and, through pursed lips, syphoned a bit of foam off the top of her IPA.

His eyes narrowed and he looked down at the blank screen of his phone. "Mmm. Larry told you about Nicole?"

"Forget it." He wasn't listening. She was irritated and hurt. She wanted him to sweep her into his arms, say he'd never leave again, that the wedding was on. Not something about Nicole. Larry had warned her. She was too late. She sipped her beer from where the spot of foam was missing. It was too bitter for today.

"But Larry told you we were back together? That why you're not wearing my ring? Because Larry said I was with Nicole?"

Her ring! She looked down at her hand resting on the bar, waiting for his touch again. She stared at the pale circle of flesh where it had been just a couple of hours ago.

"I gave it to Larry," she said.

"My ring." Jake's voice had gone flat and cold.

"Technically, it's my ring. But it's more like he took it." Oh boy. There was no good way to explain this. "I have to go back. To get it." Sliding off the stool, Celeste reached into her pack to find her wallet. "Hey, Seamus, can I pay?" She pushed a ten-dollar bill across the bar.

Jake grabbed her arm, hard. "Not now. Stay. Finish that beer with me. Please. We're celebrating, right? Like old times." Now Jake was pleading, and there was something in his voice she'd never heard before. Fear?

"I know, but I have to go back. I'm not giving up my ring. Your ring." She paused and looked at his strained face again. "Don't you want me to have it?"

"Yes, I want you to have it. But please don't leave me now. That's all." Jake put his hand over hers and pressed down as if he were trying to pin her to the bar. "He might keep you. Can't trust that guy."

"I know." Here it was again. That refrain she'd heard over and over before Jake moved out.

"Rather get you another ring than let him drag you under again." Now he leaned in close so their noses were almost touching. "Stay here. Don't go back to Larry's." His breath was warm, laced with whiskey.

"I'll be right back. Wait for me," she said, forcing herself to lean away from him. Behind her the bar door opened, and a rowdy group of hipsters from the college down the road came in, laughing, jostling each other, calling out "Ahoy!" Kids. The moment was over. Celeste pulled her hand back out from under his. "If I don't get it now, Larry *will* still have a hold on me."

Jake blew out a long breath. "Haven't changed, have you? Still doing what you want. Only this time . . . " He drained his glass. "Listen to me. Please." His voice was colder, clipped, with an edge she remembered from all the fights they'd had over Larry. But now, underneath, she sensed something else, something tight and almost desperate.

"What's wrong, Jake?"

"I can't stop you." He glanced at the stricken Celeste, and his face softened, the lines she loved falling into place, the soft creases around his eyes, the soft full lips she was dying to kiss. "Sorry. Sorry," he whispered, his words warm inside her like hot buttered rum. "Please, Celeste, don't go back there. Not today. Not now."

Everything in her wanted to stay, to feel his breath in her hair, to have that familiar sensation of her heart beating against his chest. But if she didn't get that ring back this afternoon, when her resolve was high, she didn't know what would happen. She'd be afraid to go, or worse yet, she'd go and, like Jake said, Larry would snare her again. He'd done it before.

"I'm sorry too," she murmured, "but I'm going. Maybe while I get my ring, you can get your truck from Nicole's." No! She hadn't meant to say that.

Jake let go of her hand. "She just needed . . . " He stopped. "Never mind. Go."

"Wait here! Order me another, or champagne, so we can really celebrate! I promise."

He nodded but, staring down at his phone again, never looked up, even as she turned at the door to wave.

Celeste walked as fast as she could, retracing her steps back to Larry's house, her mind churning through the events of the day, wondering why Jake had been so adamant that she not return for her ring, *his* ring. Larry and Jake clearly hated each other, but she could never get either one to tell her why. She guessed it had to do with Nicole.

"He's no good for you," Larry had pronounced when she'd finally gotten up her courage to tell him about Jake. She'd thought he'd be thrilled that she'd actually allowed herself to fall in love at last, had finally broken through her fear and found happiness waiting for her on the other side.

Larry, though, did not sanction any relationships outside the circle of Dreamers. She could still hear the cold disapproval in his voice. "You got no idea what he's really like. Another weakling, like all the other guys in your life, Cel. I got way better men for you. If you'd give in," he'd said.

There was more to it, though. Jake wasn't just someone. He was Nicole's ex, the man she'd left to become Larry's right hand, his queen of the Dreamers. But that couldn't—

A horn blared. Celeste stumbled back on the curb as a sleek black SUV screeched to a halt inches from where she stood. She waved an embarrassed apology, but the car squealed away before she could get a glimpse at the driver. He hadn't even bothered to look back. Celeste stared after the car, wondering if it was from out of state, someone unaware that in Riverton Falls, pedestrians ruled. No, the license plate was the familiar two-tone rectangle sporting some old hippie vanity message, PC2U.

"You too, buddy," she called after him, then looked both ways before venturing again into the now-empty street in front of Larry's house. She glanced at her watch. Ten till three. Whoever had this hour's appointment with Larry must be about done.

"*Awk! Awk!*" She looked up. Overhead, Pete beat the air above the hedge, the tips of his blue wings slashing the gray sky. She kept her eye on him as she started up the flagstone walk, wondering how he had escaped and if she should try to corral him somehow.

Another voice, a high-pitched rasp, brought her attention back down to earth.

There before her stood Adam, pausing in the open doorway. He looked around from the threshold, his eyes wild,
visibly startled at the sight of Celeste. "What . . . Why are
you . . . ?" Celeste asked. But Adam didn't answer. He slammed
the door behind him and took off up the boulder-strewn hill
behind the house. Puzzled, she watched him scramble over the
rocky ledge, his greatcoat flapping behind him like the wings
of another frightened bird.

CHAPTER FIVE

TUMBLING DOWN

Celeste turned the handle on the door, slowly pushing it open, afraid that Larry might be on the other side, about to rush out to chase after Adam. The waiting room was empty. It looked the same as when she'd left it just a couple of hours before, not a doily or a single pillow disturbed. The air, though, seemed charged with tension and hinted of something sweet and flowery. Leaving the front door wide open in case Pete wanted back in, she tiptoed to the inner half-open office door. "Larry?"

At first she didn't understand what she was seeing. There, on the floor, his big belly spilling out between his jeans and his flowered shirt, lay Larry, his face ashen, pale as his hair and stubbly beard. Had she really given him a heart attack? Or a stroke?

Then she saw the blood. It pooled beneath his head, soaking into the beige carpet. Celeste grabbed onto the door frame. She tried to keep herself upright, but her legs felt like waterlogged sponges. Just the mention of blood had always made her woozy, but now the actual sight of it and the raw, metallic smell forced her, gagging, to her knees.

Run, she told herself, get help! But, as Larry had so often reminded her, she rarely followed her own best instincts. Instead of running away, she found herself crawling over the threshold, inching closer to the first dead body she'd ever seen. At least he *looked* dead. He didn't seem to be moving. The crystal she'd been holding just two hours earlier lay in the sticky puddle of blood, its sharp gray edges smeared with red. The gore sent another wave of nausea rushing into her throat.

Celeste swallowed hard. She'd gotten close enough to touch him. She felt blood seeping, wicking into the knees of her corduroy pants, growing damp and sticky against her skin. Daring herself, she reached out, trying to steady her hand, to push it just that much further across the small space separating her from Larry's body. Suddenly, Larry's head rolled to the side. Her hand snapped back straight to her mouth, muffling a scream. At the strangled sound, Larry's eyelids twitched open, and she found herself looking straight into his unfocused blue eyes.

"Not you," he managed to hiss before his eyelids dropped again.

"Larry! Oh my God, Larry! What did that guy do to you?"

A blue tinge was spreading around his lips and he gasped and gurgled with each shallow intake of breath. What was she supposed to do?

She knew CPR, part of her restaurant training, but she'd never had to use it. Besides, the thought of putting her lips on Larry's was repugnant, even if he was dying right here in front of her. No, she needed to get help. Testing her legs, she slowly stood up and stepped over Larry's protruding stomach, her boot landing in a bloody patch of carpet. She fumbled for the phone on the desk and dialed 911.

It rang once and a woman answered. "What is the nature of your emergency?"

Celeste clutched the phone as if she were clinging to a real person. "Someone's tried to kill Larry. Hurry! Please!"

"Larry Blatsky?" The voice was still calm. Celeste was glad someone was keeping her head.

"Yes, you know him?"

"Honey, everyone knows Larry. Okay, forget I said that," the woman whispered before returning quickly to script. "Can you give me Larry's—I mean the victim's—condition? Is he still breathing?" asked the operator. "Still conscious?"

Celeste looked to Larry to check. His eyes were closed again, but gurgling sounds came from his throat. "I don't know. It sounds like he's drowning!" She was wailing now.

"Stay where you are, ma'am. The police and the ambulance are on the way. I'll stay on the phone with you until they arrive. Can you do that?"

Celeste nodded.

"Ma'am, can you do that? Can you give me your name, please?"

Celeste put the receiver down on the desk without answering. What was she doing? She'd come to get her ring back, and now she was in the middle of what looked like a murder. If she didn't find the ring right away, who knew what would happen to it?

She'd seen Larry drop it into that little wooden box next to . . . The computer was gone! Instead, where it should have been, where it had always been, there remained only a polished square of desk top surrounded by a faint outline of dust. Worse, the box was gone too. She began to search the desk, lifting piles of typed dreams, running her hands over the wood marled with milky water rings and grease spots. She knew she shouldn't touch anything. She was probably disturbing some kind of evidence while leaving her own fingerprints behind, but she had to have that ring. She knelt down and crawled under the desk.

There it was, the box, on its side, on the floor, its contents spilled across the carpet. She pawed through a few Chinese coins, a bracelet that looked just like one she'd brought back from Nepal and given to her friend Gloria years ago. A set of dog tags. And three gold wedding rings, one clearly a man's. None of them hers. She lay on her belly and squirmed toward Larry's chair, hoping her ring had fallen further back. The sirens grew louder, coming closer now; she needed to find it. But the ring was gone, plain and simple. No matter how hard she searched, it wasn't there.

"Ma'am, ma'am, are you all right?" Celeste jumped at the sound of the distant voice coming through the phone, banging her head on the underside of the desk above her. From behind her, she could hear Larry struggle for breath, gulping for air. "Wait there, ma'am, they're coming," the soothing voice of the 911 operator piped through the receiver.

Celeste backed out from under the desk. She stood up and rubbed the lump rising on the crown of her head. She still had a choice, and she had to make it fast. What if the cops came and thought she'd done this? She could still run, like Adam. She hadn't told the operator her name; maybe she could still get away and pretend she'd never been there.

Then she turned and saw the bloody trail of footprints she'd made across the carpet, the pattern of her Vibram-soled hikers clearly visible, and she knew then that running away was not an option. Unless she really did want to look like a suspect. No, she'd wait.

The door crashed open, smacking against the office wall, and the EMTs raced in. Celeste recognized them, Fritzi and her partner Charlene, the bartenders from Jackie-O's, but she'd never seen them in action like this, brandishing an oxygen tank and a defibrillator. Behind them stumbled Wally DeTouche. His button mouth quivered on his pale, plump, dumpling face as he dropped to his knees by Larry's head. He pushed Charlene's hand away before she could strap the oxygen mask over Larry's now purpling face.

"Larry, it's me, Wally. Who did this to you, man? Can you tell me anything?"

"Hey," protested Charlene, but the cop shushed her just long enough for them all to hear Larry's last words.

"Her . . . her . . ." He pushed the condemnation out with his last bubble of breath. As his head lolled to one side, he stared straight at Celeste just before the light went out of his eyes.

Outside, a gaggle of neighbors huddled in front of Larry's house, whispering to each other, staring as DeTouche propelled Celeste down the walk toward the squad car, his hand hot against her neck. Its warmth made her feel sick and sordid. She willed herself to keep walking, wishing she could disappear.

"Is that a bad lady?" Celeste overheard a little girl in a pink parka ask her mother as DeTouche pushed her past them into the cruiser. He shifted his hand now to shield her head, pressing too hard on the fresh, throbbing lump as he jostled her into the backseat. He slammed the squad car's door. Though she hadn't done anything wrong, Celeste felt guilty. Like she had when she'd woken from her weird dream that morning—the dream that for some reason had frightened Larry enough to kick her out. Somewhere deep down, someplace she didn't want to look, she had a sickening suspicion that the murder must somehow be her fault.

Shame, shame. Larry's voice ripped through Celeste's head. *The Shadow's been waiting for a chance to swallow you up. Now here it is, in spades!*

She clutched the little mermaid in her pocket.

The ambulance, siren blaring, already rushed toward Hospital Hill, though speed wasn't going to do Larry much good. He was already dead before Fritzi and Charlene took him out. Anything Larry said to her now was simply an echo of something he'd said in the past. How long would he haunt her like this, his words a buzz of bees at the base of her skull? Her dead parents' voices still stung, though their onslaught of drunken taunts and criticism were softening. She was sure that Dad, Mom, and Larry would all be happy zipping around together in the hell of her skull.

So instead of shouting "I didn't do anything! I'm only a witness!" at the frightened and frantic gawkers the way any normal person would, she slumped deeper into the backseat and its stale stench of vomit as Wally DeTouche clambered into the driver's seat and started the car.

Stop being so pathetic, her father said. *Don't let them see how you feel or you'll just screw it all up as usual.*

Yes, dear, just go ahead, give up. You have nothing to lose. That was her mother, her voice chiming in loud and clear over the tinkle of ice in her gin-and-tonic.

Dig deep, Larry countered in her head. *Sink into the guilt!*

Yep, there they all were, right on cue. Listen to her father, and shove the feelings back under the rug. Pay attention to her mother, and long for a stiff drink. Listen to Larry, and drop into the terror that festered now below her diaphragm, making her feel even sicker than the smell inside the car had already done.

She wriggled in the uncomfortable molded plastic bucket of a seat, wondering how many drunks had thrown up in there, the stink of it almost unbearable. Through the window, she watched two other cops, one questioning the neighbors, the other stringing yellow crime-scene tape around the lilac hedges. A photographer snapped pictures while a state trooper in a khaki Smokey the Bear hat busily scribbled in her notebook, evidently taking down a statement from the mother of the scared little girl.

Through the scratched plexiglass barrier, Celeste could hear Wally mutter something into his radio as he gunned the engine, and then the squad car peeled out of the driveway, spraying gravel in its wake, its blue light flashing, but no siren blaring, thank God.

As Wally drove, Celeste peeked out at the high school kids playing Ultimate Frisbee on the green in front of City Hall. They darted around in shorts and T-shirts, and Celeste thought about how easily they seemed to shrug off the dipping temperatures of the dying November afternoon. But just then the game stopped mid-throw and they all turned to stare after the cruiser. Sliding even further down in the backseat, Celeste tried to hide in the shadows, struggling to fold her long, gangly frame into the cramped space. She wished she had long straight hair to draw across her face like a curtain instead of the easily recognized, unmanageable frizz that stuck up for all to see over the edge of the window.

Wally still hadn't said a word to her in the car, but his shoulders heaved up and down, and even through the plexiglass she could hear him sobbing. With only three cops in town, she hadn't been too surprised when he'd shown up just as Larry was taking his last breaths. Wally had been one of Larry's most dedicated Dreamers; he'd worshipped Larry. But then, so had she, at least for a while.

Outside the cruiser, the same solid, orderly rows of three-story brick buildings that had felt so friendly and familiar only a few hours ago seemed now to glower down at her through tall, arched windows as DeTouche maneuvered the car past storefronts displaying frumpy cold-weather fashion and used books. At the corner of Maple and Main, he slammed on his brakes at Riverton Falls's only traffic light. From the sidewalks, the homebound rush-hour crowd waiting to cross the street stared in at her with curiosity and even alarm. Celeste usually enjoyed meandering through town, stopping to chat with Dreamers about their homework or share news with other Broken Gate regulars. Now she couldn't move through town fast enough and only hoped no one she knew caught sight of her scrunched in the rear of the police car, shame overtaking her once again.

She peered out the window. A couple of suits from the Broken Gate, lawyers or bankers or whatever, were looking at her in what she hoped was disbelief. She sank back down, but not before catching the eye of Victor, the ponytailed, bespectacled librarian, standing on the corner, his canvas bag of mysteries slung over his shoulder. Oh boy, once he got back to the library and told Joanie, it would be all over town. Joanie, her favorite librarian, the one who signed her in whenever she'd come in to check her e-mails on the computer, had her finger on the pulse— as the saying goes—of Riverton Falls, and any gossip that passed by Joanie's desk flew all over town in a matter of hours.

Cheep! Cheep! Cheep! sang the electronic birds that prompted pedestrians to cross, but no one moved; they just kept staring into the cruiser. Face buried in her hands, Celeste sank down as far as she could, wishing this was another bad dream. An image of Adam fleeing up the hill swam to the surface. Maybe he was simply a thief in a robbery gone wrong, but in the back of her head Larry whispered *No such thing as coincidence* just as Wally swung the car into the lot behind the police station.

"Damn," she said looking up as they passed under the big picture window of Fast N' Furious, her gym. Celeste knew from all the hours she spent working out that anyone on an elliptical in the row of trainers lined up at the full-length picture window had no choice but to stare directly into the alley where she now sat stuck in the back of the squad car. Sure enough, there was Tony Pritchett, local reporter, gaping at her, his mouth actually hanging wide open. She'd always wanted her name in the paper, but listed as a by-line, not a murder suspect. She looked away quickly as they stopped in front of the double-wide metal garage door, or "sally port," as she heard Wally call it when he announced their arrival over his radio. They waited as the door rose, squealing, metal on metal.

Still sniffling, Wally DeTouche led Celeste through the station's back door and down a harshly lit hallway of green linoleum and smudged beige walls. As they turned a corner, she got a strong whiff of bleach and then glimpsed the stainless steel shine of a lidless toilet next to a narrow wooden bench. The holding cell, waiting for her. Her shoulders dropped a notch with relief as he pushed her past the cell and into a tiny windowless interrogation room instead. The cinderblock walls were completely bare except for a white dry-erase board, staring blankly inside its wooden frame. Three utilitarian chairs and a metal desk filled most of the space. A blue light blinked on and off near the ceiling in the right hand corner of the room. Glancing up, she realized it was a surveillance camera looking down, aimed directly at the metal chair where Wally motioned her to sit. Then he collapsed onto a rolling chair on the other side of the desk. His eyes red-rimmed and his breath ragged, he grabbed a handful of tissues from a big box on the desk and mopped up his dripping pug nose. Celeste looked down at her hands, waiting for him to speak.

"Why'd you do it, Cel? Why'd you kill Larry?" His voice was a quivering whine, his face, like a baby's, bunched and splotchy from crying.

Celeste looked up, alarmed. "Me? You don't think—"

"We all knew you were a Doubter, gallivanting around with that Jake Kelly. It was only a matter of time." He blew his nose and tossed the wet wad of tissues into the wastebasket under the desk.

"Doubter?" She had no idea what he was talking about. "Look, Wally, I know you're upset. We're both upset, for God's sake! But you know me! You know I wouldn't . . . couldn't . . . " Her stomach knotted into a fist with a fuck-you finger of fear reaching into her throat. "Wait! I'm not here as a witness, am I?"

Wally grabbed the desk and pushed himself to his feet, squaring his shoulders. "I need to inspect that pack," he commanded, switching instantly from Dreamer to interrogator.

Celeste placed her bag on the desk and he began to rifle through it, pulling out her brush, her wallet, a fistful of crumpled-up dollar bills. He dug in again. He fished out her journal. She cringed as Wally flipped through the pages, scanning her dreams, and then threw them down on the desk, in what looked like disgust. The book landed open and the kretek she'd placed inside for safekeeping rolled out. He picked it up, sniffed it. "What's this? Drugs?"

"No, it's not drugs. It's just a cigarette I got from . . ." She stopped herself.

"From who?" He wasn't going to let her get away with anything.

"From Adam."

"And he is?"

"The tarot-reading guy. The one I told you to look for when you questioned me back at Larry's. The guy I saw running away when I got there."

"And he gave you this . . . cigarette? When was that? Before or after he helped you kill Larry?"

"No, that's not . . ." This didn't look good, but this was Wally, a fellow Dreamer, or maybe now only a former fellow Dreamer. Still, she had to be able to get through to him.

"Your phone, where's that at?" His doughy chin quivered as he held out his hand.

"I don't have a cell phone."

"Everyone has a cell phone."

Actually, he was right. She did have a phone, one of those too-smart things that made her feel so dumb. Jake had bought it for her, a two-for-one deal at the phone store, he'd told her. He'd spent a good hour trying to get her excited about all the great features—e-mail, camera, YouTube, games galore. The list was endless. He'd loaded a dozen confusing apps she knew she'd never understand, and the day he left she'd stuck it in a drawer and hadn't taken it out since. As far as she knew, Jake was still the only one who had the number.

"I don't use a cell phone. Privacy thing. I don't want anyone spying on me."

"Got something to hide? Running away from something?"

Celeste shook her head. "Wally, we've processed enough dreams together. You know I'm always running away."

"Listen, in here I'm Officer DeTouche. And you're Miss Fortune." He gave a strangled laugh. "Appropriately named."

She'd heard that one too many times. She wasn't about to rise to the bait.

"Must have been hard on you, the way Larry shared everything about everybody, since you're so into your *privacy*." DeTouche drew the word out as if it were something dirty. "Was he about to share something you didn't want us to know? Is that why you did it?"

"I didn't! You're not making any sense," Celeste said. In fact, DeTouche had hit a sore point. She hated the way Larry wanted everything out in the open. For Celeste there was nothing more private than what really went on in her head, there was nothing more revealing than the images that emerged in her sleep. She didn't mind telling people about the dreams that scared her, like rapists, wolves, or quicksand. But the dreams she had about *real* people, especially her dreams about Jake, were dreams she never gave to Larry or the Dreamers.

DeTouche shook his head, dropped the kretek back into the journal. "I'm going to need your boots. Evidence."

Celeste bent over, unlaced her boots, and pulled them off, avoiding the bloody soles. She handed them over to DeTouche, and he started out the door. She watched as her pack and her boots left the room, dangling by their straps and laces from either hand of Officer DeTouche.

"Wait, can I at least have my dream journal? That *is* private."

"Nope, evidence." He turned his head and glared back at her as he walked out. "And don't think there's any such thing as privacy when you're in as deep as this."

Celeste slumped back in the chair. That guy Adam, wherever he was, whatever he did, had been right. Everything was tumbling down—Larry, the Dreamscape, even Jake, everything imploding, and it was Adam's fault, or at least that's how it looked.

She should have skipped her appointment that morning, just not shown up. After all, she had gone in to quit, so why hadn't she simply stopped going? Probably because under all that anger she'd carried into the office, there was a piece of her that still wanted Larry's approval. Hard as it was to admit, she'd wanted to hear that he would miss her, that her presence mattered. She'd even wanted to thank him, because—no matter how far the Dreamscape had deteriorated for her—Larry had changed her, just as he'd promised on her first visit. That was the problem. She'd changed, and he didn't like it. Hadn't liked it. And now she'd never have a chance to confront him about it as she'd planned.

CHAPTER SIX

LEARNING TO DREAM

Alone in the interrogation room, Celeste folded her arms on the desk and lay her head on them. Her thoughts swirled back to those early days, when she'd first arrived in Riverton Falls and landed her job at the Broken Gate, where the name Larry Blatsky rippled every night through the crowd. The bar, dressed up to look like a Gay Nineties saloon, was the Dreamers' favorite watering hole. Red brocade wall paper, art nouveau chandeliers, and a mahogany bar rumored to have come from a Boston brothel. The place had a kind of womb-like, comfy feel about it that drew in this strange bunch of drinkers who'd sit pulled up to the bar on their high-backed, red velvet stools, downing Celeste's classic cocktails, discussing their therapy sessions. Half the conversations began with "Larry says," or "Larry told me," or "Larry wants me to . . ."

Celeste had lived in a lot of places and worked a lot of bars, but she'd never run into people so openly sharing their personal therapy sessions with each other over drinks at happy hour. Not that she understood anything they were talking about. Vital Self, Demon Mind, Golden Prince, Dark Mothers—they spoke in a code she couldn't crack. At least not then. But still, she grew curious about this guy who drew in everyone from locavores to lawyers to construction workers. Whatever it was, these Dreamers, as they called themselves, had something special—a community, a close connection missing from her own lonely life.

"So what's the story on this Larry guy everyone keeps talking about?" she'd asked Allegra Pippin, the other bartender on her shift, while they set up for the five o'clock rush.

As Allegra reached across to vigorously polish the far side of the already gleaming bar, Celeste couldn't help but stare at the intricate tribal tramp stamp that peeked out between the bottom of her too-tight T-shirt and the top of her tiny black skirt. No wonder guys had nicknamed her Allegra Pipin' Hot.

"Larry Blatsky? You mean the dream guy? Everyone goes to him. Only therapist in town. Or maybe not, but seems like it." Allegra shrugged her luscious shoulders, then added, "Besides, they say he's not really a therapist, more like a spiritual guide or something." She reached for a sharp knife and began to cut fresh limes into wedges while Celeste surrounded tiny bowls of smoked salt with pink and white baby radishes.

"Everyone? Everyone goes to the same guy?"

"Yep, pretty much. Pass me those olives," Allegra said. "But those regulars we have in here, the ones they call Dreamies or whatever, they're part of some kind of special, I don't know, like a fan club," she called over her shoulder as she distributed ramekins of olives to the tables around the room. "They even have a clubhouse right outside of town, big fancy place in the woods."

Celeste listened, mopping up rings and spills on the glass shelves lined with liquor bottles behind the bar. As she picked up each bottle, she held it briefly to the light. She loved their jeweled tones, the emerald Tanqueray, the amber Dewars, the diamond flash of Don Julio. Bars had been the one constant in her life—places she could go in almost any city across the globe and still recognize the same bottles, like old familiar faces, remeet the same drinks. Nairobi, Penang, Berlin—wherever there were Germans, Americans, even Japanese tourists, she'd find a hotel bar that needed her, where she could pick up enough cash to hit the road again, and then move on to the volunteer refugee work she loved but could never commit to long enough to land a real job. Sometimes she'd pick up work as a stringer for the *Toronto Globe*, Pacifica, even NPR, and she'd dream of being a real reporter—until her confidence flagged, and she ended up looking for another bar again, the only place she felt like a professional.

"So you don't go to Larry?" she asked Allegra's reflection in the gaudy gilt-framed mirror behind the bottles.

"Nah, I'm not going to waste my money on some crackpot. I hear enough about him working here. Bunch of crap if you ask me." Then Allegra lowered her voice to a whisper, though no one was around except Celeste. "Besides, there's something really creepy about it all."

"Creepy?"

Allegra bent down to stock the cooler under the counter with bottles of white wine, the black swirls of her tattoo now fully revealed. "Whatever. At least they tip good."

Celeste should have listened to Allegra, but her curiosity got the better of her. And though she didn't want to admit it, she was beginning to feel desperate. She had no idea what she was looking for, but she suspected it was more than just the right place to live after years of wandering. She'd never thought about going to therapy before, but after almost two decades living as an expat, she had a nagging feeling that her life was about nothing more than being on the move.

Until she landed in Riverton Falls to be near her friend Gloria, who had written to her about this rare place where people stayed because they wanted to be there, not because they had no other choice. Unlike the rest of the strip-mall-ridden America Celeste had encountered on her return to the States after years overseas, Riverton Falls still had old-fashioned character and charm. It reminded her of the small town in Ohio where she'd grown up. People greeted each other on the streets. Kids rode bikes up and down the neighborhoods and played Kick the Can on summer evenings. Families went to band concerts on the green and basketball games at the high school for entertainment. But Riverton Falls was far from provincial. It had three indie bookstores, a great little artsy movie theater, and for some reason, an incredible number of really good musicians of all kinds, some of whom played right there at the Broken Gate every weekend. The town, she thought, was almost perfect.

The only thing missing was the ocean. It took three-plus hours to reach the coast. But for a kid from Ohio, that seemed like nothing. Summers, when she was a girl, her family would make the long drive overnight to her grandparents' place on Cape Cod. That cottage and the ocean steps away from it were all she and her mother ever had in common. They'd race each other from the porch and across the sand to the water's edge, then dance together in the surf, splashing and laughing.

"My little mermaid," her mother had called her, and Celeste still treasured the tiny bronze mermaid her mother had given her for her tenth birthday. Wherever Celeste had traveled, the tiny mermaid, hair cascading down her back, hands clasped beneath her chin, had gone too. Celeste still longed to live where the air smelled of salt and seaweed, where she could fall asleep to the sound of crashing waves. For now, though, the mossy scent of the West Branch and the thundering falls of the Pelletier were close enough.

As she began to settle down for the first time in years, she couldn't ignore the underlying thrum of anxiety and self-doubt that had become the background noise to her days and nights. It wasn't as if there was anything really wrong, she told herself, nothing a few drinks or a couple of tokes didn't usually take care of. Really, she was fine—a little lonely, a little empty, a little depressed, but basically fine. But now, with forty looming ahead, it might be time to take a closer look at where she was going. She wanted the second half of her life to be about something more than where to move next. So she'd taken the leap and made that first call to Larry Blatsky.

"Yup, I can squeeze ya in. One month, okay?" He sounded brusque, but he was probably a busy man. "Bring some dreams. Write 'em down. See ya then." He hung up without another word.

Write them down? How do you do that? she remembered wondering back then, completely at a loss. Weren't dreams just something to wake up from? She asked her old friend Gloria for advice; Gloria had been in the Dreamscape herself, but she'd quit soon before Celeste had followed her to Riverton Falls.

Gloria had given her a sour look and said, "*Don't* get involved. The guy's a whack job. I'm warning you, don't go." And that had been the end of the conversation and, as far as Celeste could figure out, the beginning of the end of a friendship that reached back to their college days.

Bruce Nussbaum, a lanky, anxious Dreamer, a regular at the bar, had been the one to help her figure out how to capture her dreams. He'd been going to Larry for almost a decade. As Bruce saw it, Larry had turned him from a low-life ski bum into the self-proclaimed successful lawyer she now saw propped at her bar every evening downing a couple of mojitos, his drink of choice even on the coldest nights when everyone else had switched to bourbon. Seemed Larry didn't have anything against drinking, based on the hours and dollars his clients put in at the Broken Gate. That was good. She liked to drink—a lot.

"You need the right equipment," Bruce had advised her, stretching across the bar to get right in her face. "A notebook and some kind of pen that writes really fast. Like a Rollerball. Put them by your pillow when you go to sleep so you can grab them the second you wake up. Then just write what you remember. Don't think. Just write." To demonstrate, he wrote the word "dream" with his long tapered index finger in the condensation from his mojito on the bar. "Like that. Don't open your eyes. Write blind. Otherwise the dream will . . ." He searched for the right word. "Evaporate. Keep yourself inside the dream as long as you can. I'd be happy to show you some night," he added, inching even closer. Celeste tried to smile. Bruce was one of those fit, runner kind of guys with the pinched face of a know-it-all. Not her type at all.

"Thanks, I got it. But how do I write without opening my eyes?"

Bruce dipped a radish in the salt and licked it. "You'll figure it out. Can't wait to hear how it goes." He winked and threw down a $10 tip before heading out.

A bit doubtful, Celeste did what he advised. After a couple of false starts, she began waking up more regularly and automatically, frantically jotting down whatever ragged remnants she could grasp before the dreams dissolved. Finally, on the morning of her first appointment with Larry, she managed to capture one dream almost whole. She'd written it down as fast as she could, happy she'd have something to bring in even if she wasn't completely sure this would be more than a one-shot deal with Larry Blatsky.

She remembered entering that waiting room for the first time, how she followed behind as Larry led the way into his utilitarian office.

"Sit," he said, and she lowered herself onto the chair closest to his desk without taking her eyes off the strange man in front of her. This was the famous Larry Blatsky? He looked like a displaced beach bum in his cut-offs, flip-flops, and Hawaiian shirt, which barely hid the incipient paunch Celeste would watch grow into a bulging belly over the next four years. She wasn't sure what she had expected, but his unkempt appearance made her wonder why he didn't even try to look professional.

"Feel the pain! Feel the pain!" She jumped at the sound of the command then turned to find, in the corner, pacing freely along a perch, a bobbing parrot.

"Shut up, Pete!" Larry admonished his pet before turning the full force of his attention on Celeste. "Okay, let's see here. Celeste Fortune. That's some kinda name all right. Were you born with that or did you acquire it?"

"I'm not married if that's what you mean."

"Nah, just thought it was kinda like the name of a, let's say, stripper I used to know. And you do look kinda familiar. Not sure why." Larry laughed. "So what's your problem?" he rushed on without waiting for her to respond. "Why are you sitting here today?" He crossed his hands over his belly, leaned back, and put his feet up on the desk.

"Mostly curious, I guess." Celeste tried to sound nonchalant. "And maybe to work on some minor issues that have come up recently?" She hadn't meant that to come out as a question, but he already had her flustered.

This had always been his game, to knock her off balance right from the get-go, every time she sat down across from him. Then he'd peer at her over those half-rim glasses, his chin resting on his hammy hands, never nodding or giving any indication that he'd heard her, just like on that first day. She'd finally figured out it was one of those therapist tricks to get you to say more than you intended just to fill up the silence. Right from the beginning, she was a sucker for it.

"Actually, I guess I've been feeling a little depressed, sort of unsettled. I thought maybe seeing you would give me some motivation to make changes in my life?"

Larry smiled, looking like he understood exactly what she meant. "I'm willing to bet there's a lot more to it than that. Let me tell you what I see in front of me, then you tell me if I'm wrong."

Celeste nodded, wondering what he could possibly know about her. She'd hardly opened her mouth.

"I see a woman too scared to go after what she really wants in her life, who doesn't believe she can get it anyway, and who covers it all up by pretending everything's hunky-dory. All the indicators of what I call false independence." He paused for a breath, scanning her astonished face. "Besides, I'm willing to bet you have a lot of guy issues, so I'm not completely convinced this will work out between us, but I'm willing to give it a try if you are."

This man had X-ray vision. He'd seen through her faster than anyone she'd ever met. No wonder he'd considered rejecting her right off the bat. He'd probably known from the start that she'd be trouble. Somehow, though, she'd managed to hang on.

"So, Cel, tell me, what do you know about the Dreamscape?"

Cel? No one called her Cel. Not since her father, and she'd never liked it when he had. She should have said something right then, corrected Larry, let him know her name was Celeste. She'd never been able to stand up to him, though. Within six months, even the damn bird called her Cel, and by then she was already so unsure of herself that she was embarrassed to say anything about it.

"The Dreamscape?" She shrugged her shoulders. "Only what I've heard from some of your . . . clients. At the bar. Where I work."

"So, not a lot then. Figures." Larry furiously typed a few sentences into his computer. Celeste noticed he used only a couple of fingers to type, but, boy, was he fast. "Let me give you a quick rundown. But first, I need you to sign this." He pushed a form across the desk at her.

Celeste glanced at it. "You want to copyright my dreams?"

"Doesn't mean anything. Allows me to type them up, that's all. Just sign it." Larry passed her a pen. She shrugged and scribbled her signature across the bottom line.

"Touch down! Touch down!" Pete croaked from his perch.

"Shut up, right now!" Larry yelled back. He pulled a plate of chocolate chip cookies from the drawer. "Want one?"

"Sure, thanks." The cookies tasted homemade, soft and gooey with melting chocolate, the way she liked them.

"The Dreamscape," he began, "is something I've been developing for about twenty years now. The shortest way I can describe it is this." He stood up from the computer, walked over to the window, and half-sat on the sill, arms folded as he began to lecture. "The dreams, Cel, are the way we're going to discover who you really are. They're the gateway to your Vital Self. Ya gotta go way down deep here, Cel, way down below your thinking mind, below your subconscious, down to your heart and soul."

Celeste tried to listen as she chewed, but her mind kept wandering as the words sailed past her—*collective unconscious, archetypes, Demon Mind, Vital Self, gestalt.* She gazed at the lilac blossoms bobbing in the late May breeze outside the window as his voice got louder, more insistent, demanding her attention.

"The dreams are your healing guides," Larry said, his mouth full of cookie. "They're going to help me rip off that mask of false independence and find the sad little girl you stuffed away long ago." Celeste had no idea what girl he was talking about. Maybe this was too far over her head. Maybe she shouldn't have come.

Larry stood up and leaned back against his desk, staring into her eyes. "Now I want you to relax. Breathe deeply."

Celeste tried to melt into the chair. Relaxing was not something she did well. Anxiety had become the scaffolding that held her up, but she tried to keep herself together and follow directions, inhaling and exhaling audibly.

"Now close your eyes."

Tired after working late the night before, she nodded sleepily in the chair. A loud slap startled her. Her eyes flew open. Larry was walking toward her. As he came closer, the room darkened, as if a cloud had passed over the sun. Celeste watched, transfixed as the short, stocky man seemed to transform in front of her, growing taller, the edges of his body shimmering with a glacial blue light. His eyes bore into her as he stepped closer. She cowered in her chair. Larry hovered above her, filling the room, until the walls fell away and they were where? On an empty plane, wind whipping about her as she looked up into the face of an ancient shaman or a bearded prophet filled with fire, calling her name. "Let go now," the giant figure bellowed. "Drop that mask. Drop the costumes you wear to cover the nakedness of your heart. Show me the girl who is hiding in you! Bring her forth and let her dance on this altar we are building together."

The voice crashed through her, like an axe splitting a log into kindling.

"This woman must crash and burn. Stoke the fire, step into the flames!"

A hand landed on her shoulder, pinning her in place. Heat rose, shooting down her arms, racing through her body. Sweat trickled down her back. She ran her hand over her flushed face as the towering figure commanded, "Let the soft, vulnerable creature of your heart climb up through the ashes."

A hot wind blew across her face and circled her head, ruffling her hair.

"The Dreamscape is demanding. The Dreamscape is dangerous. It will force you to face yourself, to face the truth of your life. Step into the dreams, Cel. Let your authentic life begin!"

"Yes, yes, that's what I want!" Celeste heard herself say. Desire surged through her, white heat pulling her to this alluring magician. The boundaries of her body dissolved with longing for whatever it was he was offering. The room filled with magnetic energy, crackling with static electricity.

"Take this chance to become who you truly are! Tear down those walls and free that girl! Together we will take her from the darkness and bring her back to the light."

Larry slapped his desk again and just as suddenly as it had begun, the show was over. Sunshine streamed through the window. Larry was once again the squat man with bad hair and a three-day-old beard. All the exciting energy ebbed as Celeste's familiar defenses reassembled around her, as if Larry had flipped a film into reverse.

"Did you bring a dream?" he'd asked, back in his chair as if nothing had happened.

She nodded, afraid her voice would sound weak and squeaky. From her pack, she pulled her journal, wondering what in the world would happen next. She began to read.

"There's a girl in a shack with lots of little children, siblings? Her mother is lying cold and dead on the bed. A woman is outside, pounding on the door, trying to get in. Muddy water is seeping under the door. The girl holds the door shut and won't let her in. She's afraid she will drown. She's afraid the woman is cruel. The children are crying."

Larry banged the words into his computer. When he finished, he spun around in his chair and peered at her over his glasses. "That's it? That's the whole dream?"

Celeste nodded again, feeling ashamed that she hadn't brought something more complex. Maybe other people brought pages of dreams. Maybe her dream wasn't good enough. Maybe Larry had already discovered how shallow she actually was.

"Okay, that's a good start. Thought it wasn't good enough, didn't ya?"

Celeste was so used to hiding, she had no idea how to handle this guy who seemed to walk right into her mind.

"Ya gotta trust yourself, Cel. Now let's ask that kid some questions."

She swallowed, nodded again, then managed to ask, "What if I don't know the right questions?"

"Hey, it's okay. You don't need to know the questions. The Shining Spirit gives them to me, and I give them to you. They come right from the Source."

Oh great, now he's going to channel God, she thought, her natural cynicism sweeping in, blowback to her shame.

"I know," Larry continued. "People think this part is weird, but give it a try before you dismiss me as a crackpot, okay? I'm gonna tell ya what to ask that orphan girl. Then you're gonna switch chairs," he pointed a meaty finger at the ladder-back chair just a few feet to her left, "and she'll give us the answers *through* you. Got it?"

"I guess." Celeste shrugged, still confused about the point of jumping from chair to chair. Waiting, she stared at the empty wicker seat across from her.

"Ask her 'What part of me are you?' and then switch chairs, see what comes up."

Celeste pictured the shabby little girl from her dream sitting across from her, dusty feet swinging. Feeling ridiculous, she mumbled, "What part of me are you?" Then she stood and shuffled the few feet across the rug to the other chair, wondering how she would ever pull this off. In the background, she could hear the clickety-clack of Larry's keyboard.

She closed her eyes to think. Instantly words formed somewhere in her chest, right above her diaphragm, rushing up and out of her mouth in a high, clear, little girl's voice. "I am the part that doesn't let anyone in. I'm the part that's fighting to protect you from everyone." Celeste's throat constricted and tears edged into the corners of her eyes. Trying to hide them, she shuffled back to her original seat, bewildered by what she had just experienced. The girl with her dirt-streaked face and tangled hair had her own voice and her own answers.

"Why don't you let the woman help you?" Larry prompted.

Celeste repeated the question to the dream girl across from her and then began the musical-chairs routine again. No way was that orphan girl's voice going to come from her mouth again. It had to be some kind of autosuggestion. This time she would pay better attention to the trick. But as soon as she sat down and looked back at her empty chair, she felt the transformation, as if a warm shawl had been pulled over her shoulders and across her chest. From somewhere within, somewhere she barely felt belonged to her, the thin voice of the girl emerged once again.

"Because I can take care of all these children all by myself. If I open the door, the water will pour in, the woman will sweep us away." Now tears rolled down her cheeks, and as she made her way back to her chair she realized that the voice was familiar. It was the voice behind her loneliness, the one that locked out love and even friendship, the voice that said "Run!" whenever anyone got too close.

"Okay, good." Larry stopped typing and pushed the box of tissues across the desk to her. "Now I know what we've gotta work with. You're a lost and lonely orphan. To cover up all her hurt and fear, you pretend you've got it all together. You don't need anybody. See it a lot in you older single gals. Like I said, false independence."

Celeste giggled, uncomfortably exposed, as if she'd just ripped off all her clothes in front of this strange little man.

"Now I want you to put that social worker in the hot seat, and I want you to ask her 'What part of me are you?'"

"Again?" Celeste blew her nose.

"Everything in your dream is part of you. Even that door they're both pushing on. So ask."

Celeste followed his directions. Now she heard a new voice, quiet and gentle, come from her mouth. "I am your heart. I am here to support you, I am here to guide you, I am here to love you. But you have to open that door and let me in."

She closed her eyes. The door opened. A trickle of brackish water swirled around her feet. She watched the girl falling into the strong embrace of the woman, the children laughing behind her. The flood she feared was only a puddle, the woman, not angry, but warm and welcoming. For the briefest of moments, she felt something she had never known before.

"What?" whispered Larry.

"I feel loved," she whispered back, but the spell was broken, the feeling was already gone.

"Exactly! Sure you've never done this before?" Larry looked at her, eyes narrowed. "Something about that dream reminds me . . . You're sure we've never met?"

"I'm sure." She'd already told him that.

"Never mind." Larry checked his computer. "Now for your homework. I want ya to keep living in that moment. Go back to it ten, fifty, a hundred times a day. Live in the dreams, Cel, and they will free you."

CHAPTER SEVEN

PEARL OF A GIRL

A knock on the interrogation room door hurtled Celeste from her memories back to the miserable present. She shook her head, trying to clear away the image of Larry. The blood. His final blank stare. From the hallway came voices, arguing.

"Conflict of interest . . . Not just your case," a woman said.

"I know, but . . ." DeTouche whined.

". . . waited for me," replied the woman. She opened the door and backed into the room while ordering the chastened Wally DeTouche to get them some coffee. She turned and smiled at Celeste.

"Ms. Fortune? I'm Detective Jean Pearl, State Police."

DeTouche hovered by the open door, his round face bunched and pink splotched.

"Cream?" Pearl asked Celeste, who shook her head. The door closed and DeTouche's boots clacked down the hall. The detective sat down across the desk from Celeste and smiled again.

"I'm sorry about Officer DeTouche. I understand you two know each other, so he shouldn't have been the one questioning you. I've been brought in to help with the investigation of Dr. Blatsky's death. I'd like ask you some questions about what you experienced this afternoon, but first let's take a moment to regroup." She reached for the tape recorder on the desk and spoke into it. "Detective Jean Pearl, interviewing Celeste Fortune, five p.m., November 6, 2015."

Celeste breathed a sigh of relief and sank back in her own seat, realizing she had been holding herself rigid throughout Wally's interrogation. She had no reason to think things were looking up at that point, but it gave her a sense of hope just to have another woman involved, as long as she wasn't one of Larry's clients too. Besides, this woman, even in her neatly pressed tan uniform, hardly looked like a cop. She's almost too pretty, everything about her sleek and shiny as a seal, thought Celeste, taking in her cropped black hair, her fine features, her porcelain skin. Detective Pearl wheeled her chair to the side of the desk so they sat almost knee to knee. Instead of pulling away, Celeste leaned toward the younger woman, focusing her eyes on the tiny silver Buddha hanging from a black silk cord around the detective's neck. This woman radiated compassion and kindness. Celeste burst into tears, giving in to the fear and grief that she'd been holding in since discovering Larry.

"Until Larry, I hardly ever cried," she said. "Now I can't seem to stop." She sniffled again, embarrassed by the tears and snot flowing down her face.

"Here." Detective Pearl handed her a handkerchief, folded and fresh, probably straight from the Buddhist laundry. "Feel better now?"

Celeste blew her nose, then slumped in her chair, limp, depleted. "I didn't do anything to Larry. I'm not sure if Wally— Officer DeTouche—believes me, but please—"

Detective Pearl said, "I want you to feel at ease so we can find out what happened today. But first, Celeste—that's what you want to be called, correct? You can call me Pearl. Most people do."

Celeste nodded.

"Why don't you just take a moment? Breathe, get centered."

Celeste did as Pearl instructed and felt the fog of fear in her head begin to clear a little. That simple bit of kindness was exactly what she needed. "You have to find that guy Adam, find out why he was there."

"The person you described to Officer DeTouche back at Dr. Blatsky's office?"

Celeste nodded and blew her nose again, not sure if she was supposed to give back the hankie, now crumpled, wet, and slimy.

"We're looking for him. But right now, I'm here for you," Pearl responded in a low, hushed tone. "So while we wait for that coffee, why don't we chat a little?" She picked up the tape recorder, which was still going, clicked it off and then back on. She continued, "I have so many questions to round out my picture of what could have happened, and I'm counting on you to help me."

Celeste pulled back, away from the detective's gentle gaze, telling herself not to get fooled. This could be a good cop/bad cop setup.

"So you don't think I did it?" Celeste asked.

"Let's just get through some of these questions, okay? How long have you been seeing Dr. Blatsky?"

"About four years. But he's not a doctor." She looked down at her stockinged feet. The tip of her right big toe poked through the well-worn wool. She covered it with her left foot.

"No?"

"He called himself a spiritual healer. I don't think he had any official training or anything."

"I see." Detective Pearl pulled out a small Moleskine notebook from the pocket of her jacket and began to write. "So he was a bit unconventional, I gather. Not your typical therapist?"

"You don't know anything about Larry?" That was hard to believe. Everyone in Riverton Falls knew Larry. Or so it seemed.

"I'm new around here. Sounds like he was quite an interesting fellow, though."

Celeste winced at hearing Larry referred to in the past tense.

"He also seems to have had quite a following. You know, I have a spiritual teacher. Thich Nhat Hanh?" She pointed to the little Buddha that nestled at the base of her throat. "He does training for police. So I think I can understand some of your attachment to Dr.—Mr. Blatsky."

Celeste rolled her eyes. "I don't think it was quite the same thing."

Detective Pearl wrote a few words in her book. "Would you like to tell me more about that or should we move on?"

"Look, I just want to get out of here."

Pearl nodded and wrote something in her book, then looked up. "Now," she said, sounding harder, more like a cop, "let's pick up where Officer DeTouche left off. You say you left the office around one o'clock, but then returned at around three, correct?" She looked at her notebook, and Celeste realized that Wally must have already given her his version of events.

"I forgot something and had to get it." Celeste twisted the soggy handkerchief in her hands.

"Must have been pretty important if you couldn't wait until your next appointment to retrieve it."

Jean Pearl waited patiently while Celeste formulated a response. She did not like the direction this was going.

"My engagement ring." She didn't need to tell Pearl that she hadn't planned on another appointment. She didn't need to tell her about the whole mess with Larry and Jake, how she was being torn in two, how Larry had messed up her life.

"Oh, so you're engaged! Congratulations! Who's the lucky guy? Or gal?"

What was *with* this woman? Either she was using this girl talk as a ploy or she was really as nice as she seemed. Either way, she was still waiting for an answer.

"Jake Kelly, local guy. Maybe you've seen him playing guitar in some of the bars around here?"

She wrote another note. "Could this Mr. Kelly be related to a Nicole Kelly? Nicole Tromblay Kelly?" Detective Pearl asked, flipping quickly through her little black notebook.

This wasn't looking good. "They used to be married."

"Hmmm." Detective Pearl wrote a few words then looked up.

"But I don't see what that's got to do with anything." Celeste's stomach tightened. The last thing she wanted to do was drag Jake into all this.

Celeste looked down at her hands, wringing the handkerchief. The motion seemed strangely familiar. Something in that dream, someone's hands pulling on something, fists clenched, moving toward the back of the woman, bending and straightening in front of the window.

"Celeste?"

She looked up and the image vanished as quickly as it had come. "Sorry. I don't understand what that has to do with Larry being killed."

Pearl nodded, then wrote a few more words in her book. "So you were saying you went back for your ring. I can see why you were in a hurry to get it. Is there some reason you left it there in the first place?"

"Larry asked me for it." Uh-oh, she could feel the slope growing slippery.

"I see. That must have made you upset, angry perhaps?" The detective waited, leaving a big trough of silence for Celeste to stumble into.

"That doesn't mean I—"

"And it seems," Detective Pearl went on, looking down at Celeste's bare left hand, "he didn't give it back. That must have made you even angrier?"

"No, that's not what happened! Larry was on the floor, bleeding, almost dead, when I got there. And the ring was gone, along with the computer. They might have been the only two valuable things in the whole place." Her mouth was dry and the palms of her hands prickled. "I didn't have anything to do with this! I don't have the computer either. Obviously someone, probably that crazy Adam guy, stole it!" She wanted to reach over and shake Jean Pearl.

"Calm down," Pearl said, her soft voice almost inaudible.

"That tarot guy, he must have taken it. Maybe dumped it in the woods. I don't know." Her words emerged as a squeak. "Don't you believe that I saw him?"

Pearl smiled then jotted some words in her notebook. "Let's just concentrate on your story, shall we? I want to make sure I've got this all straight. You went to your appointment. Officer DeTouche tells me you left there early and saw no one else at Mr. Blatsky's house at that time. We do, however, have reports that some kind of altercation took place between Mr. Blatsky and someone with a higher-pitched voice, possibly a woman. You're sure you didn't see another woman there?"

"No, I told you, only that crazy guy." What was happening here? "He had a weird voice, kind of high, I guess. Maybe they heard him? I don't know!" The handkerchief fell to the floor as Celeste stood up out of the chair.

Detective Pearl again jotted something in her little black book, then looked up at Celeste. "Please remain seated," she said. "I can see that I've upset you. Is this how you felt when Mr. Blatsky took your ring?"

"No! Why can't you listen to me!"

A knock on the door made her jump. She turned to see Wally coming in, a white paper coffee cup in each hand.

"Thanks, you can set them on the desk," said Pearl, glancing sideways rather than looking directly at DeTouche. "You can leave us." She waited until he was gone before picking up her cup.

Celeste flopped back down into her chair. "I think this is when I ask for a lawyer."

"Do you think you need a lawyer? I thought things were going rather well."

"No, I definitely need a lawyer." She reached down, picked up the hankie, and put it on the desk between them. This woman had tricked her and she'd hardly seen it coming. She'd seemed so kind and empathetic. Too good to be true.

"You understand that our conversation will have to end here? That you won't have another chance to clear yourself today?"

"I understand."

The detective's smile tightened. She wasn't pleased with this turn of events. "Do you have someone in mind? A lawyer you want me to call?"

Celeste rolled her eyes to the ceiling, trying to think what to do. There was Bruce Nussbaum, but he wasn't about to help her. He was probably up at the hospital with all the other Dreamers right now, walking the corridors, cursing her. Only one other lawyer came straight to mind. "Gloria Cross," she said, as if she were certain Gloria would talk to her, let alone represent her. Celeste's old friend had hardly spoken to her since she'd joined the Dreamers. "Her office is right around the corner."

"Cross?" Detective Pearl cleared her throat and flushed.

"Do you know Gloria?"

Detective Pearl didn't answer.

"Can you please get her in here?"

"All right. If that's what you want." Pearl looked at Celeste and shrugged. "I'm sorry you won't be able to explain what happened. At least not today." Detective Pearl stood up, sighed, shut her Moleskine, picked up her coffee, and walked out the door.

CHAPTER EIGHT

GLORIA! GLORIA!

Gloria Cross exploded through the door like an elfin super-hero, her bright red hair blazing behind her as she strode into the middle of the interrogation room. "What the hell are you doing in here, Celeste?" she boomed.

She had a huge voice for such a tiny woman. In her purple coat, orange mohair tunic, and turquoise leggings, Gloria didn't look much like a lawyer; in fact she looked more like some kid who'd refused to change out of her Halloween costume. As usual though, Gloria managed to take over the space with practiced authority. She might have been small, but she knew how to put people in their place right off the bat. There was no messing around with Gloria Cross.

"I don't know what she's told you, but I've known this woman for more years than I can remember, and I can guarantee you that she had nothing to do with killing Blatsky the B—"

The *bastard*. Celeste could almost hear the word Gloria cut off just in time. She always called him "Blatsky the Bastard," at least the few times they'd actually spoken with each other about Larry. "I can tell you right now, this interrogation is over, unless you're going to throw some bogus charge at my client." Gloria glared up at the two police officers, tossing her thick mane of hair for emphasis.

Celeste smiled at the floor, half embarrassed by Gloria's audacity and half relieved that she'd summoned such a brash champion to her side.

"We're waiting for forensics, so right now she's a witness with a lot of circumstantial evidence piled up around her. Go ahead, take her, but don't think we're done with her yet," DeTouche said, glancing over at Detective Pearl, who watched Gloria with a shy smile.

"Oh no, you're done. I would advise you to stop wasting your time on my client and start looking for the real culprit." Gloria is actually good at this, Celeste thought as she zipped up her vest.

"Stick around town. No running away." DeTouche smiled at her as if this were some private joke, which in a way, she guessed, it was.

"Don't worry, Wally, I'm not planning on going anywhere. At least not yet. Besides, I wouldn't get too far without my boots." Celeste looked down and wiggled the bare toe poking through her sock. "And my pack?"

"Get this woman some shoes!" Gloria demanded. "You must have some around here for cases like this?"

DeTouche waddled back toward the interrogation room while Celeste followed Gloria and Detective Pearl down the shabby hallway, glancing at the big red letters splashed across the DARE poster and at the yellowing photos of the station's softball teams. Gloria laughed at something Pearl said as the detective unlocked the heavy fire door and pushed it open.

"Found some shoes!" DeTouche thrust a pair of men's running shoes toward Celeste. "This is all I could find."

They were beat up and smelled of dirty feet. Celeste reached for them, wrinkling her nose, then slid them on, relieved they fit.

"And here's your . . . bag." He dangled her pack from one finger.

Celeste grabbed it from him, hoping he hadn't been reading through her dream journal. With Gloria at her side, she walked out into the bright fluorescent lights of the front foyer, blinking against the glare and lurching forward awkwardly as Gloria practically shoved her toward the glass doors that led back into the normal world.

"Let's get outta here—now!" Gloria said, giving a quick, almost surreptitious wave to Detective Pearl.

Before they made it any further, however, a fist of cold air punched its way into the station. Just then, a woman bundled against the weather stepped inside through the open glass door. Once inside the warm enclosure, she pulled off her knit cap and shook out her long, sable-colored hair. Nicole.

"We've come to get you," she said, walking straight up to Celeste, her high-heeled boots clicking across the floor. First Celeste noticed her red-rimmed eyes, and then she heard how Nicole's voice quavered, as if she were trying hard to get the words out without crying when she said, "You need to be with us right now, Cel."

Before Celeste could react, Gloria stepped into the space between them and looked up, hands on hips, scanning their faces as if trying to figure out what was going on between the two much taller women. "That's the last place she needs to be, Nicole. Do you actually believe the minions in your little cult aren't out for her blood? Quite mistakenly, by the way."

"Gloria," Nicole looked down at Gloria's upturned face, "you have no idea what Cel needs right now."

"I know it's not a bunch of angry Dreamers looking for someone to blame."

"That's exactly why she needs to face them. Cel needs to . . . Never mind. You wouldn't understand."

"Oh, I understand all right. It hasn't been that long. Right now, Celeste is going with me. Not with you, not with your groupies."

Color flooded Nicole's face. "We want to know what happened. I think we deserve that, don't you, Celeste?" She bent toward Celeste, her face open and pleading. Celeste could see the tears gathering along Nicole's lower lashes, the smudges of mascara darkening the delicately lined skin beneath her eyes.

Celeste looked down at the floor. She scuffed one beat-up sneaker back and forth, trying to think of what to say, what to do. Nicole was right. She should talk to the Dreamers. They'd been her friends, they'd been everything to her. But what if they really believed she'd killed Larry, like Wally seemed to?

"Celeste, you don't have to answer that. As your *lawyer*," Gloria drew out the word so Nicole would get the full import of her status here, "I would advise you to keep your mouth shut and avoid these nutcases at all costs."

Celeste nodded, glad that Gloria was in charge, making the decisions she felt powerless to make.

"Besides, Nicole, I'm sure the cops are going to want some kind of statement from you, so I'll bet you'll be here for a while." It wasn't hard to hear the edge of sarcasm in Gloria's voice.

"From *me*?" Nicole's face went a deeper shade of pink.

"Sure," Gloria said, "you Dreamers are like Larry's family. And who do they usually suspect first?"

"Don't be ridiculous." Nicole's icy calm was returning. "But if you want to travel along those lines, Gloria, why don't we look at those family members who have strayed from the fold?"

Celeste wrinkled her forehead. Were there others besides Gloria who had left? She'd never heard anyone mentioned. In fact, she'd never even heard the Dreamers mention Gloria, but then again, she'd broken away years earlier, and they'd probably forgotten about her.

"Now look at who's being ridiculous." Gloria pulled herself up to her full height, and Celeste had a bad feeling she was about to punch Nicole right there in the police station foyer.

"Okay, you two, calm down." Celeste looked back and forth between the two women fighting over her.

"Ms. Kelly?" All three women turned at the sound of Detective Pearl's voice. "Are you Nicole Kelly?"

Nicole nodded.

"We were just about to call you in for a statement," Detective Pearl said, looking at her little black notebook.

Nicole looked surprised, then nodded before turning to Celeste. "What have you been telling them?" she hissed at Gloria and Celeste.

Before Celeste could reply, Nicole turned and said to Detective Pearl, "Back there?" She pointed to the door Gloria and Celeste had just come through.

"That's right." Pearl smiled. "Just a few questions for you. So we can help you find out who did this to Larry." Detective Pearl nodded, pulled the door open, and the two of them disappeared down the hall.

"What'd I tell ya?" Gloria looked triumphant. "We are outta here, Celeste."

Celeste heaved her pack onto her shoulder and followed Gloria out into the already dark November night.

"Celeste!" a voice called. Beneath the street lamps, leaning against a parked car, two Dreamers waited. Even from the steps of the station, Celeste could hear Ingrid's Swedish-accented murmur. Her husband Bill stepped forward into the light that leaked from the station doors behind Gloria and Celeste, his bald head and fringe of white hair glowing in the harsh fluorescence. She should have guessed they'd be here. Nicole never went anywhere without her cadre of Dreamland guards.

"What happened, Cel? What did you do to Larry?" the two asked in unison, Bill's husky, rumbling voice almost drowned out by Ingrid's almost hysterical screech. Had they come to blame her or to claim her? She couldn't tell.

"I have to talk to them, Gloria. I want them to believe me." She started down the rain-slicked granite steps, but Gloria grabbed her vest and pulled her back.

"Don't be an idiot. They're not your friends."

"What do you mean? Of course they are!" Celeste tried to pull away. "They know me better than anyone. I have to convince them."

"If they really knew you, they would already know you're innocent. You didn't have to convince me, remember? The Dreamers are loyal to one thing only. The Dreamscape."

Celeste looked out at the two people who should have been her allies, wondering if Gloria was right. Ingrid glared back, while Bill, his arm around her broad shoulders, looked down at his feet. They couldn't have suddenly turned on her. She had brought them to Larry in the first place, even if it had been under somewhat false pretenses.

It was the morning, two years ago now, that she'd had her second close encounter with Jake; she remembered that clearly. She'd been in line at the Corner Cup when behind her she heard, "If it isn't the heavenly Celeste." She spun around and there he was, even more handsome than he'd been in the dreams she'd already had about him. He looked leaner, his gray eyes brighter under his floppy forelock of dark hair.

"Hey," she said as the barista with the green dragon tattooed on her cheek asked for her order. "Americano," she said, turning away from Jake, glad for an excuse to hide the blush that shot up her neck, warming her face. She paid, then moved to the end of the splattered counter to wait for her coffee.

Jake stepped out of the long line and walked over to her. "I'd been hoping I'd run into you again somewhere."

Had he really said that? Celeste smiled and tried to answer, but her "me too" came out as a croak. Since she'd met him at The Castaway, she'd caught glimpses of Jake around town, but she'd never gotten up the courage to approach him. Especially after she'd found out he was married. To Nicole, Larry's right hand.

Then, loud enough for half the coffee shop to hear, she asked, "How's your wife?" Oh God, what a dumb thing to say! He'd never mentioned Nicole when they'd met. Now he'd know she'd been checking up on him. Discovering his connection to Larry had been even more surprising than finding out he was married.

He tilted his head, thought for a second, then actually answered. "Fine, I guess. We split up, though."

Celeste swallowed hard. Either this was her lucky day or he already had someone waiting in the wings. "I'm sorry, I guess. Or, congratulations?" She wasn't quite sure which way he was taking this.

"Yeah, I guess it's a bit of both," he said in that smooth-as-silk voice she'd fallen for all those months ago. "It was a long time coming."

"Americano, with room," the barista called. Celeste reached over and grabbed the paper cup, then took a sip so hot it burned her tongue. She spluttered.

"You okay?" Jake put his hand on her shoulder, and she could feel the warmth of his palm radiate straight into her chest.

"Sure. Gotta go! Nice seeing you again." Wait, wait, a voice inside her screamed. But her feet were already rushing her toward the door then out into the warmth of a summer Saturday. *Heavenly Celeste*? Had he really said that? She'd kept turning the phrase over in her mind as she crossed the street to the farmer's market. It was already bustling as shoppers sauntered through, sampling goat cheeses and kimchi, filling their bags and baskets with organic veggies and loaves of hearty bread.

In the midst of the chattering throng, she heard someone call her name for the second time that morning. At the picnic table next to the wood-fired pizza wagon sat her landlord, Bill, loaded down with string bags bursting with Happy Girls Farm tomatoes and an assortment of Jumpin' Jeff's greens. Next to him sat Ingrid, trying hard to restrain her giant mutt Pogo, who was pulling toward the toothpicked cubes of grass-fed bison samples.

"Come. Sit!" Ingrid called.

Celeste made her way through the crowd. Ingrid looked up, scanning her face. "My, you look wonderful," she'd said in her accented English. "Doesn't she look, how do you say, radiant?" asked Ingrid, turning to Bill. He looked Celeste up and down, nodding.

"Must be my therapist," Celeste remembered answering, not wanting to reveal that her radiance probably had more to do with her encounter with Jake in the coffee shop. "Larry Blatsky, the guy everyone goes to."

"Blatsky?" Ingrid looked puzzled, mashing her straw hat down on her head to keep it from blowing away. "Bill, didn't he used to fix our computers?"

"That's him," Celeste said. "You should check him out. He's pretty amazing."

Bill and Ingrid, it turned out, were whizzes at the Dreamscape. Within six months, they'd already been inducted into Dreamland while Celeste still struggled with her beginner dreams, slogging through muddy streams, chasing after twisted, ape-like children. When she'd finally made it to Level Three and been inducted into the Dreamers, they'd been chosen as her Dreamscape guides, helping to initiate her, holding her hand each step of the way.

Maybe that was the problem. They had probably sensed her growing disillusionment over the past few months as she began to question some of Larry's harsher dictates. She'd tried hard to hide it from them, but now here they were, in front of the police station, accusing her of killing Larry.

"I didn't do anything! I just found him there!" Celeste protested, pulling against Gloria's restraining hand.

"Celeste, shut up, right now. You don't owe them any explanations. Come on, let's go."

"Yes, you just go," called Ingrid. "You just go off with that—"

"Ingrid! That's enough." Bill looked alarmed, and he tried to pull his angry wife away.

"That's right, Ingrid. She's going off with me, like it or not." Gloria grasped Celeste's wrist and steered her in the other direction. Bill and Ingrid continued to call after her even as Gloria tugged her toward the street.

Celeste glanced at her watch. Seven o'clock. "I was supposed to be at work an hour ago," she said.

"I don't think you're going in there," Gloria answered, pointing across the street to the crowd of Dreamers gathered at the entrance to the Broken Gate, where Celeste was scheduled to be behind the bar. Bill and Ingrid had arrived at the edge of the group where arms reached out and pulled them into a communal hug, one great collective sob arising from its center.

"But what about work?" Celeste asked. All she needed now was to get fired for not showing up, but there was no way she was going to face the Dreamers en masse tonight.

"I'm already on it." Gloria held her cell phone up to her ear. "Hi, who's this?"

Celeste could hear the irritated voice coming through the speaker. "Allegra Pippin. Who's asking?"

"This is Gloria Cross. Calling on behalf of Celeste Fortune."

"Yeah, well, she better get her ass in here right now. This place is swarming with people looking for her, and I can't keep up alone."

Celeste imagined Allegra trying to talk on the phone while mixing a Dark and Stormy. She could almost see her there, totally pissed off because she was stuck serving the happy hour crowd and the influx of unhappy Dreamers all by herself—stomping around behind the bar, her miniskirt twitching over her smooth, muscled thighs, her hennaed hair spiked and stiff with styling gel.

"What the hell did she do anyway? I heard she knocked off Blatsky. I told her—"

"She didn't kill anyone, and she's not coming in. Call a sub if you have to."

Gloria clicked off the phone before Allegra could protest. Thank God for Gloria. Celeste didn't have the strength to know what was good for her right now. Across the street, in her bar, were the Dreamers, the people who had been her world, gathering to mourn the man they had worshipped. Until this morning, she would have been with them, but now the world had turned upside down. Instead, she stood out here in the cold, with her old friend Gloria, going to bat for her now, even though they'd hardly spoken since Celeste started seeing Larry.

"I need a drink, Gloria."

"That's just what we're going to do. In private, so you can tell me how you got into this mess. Then we're going to figure out who killed Larry."

CHAPTER NINE

CELESTE CONFESSES

Avoiding the Dreamland crowd at the Broken Gate, Gloria and Celeste headed up Bank Street to Gloria's cubbyhole of an office in the back of Arts and Herbs!, the herbal apothecary and feminist art gallery. The wind chimes over the door jingled as Gloria unlocked the door then flipped on the overhead light. Following Gloria to the back of the shop, Celeste perused the dusty shelves of glass jars filled with faded flowers and desiccated mushrooms. She breathed in the overpowering scent of lavender, sage, and something that smelled like stinky cheese.

"*This* is where you work?" Celeste asked.

"It's all I can afford until my business gets off the ground. Taking you on is not going to help much, I have a feeling." Gloria bent to unlock the door. "Read that sign, Celeste. See what it says?"

Celeste scanned the words in carved gold letters flanked by sheaves of wheat or maybe bundles of dune grass like natural quotation marks.

"Got that? 'Gloria Cross, Conservation and Environmental Law'?" She pushed open the door to the cramped back room. "Wind power, water rights, that's what I do now. I haven't touched criminal since I was a paralegal back in Akron."

"I know, Glor," Celeste said, flopping onto the faded red futon couch that took up a good portion of the office. She trained her eyes on the double-hung window at the far end of the makeshift couch, trying to ward off the sense of suffocation that overtook her in small, crowded spaces. "But you're the only lawyer I could think of. And besides, I need a friend right now." She kicked off her borrowed sneakers and held her nose as they thumped to the floor.

"Oh, so we're friends now, are we?" Gloria rolled her eyes, then bent down and pulled open the bottom drawer of her beat-up wooden file cabinet. She brought out two water-spotted glasses and a bottle of fifteen-year-old Laphroaig Scotch. Right away, Celeste noticed the bottle was half empty.

"How very Bogart of you," said Celeste as Gloria poured. She reached for her glass and took a long swig, letting the flavor linger on her tongue. The peaty aroma pushed her right back to their college days when she could tell Gloria anything—Gloria, the main reason she'd ended up in Riverton Falls after all those years of wandering. But somehow they'd both let Larry and his Dreamscape come between them. "At least we can be drinking buddies."

"If you say so. Cheers!" Gloria raised her glass and downed half of it in one long swig.

Celeste followed suit, savoring both the Scotch and this rare moment of camaraderie.

"Now that we have that under our belts," said Gloria,

setting her glass on the desk with a solid thunk, "it's time to get to work. I still think you need another lawyer, someone in criminal, but since we're here, and I'm the only lawyer you've got for tonight, I'm going to ask you a few questions so at least we can figure out what to do next."

"We? So you're going to help me?" Celeste sounded hopeful.

"Against my better judgment. Before we get too drunk, just tell me what happened today, starting with this morning." Gloria pulled a yellow legal pad from her desk drawer and waited, pen poised.

Celeste drained her glass. As the Scotch warmed her up, the strong arm of fear loosened its full-nelson grip on her. While Gloria scribbled furiously, she dove into the day until she finished with Gloria's arrival at the police station.

"Let me see if I've got the main points here." Gloria counted up the steps of Celeste's story on her fingers: "First you went to tell Larry you were leaving, then you gave him your ring, told him a dream, and, for some reason you don't know—something about that dream—Larry kicked you out, saying Jake put you up to it. Right so far?"

Celeste nodded, running her finger around the rim of her glass.

"Then you met the tarot guy—"

"Adam."

"Yeah." She made a note. "You saw Jake running down the street, saw his truck at Nicole's. Caught up with him at Castaway. He noticed your ring was gone. You wanted to get it. Jake tried to talk you out of it, but you went back to Larry's anyway in time to see the bird and this Adam guy flying away. Larry was on the floor, dying. No ring. No computer. Called the cops, they took you in, and now you're here. Is that about it?"

"Yep, right up to the minute." Tallied up on Gloria's fingers it all sounded so mundane. Where was the part about

Larry's face turning blue, the blood on the floor, the terror of watching him struggle to breathe? Celeste's glass was empty, drained in two big gulps. The buzz from the alcohol circulated through her body, loosening her shoulders, melting the knot in her stomach.

"Can I have another hit of that Laphroaig?"

Gloria poured enough to cover the bottom of the glass. Celeste swirled the chintzy bit of Scotch and gave Gloria a dirty look. Gloria knew her too well. Given half a chance, Celeste would have downed a second tumbler in seconds. She was not what you'd call a moderate drinker, a fact Gloria knew all too well from years of steering her out of some embarrassing or even downright dangerous situations.

"You seem to think it was this guy, Adam." Gloria perused the pad she'd been writing on. "But I'm wondering what he would have done with the computer."

"The computer? Hid it in the woods before I got there?" Celeste shrugged.

"Maybe. Seems a bit unlikely. You'd never seen him around Larry's office before?" Gloria leaned back in her chair, put her feet up on the desk, and closed her eyes, waiting.

"No, but now that I think about it, there might have been some connection."

"What do you mean?"

"When he was reading my cards," Celeste took a tiny sip from her glass, "something about him reminded me of Larry. He had me do this little gestalt thing with one of my cards, pretend I was The Fool. Then he talked about archetypes. I thought it was kind of weird at the time."

Gloria didn't seem convinced. "Maybe. But tons of people do that stuff. Larry wanted you to think he made it all up, but those are pretty standard therapy techniques. Maybe the guy had a lot of therapy. I mean, he sounds a bit off, to say the least. Still, could be something there." She grabbed her pad and wrote a few more notes.

Celeste held out her empty glass. "One more?"

"Not yet. Anything else you can think of?"

"He left me a kretek, you know, one of those Indonesian clove cigarettes I used to smoke? That seemed strange. And," now she hesitated, not sure if she should tell Gloria the next part, "he kind of took off when Jake went by. Could be that my time was up, and he was leaving anyway."

"Kind of—"

A thump and a crash from somewhere out front in the apothecary rattled the door. Startled by the noise, Gloria swung her feet off the desk, kicking her notes to the floor.

"Who's out there?" she called loudly.

No answer. The two women stared at each other for a frightened second. Before Celeste could protest, Gloria jumped up and flung open the door. Except for the crowded shelves and the paintings of breast-feeding mothers on the walls, the shop seemed empty. She took a step, Celeste right behind her.

"Stop right there!" a voice said. A big-headed shadow slid across the far wall. Celeste gasped as it moved toward them, growing larger, bat-like wings outstretched. Then, out from behind the shelves leapt Juniper, the herbalist, her purple turban threatening to fall from the rapid movement. The three women stared at each other before bursting into nervous laughter.

"Jesus, you scared me! What the heck are you doing here this late, Gloria?" Juniper reached up and straightened her wobbling headpiece, her arms emerging from the thick woolen cape she wore.

"Me? What about you? You're either very stupid or very brave to check it out yourself, young woman." Gloria sounded like a stern older sister.

Juniper gave her the finger. "I saw the lights on, and after everything that's happened today, I freaked." She stared at Celeste, making it clear that rumors were already circulating around Riverton Falls. "I still can't believe he's actually dead. After all he—"

Had she known Larry too?

"Believe it. I guarantee you it's true," Gloria quickly interrupted her. "We're all on edge. But we're just talking, having a drink. Nothing to worry about in here. I promise we'll close up tight when we leave."

"Nighty-night then. But be careful!" Juniper said, sliding her eyes from Gloria to Celeste, before heading out the door.

"I'm not going to hurt Gloria if that's what you're—"

Gloria didn't give Celeste any time to go down that road. She pointed to the office, saying, "Back to work."

Celeste hurried in ahead of Gloria, grabbed the Scotch, and filled her glass almost to the rim. "That was scary."

Gloria shook her head and sighed. "Looks like Larry didn't change you that much."

Celeste lifted her glass. "At least I held onto my bad habits. Cheers!"

CHAPTER TEN

DRINKING AGAIN

Celeste sat back down on the futon and picked up where she'd left off. "It had to be Adam. I saw him running away. And maybe the ring was the only valuable thing there. Or maybe he took more?"

"Hmm." Gloria made another note. "So what was that dream, anyway? The one that got you kicked out."

"I have no idea, except it wasn't a normal dream."

"And what would you consider a normal dream?" Gloria stood and stretched her arms over her head in the narrow space behind her desk.

Celeste took a long pull of Scotch, swishing it around in her mouth before swallowing. She wasn't sure how to answer. "You know, Glor. The kind where you're the star and things happen to you. Even if you don't look or feel like yourself, you still know it's you in the middle of the dream."

"Sure." Gloria sounded doubtful. "And you know I think the Dreamscape is a bunch of bull, that dreams are just chemical reactions, synapses crackling and all that. Your brain's way of integrating information, filing it away."

Celeste didn't buy that theory though. On her travels, she'd encountered plenty of shamans, mystics, and healers who claimed to use dreams as bridges between the world of the living and the larger realm of the spirits. She hadn't completely understood what they were doing until she met Larry. Larry used dreams to force her below the surface of her jitterbugging mind, to make her confront that subterranean fear, that Demon Mind that kept her on the run. Now she understood that, like the drum-banging shaman she'd tripped with in the Amazon, Larry was creating connections between what she believed and what was true.

"Yeah," Gloria said, leaning over and touching her toes, "you're still under Larry's spell and all those crazy notions the Dreamers have stuffed into your poor little brainwashed cranium."

"Let's not argue. I'm only saying this particular dream was different somehow. It's like I was dreaming someone else's dream."

"Sounds like you've reached the pinnacle of success then, honey. You know Larry was always hoping the Dreamers would begin dreaming the same dream. That wouldn't be so surprising with all that psychodrama crap they do, acting out each other's fantasies." She stopped moving and leaned on the back of her chair toward Celeste. "Like I said, integration of information. Or maybe autosuggestion."

"I never actually believed it could happen either. At least it never happened to me. But this dream wasn't like that. I mean *I* wasn't in the dream. *At all.*"

"Tell me the dream and maybe we can figure it out. Combined we have a good decade's worth of practice to go on. My six years and your four."

"That's the problem. I hardly remember any of it, except

that it felt different. I woke up upset, feeling guilty, but I don't know why. I couldn't get my breath, like someone was choking me, or whoever the dream woman was." As she spoke, little shreds of the dream came floating back. The images came into focus, as if the fog that had covered them that morning was finally dissolving. Now she could see the woman was slender, skinny even. She wore an apron tied around her neck. "I think I'm seeing this woman through someone's eyes. Someone walking toward her at a window." Celeste tried to continue but she couldn't breathe. Her throat closed, something was around her neck. She tried to yell, but only a gasp came out.

Then Gloria was next to her, shaking her.

"Celeste!"

As suddenly as it had come, the dream lifted and she was back in Gloria's office.

"That's all I can remember," she whispered, rubbing at her neck. "But it sure felt like a panic attack."

"Jeez, no wonder you scared the shit out of Larry. You scared the shit out of me. I thought you were being strangled!"

"Nothing like that happened in his office. All I did was read out loud what I'd written down." She coughed, still trying to get her breath back. She grabbed her glass, but now the Scotch burned going down as if she'd actually been strangled. They sat in silence, regrouping.

"Why do you think Larry thought Jake had something to do with it?" Gloria asked as she went back to her desk and picked up her legal pad.

"I have no idea. He blamed Jake for everything he didn't like about my life."

"What time did you see Jake running down Maple?" Gloria was pacing, three, four steps then spinning on her toes to turn back.

"What are you saying? Jake didn't kill Larry!"

"Calm down. If you want me to help you, then you have to let me do my job, and that means everyone's a suspect except you." Gloria returned to her chair and put her turquoise-stockinged feet up on the desk. "Why do you think Larry thought Jake had something to do with the dream?" she repeated.

"How the hell should I know?" Celeste took another swig of her Scotch and set the tumbler down hard on the desk.

"It's a clue. It's got to mean something."

"No, it doesn't. I didn't have anything to do with killing Larry, if you remember, so why should my dream be a clue?" They were squabbling, back and forth, as they used to when they were friends. It felt familiar. It felt like old times. "You think Jake's a suspect?"

"Come on, Celeste. After all he'd gone through with Larry stealing Nicole. And now you. Obvious choice, I'd say. They hated each other, right?"

Celeste nodded, not wanting to hear what Gloria was saying.

"Plus, you said he was running down Maple, which means he could have been coming from Larry's around the right time, correct? And later, at Castaway, he didn't want you to go back to Larry's?"

Celeste shrugged, looking down at the hole in her sock.

"Besides, who else would have taken your ring and not the rest of the stuff that was in the box? Gotta cover all the bases here, Celeste. Unless you want them to book you."

Celeste looked out the window, trying to hold herself together.

Gloria grabbed her glass, came around the desk, and sat down next to Celeste, pulling her feet up under her.

"You think you were the only one who had issues with Larry?" Gloria sloshed the Scotch around in her glass.

"It sure felt that way." How could she tell Gloria all that

had happened over the past year since Jake had come into her life? About all her doubts, the loneliness of keeping them to herself; about her attempts to talk about them with Bill and Ingrid; about their rebuffs, the way they threw it all back at her as if her questioning was simply her inability to see the truth of the Dreamscape. Her Demon Mind, they'd warned, before giving her that pitying, judgmental look, as if they had the keys to the Kingdom, as if she obviously hadn't worked hard enough to get there yet. As if she hadn't done her homework, hadn't delved far enough into her pain, had let her head get in the way of her heart. After all, she'd allowed the outer world to overcome her inner light and the truth of the dreams, they'd said. Worst of all, she'd fallen for Jake, and for some reason she could never figure out, Larry and the Dreamers could not accept that.

Celeste pulled up her long legs and hugged her knees to her chest, closed her eyes, and burrowed back into the futon. "Maybe they were right. My Demon Mind won. I failed the Dreamscape." She hid her face against her knees, and the tears slid down her cheeks again. She felt Gloria's hand on her arm.

"You don't have to defend those Dreamers anymore, Celeste. Not to me. But I do want you to look at the possibility that there could have been other Dreamers or people who went to Larry who struggled like you did."

Celeste wiped her hand under her nose. "Besides you?" She opened her eyes and looked straight into Gloria's concerned face. "I've never heard of a Dreamer who'd had doubts or had actually left the Dreamscape. Except you. And you've never even told me why. There are others?" Nicole had mentioned something like that too, back in the station.

Gloria straightened up quickly and went back to her chair. "Just sayin'." She sat down hard and immediately began organizing the pens and pencils she kept in an old mug on her desk.

"But the Dreamers are like a family!"

"And what did I say about family? Always the first suspects?" Gloria looked up and shrugged.

"What about his real family? Didn't he used to have a wife who ran off with some guy? The last thing Larry said was 'her.' Maybe that's who he meant, not me!"

Gloria quickly shook her head. "I don't think so. She couldn't get away from him fast enough as far as I could tell."

"You knew her?"

"Not really. Saw her once in a while, in the kitchen, going out the door, never talked to her." Gloria was mumbling, picking up papers she'd knocked from her desk, no longer looking at Celeste.

"Why do I get the feeling there's something you're not telling me?" Celeste sighed, straightened her legs out to one side, and lay down along the full length of the futon couch, suddenly exhausted from all the questions. All she wanted to do was grab the almost-empty bottle and keep drinking until this day became nothing but a drunken blur. She tipped her head back to look out the window at the overcast night sky, clouds tinged a ghastly peach by the lights of the town.

"How long has it been, Glor, since we were really friends? A few years?" She exhaled a long sigh, knowing she was tiptoeing into an area they'd been avoiding for quite a while. Maybe they were drunk enough to do this.

"Too long," Gloria admitted. "I know, I know. I've never wanted to talk about my time with Larry."

"Except to say I should stay away from him."

"And I'm not going to say I told you so." Gloria came back to the couch and sat on the edge, leaning against Celeste's outstretched legs. "When I first started seeing him—seems like a million years ago—he was still fixing computers, just doing the dream stuff on the side. His head hadn't swelled quite so big. But," she stared at the ceiling, "I knew from the beginning he had something special, a gift. He helped me find parts of myself I'd buried for years. A lot of times it hurt like hell, but then came these great surges of joy and freedom after I'd let go of all the crap I'd been carrying around trying to fit in." She put a hand on Celeste's ankle.

"You were never good at fitting in, Gloria." She liked feeling the warmth of Gloria's hand, even though she usually pulled away from such close physical contact. Gloria's touch had always felt safe. She knew Celeste's tricky boundaries, dared to go right up but never past them. Like Jake. They knew where her wounds lay, and they knew not to probe them.

"I know that now," Gloria said. "But I kept trying, pretending I could do it, contorting myself into all sorts of shapes to cover up the fact that I'm basically nuts. No way around it. And Larry cheered on my crazies. He helped me see the only way I would ever get anywhere was to dive head first into the pain I felt trying to be normal. I'd been running away from it for years."

Celeste nodded. "Same with me."

"At first I thought he could see right inside me, like someone finally discovered the place where I'd been hiding the secret of who I really was, not who I pretended to be."

"Same with me," Celeste repeated.

"And I bought it all—hook, line, and sinker—just like you. Until I got strong enough to think for myself and realized he was trying to stuff me into some new box. Only I wasn't about to climb in and slam the lid on myself. I'd finally started to live the life that made sense to me. I owned up to who I was—to the fact that I like women, and the fact that I wanted to go to law school and save the world. And that's when everything began to go to hell with Larry. I started to actually feel my power, to not need him anymore. He didn't like it. He set me up and then shot me right back down."

"I know! That's exactly how Larry made me feel when I

fell in love with Jake! Why I had to get away. But you're the first person who has said anything like this. All the Dreamers, all the others always go along with it. Why didn't you tell me all this before?"

"Because you wouldn't have listened. You needed to find your own way out."

Celeste turned onto her side and propped her head up with her hand to look directly at Gloria.

"He got to you way worse than he ever got to me, though." Gloria reached over, grabbed the bottle from the desk, and poured the final sips into their glasses. She handed one to Celeste. "We did a number on that. Bottle's empty."

Celeste sipped lightly, glad now that Gloria had rationed her earlier, figuring she'd be somewhere on the floor if Gloria hadn't kept full control of the bottle. "You were always the bigger bitch. I was never as strong as you, Glor. I was trying to find out who I was, why I'd messed up my life so badly that I'd ended up alone with no money and no real place to call home." She set the glass down on the carpet and flopped onto her back, looking again out the window over her head. "I wanted to be more like you, someone who knew exactly who she was and where she was going."

"That's a bunch of BS and you know it. You were always one of the most original people I knew, someone who dared to strike off on her own, not follow anybody's rules."

"False independence, Larry called that."

"Well, I call it guts, and it's what makes you special."

"Thanks, I guess."

Gloria wasn't done though, and Celeste knew there was no turning back until every last pent-up word was out in the open. "You think I had it all together? No way. But at least I had some idea that I was fundamentally all right. When Larry tried to take that idea from me, when I'd begun to pull away from him, I fought back. You could have too. I would have helped you. But I lost you, C, and I had to sit around and watch you lose yourself." Gloria took a deep breath and rushed on. "Everything that was great about you, things I'd loved since we were kids, like your sense of adventure, your willingness to go for things that I wouldn't dare consider, like counting turtles in Zanzibar, or teaching English in those god-awful refugee camps in Beirut. A normal job? Really? That's what you were supposed to want? Sure, you could have used a few tweaks here and there, a bit of aging, but who couldn't? I loved the Celeste who was funny and brave and ballsy enough to take on the whole world on her own terms."

"But that wasn't really me, Glor. That's what I learned from Larry. I was jumping from experience to experience so I wouldn't have to feel anything."

"I don't believe that. You did a lot of good out there in the world. You've made a difference. You don't need to feel ashamed, like that was all a mistake." She drank. "We all have crazy reasons and rioting pathologies to struggle with. Instead of trying to kill them, like Larry did, we need to recognize them and love them as part of the bigger picture of who we are."

"I know. That's what Jake says too."

"So listen to us! Listen to yourself! Larry was holding you captive. He sucked all the stuffing out of you, sweetie. And all that was left was some weepy woman who couldn't make a decision about the man she loved without Larry's approval."

"There was more to it than that. I couldn't figure out why Larry hated Jake so much."

Gloria cleared her throat and again looked away from Celeste, staring into the bottom of her now empty glass.

"I know there's something you're not telling me, Glor." Celeste pulled her knees to her chest and swung herself upright. "What do you know about them?"

Gloria cleared her throat again. "Nothing. There's still some things I can't tell you. Yet."

"Like?"

"Not now." Gloria stood up, stretched, then yawned. "Time to call it a night."

"Wait, you can't *not* tell me!"

"Tomorrow. I promise. But let's get out of here and get some sleep."

Celeste was too tired and woozy to fight. She wondered if she could take in any more information anyway. She pulled on her vest, stretching her arms through the armholes, wriggling her fingers.

Gloria tossed the empty bottle into her recycling bin and tucked the glasses back in the drawer. "Deal with washing those tomorrow. Glad we had this talk. I might not be the right lawyer for this, but we're going to work together somehow, okay?"

Celeste nodded, relieved. She pulled the sneakers on as Gloria opened the door and the scent of dusty roses and chamomile flooded in. She got up and the two old friends walked back into the apothecary.

"We're in this together, you know. I won't let you down," Gloria said, shutting the door behind them.

CHAPTER ELEVEN

HEADING HOME

Outside, a cold drizzle fell and the streetlights reflected off the icy pavement as Gloria and Celeste headed back to the parking lot in front of the police station, holding on to each other for support.

"Not smart to drink on nights like this," Gloria said as they inched along, warily watching for frozen puddles. As they rounded the corner, they both glanced toward the Broken Gate. The Dreamers were gone, replaced by a couple of smokers huddled under the restaurant's black-and-white-striped awning, their cigarettes flashing like orange stars in the dark.

"At least those crazies have left," said Gloria as she slid in behind the steering wheel. She leaned across the passenger seat to open the door for Celeste. "I probably shouldn't be driving, especially right under the cops' noses," Gloria said as a cruiser pulled in and parked a few yards away. "But I did promise to get you home."

"I trust you implissily!" Celeste responded. The Scotch was tying up her tongue, but she felt strangely sober, hyper-alert to the lights and the sounds of slamming car doors and the beat of freezing rain on the windshield. All she wanted to do was to fall into bed and put an end to the day. She leaned back in the seat, taking in the lingering smell of Gloria's shaggy white malamute after one of his outings spent swimming in the reservoir: wet and funky.

"What'd you do with your poor dog? He must be going nuts by now."

"The neighbor kid walked him. I'm sure Zion's sound asleep, like you should be." Gloria revved the engine, then pulled out onto the empty street.

"And you." Celeste yawned without bothering to cover her mouth. She shook her head and let the big hit of oxygen push away some of the fuzz in her brain.

"My mind's going a mile a minute, but maybe it will come up with something we can act on by morning. We're going to figure this out, C, come hell or high water."

"I know. That's why I called you." Celeste leaned her head against the cool glass of the car window and closed her eyes. When she opened them again, Gloria was pulling into the driveway in front of her building. She looked up at the dark, imposing Victorian mansion that had long ago been broken up into apartments. Tonight the tall windows glowered like great black eyes under the heavy brows of the cornices.

"Do you want me to come in with you? To make sure?" Gloria reached over and grabbed Celeste's arm before she could stagger from the car.

"Sure of what?" Celeste already knew what Gloria was going to say.

"Sure there's no one waiting for you in there. A murderer is on the loose, in case you forgot. And you might be the only witness. Really, Celeste, you should be coming home with me, not going in there alone." Gloria used her bossiest tone.

Celeste turned to look out the window at the house again. All she'd been worried about were the Dreamers and their accusations. Now Gloria was scaring her, but she wasn't going to show it. "I'll be okay," she said, realizing as she did that the "false independence" mode that Larry accused her of hiding behind was not what was needed at this moment. Still, she plunged on. "This is Riverton Falls, for Christ's sake."

"And that means you probably didn't even bother to lock your door when you went out this morning. Right?" Gloria's hand tightened on Celeste's arm, as if she were trying to hold her back.

"Why would anyone be after me?"

The tight smile on Gloria's lips told her Gloria saw through her bravado. The idea that someone might already be inside was much more terrifying than the possibility that someone might show up later.

"Maybe you could stay out here a while, until I get the lights on?"

"If that's the best you can do, I'll wait." She paused. "Sure you don't want to come home with me?"

Celeste shook her head. "I know it sounds crazy, and don't think I don't appreciate the offer, but I need to be alone right now. Way too many people in my space for one day."

"You really haven't changed, have you? But you'll have to come out and wave or something so I know you're all right. Or I could come in with you?"

"Nah, it's fine. Thanks, Glor. But stay here . . . 'til I get all the lights on, okay?" She was such an idiot. Couldn't even accept help in the most dire of circumstances. Celeste reached over and patted Gloria's hand, which still clung to her arm. She could feel it trembling. Or maybe the trembling was her own hand.

From the driveway, Celeste scanned the broad porch that wrapped around her first-floor apartment. Wary, she walked beneath the gingerbread portico, watching for any movement in the shadows, someone hiding behind the sturdy white pillars. Before Gloria had shoved the question of safety in her face, Celeste had been pining for home as a haven, looking forward to collapsing in familiar territory. Now she was afraid to open the door. She wished Gloria hadn't let her do this. She'd always hated coming home to a dark apartment and wished right now she'd left a light on, as she usually did when she went to work. But she hadn't known she'd be out all day. She wished she'd locked the door. But she hadn't even thought about it. Too late now. Her legs were so heavy with fear she could barely lift them. She wished someone else in one of the apartments was still awake, but mostly she wished the day had never happened.

"Breathe," she told herself out loud. The air was cold, scraping down her windpipe into her lungs, providing the lift she needed to shove open the door and step into the high-ceilinged hallway. She stood still, listening for any little sound or sense of movement. She pushed the old-fashioned button switch. The lights flickered into a cold fluorescent glow.

"See, no one," she reassured herself, as loud as her voice would go. The muscles in her chest tightened painfully. A panic attack, that's all it is, she thought, trying to calm herself, her breath staccato and grating. She could hear her father's voice sneering through her fear. *Don't be such a baby!*

"I'm not!" she said, as she picked up the collapsible umbrella that hung on a hook by the door. It was a flimsy thing, one of those jobs that turn inside out at any whisper of wind, but its slightly pointed tip was the nearest thing to a weapon she had at hand. Thrusting the umbrella in front of her like a ship's prow, she forced herself to walk down the hall to the kitchen. See, she wasn't a baby. She had every reason to be afraid, though. Anyone could be in here. This was real and this was happening to her.

Quickly, she switched on the kitchen lights. No hidden corners there. The room looked the same as she'd left it that morning. A lifetime ago. Toast crumbs littered the yellowing counter, a single blue plastic dish and her juice glass, strings of orange pulp clinging to its rim, waited in the sink along with her Carpe Diem coffee cup—remains of the last meal she'd eaten, she now realized. She glanced over at the card table covered with a faded floral tablecloth, and beside it, her two folding chairs, one pushed in, the other slightly askew. Is that how she'd left them? She rarely sat at the table, ate most of her solo meals standing over the sink. Had someone been here? Then, from somewhere, she heard—what? who?—a slight rustling movement. Holding her umbrella in front of her, she shuffled down the hall. The rustling grew louder, but she still couldn't tell where it was coming from. Under the bed? Slowly, she pushed the bedroom door open, heard its familiar creak.

She switched on the overhead light and held her breath as the small room lit up. Again, the room seemed empty. There was the bed, still unmade, the mess of magazines and books littering the floor, clothes flung over the chair. But she could still hear the rustling, faint as breath. Her heart jamming against her ribs, Celeste bent down, tilted her head, and peered into the dark space beneath the bed. Nothing. She let out the breath she'd been holding, then inhaled. The rush of oxygen made her dizzy, light-headed. She laughed out loud. Nothing had changed since she'd gotten up. She was just being paranoid. No one was in the bedroom. No one had been there since Jake left. She knew the feel of its loneliness.

But still, someone could be hiding in the bathroom. She screwed up her courage once again, reached in over the sink to grab the pull chain hanging from the light above the medicine cabinet and gave it a yank. Then, with the hook of the umbrella handle, she whipped back the plastic shower curtain. No one. There's no one, she told herself, backing out into the hall, then turning toward the living room.

The rustling—it had to be coming from in there. A flicker of movement caught her eye. In the faint light spilling from the bathroom, she could see a shadow moving across her own, slanting over the floor in front of the French doors to the porch. A long spindly arm shot up along the sheer curtains. Another reached out, close enough to grab her. She jumped back into the hall. Fear caught in her throat. "Who's there?" she tried to say, but nothing came out. This time, she wasn't imagining it. She swallowed hard and dared herself to step forward. One . . . two . . . three . . .

"Idiot!" she said aloud. Celeste stood still in disbelief, her heart still racing. She walked over to the corner, where the *wayang* marionette from Indonesia had always lived. It stared back at her, its long skinny arms, propped wide on their sticks, stirring in the light draught that snuck in through the cracks around the French doors. At its feet, the *New York Times Book Review* lay open where she'd left it, a few loose pages on top fluttering softly, rustling. She fell back against the wall, slid to the floor, and began to laugh, her sudden, nervous, high-pitched, hysterical peals echoing through the empty apartment.

Celeste used the umbrella like a cane to hoist herself up and managed to get to her feet, then pulled open the French doors and stepped out into the cold. From the porch, she could see Gloria's headlights still illuminating the big bushy rhododendrons that lined the drive. Celeste waved the umbrella over her head.

"Coast clear!" she called, hoping Gloria could hear her. Two short beeps of the Saab's horn came in response. Gloria flashed her headlights and the engine rumbled. Celeste almost ran after her friend as the car backed out of the driveway, but the taillights headed down Bartley Street, and the ruff-ruff of the old Saab disappeared into the night.

Closing the doors, Celeste backed into the living room, inching her way through the dark until she reached the standing halogen light in the far corner. The lamp clicked and hummed before the harsh white glare burst from its bowl, lighting up the puppet, who seemed to be nodding his sharp-nosed leather face at her. Grabbing the supporting sticks from under his outstretched arms, she lowered them against his brown-and-white batik sarong.

"You scared me to death!" she said, giving his head scarf a pull. She sank down on the cracked Naugahyde couch, sucked in a long breath, and then let it go with a loud gasp somewhere between a laugh and a sob. Stupid, she admonished herself—stupid, stubborn, and scared to boot. The fear, she realized now, had knocked the worst of the drunk out of her, and all she could think about was another drink. She hauled herself up and made it over to the built-in cabinet in the corner, where she kept her booze on the bottom shelves.

Captain Morgan Spiced Rum. That's what I need, she thought, pouring two fingers into one of the wine glasses she kept in the upper section. The tumblers in the kitchen were too far away. She took a sip, savoring the spicy caramel aroma trickling down her throat as she leaned back and again slid down against the wall onto the floor, too tired to even get back to the couch. She pulled her knees up to her chest. Her tears returned, and she let them shake through her as she huddled in the corner against the cold plaster.

Every time she shut her eyes, the movie of Larry lying in his own spreading blood played against her closed lids. She kept seeing his eyes on her, hearing his last whispered word—"her." She leaned her head on her knees and took another deep breath.

Immediately her nostrils filled with that same raw, metallic odor that had assailed her hours earlier. Her eyes flew open as she recognized the scent—Larry's blood, dried, cracked, and flaking—on the knees of her cords.

Horrified, she jumped up, dashed to the kitchen, stripped off her pants and threw them straight into the kitchen sink. Cold water for blood, she thought as she turned on the faucet, rubbed dish soap on the stains, then scrubbed the dark patches against each other, watching the rust-colored water swirl and disappear down the drain. Celeste wrung out the pants as hard as she could, then she draped them over the towel rack by the table to dry. Back in the bathroom, she pulled on the flannel pajama bottoms that hung on a hook behind the door, and then she scrambled back to the living room where Captain Morgan waited for her. A few more dances with him would help her finally get some sleep. Actually, she thought, settling on the couch, putting her bare feet up on the glass-topped coffee table (she thought it probably used to be someone's patio furniture), what she really needed was some food, but the fridge was close to empty. Usually, she ate at work, and also, without Jake around, she'd pretty much stopped buying anything but breakfast food. A couple of eggs and some bread would do, but she couldn't get herself up to make anything.

Too many nights she'd sat on this couch, alone, wondering where Jake was and what he was doing. She looked at the wall clock. Almost midnight again, she noted, letting her glance stray to the only framed photo in the room. There they were, she and Jake, smiling at the top of Hunger Mountain. She saw her own hand, held up for Jake's cell phone camera, the sapphire ring sparkling in the early summer sun. They looked so fresh, so pleased with themselves, just engaged seconds before he snapped the selfie.

Right now the people in the photo looked only vaguely familiar, like friends she'd lost touch with long ago. What had happened to that guy, Jake, the first guy she hadn't fled from at the earliest inkling of love? What had happened to that Celeste, the one who looked so dazzled and excited, pink-cheeked from the climb? Somehow they'd morphed into two bitter and wounded people. She wanted to blame Larry, but she knew she'd set it up herself. She was the one who had lied to both Larry and Jake, trying to keep them both, never guessing she'd end up with neither.

Celeste lay on the couch trying to calm her mind, but memories of Jake kept flooding in. After the encounter in the Corner Cup, Celeste had seen him around town a few times. He'd bought her a beer one evening at The Castaway, where all she could do was mouth "Thanks!" over the boisterous crowd. She'd bumped into him at Winzer's, where he helped her pick out a low-flow showerhead, then again at the Buddhist laundry, where she'd lent him her fabric softener. After each chance encounter, her nights filled with dreams of men who looked like Jake getting close, calling her name, running after her as she backed away. She never told Larry about these dreams. They belonged to her.

Then came the day a little over a year ago after she'd hiked solo through the forest to the bald expanse of gray rock at the top of Hunger Mountain. She was standing there, looking out at the group of kettle ponds below, eating a PB&J sandwich, taking in the view, when he came up behind her. "Celeste?"

They'd talked for hours, sitting on the sun-warmed rocks, eating gorp and oranges, looking out over the red and gold damask of peak foliage below them, watching the sun move from east to west. Jake had gradually sidled over, closer bit by bit, until his shoulder and thigh pressed against hers, until she felt as if electricity sizzled though her veins, then exploded like little star bursts in her stomach. He put his hand, calloused yet tender, on her cheek, turned her face toward his, and kissed her for the first time. His lips were soft. He smelled of wood smoke and tasted like caramel. The kiss went on and on and she hoped he'd never stop kissing her.

As the light faded she'd followed Jake back down the mountain. And after they'd gotten into their separate cars, she'd kept right on following him down the rutted dirt road alongside the river, terrified her car would slide down the embankment into the freezing water. She remembered rounding the bend and seeing the house for the first time—a simple shack of weathered wood under a green metal roof, the steps winding down to the river that rushed over peninsulas of granite worn smooth over the years by the current. A sense of familiarity swept over Celeste as she pulled her car in next to Jake's truck. She'd dreamt about this place, or one just like it, where the water flowed clear, not full of the mud and debris that usually sullied the ponds and rivers of her dreams.

He'd brought in wood and laid a fire in the cookstove, then fried up eggs and bacon while she chopped vegetables for salad. Side by side on his couch, they ate, shooting shy glances at each other, wondering what would happen next.

Everything was perfect, until she mentioned Larry. She'd tried so hard not to say anything about him, afraid that Larry's name would summon memories of the break-up of his marriage to Nicole. Until something about her dream had slipped out. "I dreamt about this place a few weeks ago. Larry called it my heart home."

Jake glowered as she said it, then got up to stoke the fire, pushing the poker around in the woodstove. With his back to her, he'd said in a low, tight voice she hadn't heard before, "I'd stay away from Larry if I were you. He's nothing but trouble."

"Because of what happened with Nicole?"

"Among other things." He threw another log on the fire, so hard that sparks jumped onto the granite hearthstone.

"Would me seeing Larry be a deal breaker?" Celeste held her breath, afraid to hear the answer.

"Long as you don't go join that Dreamer group, I can live with it." He stood and wiped his hands along the length of his thighs, rubbing off the soot on his jeans.

When he turned back to her, he gave her a strained smile, but then he picked up his guitar and began to play as if nothing had happened. In a low, mellow voice he sang songs she'd never heard, about loneliness and love, songs he'd written himself, not like the rollicking tunes she'd heard him strum weeks earlier as she tried to hide in the back of the burrito shop where he had a weekly gig.

After a few tunes, they snuggled together on his couch, talking and laughing, finishing off a bottle of white wine before falling onto his lumpy double bed, happy, high, and hungry for each other.

That night, in Jake's arms, surrounded by his strong, comfortable body, she dreamed she was standing in a glass house on a cliff above an ocean. Far off she could see a great blue wave, a tsunami, gathering speed and strength, rolling rapidly toward her, a gigantic wall of water that shattered her window into a million spangled pieces, all floating around her as she was swept away inside the wave.

The next day, she told Larry the dream, knowing she had finally broken the barrier to her own heart. But instead of praising her, as she'd expected, Larry looked at her quizzically. He shook his head as if trying to clear it and mumbled something that sounded like, "That's why . . . familiar."

"Excuse me?"

"A blue wave? Swept away by a blue wave?" He looked surprised.

"Came right through the glass, the barrier. Does that mean anything?"

He coughed and typed something into his computer, but didn't answer her question. Finally, he turned his attention back to her.

"That was the dream we've been waiting for, Cel!" Larry said, suddenly all smiles, rubbing his hands together. "I knew we'd get there eventually. I've had to work hard, but it's paid off. Time for you to join us at Dreamland."

"Really? You're letting me be a Dreamer?" She was stunned. Here it was, the goal she'd been working toward for the past three years. But the memory of Jake's words about joining the Dreamers trampled the excitement and happiness she'd expected to feel.

Larry was grinning at her, crowing about their joint achievement. Celeste forced herself to smile back and clap her hands together.

Then, for the first time, she told Larry about Jake. In seconds everything changed. Larry jumped up from his chair, knocking it over, and banged his fist on the desk so hard the mug crashed to the floor. *"Awk!"* screeched Pete, fluttering frantically over his perch.

"You don't know anything about that guy. He's not who you think he is." He walked over to the window, breathing heavily.

"Why not?"

Larry reacted like Jake had the night before, only worse. "Stay away, that's all," Larry answered, echoing Gloria's long-ago warning about Larry himself. He turned to face her, clearing his throat, gathering himself. "Jake's another distraction." He sat back down and crossed his arms. "That dream's not about him. You're opening your heart to the Dreamscape."

Celeste looked away, out the window, wondering what Jake and Larry had against each other. Nicole—it had to have something to do with her.

"Don't get off track. Now's the time to discover your true heart. You have to decide, Cel. The Dreamscape or Jake, but not both."

But she'd wanted both. So she decided not to mention Jake to Larry and not to tell Jake about becoming a Dreamer. It had worked fine for quite a while after that. Until Jake moved in, and then it had all blown up in her face and left her all alone, which is where she was now on the worst night of her life.

Celeste threw a shot of rum down her throat, the spicy burn distracting her from the memory she kept trying to push away: As a surprise, Jake had come to pick her up at the bar. Only she wasn't working that night as she'd told him—the lie she'd been telling him for months, whenever she headed out to Dreamland. She knew Jake never went to the Broken Gate. Always avoided Dreamer overload at the bar. She'd come home that night to find Jake, silent and stony, shoving flannel shirts and grubby work boots into his Army Surplus duffel. She'd stood in the doorway to the bedroom, frozen, unable to make herself reach out for him. A voice in her head screamed, "Stop! Don't leave me!" while Jake kept right on packing.

"Can't you see what Larry's doing? The guy's evil. He's manipulating you like all those other idiots he calls Dreamers." He brushed past her and stormed into the bathroom where she could hear him rattling shelves in the medicine chest. Back in the bedroom he threw his toothbrush and toiletries into his bag. "Schemers, more like it. You all think it's about salvation. But there's something else going on."

"What do you mean?" she managed to whisper.

"He's using you. Believe me. I know how this guy operates." Jake zipped the duffel and the tearing sound made her cringe. "He destroys people. You think that the Nicole you know is the one I married? I don't even recognize her." He turned to look at Celeste, his face contorted with rage. "And that's nothing compared to what he did to his own wife."

"His wife? I thought—"

"Forget I said that."

You don't know who Jake is, Larry's voice flashed through the back of her mind. *You can't trust him.*

"Okay. Go," she'd so stupidly said. "I'm not going to be in the middle of your damn feud with Larry. If you loved me, you wouldn't let him come between us." She folded her arms across her chest. These two men had her trapped and she had no idea which one to believe.

Jake dropped the duffel and started toward her, his eyes full of pain, anger suddenly replaced by grief. "I have to go because I don't know any other way to get through to you."

He grabbed her arms, pulling them to her sides, then pinned her against the wall. His body softened against hers. He buried his face in her hair and choked, "Don't let him take this away from us."

She breathed in the rich coffee musk of his neck, her body rigid. Larry's voice thundered through her saying, *Jake's what's holding you back. You don't need him. You can't trust him. So close, Cel. So close to the Divine. Don't throw it away.*

She wrested herself from Jake's grasp. "I can't!" she said, her voice a deep moan.

Jake stepped back, bit his lip, and shook his head. He shouldered his bag and, without looking at her, walked to the front door. Celeste followed, wanting with every fiber of her being to yell "Stop!" But she couldn't get out even that single word.

Stepping into the foggy night, he turned. "Me or him, Celeste," Jake said. He looked her straight in the eye. "Let me know when you decide. But I'm not going to wait forever."

If she believed Larry's story about his reunion with Nicole, he'd only waited six weeks.

Loud, insistent pounding rattled the French doors, startling Celeste out of her reverie. She jumped up, barking her shins against the coffee table. She fumbled for the umbrella, then she spun toward the noise. Her own reflection shivered on the darkened glass. Screwing up her last remaining ounce of courage, she inched closer to the sound. She focused on the darkness, looking through her own reflection. Against the glass panes, between the hammering fists, a face emerged, a twisted mask of fear, framed by flying dreadlocks and the collar of an oversize coat. Celeste opened her mouth and screamed.

CHAPTER TWELVE

THINGS THAT GO BUMP
IN THE NIGHT

Celeste's scream vibrated through her body. She could see Adam outside, flapping his hands up and down as if he were trying to lower the volume. In his right hand fluttered a scrap of paper. As her scream died into a whimper, she watched him desperately press the paper against the glass. "HE'S AFTER ME!" She focused in on the note and its big block letters and tried to get herself under control. Before she had time to think, a black shape thundered past the window, heavy footsteps pounding across the porch, chasing Adam away.

Celeste collapsed. She hit the floor and sat there, staring out into the sudden emptiness, teeth chattering as she hugged herself, rocking from side to side, hoping it was over. Until the footsteps shook the glass doors again. Forcing herself to her knees, she crawled to the other side of the couch, trying to hide. She peeked out as the black shape bent down and scooped something from the porch. She shrank back, terrified, listening to the sound of boots now crunching across the gravel driveway. The creak of the front door opening. She hadn't locked it after she came in, afraid someone might be hiding inside. Now it was too late. Cold wet air rushed in. Boots scraped against the coir mat, followed by two heavy thumps, then the *brush, brush* of someone walking toward her.

"Get out!" she tried to scream, but nothing came out. She clutched her pathetic umbrella, waving it back and forth, eyes closed, not wanting to face her own murderer. Hands grabbed her shoulders—shaking her—then pulled her hard against a body that smelled of wet wool and damp leather. "Don't hurt me," she whimpered.

"Hurt you? Jesus Christ, they've done a number on you."

Celeste opened her eyes. Jake looked back. Rain dripped from his brows into his dark eyes. She struggled against his hold, but he gripped tighter, his hands close to her neck.

"Let me go, let me go!"

Gloria's words pulsed through her mind: *He had the most reason.*

"Calm down. It's okay. It's me!" He released her arms and she backed away. "What the hell's wrong with you?"

"He said you were after him!" Celeste tried to control her voice.

"Who said?"

"Adam. He had a sign."

"You mean this?" Jake held up a crumpled ball of wet paper that dripped red ink. "I got this off the porch."

"And at The Castaway," she rushed on, her fears tumbling out of her mouth. "You didn't want me to go back and get my ring. You already knew. Is that why you were chasing Adam—he saw you kill Larry?" Pieces were falling into place, but not the way she wanted them to. Trying to read his expression, she saw the man she loved looking back at her, perplexed, worried. Not a murderer. Impulsively, she reached out to run her hand over his cheek, to feel the roughness of his beard against her palm. "I'm sorry. I don't know what or who to believe. What to think. What or who to trust."

Jake put his arms around her, gentle now, and pulled her close. This time she let herself melt into him, listening to his heart pound over Gloria's suspicions and Larry's warnings.

"I know. It's okay. I'm here now." He stroked her hair and kissed her forehead. Everything she'd been hoping for, but not this way.

"You didn't do it, did you?" She couldn't believe she was asking this again, but she needed to hear it from him.

He let go of her and sat down hard on the couch, his face dropping into his hands. "I thought you knew me. Trusted me."

She started to go to him, but stopped. From the corner of her eye, she caught an image of Larry—his arms folded across his belly, stubbled chin tilted toward her—hovering on the other end of the couch. The anger she'd felt propelling her toward Larry's office that morning now buzz-sawed through her again. There he was, crouching, ready to pull her away from Jake in the tug-of-war that hadn't ended even with his death. These two men had ripped her apart, letting their mysterious hatred for each other play out through her. "How could you do this to me?" she hissed under her breath at both men.

Jake raised his head, forehead furrowed, brows knit.

"You thought I knew you?" Celeste said. "Thanks to you and Larry I don't even know myself. Trust you?" She stopped, watching his face. She'd expected anger, but what she saw was weariness and confusion. Of course she was wrong. Gloria was crazy. Larry was a monster. Here was Jake, back home, with her, what she'd longed for all along.

She went to him, ran her hand through his hair, her fingers across the soft nape of his neck. She crawled onto the couch, sinking into the cracked, duct-taped pleather. Laying her head on Jake's shoulder, she whispered, "I'm sorry. It's all been too much."

He lowered his head to hers, the weight of it pushing her cheek against the damp, rough canvas of his jacket. He put an arm around her waist and tenderly pulled her in. Celeste took deep quaking breaths, trying to trust the touch she had missed so much. She wanted to close her eyes and fall asleep right then and there in the familiar comfort that surrounded them, but even in Jake's arms, the doubts kept bubbling up. Celeste struggled to put her thoughts into words.

"I feel like I'm stuck in the middle of some game and I have no idea what is—what the rules are. I don't even know who's playing, or what side anyone's on."

"I wish I could tell you."

She lifted her head and pulled back to look at him. "Tell me what? Why can't you tell me?"

"I don't have the answers, not all of them, anyway. But I'm trying to help you. Trying to figure this out."

She wanted to push him for more, but hearing the weariness in his voice now, she lay her head back on his shoulder, and just let silence envelop them.

Finally, she sat up and spoke. "Do you think he did it, the tarot guy? Is that why you were after him?"

"After him? I was on my way here to make sure you were all right."

She searched his eyes to see if he was telling the truth. "The sign. And when he saw you today, when I was getting my tarot read and you came down the street, I thought he seemed scared of you. Do you know him?"

Jake cleared his throat and hesitated. "No." He shook

his head, raindrops scattering on his shoulders. "Seen him on the streets. Something about him . . ." he trailed off. "Never mind. Nothing."

She wondered what he wasn't telling her. "Then who did he mean was after him? And why was he here, at my window?"

Jake shrugged. "Not me. He must have meant someone else—someone who's still after him. But that guy's involved in this somehow. Didn't catch him, anyway. He disappeared." He took off his wet coat. "Dropped something else though."

He rummaged through his pocket, extracting a soggy clump of paper, hesitating, before shoving most of the wet wad back into his pocket. Then he held out a soggy tarot card. "Found this with the note. Mean anything to you?"

"The Hermit," she read, looking at the drawing of a tall, thin monk enfolded in a brown robe, a lantern in one hand, cane in the other. "One of his tarot cards. Maybe it means Adam's a hermit? He looks like a hermit."

"Or a monk." Jake perused the wet card then put it on the coffee table next to Celeste's empty, rum-rimmed glass.

"Anything else?" She reached across the couch and tried to insert her hand inside the big patch pocket on his Carhartt jacket, but Jake leaned away.

"Junk. You know how I am, stuff all those receipts in there. Had to get some paint brushes, rollers, things like that. Receipts from Winzer's."

Now she knew he was lying. Jake never said more than he needed to, and this explanation, short as it was, was too long for him.

"Stuff you bought after I saw you in the bar today?"

He cleared his throat before responding. "Guess so." Then he quickly changed the subject. "You have no idea why that guy was at your window?"

Celeste sucked in her breath. "I think he killed Larry."

She let the words out fast. "Or at least might have killed Larry. He was running away from Larry's house when I got there, when I went to get my ring."

"Did you tell the cops this?"

"Of course! They acted like I made him up. Probably should call them right now."

She started to stand, but Jake grabbed her arm and pulled her back down, next to him. "He's long gone. You can tell them in the morning."

"But how do you know? What if he comes back?" Jake was making her nervous. Something didn't feel quite right, no matter how much she wanted it to. The old metal radiator clanged and groaned, and she flinched, though most nights she hardly noticed the noise.

Jake picked up the tarot card, leaving a bit of wet backing stuck to the glass coffee table. "Maybe he didn't just drop this. Might have left it on purpose."

"Like a message?"

"Is that what you think?"

"You sound like a therapist."

"What makes you say that?"

"Stop it!" Celeste landed a light punch on his bicep. Usually she hated it when he played this game on her, but tonight she read it as another sign that he was trying to draw her away from her suspicious thoughts and into the sort of banter they used to always bat back and forth on this old couch.

"Just messin' with ya." Jake put his arm around Celeste. She let herself be pulled in, pressing her cheek against his shoulder. Celeste had been wanting for too long to feel his arms around her to let some niggling doubt keep her from what she needed more than anything right now. The warmth of Jake's body seeped into hers, and she melted into his arms, her muscles aching as her body let go of the fear, anger, and grief she'd struggled to contain all day. "I'm all mixed up, I can't stop thinking about Larry, finding him."

"I know." Jake hugged her closer.

Celeste was limp, drained by the horror of the day that had started out so differently. She wished he'd hold her forever.

"I can go now," he said, "but I'll stay if you need me."

"What do you want to do?" she asked, her voice a weak whisper.

"Nope, this one's up to you, Celeste. Sometimes you have to ask for what you need."

She swallowed hard, thinking back to the night he'd left. She gripped his hand. Such a simple, impossible request—*Ask for what you need*. She looked down and the floor seemed to open up beneath her, revealing a deep, gaping hole. She hurtled into black space, naked, undefended, grasping for words as if they were a rope she could catch to stop the free fall. She opened her mouth and a small voice emerged. "Please stay with me, Jake. I need you."

"Okay." He kissed the top of her head.

The room reassembled around her, and she was back on solid ground. It seemed so easy. She was actually getting what she wanted. All she had to do was open her mouth.

"Wasn't so hard, was it?" Jake asked. "Probably took more guts to confront Larry. Right?" He hugged her. "You're brave and you're strong. And those are only two of the things I love about you."

There it was again. He loved parts of her, not all of her. Still, he knew her foibles, and he hadn't given up on her. At least that's how it seemed as she sat, folding herself against him on the ratty old couch. Still feeling exposed, she worried she'd shown Jake too much. Especially if Larry had been right about Jake and Nicole.

"I'll stay out here on the couch in case that nutcase comes back. Got anything more threatening than that umbrella?"

Out here? He wasn't going to follow her into the bedroom, their bedroom, even though that had been her goal when she'd set off to see Larry that morning. Things had changed; tonight all she needed was his presence, his breathing self, in the next room, keeping her safe.

CHAPTER THIRTEEN

DREAMING AGAIN

Celeste blinked against the bright morning light slipping in below the half-drawn shades. She looked up, stared at the ceiling, then inventoried her hungover body: Throat sore. Mouth like cotton. Head pounding. Under all that: Fear. Her T-shirt stuck to her back, soaked with sweat. Her hands hurt; she gingerly touched the indentations her nails had made along her palm. The dream had come again. More this time. She remembered seeing through the eyes of the woman—a lump of dough between her hands, a blue jay in the hedge outside the window—then feeling something tight around her neck. Her hands transformed into the hands of the other, the view shifting to the back of the woman's head. Her scream shot Celeste back into waking life.

She rolled over and automatically reached for her journal. Celeste wrote as fast as she could, the horror of the dream dissolving into the horror of the day before, now flooding in to fill that moment of oblivion between sleeping and waking.

Her fear had a name and a reason. Larry was dead. No one cared what her dream had been. No one was going to interpret it, or feed her questions for the gestalt, or tell her how tricky her Demon Mind could be. Instead of that momentary burst of euphoria she experienced after Larry kicked her out, she felt adrift, left scrambling to get her sea legs. Funny, Larry had been trying to get her to feel this way for years—vulnerable and wide open to the very feelings she'd always longed to flee.

Celeste closed the journal. It wasn't her ego or her Demon Mind that had to die so she could be free. It was Larry. Someone had to actually murder the guy before she could grasp what he'd been trying to get her to feel all along. She smiled at the irony. Jake had warned her. "Larry and the Dreamers are smothering you," he'd said, but she'd been too stubborn and probably too brainwashed to listen.

Jake! Was he still out there on the sofa? Celeste tiptoed to the bedroom door and peered into the living room. Snoring away, he lay on his back on the couch, under their blanket. Like the old days, she thought. Jake had spent his share of nights on that couch after drinking too much Jameson, the Irish whiskey that made him snore like a freight train. Her kicks and pleas for silence sent him stumbling out of bed to the living room.

She crept past him into the kitchen to get Mr. Coffee up and going. In the light of day, Jake seemed like Jake, big and bear-like. Not a murderer, Gloria! She pulled the last two slices of thick grainy bread from the fridge and slid them into the toaster oven. Then, after pouring a mug of coffee, she glanced back into the living room, thinking about the way Jake had turned away from her last night as he went through his pocket before producing The Hermit card that now lay on the coffee table. Jake was hiding something.

She could sneak back into the living room and go through the pocket herself. He'd draped his jacket across the plastic lawn chair to dry by the French doors. She padded softly from the kitchen into the hall. She was sure to wake him if she went snooping now, but she couldn't help herself. She waited, watching.

Jake was still sound asleep, but the jacket was gone. Her eyes searched the floor around the chair, wondering if it had slipped off in the night. No mustard-colored Carhartt. Puzzled, she turned back toward the kitchen. Then she saw it, hanging on a hook in the entryway, next to the front door. He must have hung it up after she'd gone to bed. She reached for the jacket, stumbling slightly over the old leather work boots he'd tossed against the wall when he came in. Clumps of wet, gray mud covered the soles. He must have chased Adam all the way into the neighboring woods in the rain in order to get them that dirty.

Celeste eased her hand into the damp right pocket. As Jake had maintained, it was stuffed with crinkled receipts. Stop and Shop, Winzer's, The Castaway. The guy is a walking trash can, she thought, softly balling up the slips of paper so she could slide them noiselessly back in. Looked like he'd been telling her the truth after all.

He's right, I need to trust him, she thought, even as she reached her fingers deeper into the corner of the pocket, fingertips grazing crumbs and pennies. Still nothing. From the kitchen wafted the smell of toast beginning to burn in the unreliable toaster oven. She ran her hand over the coat and then, hesitantly, reached into the left pocket.

Right away, her fingers encountered a soggy piece of card stock. Probably whatever Jake had picked up on the porch then sneakily shoved in his pocket while she sat next to him on the couch the night before. Then a little further down, jammed in the corner, something else. Holding her breath, Celeste ran a finger across the familiar shape, knew immediately the tiny prongs and the smooth, cool surface. Pinching her fingers around it, she pulled it out and opened her palm to see what she was afraid to see. There, glowing in the center of her hand, sat her ring, as blue and sparkling as when she had pulled it from her finger and dropped it into Larry's outstretched palm. That seemed like ages ago, though it had been less than twenty-four hours since she sat in his office for the last time.

She froze, not knowing what to do. Put it back? She looked down at the floor. The card had fluttered to her feet as she pulled out the ring. She squatted to pick it up. "Rowan McNeil," she read, whispering to herself, "www.BlueWave.com." No phone, no physical address. This guy, whoever he was, must live in cyberspace. She turned it over and was surprised to see three lines of kanji across the back. She recognized the Japanese letters right away. It was the kind of card that every Japanese businessman carried. She had collected quite a stack of them as a hostess at Café Absinthe in Osaka. But the name on the card was clearly not Japanese. Rowan McNeil. It rings a small, distant bell, but not one that has to do with Larry, she thought, leaning against the wall for support. But *Blue Wave*? Her tsunami dream, and Larry, repeatedly asking her if her dream wave was blue. Probably just a coincidence.

Ring in one hand, card in the other, she walked in a daze back to the kitchen. A wisp of smoke escaped from the toaster oven. She jerked it open and pulled out the two pieces of toast, slightly charred around the edges. Mr. Coffee sputtered the last few drops into the carafe. Celeste put the ring and the card into her pajama-bottom pocket. She stood in the middle of the room, wondering what she was going to say to Jake, then she picked up her mug and sat down at the table. She took a few sips and tried to think. First she pulled out the card and placed it down, English side up, then she reached back into her pocket for the ring. She slipped it onto her left ring finger and held up her hand, turning it this way and that toward the light as she had the first time she'd worn it. Jake must have picked it up from the porch and hidden it from her for some reason.

Now she was certain that Adam killed Larry, but she couldn't figure out why he had been on her porch. Looking for refuge or rescue from whoever had been "after" him. That seemed clear. But why come to her? Maybe he'd wanted to give back her ring, though she had no idea how he'd even known it was hers. Or why Jake had kept it from her.

A groan came from the living room, and she could picture Jake coming back into his body from wherever the previous night had taken him. Celeste had watched him reenter so many times. Instead of shooting up out of his dreams the way she did, Jake always woke slowly, letting the day gradually seep into him. She'd often wondered where he'd been, what he'd seen, but in the year they'd been together, he'd never told her a single dream. Like Gloria, he maintained that the dreams themselves were irrelevant—synapses popping away, disposing of the detritus of daily life while transforming the encounters and thoughts into memories.

From her chair in the kitchen, Celeste heard the familiar, soft rasp of Jake's whiskered cheeks as he ran his hand over his face. Or was that a memory? She got up, put the card and the ring back in her pocket, and went to the counter to butter the cooling toast. She still had no idea what she was going to say.

Jake groaned again, and she guessed he was pulling himself up from the couch, stiff from a night crammed head to toe between the armrests. *Mr. Bones,* dead Larry chuckled. *Not long 'til we're all with Mr. Bones.* Guess he was right about that one. Her breath caught somewhere between a giggle and a sob.

"Celeste? Did you burn the toast again?" Jake shuffled into the kitchen, coming up behind her and putting his arms around her as he'd done so many mornings before. She let herself ease back and snuggle against him, closing her mind to everything else but the solid feel of his body against hers. Here was the one man who knew how to hold her, not too tight, leaving enough room for her to pull away if she started to feel trapped. His hands moved slowly from her stomach down to the tops of her thighs and she wanted to go wherever he was taking her. Instead she wrenched herself away, afraid he'd discover the ring in her pocket.

"Coffee?" she asked, trying to control the quaver in her voice.

She could see the flicker of hurt cross his face, a shadow of what she'd seen that final night. He turned from her, nodding, and went to the door to retrieve Celeste's copy of *The Riverton Spectator*, the town's increasingly skimpy daily paper. She took a mug off the shelf and poured him a cup, wondering how she was going to broach the subject of the ring and this Rowan McNeil fellow. Or what she was going to say about going through his pockets in the first place.

"Headline news," Jake said as he reentered the kitchen. "Guess it would be, considering it's the first murder in this town in," he perused the columns, "fifty-seven years? Wow."

He held up the front page for her to read. "Local Therapist Murdered" ran the headline over a photo of Larry's brick house with the yellow crime-scene tape crisscrossing the front door. In the far right-hand corner of the picture, she noticed the cop car, Wally at the wheel, her own silhouette barely visible through the rear window. Celeste grimaced. She hoped the picture was too indistinct for anyone to recognize her—not that there was anyone left who didn't already know all about it. She watched Jake skim the article, scanning his face for clues to the contents. God, I hope they don't mention me, she thought, as he began to read aloud.

"'Alerted by a client . . .' How do they know that?" He looked up at her. She shrugged and handed him his coffee. "Northern

Rivers Hospital . . . pronounced dead . . . blunt trauma to the head,' blah, blah, 'Anyone having information,' blah, blah, blah."

"That's it?" Celeste asked as she put a dollop of his favorite strawberry jam on his toast. She wanted him to keep reading so she could figure out her next move.

"Let's not read this crap right now," Jake tossed the paper onto the table. "I'd rather talk about us." He took a bite of toast and washed it down with coffee. "There are a few things I need to explain and—"

"Like why you didn't tell me about the ring?" Celeste said through tight lips, ripping her toast in two.

"Ring?" She could hear the wariness in his voice.

She put her hand into her pocket. "I found this," she waved the ring in front of his eyes, then reached back in and pulled out the card, "and this, in your coat."

"Were you going through my jacket?" He thumped his mug down on the counter, coffee sloshing over the rim, running down the mug's washed-out drawing of a black lab carrying a flag in his mouth.

She had to tell him the truth. "You're hiding something from me. I can tell. If you want me to trust you, you need to tell me what's going on." Her voice was high, imploring. "I'm so confused I don't know what or whom to believe at this point." She waited for the floor to open up once again and swallow her for good this time.

I told ya, ya can't trust that guy, Larry whispered in her ear. She pushed her hand through her hair, trying to brush his voice away.

Jake looked at the ceiling and sighed. Curiously, he sounded relieved. "Yes, I picked them up from the porch." He took another bite of toast. "I didn't mean to lie to you."

He was lying again. She was sure of it, but she couldn't explain how she knew, except he kept avoiding her eyes. *See, ya don't know anything about Jake at all,* Larry insisted.

"I don't know what to believe. I want to believe in you, Jake, but Larry—"

"Stop it, Celeste," Jake said. "When are you going to get that Larry deliberately put all these ideas about me in your head? They're not true, whatever they are."

"Oh, so it's not true that you're seeing Nicole? Getting back with her?" There it was, the thing that had been lurking beneath her mistrust all along, slithering out of her.

"It's not what you think." His voice was flat.

It was true, then, not simply more of Larry's poison. "So you have?"

"Don't let Larry keep ruining this for us. He's dead, he's gone. We got another chance. If we can trust each other again."

"But you *are* seeing her."

"I told you," tension in his voice as he repeated himself, "there's nothing going on. Nothing I can explain right now." Then his voice softened and lowered a notch. "It's one of those times we talked about. Needing to work things out on our own? Telling each other, promising to be back when we could?" Finally, his eyes were on hers again and the intense, earnest expression she knew so well—brows knit together, gaze direct and open—settled on his face. "This is one of those times. Let me do what I need to do."

She nodded, ashamed of her jealousy—jealousy Larry had fanned into flame.

"What about the card? This Rowan guy? Did Adam leave that too?"

"Some guy he read the tarot for? Who knows." Jake took another bite of toast and swallowed the last drop of coffee. "Gotta go. Call Gloria. She'll help you figure it out."

"Gloria?"

But Jake was already heading toward the door.

She trailed after him. "Jake, do you want me to keep the ring?"

He bent down to pull on his muddy boots, a lock of dark hair falling across his broad forehead. Celeste's palms began to sweat.

"It's up to you," he answered, head still down as he tied up his laces.

He hauled himself upright, still stiff from the couch. "Can't tell you what's going to happen between us. But I do still love you. Time to start believing me." And without a good-bye kiss or another look, he headed out the door and down the steps.

He said it! I love you! Smiling, she watched him trudge across the lawn to his truck. Funny. She hadn't heard him drive in the night before. She knew the sound of his engine, the one she had been waiting for weeks to hear. But then with Adam pounding on the doors . . .

As the engine revved, Celeste forced herself not to run after him. Instead, she looked at the ring, at home on her finger again, and wondered where Jake was heading now. Back in the kitchen, she poured the last of the coffee into her mug, then began digging around for the cell phone, lost somewhere in the back of the spatula drawer. She plugged in the phone and was surprised to see it still had a charge. She dialed Gloria. No answer.

"Damn, Gloria, what haven't you been telling me?" she asked the voice mail. She couldn't sit around waiting for Gloria to call back. She knew where she needed to go.

CHAPTER FOURTEEN

DREAMLAND

Dreamland emerged from the dense growth of pines and birch, a gleaming temple at the end of a rutted Class Four road. The gold-flecked clapboard siding shimmered even in the gray November light, and the copper roof reflected the few rays of sun breaking through the clouds. Beneath the tallest gable, a round stained-glass window glinted rose and blue. Nicole had had it specially made by French monks along with the four rose-tinted windows on the sides of the building and a floor-to-ceiling tapestry depicting Nicole as Snow White, in her glass coffin, waiting for her prince. Dreamland, the Dreamer's forest retreat, had cost her a fortune to build and furnish.

"Millions," Jake had told her. "Almost everything she made investing in the start-ups that went wild in the dot-com boom. Sold out before the big bust. Gave it away to that—that Svengali," he'd said one of the few times he'd ever actually opened up about his marriage or his divorce.

Celeste followed the path of paving stones engraved with various mythical and fairy-tale symbols—a soaring swan, a twisted beanstalk, a glass slipper—then hesitated in front of the massive oak doors, not sure what she might find waiting inside for her, accusation or understanding.

She grasped the ornate brass handles and slowly opened the doors. She tiptoed in. The foyer smelled of damp coats and wet wool scarves, and she breathed in the familiar scent. Just inside the doors, she traded her boots for a pair of the wool felt slippers the Dreamers were required to wear to protect the parquet floors—the floors she'd spent hours polishing on her hands and knees. Rather than pay the required monthly upkeep fees like most of the Dreamers, Celeste had pledged to clean four hours a week, telling Jake she'd picked up an extra job, that she'd begun cleaning the house of an elderly bar patron. And he had never questioned her.

For a few moments, she stood in the entryway, straining to hear what was going on behind the door to the Sanctuary. It sounded like they were talking about her. She finally gave up trying to decipher the murmurs sifting through and inched open the double doors to peek inside.

Straight ahead, at the opposite end of the great hall, the overcast sky pressed against the triangular window that soared to the peak of the cathedral ceiling, framing Hunger Mountain in the distance. A dozen Dreamers sat in their assigned rows. Fifth Level Dreamers sat up front, lower levels behind. They were all dressed in their usual flowing Dreamer attire, although now, instead of wearing their rainbow colors, they wore black tunics and pants. Otherwise, this looked like the beginning of any Dreamland gathering—the Dreamers waiting patiently for Larry and Nicole to enter from their private room and take their places on the two leather armchairs on the dais in front of the picture window. Today, at least one of those chairs would remain empty.

The whispered repetition of Larry's name mingled with the rustling of tissues, noses blowing, and occasional deep sobs followed by quick little intakes of breath. Hunched and huddled, the Dreamers looked as lost and confused as she felt. As her eyes adjusted, she began to pick out individuals. The Romano sisters swayed from side to side, humming a low, mournful chorus. Bill and Ingrid leaned into each other, her blonde curls cascading across his trembling shoulders. There was Porter, flanked by his fiancée Julia and his soon-to-be-ex-wife Karin, his arms around their shoulders, pulling both women to him, the collective trio shuddering and sniffling simultaneously. In the front row, Angus, Barb, and the other old hippies held hands. Alone in back, now that Celeste was no longer seated next to him, Bruce Nussbaum stared down at his tasseled loafers. If Larry had had his way, she might now be comforting the anxious, disheveled lawyer who dreamed about her. Poor lonely guy. No sign of his pal Wally DeTouche. And no Nicole either.

Celeste cracked the door open another inch. For more than a year, this sad and forlorn bunch of characters had been her world. Weekly gatherings at Dreamland, daily meet-ups at the Corner Cup, and the steady flow of intimate e-mail, the threads that pulled her in each afternoon during her computer session at the library. She knew these Dreamers inside out. She knew their fears, their shame, their Dark Mothers, Magical Children, Golden Princes. And they knew hers. She dreamed about them; they dreamed about her. In this Sanctuary, they all dreamed together, weaving together their individual lives. Celeste had believed she'd found the family she'd longed for, one that surrounded her with wisdom and warmth. She remembered how excited she'd been at her initiation into the Dreamers only one year ago, when she stood at this very same door on a cold November evening, her stomach knotted with anticipation.

She'd waited in the foyer, adjusting the scratchy mandarin collar of the floor-length crimson robe Nicole had draped around her shoulders. She could remember the doors opening; how Bill and Ingrid had escorted her, like a bride, to the center of the Sanctuary; how otherworldly and ethereal it appeared, just like her own dreams. The room glowed in the flicker of candlelight; the scent of cinnamon and cardamom enveloped her. The Dreamers danced in their jewel-toned robes, circling around her, their whispered welcomes almost lost in the swish of silk. On the dais, the three Romano sisters, their faces perfect ovals in the candlelight, sang haunting harmonies. Celeste stood in the center of the great hall, swaying to the sounds and lost in the sensations, filled with an unfamiliar calm.

Nicole, radiant in an amber robe, took her by the hand. "Larry is waiting," she whispered.

Nicole led her to the rear of the Sanctuary, guiding her toward a large gray cube that filled the back third of the hall. Like a cross between a miniature Kaaba and a confessional, the box dominated the Sanctuary. It had to be over eight feet tall and equally as long and wide. Soft bluish light flickered around the edges and through the square of decorative latticework on its front facade. When Nicole pressed on this wall, a small door opened. At Nicole's urging, Celeste stooped, then stepped through the door and into the box.

There sat Larry, covered from head to foot in a hooded green robe, his fleshy face peering at her in the eerie blue light. When Nicole closed the door, Celeste waited for claustrophobia to overtake her. Instead she floated on the sense of deep calm.

"Welcome, new Dreamer. We've been waiting a long time for you. Sit down," said Larry, pointing to a three-legged stool at his feet. He towered over her, and it took her a moment to realize he was seated on a raised platform almost hidden beneath his robe. "What you are about to experience must never be discussed outside this building. Understood?" His voice was like a far-off breeze, and he spoke in a lofty tone she'd never heard him use before.

The tiny room darkened.

"Close your eyes," Larry instructed. He hummed and chanted, his wavering voice almost drowned out by a whirring sound while Celeste shifted nervously on the stool.

"Now open."

She blinked hard, wondering what she was seeing. Larry floated in the space above his seat. Transfixed, Celeste shrank back as his feet and hands morphed into great furry paws, and his mouth and nose elongated into the muzzle of a lion. Before her eyes, his hair and beard grew long, thick, and wiry, merging at last into a magnificent golden mane. The only hint of Larry were the eyes, which bore into her as he opened his huge maw and blew forth a gust of turquoise wind, unfurling from the chasm of his lion mouth against the star-studded night that now surrounded them.

In the midst of this howling banner of breath sprouted a tiny green seed that grew rapidly and unfolded into the shape of a mermaid that swam in the star-spangled firmament above. The mermaid's silvery tail shimmered in the great ocean of lion's breath, flicking in and out between sharp, shiny teeth. Slowly, the mermaid spun around, revealing her face, Celeste's own face, or more specifically, the face she'd worn as a thirteen-year-old girl. Small, pink-nippled breasts budded from the mermaid's naked torso.

She laughed, her tinkling voice high, watery, and melodic, and then she wiggled her tail and began to sing in a voice like shimmering glass—high and fragile and heartbreakingly beautiful, though the words were in another language. The song washed over Celeste, flowing through and across her body like ocean waves, soothing even her deepest wounds. The warring voices in her head stopped as her mermaid drew closer, closer, riding on a towering blue wave, the wave she'd dreamt about that night with Jake.

The wave lifted her into the arms of the mermaid, but instead of comfort, fear swamped Celeste. She forced her gaze away and tried to latch onto something solid. She stared down at her lap. The boundaries between her legs and the stool dissolved, atoms bouncing and weaving wildly between them. She held on tight to the seat as the soft, liquid laughter of the mermaid filled the tiny space.

Then, as if someone had pulled the plug from the kitchen sink, the whole vision—mermaid, lion, and starry night—spiraled down an invisible drain between her feet and Larry's. Celeste looked up. There he was again, sitting right in front of her, the same man she visited every week in his plain old office in the back of his plain old brick house.

"What was that?" she asked, barely able to open her mouth. Her body tingled from head to toe as if the molecules still danced between her skin and the air.

"Your totem, 'The Little Mermaid,' the one who traded away her true voice, her Vital Self, for a pair of human legs, and ya know what that got her."

Celeste nodded. The Hans Christian Andersen fairy tale her mother had repeated for her every year on Cape Cod. "Each step was like walking on swords. And she never got the Prince." But how had Larry known? Celeste was certain she'd never told him about that bond with her mother or about the mermaid she often carried in her pocket for luck. At least, she couldn't remember telling him anything like that.

"Ya gotta hold on to your Vital Self if you want love. Quit denying the pain of those swords, the pain of pretending you're something you're not. Cel, get rid'a those fake legs, that false bravado, and start swimming with your mermaid's tail."

Larry didn't realize that if she did, she'd swim straight for Jake, and that once he'd slipped that ring on her finger, she'd keep on swimming away from the Dreamscape.

A great sob ripped through the Sanctuary, startling Celeste back to the present. Through the crack in the door, she watched the new kid, Arun, hurtle toward the dais, his chair clattering to the ground behind him. He threw his lanky, black-robe-draped frame across Larry's empty armchair, weeping and gasping like some stranded fish. Behind him ran his sister Sarabande, camcorder pressed to her right eye, capturing each wracking sob.

Celeste could hear someone tsk-tsking. Bruce shook his head, and she thought she heard him mutter, "Drama queens." The pair of young newbies had been a contentious puzzle ever since Larry brought them into the Dreamscape after only two office sessions. A couple of weeks later, they managed to leap-frog from the back row next to her up to the front row, where they sat beside the most experienced Dreamers, Angus and Barb. The two gray-haired hippies had been with Larry since those two were still in diapers. "Larry's pets," some Dreamers called them. More like Larry's *pests,* thought Celeste.

"We need more diversity," Nicole had explained to the disgruntled Dreamers. "We need to be more than a bunch of middle-aged white people."

"Affirmative action? That's how they got in?" Bruce had whined from his place in the last row.

"Sort of," Nicole answered, looking at Larry, who was once again off in a corner whispering to the twenty-something sibs with their matching hairdos—shaved sides with buns on top of their heads.

Now Sarabande maneuvered around Arun, then lay on

her back as she filmed his anguish. The whole thing was nothing but a video op for her.

Suddenly, someone pushed hard against the door from the inside, knocking Celeste back.

"What the hell are you doing here?" Angus glared at her, his skinny gray braids flapping against his black flannel tunic. He held the door wide so everyone could see the intruder, and the Dreamers all turned in their seats to stare, their faces twisted in rage and hatred.

Celeste stared back at a roomful of people she hardly recognized. For an instant, she wondered where these angry people had come from. But she knew the anger had been there all along. Once she'd felt just like them, ready to lash out and wound anyone who questioned her attachment to Larry and his Dreamscape. Like Jake. Like Gloria.

"You're not welcome here anymore, Celeste," Rain Romano hissed at her.

"Yeah, Celeste," she heard familiar voices echoing through the hall.

"But I didn't do anything! All I did was find him!" She stepped past Angus into the Sanctuary.

Bruce stood, put his hands on his hips, and narrowed his eyes behind his black-framed glasses. "You had it in for him—all because he wanted you to be with me."

"We knew you were one of the Doubters," Angus said.

"We all have doubts once in a while, right?" Celeste asked the crowd.

The room buzzed with noisy indignation. Celeste looked at Ingrid and Bill, hoping for sympathy. They both turned away. Even they had never really been her friends. Suddenly, it was all too clear.

"I had a few issues with Larry, sure! But you can't possibly believe that I killed him. You can't!"

Her voice was strangely steady and strong, a voice that hadn't emerged from her throat in years. It sounded like the voice she'd had once but had since given up, just like her ring, to Larry. "I thought you cared about me. That we cared about each other, but it's all a big lie. The emperor had no clothes."

For a moment the room was silent. Then it erupted into a blizzard of taunts and threats that flew about her ears. "Doubter" was the only word she could pick out in the frenzy.

"Leave her alone."

The Dreamers turned. The noise stopped. Nicole stood on the dais—a Nicole none of them had seen before. No makeup, no stilettos, merely a woman looking as grief-stricken and lost as they all felt. Her face was pale and luminous, the skin around her red-rimmed eyes drawn tight, her long dark hair limp and tangled around her face. The blue tunic she wore was stained and wrinkled as if she'd been wearing it for days.

"She didn't do it," Nicole said.

The Dreamers leaned toward her, trying to make sure they'd heard right.

"She didn't do it," Nicole repeated, louder this time.

"You don't know," Arun said, challenging Nicole's assertion in a way he never would have dared challenge Larry. "Unless they caught someone else?"

"Yeah, if she didn't do it, tell us who did!" Sarabande demanded, lifting her camera to record the answer.

"I've had some dreams," Nicole said, again so softly Celeste wasn't sure what she'd actually heard. Then louder, "You can put that camera down now, Sara. No more videos. We're done with that." Nicole shook her head, then sank down wearily into her wingback chair. "Let's not turn on each other. Right now we need to be thinking about Larry and all he gave us."

Nicole's voice strengthened, but Celeste could see her fingers digging into the arms of the chair.

"I said put that damn thing down, Sarabande!"

The younger woman lowered her camera and glared at Nicole. "This was Larry's project. This is how I'm honoring him. You can't tell me to quit."

Again, a buzz went through the Dreamers. Larry had never explained why he had given Sarabande and Arun permission to videotape the Dreamscape Actions that were the core of what went on in Dreamland—Dreamers acting out each other's nightly visions, reentering their dreams through another portal to find deeper meaning through orchestrated psychodramas. Or so Larry explained it. Celeste had watched dozens of these reenactments, and she'd acted out other Dreamers' dreams—but not until she had been called to the stage to relive her own dream had she fully understood the impact of these theatrical dramas.

Celeste's tsunami dream, the one she'd had that first night with Jake, had been filmed by Sarabande and Arun. Sarabande, camera in hand, caught each ungainly movement as Angus and Barb wriggled across the floor toward Celeste, their bodies heaving up and down in their imitation of the giant wave. Arun kept his camera focused tightly on Celeste's face as the three Romano sisters, all big-boned women, stood in front of her, pretending to be the plate-glass window. Sarabande zoomed in as Angus and Barb struggled from the floor and rushed forward, breaking through the human window and surrounding Celeste. Wrapped in their arms, she was transported back to the dream, only this time her legs fused into the mermaid's tail as she swam effortlessly out to sea. The water was warm. She could taste the salt, as if the dream had come true.

Arun had broken the spell that day, jumping around with his camcorder, as irritating as Sarabande seemed now.

"Do what I say, Sarabande," Nicole commanded. "Larry isn't here anymore. He doesn't need your silly little movies and neither do I."

"I don't think that's up to you, Nicole." The two women stared across the room at each other. The Sanctuary was silent, as if the Dreamers held their collective breath, waiting to see who was in charge now.

Finally, Nicole spoke. "That's enough. We need to think of Larry right now."

Sarabande lowered the camera and dropped her gaze, muttering to Arun who stood at her side. Celeste wished she could hear what they were saying. This power struggle had been going on ever since these two entered Dreamland. No one could miss it now.

"But we *are* thinking of Larry." Bill stood up, his tall, thin frame rigid as he turned to catch the eyes of all the Dreamers. "We're thinking there's someone out there, or perhaps in here, who knows exactly what happened to him and why." He looked over his shoulder straight at Celeste, and all the heads in the room turned to follow his gaze.

Shying away from the venom directed at her, Celeste turned to Nicole.

"Go!" Nicole mouthed the word, her lips, without their usual red lipstick, as pale as her face. "Go!"

Celeste backed against the door, feeling the anger and mistrust of the crowd pushing her from the Sanctuary. "I didn't. I didn't," she said as she retreated, knowing she would never set foot in Dreamland again.

CHAPTER FIFTEEN

DEJA VU ALL OVER AGAIN

Celeste stumbled out of Dreamland. Snow crystals whirled about her in the blustery wind, stinging her cheeks. She felt sick to her stomach. Doubter! Her ears still rang with the violence of their voices. The Dreamers' voices. She had to escape them. She could get in the car, lock the doors, curl up, and allow the hurt and fear to sweep through her, and then explode into a long Primal Scream right outside the doors of the retreat. That's what Larry would have advised.

"The way out is through," he'd often said. And plunging into the darkness had always led her to the other side. But only after she'd traversed a shadowy valley of tears and misery, which was the last thing she needed today. This was not a good time to fall apart.

Fresh air and a clear head, that's what she needed now. Shivering, she stamped her feet. She watched the snow collecting in the imprints her shoes had left. She missed her boots.

She wasn't dressed for the cold, but she headed toward the Dreamland meditation path anyway. Often she'd followed it through the woods to the old cemetery, losing herself in the play of light catching on the leaves, the flute of the hermit thrush, and the scolding of squirrels as she passed beneath their ragged nests. She'd walked slowly, practicing her homework, revisiting her dreams to retrieve the feelings and images they stirred up. Or thinking about Jake, wondering how she could ever tell him the truth about joining the Dreamers.

After what had just happened inside, today was probably her last chance to hike through the forest where she'd spent so much time.

Trying to escape again, huh, Cel? There it was, right on cue—Larry's voice wriggling into her thoughts. *Always lookin' for a way around the pain.*

Shut up, Larry! Yes, she was running away from the hurricane of hurt the Dreamers had stirred up inside her. Well, so what, Larry? There's more to life—and death—than being in constant touch with my puny Vital Self.

"I am not your hostage anymore," she said into the wind. "I'm following my own damn voice, and it's telling me it's time to reclaim my life." She shoved her cold hands into her vest pockets and followed the trail into the woods, stepping around two sets of boot-prints, one small, one larger—father and son?—lightly outlined by snow. Hunters out for the first week of deer season? She'd forgotten. Here she was, alone, without a scrap of fluorescent orange to distinguish her in the eyes of hunters from an unsuspecting deer. Her green vest would only make her blend in with the pines.

"Ready or not, here I come!" she called, hoping her voice would alert anyone out there to her presence as she made her way along the path. She stepped over downed branches and around patches of slushy leaves. Several times, she stopped, listening for voices or the sound of a rifle being cocked. Briefly, she considered turning back, but there was too much she needed to sort out, and this trail through the birch, beech, and pine had always offered comfort and solace.

But not today. The woods felt anything but welcoming. The trees surrounding her creaked in the wind. The bare branches of the skeletal birches scratched against the ominous gray sky. Around her ankles, little cyclones of snow rose from the ground—tiny twirling ghosts. Celeste clutched the collar of her vest against her throat. Like the Dreamers, the forest had turned on her. Around her, the wind whistled, echoing, *Doubter! Doubter!*

Head down, she threaded her way through the underbrush, lost in her thoughts, wondering why she'd never heard the term before. Clearly, the rest of the Dreamers knew the word. They had it ready and waiting like an arrow in a quiver aimed directly at her. They must have used it on others before her—unnamed Doubters who'd also been cast out, with that word reverberating behind them as they went. Who were these other Doubters and why had she never heard any mention of them? Gloria must know. She'd mentioned something last night, in her office. Celeste couldn't remember now; it was lost in the haze of shock, lost in the lingering, buzzy daze of Laphroaig.

She stopped, looking up. This wasn't her path. She must have turned onto one of the deer trails that branched out from her usual well-traveled route, must have followed it into the middle of the forest. Hunters might be out hiding, in a blind, waiting for movement. She listened. A woodpecker cackled in the distance. Beech leaves shivered, hanging down from limbs like copper-colored bats. Behind her, she thought she heard someone call her name. The hairs on her arms and the back of her neck bristled. She wanted to run, but her legs were clumsy with fear, like they were in her nightmares of rapists and wild animals. Her feet, in the wet shoes, were numb with cold, and she kept slipping on the light coating of snow that dusted the path. She pushed on, listening for voices or footsteps. But all she could hear was the wind whistling through the trees and her own wildly beating heart throbbing in her ears. A fallen branch caught her foot. She scrambled to keep herself upright, then plunged ahead along the narrowing trail beneath the dense canopy of evergreens.

"Don't shoot! I'm a person!" she yelled, hoping her voice would carry in every direction. She didn't know which way to go to get back on the right path. She spotted a pile of boulders, the tumbled remains of an old stone wall, and decided to follow along it, hoping it might lead her to the cemetery. Ahead, a branch cracked. She stopped. Just steps away from her stood a doe, stock still, watching her, its right foreleg lifted, ready to run. They both waited. Neither moved as they looked into each other's eyes.

The thrum of a car engine rumbled through the forest. She heard wheels spinning through mud. The doe bolted, leapt away, white tail lifted. Celeste turned toward the sounds and caught a flash of blue through the trees. The Dreamers' gathering must be breaking up. They were heading home. She wasn't lost after all. On the other side of the old stone wall she could just make out Beaver Pond Road, the rough dirt road she'd driven along to Dreamland, running parallel to the meditation path.

She continued to follow the wall, staying near the road, where any hunters were likely to be staked out. A few more cars went by. Then the forest was quiet again, and she relaxed a bit. Ahead, she glimpsed the lighted clearing. Relief washed through her. Up there, in the open, any hunter could see she wasn't a deer. Unless the voice hadn't belonged to a hunter. Unless the murderer had followed her, and now waited in the woods for a clear shot at her.

Told ya not to go! Larry whispered as she sprinted uphill toward the lonely graveyard at the top of the rise. Larry was right. She should have faced her grief instead of plunging into the woods, all alone, ready bait for whoever was out there. She stopped, panting, surveying the scene. Shafts of sunlight shot through the dark clouds billowing over the leafless hills that cradled the old cemetery. In the small pull-off parking area sat a mud-spattered Subaru. Celeste looked around for the driver, realizing just then that she'd never before run into anyone else in the cemetery. There he was, sitting on the cold ground in the middle of the cemetery, leaning against the largest grave marker, bundled in a blanket. At least she wasn't alone anymore.

"Hello?" she called, hoping not to startle him. She'd been stupid for being so frightened. Still, she hesitated, waiting for some sign or acknowledgment. None came. He must not have heard her over the wind. Slowly, she walked toward him as he—or was it a she?—continued to stare straight ahead, not bothering to turn his or her head to look at her.

"Hello," Celeste called again when she reached the weathered, split-rail fence that surrounded the few dozen listing, lichen-draped gravestones. Still no response. The person huddled, motionless.

Celeste inched closer, until she stood directly in front of him. Blank, filmy eyes stared at her through a tangle of snow-covered dreadlocks. A trickle of clotted blood ran down his chin. His face was paste white, his swollen tongue hanging between pale lips pulled back in a grimace. He was wrapped in the same dirty green blanket she'd sat on the day before.

"Adam," she whispered.

Then, from behind, a hand grabbed her shoulder, yanking her off her feet.

CHAPTER SIXTEEN

TURN OF THE TAROT

"Let me go!" Celeste yelled as she struggled to regain her balance.

"Quit yelling. It's only me."

The voice was familiar, but in her panic she couldn't make sense of what was happening.

"Stop it, Cel. Look at me." The hand let go. She didn't dare look up, but she could see brown tasseled loafers, loose linen pants, the bottom hems blowing around skinny ankles.

"What the hell are you doing here?" she asked.

Bruce Nussbaum stood in front of her, his eyes hard and accusing. A look she'd never seen before—a look that scared her.

"You can't keep running from me. We're supposed to be together."

"Seriously? This is what you wanted to talk about? Now?" She stepped away from him, offering him a full view of the body behind her.

"What, what is that?" he whimpered, suddenly looking and sounding like the old Bruce again.

"He's dead," Celeste said.

Bruce lowered himself down, steadying himself with one hand on the weathered gravestone, to squat beside the body. He touched the corpse's stiff, white hand, and then drew quickly back. Overhead, a murder of crows landed on the birch trees, flapping their wings and cawing.

"Dead?" Bruce's high, frantic voice seemed to shatter against the cold wind. "What have you done now, Cel?"

"Me? I didn't do this," Celeste protested.

"Then maybe he froze to death?" he said.

"Froze?" She bent down next to Bruce, swallowed hard, and then reached out and pulled the stained blanket from Adam's shoulder. As it fell to the ground, the filthy greatcoat opened. A glossy crimson stain covered Adam's chest.

Bruce gagged and shot to his feet. "Oh my God!" he wailed. He swayed as his knees buckled. Down he went, his head grazing the gravestone as he collapsed with a thump on the frozen ground.

"Bruce!" Celeste tried shaking him. He was as unresponsive as Adam, but not quite so cold.

She squatted between the two bodies, wondering what to do next. If only she had a phone! Bruce must have one on him somewhere. She reached inside the pocket of his down jacket . . . bingo! It was locked, but she knew the code. The same one all the Dreamers used, Larry's birthday: 0326. Celeste hit the numbers with her frigid fingers, pressing extra hard to get what little warmth she could out of them. The screen opened. Two bars of reception. She found the phone icon and, for the second time in two days, dialed 911.

"911. What's your emergency?" It sounded like the same woman who had answered when she was in Larry's office.

"A dead body! In the West Branch Cemetery!"

"Is this a hoax? Because if it—"

"It's not a hoax, I promise. He's shot!"

"Shot in the cemetery. Can you detect any sign of life?"

Celeste clutched the phone harder, hanging on to it as if it could keep her from toppling over like Bruce. "No! But there's another guy down. He fainted and hit his head."

"All right, ma'am. Calm down. I'm contacting the police. They'll be there soon. Please, stay where you are." There was a pause. "Your name, please?"

She could hang up. Run like she had wanted to the day before. What would the cops think when they found her at the scene of another murder?

Instead she answered, "Fortune. Celeste Fortune."

"I can remain on the line with you if you like."

Bruce moaned and his eyelids fluttered. At least he was still alive.

"Gotta go." Celeste clicked off the phone and scooted to Bruce's side.

"What happened?" He sat up slowly, rubbing a small bump rising on his right cheekbone, not far from his temple. "Where . . . ?" He gulped for air, then gagged again.

"Can you stand?" Celeste asked, not sure if she could actually help him get up with her shaky knees.

"I don't . . ." Bruce shook his head and looked at her, puzzled.

"Let's sit somewhere else. Over there." She pointed to the far corner of the cemetery, to a carved granite bench. The two of them staggered across the small expanse of brown grass. The bench was ice cold, numbing her bottom and thighs in seconds. Bruce sat down next to her, his shoulder and thigh pressed against hers. Celeste edged away.

"I used your phone to call the cops. They're coming."

Bruce nodded.

"What the hell are you doing here, anyway? You scared the shit out of me."

"I needed to find you, Cel," Bruce said, his voice a nasal whine.

"You followed me?"

"I watched you take the path. I was afraid you were getting away. I wouldn't have a chance." He moved closer. "I drove over to find out why, Cel. Why wouldn't you marry me? Like Larry said?"

So it was his Subaru in the parking area. This guy was absolutely nuts!

"Just because you had a few dreams about me doesn't mean we're in love, no matter what Larry might have said to you." The feisty old Celeste spoke up again, and she pushed herself slowly to her feet, surprised that her legs actually held. She looked at Bruce, his dark curly head bowed, his arms folded across his chest, his shoulders hunched up around his ears. He looked like a wounded turtle drawn into its shell.

He couldn't help it. He was as trapped in Larry's web as she had been. She wanted to grab him by the shoulders and shake him, make him come out and see what was in front of him. She wanted to smash his Dreamer's trance, wake him up to the pain outside himself. "Open your eyes, Bruce! This isn't about us. There's a dead guy right here. The same guy I thought killed Larry!"

His head snapped up and he looked at her, hurt and surprised as if she'd slapped him.

"You know this . . . this guy? He killed Larry? With you?" Bruce's voice rose to a squeak.

"Calm down. I didn't kill Larry. Maybe this guy didn't either, but he was my best bet so far."

"But Wally told me. Larry said it was you. The last thing he said."

So it was Wally who turned the Dreamers against her. Figured.

"And you believed him."

Bruce sniffed and wiped his nose with his hand.

Finally, Celeste asked, "What's a Doubter?"

Bruce looked at his feet.

"Come on. You called me a Doubter back there. Wally did too. Yesterday."

He took off his glasses and wiped them on the hem of his linen shirt, which hung down below his jacket. Bruce mumbled something Celeste couldn't make out.

"What? I can't hear you."

"Not supposed to talk about them." He looked down and kicked at some leaves with his wet loafers.

"Them? So there *are* others?" She'd never even heard a whisper of these Doubters. "Like Gloria?"

"I hear them," Bruce said, looking up as a piercing siren ripped through the stillness of the graveyard. Celeste couldn't tell if the look of relief on his face was because they were about to be rescued or because he wouldn't have to answer any more of her questions.

Blue light flashing, a squad car barreled up the dirt road into the small parking space, braking hard as it pulled up next to Bruce's Subaru, shooting gravel into the air like buckshot. Officer Wally DeTouche and Detective Jean Pearl got out of the car, slammed the doors, and walked across the withered, snow-spotted lawn toward Celeste and Bruce.

Anger splotched DeTouche's pudgy face as he lumbered into range.

"Killed another one, did you? Catch her in the act, Nussbaum?" His hand was on his holstered gun.

Bruce looked at DeTouche, puzzled. "Wally, where were you this morning? You weren't at Dreamland with us."

As if he hadn't heard, DeTouche turned to Celeste, his button mouth quivering. "Figured you had something to do with this."

Celeste almost laughed, but choked it back. "What? Now you think I'm a serial killer?"

"I wouldn't be laughing if I were you, Cel."

Celeste turned away from Wally and shook her head. He had it in for her all right.

"Where's the body?" Detective Pearl asked.

Bruce pointed. "We didn't kill him." His voice rose, a note of hysteria sneaking in.

"Shot," added Celeste, trying to keep her own voice steady.

"The report said two down," Pearl said, turning to look around the grounds for another.

"Now one's up," answered Celeste, tilting her head toward Bruce. "The other one's over there."

Pearl looked over Celeste's shoulder toward the body, then turned her attention to Bruce. "Sir, Mr. . . . ?"

"Nussbaum, Bruce Nussbaum," DeTouche answered for the shivering man next to him.

"You know this guy?" she asked DeTouche, looking Bruce up and down. "Another one of your cult?"

DeTouche bristled. "Dreamers. It's not a cult."

"Sure. Whatever you want to call it. In any case, I'll handle the questioning from here. Go and make yourself useful somewhere else for now."

DeTouche glared at Celeste as if she were the one ordering his exile from the scene. "You're not getting away with this, I guarantee you." Like a chastised child, he retreated to the squad car, muttering to himself, kicking at the ground as he went.

"I'm sorry," Pearl said to Celeste. "If I'd known this had anything to do with you when I got the call, I would have requested another officer."

Celeste shrugged. She loved the way Pearl bossed Wally around.

The detective motioned toward the body with her chin. "Any idea who it is?"

Celeste nodded. "It's the guy. The guy I told you about yesterday? Adam."

"Can you tell me what happened here, Mr. Nussbaum?" She pulled her little Moleskine and a pen from her jacket pocket, ready to write.

"Like I said. He was like this when I got here," Bruce answered and then shuffled his feet.

"And was Ms. Fortune already here when you arrived?" Pearl made quick notes, waiting for Bruce to answer.

Bruce nodded, his head bobbing up and down rapidly, still not lifting his eyes to Pearl.

"What exactly was she doing? Can you look at me, please, sir?"

His head jerked up and then dropped again before he spoke. "Standing by it. The body. She's my girlfriend."

"She's your girlfriend?" Pearl looked at Celeste who shook her head hard. "Okay, Mr. Nussbaum. I think I've got the flavor of this."

Behind them, an ambulance pulled up next to the cruiser blocking the dirt road that led from Route 12 to the cemetery. The double doors at the back of the vehicle opened and Fritzi and Charlene leapt out, loaded down again with their EMT equipment. They wouldn't need it this time. They conferred with Pearl in quiet tones, then nodded at Celeste as they walked by.

"Fancy meeting you again," whispered Fritzi as she passed.

Oh, boy, this is getting too weird, Celeste thought with a slight shiver of déjà vu.

Pearl pulled a pair of purple latex gloves from her coat pocket, rolled them on, then from another pocket extracted one of her Buddhist laundry handkerchiefs and held it over her nose and mouth. She knelt down by the body, then tugged at one arm, able to move it an inch or so away from Adam's stomach. The body slipped sideways, and the mouth fell open, letting loose the noxious odor of death. Holding back the lapel of his coat, Pearl turned her head away, inhaling a deep breath. Then she leaned in and inspected the chest wound, probing it with her gloved index finger, rubbing her finger against her thumb. She peered at the dried flecks of blood and nodded.

Bruce and Celeste stood together silently as Pearl shifted over, moving along the body, and rolled one pant leg up over a rigid calf. She ran her hand lightly over the dark, bruised skin at the back of the pale leg. DeTouche had reemerged and waited nearby with Fritzi and Charlene, a roll of yellow crime tape in his hand.

"I'd say time of death was sometime between midnight and five this morning." Standing up quickly, she backed away, tearing off the gloves with a loud snap. "Can't say for sure yet. Definitely shot." She bent and looked again. "Could have been a hunting accident. Or not." Straightening, she looked at Celeste. "Follow me, please. I have some questions for you, too. And, Mr. Nussbaum, wait on the bench."

He shrugged, then followed her orders.

Celeste trudged behind Pearl back toward the squad car, while the others busied themselves around the body. The wind picked up again and whistled in her ears. The two women leaned against the hood of the car, wrapping their arms around themselves for warmth.

"I need to know why you are out here, why you were out in those woods in the first place." Pearl still looked stern, but Celeste could hear the softness coming back into her voice. Seemed like she had different questioning techniques for men and women.

"I was out at Dreamland, Larry's retreat center," she said, unsure of how much to divulge. "I needed to take a walk, through the woods," she pointed to the end of the trail under the pines. "To clear my head."

"Did you notice anyone in the woods?"

"Some footprints."

"Go on." Pearl was writing rapidly in her black book.

"Hunters, I figured. Now I guess the smaller pair might have been his. Adam's. And the bigger ones whoever was after him." She glanced back at the body. DeTouche was stretching the crime tape around the scene, looping it around the gravestones. Bruce sat alone, bewildered, watching him work. Fritzi and Charlene leaned against the fence, waiting with the stretcher nearby.

"Two sets of prints?"

"Maybe. Maybe more, hard to tell." Celeste shifted from foot to foot. She hugged herself and ran her hands up and down her arms.

"Someone from, what do you call it? Dreamland? Anybody live there, stay there overnight?"

"No, I don't think so. There's no bed or anything there. Maybe you could still find the prints in the woods. Probably I messed them up. But they were there."

Pearl wrote some more, shut her notebook, and then looked up. "I see you found your ring."

Celeste stood still, feeling guilty.

"Didn't you tell me you couldn't find it, when you went back to Larry's office?"

"I couldn't." Celeste covered her left hand with her right and watched DeTouche and the EMTs over Pearl's shoulder. Bruce now hovered near them, stamping his feet and rubbing his hands. His face was bunched up as he squinted through his glasses.

"But you're wearing it now. Do you want to explain that to me?"

"Detective Pearl, I need you over here!" DeTouche called. He was squatting by Adam's body, his gaze shifting back and forth, as if he were searching for something on the ground.

"We're not done," Pearl said to Celeste. She slipped her notebook back into her rear pocket, sprinted across the field, then zig-zagged between the headstones toward DeTouche and the others.

Curious, Celeste trailed behind but then waited a few feet from the rest of the group, following their eyes to what looked like a macabre game of Fifty-Two Pickup. On the ground, behind the body, a pack of cards lay scattered. Their brown crackled backs blended in with the muddy grass they lay upon. She remembered the pattern from the day before. Adam's tarot deck, cards face down—except for three, laid out nearby in a seemingly deliberate row, dried blood slashed across the pictures on each one.

Moving closer, Celeste stared at the cards, unable to look away. The images on the cards swam and shivered beneath the diagonal streak of red that ran across them, as if painted by a bleeding finger. Her knees buckled, and she sank to the ground, woozy and disoriented, her gorge rising as she inhaled the stench of blood and death that had emerged when Pearl opened Adam's heavy coat.

Around her, the graveyard, the cops and EMTs, even the body grew hazy, all of it swallowed by heavy fog. Celeste sat alone with the cards, trapped among them as they rose from the ground, now life-size. Surrounding her, they teetered on their bottom edges, their images alive, like movies on three separate screens, circling her.

Here came yesterday's burning tower. The flames' heat scorched her cheeks and screams filled the air as the dome exploded, sending bodies flailing, headlong into empty blue sky. Today the bodies seemed to have faces, faces she recognized. One was Nicole's. The other was Jake's. She reached out, trying to catch them in her hands. Too late.

A new card spun into view. She shrank back. A horned devil, bat wings sprouting from his shoulders, hissed at her, his forked snake's tongue darting in and out, almost touching her. Unkempt hair and a shaggy beard framed a yellow-eyed face—Larry's face.

"Greed," he hissed again. Chained to his hairy goat legs, Arun and Sarabande danced naked, like marionettes, beneath the devil's throne.

Then the last card. The Hermit, with his rough brown cloak flapping in a howling wind, stared at her, his face stern, unsmiling. He raised an arm, and a bony finger emerged from the folds of his robe, pointing not at her but over her head, beyond the fog, to the crows, now silent, hovering in the trees.

Celeste looked up at the crows. From somewhere way down inside, from that deep place of her gestalts, words scratched their way up. She opened her mouth, and Adam's high, cracked voice scrabbled out. "Tumbling down, it all comes tumbling down!"

Celeste slammed back into her body, ripped away from the trance. Pearl knelt in front of her, hands on her shoulders, the three face-up cards on the ground between the two women.

"Celeste, look at me!" Pearl's command hit her like a bucket of ice water.

Celeste blinked twice, hard, as Pearl shook her gently. Reality swam back in. She was back in the cemetery.

"I . . ." She tried to talk, but her tongue felt heavy and dry. She ran it over her teeth, trying to clear away the taste of rust. "I don't know . . ." She looked up at the alarmed and concerned faces that surrounded her. "I'm okay. I think." She shook her hands and blood rushed back into them. "What happened?"

"You were talking in a weird voice," said Bruce. "Something about things falling down?"

"Tumbling down. That's what he told me yesterday." Celeste pointed to the Tower card. The faces of the two falling figures were blank, generic ovals, not Jake and Nicole at all.

"Do the other cards mean anything to you?" Pearl asked.

Celeste moved her attention to the devil and his captives, three figures she no longer recognized. They wouldn't believe her if she told them what she'd seen and heard. She shook her head.

"This?" DeTouche thrust a chubby finger at the third card. The Hermit.

"That one," she stalled. "That one . . . this guy, Adam, he dropped one just like it on my porch last night." She tore through the sentence knowing she was about to blow things wide open.

"What?" She could see the chords in DeTouche's fleshy neck tighten.

Pearl cleared her throat. "Are you saying that this man," she glanced at the body, "this man you thought killed Larry was on your porch last night?"

"Banging at my windows. He was running, he looked scared. He had a note that said someone was after him."

"And you didn't think you should call us?" demanded DeTouche.

"What *did* you do? I hope you didn't let him in," said Pearl, hands falling from Celeste's shoulders.

"I wanted to call, but Jake said I could wait 'til today."

"Jake? Was there too?"

"He tried to catch Adam, but he got away. Jake found that card and my ring. On the porch. He," she nodded toward Adam, "dropped them."

"Mr. Kelly was after him?"

"No," Celeste said. "No, he didn't say Jake. Just 'he'!" Like Larry had said "her," she thought to herself. Not a specific "he."

Pearl pulled out her notebook and pen again, made some notes, paged back through, then asked, "And Mr. Kelly gave you back the ring?"

Now what should she say? She wanted to lie, to say yes, he put it back on my finger where it belongs, but she couldn't. Too many thoughts danced inside her.

"I found it in his jacket," she finally said, under her breath.

Pearl wrote some more, then looked up, pen still poised over the small square of her Moleskine.

"So you really can't be sure he picked that ring up from the porch. It might have already been in his jacket, correct?"

Pearl was right. A shiver ran down Celeste's back. She hadn't wanted to admit it. Jake might have had the ring all along.

"Does the Hermit card have any significance that you know of?" Pearl asked.

Celeste shook her head. "I thought it meant him. Adam. Maybe he was a hermit." She looked down and poked at the grass with her shoe. She didn't want Pearl or any of the others to ask about the scenes in her head—Adam scuttling away when Jake ran by. Jake thundering onto her porch. Her ring, in his pocket. Doubter.

Pearl tapped her pen on the page. "Okay, Celeste, Mr. Nussbaum, I'm going to let you go for now. I think you've had enough for today."

They were letting her go!

"But I have one more question."

Celeste nodded, relieved that this was almost over.

"Does Mr. Kelly own a hunting rifle?"

Celeste reacted quickly, almost too quickly. "Yes, but he didn't do this! He couldn't have!"

"Because?" asked Pearl, perfect eyebrows raised.

"Because he was asleep. On my couch. All night." She couldn't get the words out fast enough.

"So you were with him all night?"

"No," she admitted. "I was in my room. But he was there in the morning. He hadn't been anywhere, I'm sure! I would have heard him go out." Of course, she'd been pretty dead to the world, but still.

"And you were asleep, unaware from what time to what time?"

Celeste stiffened. She had to convince Pearl, but how could she, when all that she knew to be true was imploding?

"From around one, I think, until seven or so this morning."

"And Mr. Kelly can vouch for your whereabouts too, I assume?"

Celeste nodded. Did Pearl think they'd been out on some late-night killing spree? She felt sick to her stomach again.

"If there's anything else, I think you'd better tell me now," Pearl said in her encouraging voice, a small, almost pitying smile on her perfect pink lips. "And," she continued, "I need that ring. Sorry. It's evidence."

Celeste looked up. "Really?"

"That ring is the only thing we have connecting our . . . let's say our persons of interest."

Damn, thought Celeste, here come the tears again. "You mean me, Jake, and," she jerked her chin toward Adam's body, "him?"

"Give me the ring, Celeste." Pearl put out her hand, like Larry had the day before. Celeste jiggled the ring over her knuckle and dropped it, sparkling like a drop of rainwater, into Pearl's delicate palm, wondering if now it was gone for good.

CHAPTER SEVENTEEN

LUNCH AT MURPHY'S BAR

"Damn!" Celeste swore out loud to herself, trying to keep her hands steady as she steered the Jetta back down Beaver Pond Road. The car rattled and bumped in and out of the ruts, now slippery with the residue of wet snow. She glanced in the rearview mirror to make sure Bruce Nussbaum, who'd given her a lift back to Dreamland for her car, wasn't following her again.

She punched the radio button. "*. . . well-known Riverton Falls therapist Larry Blatsky. According to police spokesman Arnie Bond, Blatsky was attacked and killed in his office yesterday in the town's first murder in over fifty years.*"

Adam doubles the score, Celeste thought.

"*. . . leads being pursued, but anyone with information is urged to contact the Riverton Falls police department.*"

She snapped off the radio, then swerved to the shoulder of the road, where the old car coughed and stalled out. Head tilted back, she opened her mouth and wailed, "It's too much!

God fucking damn it! I didn't ask for this!" The wail trailed into choking sobs as she banged her fists on the steering wheel.

First Larry, then Adam. Her ring in Jake's jacket. The Dreamers turning on her. She felt battered from all sides, storm waves heaving her up on a rocky shore, sucking her back under every time she tried to clamber ashore. She needed a hand, someone to pull her out of the surf and back onto dry land. But no one was coming to save her. She had to rescue herself.

"Screw them all. Fuck all of you, Larry, Dreamers, Bruce, the cops, and you too, Jake!"

Breathe, she instructed herself, breathe.

All she wanted to do was crawl into the rear seat, curl into a ball, and hide. Except with all her junk, there wasn't any room back there. Even her trusty, rusty Jetta had no place for her. She popped the glove compartment, looking for tissues, anything to mop the tears and wipe her dripping nose. Nothing there except stacks of tattered road maps from excursions she and Jake had taken together way back when.

"Okay, that's enough," she reprimanded herself as the thought of Jake threatened to bring on a whole new round of sobs.

Gloria was right: the only thing to do was figure out who was doing the killing. She had to pull herself together, find that ballsy Celeste she'd known before Larry had demolished her.

She started the car again, gunned the engine, and maneuvered back onto the highway, steering toward town, foot heavy on the gas. At least Nicole seemed to believe in her. But she had been so evasive. Nicole knew something, and Celeste had a sneaking suspicion that something might have to do with Jake.

Slowing the car, she crossed the town line into Riverton Falls. Her hands were numb from gripping the steering wheel. She shook them out one at a time, missing the familiar flash of her ring all over again. Pearl was right—the ring was evidence. But evidence of what? She had to find Gloria.

Outside the car window, the town ball fields lay brown and forlorn, and in the public pool, murky green puddles collected atop a thin skim of ice. Riverton was in suspended animation—the early snow a preview or warning of winter around the corner.

Slowly, Celeste settled back into her body. Her stomach was growling, and the clock on the dash claimed it was 12:30. Only three hours had passed since she'd been sharing breakfast with Jake.

On Main Street, she parallel-parked her car into a space a few blocks down the street from Gloria's office, hoping she wouldn't have any more trouble finding her. Rummaging in the backseat, she came up with a blue knit cap. She put it on and pulled it down low over her forehead in a pathetic attempt to hide. After plunking a few quarters in the meter, she walked down the sidewalk, trying to avoid the knots of people talking together, their faces anxious and stricken under their own hats. Wait until they hear about Adam, she thought as she passed the Miss Riverton Diner. A hand-lettered sign propped in the window read WE MISS YOU, LARRY!

By the time she reached Arts and Herbs!, her hunger had turned to a sick emptiness—a feeling she knew too well. She'd spent years and a small fortune on Larry only to end up back where she'd started: that damn abyss was still there, unchanged, but the woman standing on the edge was no longer the same, she knew that. Instead of dancing around, trying to ignore the gaping hole in the center of her life, she was staring straight down into the darkness, about to do what Larry had tried to make her do all along—jump in feet first, fists flailing, ready to hit bottom.

Celeste knocked, waited a second, then opened Gloria's office door. There sat Gloria, asleep at her desk, her head nestled on her folded arms, snoring lightly.

"Gloria," Celeste whispered, not wanting to freak out her friend.

Gloria raised her head and blinked. Her face was pale, eyes puffy, her tangle of copper-colored hair as unkempt as Adam's dreads.

"Where the hell have you been?" Her voice was husky with sleep. "I've been calling you all morning. Wish you'd just carry a cell phone. You look awful, by the way."

"Look who's talking. But if you'd just been through what I've been through . . ." There was no way around it. Celeste just had to blurt it out. "Adam's dead. Shot."

Gloria sprang out of her chair. "Where?"

"Where?" That wasn't the question Celeste expected. "What do you—"

"We got a lot to talk about," said Gloria, pulling on her coat. "But I need to get outta here."

Ten minutes later, Celeste and Gloria slid into a booth at Murphy's. They both squinted, straining to read the ketch-up-stained menus under the dim light of the wood-paneled taproom that smelled of grease, clam chowder, and beer. Over at the bar, half a dozen middle-aged men hunkered over their pints and plates piled high with onion rings. They glanced up now and then at the flat-screen TV over the bar. A couple wore Bruins jackets, but the others were dressed in camou-flage and fluorescent orange—hunters who seemed to prefer the warmth of Murphy's to the woodstove heat of their rustic hunting camps.

As the waitress took their order, snatches of conversation drifted from the bar. "Head bashed in . . ." "Some chick . . . " "Blatsky, think my cousin went to him." "My last girlfriend . . . nutcase."

The words filtered through over the *vroom-vroom* of the NASCAR race on the TV. "Guess there really is nowhere to get away from all this, huh?" Celeste said to Gloria.

"No, my dear Ms. Fortune, there certainly isn't."

Celeste recognized the stentorian tones rising from the booth that backed up to theirs. Gloria shot her a what's-up look.

"Reggie Webb." Then she heard the nervous voice of his still unseen companion. "And Tony Pritchett."

"From *The Riverton Rag*?" Gloria looked up as Tony's springy curls and boyish face emerged above them, peering over the back of the adjoining booths. Next to him rose Reggie, publisher of Riverton Falls's weekly gossip rag, looking like an old bloodhound with pouchy cheek wattles and deep bags under his beer-bleary eyes. The two men had turned around in their seats and knelt side by side on the bench so they could peer over the top of their booth while lifting foam-topped mugs to toast Celeste and Gloria.

"Well, well, it seems our favorite barkeep is now a star suspect. How was your little ride in the super-cruiser?" asked Tony.

"A witness, that's all—and don't think you're getting anything out of her today," Gloria fired back.

"And you're supposed to be her lawyer, I presume?" Reggie rumbled.

"I thought you only worked for spotted owls and minnows." Tony wagged his mug at Gloria, spilling a few drops down the women's side of the booth.

"Look, can you guys leave us alone?" Celeste asked, mopping at the spill with a paper napkin from the chrome pop-up holder on the table. "I've got nothing to say to you. Nothing fit to print that is." Of all the places and times for these two to show up. Just her luck.

"But, my dear Celeste, we were hoping for an exclusive!" Reggie almost drooled over the possibility that he would have a story someone might actually read in his flimsy paper. *The Rag* was better known for its classifieds than for its stellar reporting. Still, Reggie had given her a chance at writing after Larry and her dream of a dancing fountain pen had convinced her she should actually rebuild her abandoned career in journalism instead of tending bar. She'd managed to turn in a couple of movie reviews and even a front-page story on the town's new naturopathic vet before Larry told her that he had been mistaken, and that her dreams of writing were simply another of her Demon Mind's pathological urges. He said her years as an international freelancer merely signaled a lack of commitment, not journalistic ambition. And she'd believed him.

At any rate, *The Rag* getting this scoop over the daily *Spectator* would be a real coup for Reggie and Tony.

"Listen, when we figure out what's going on, you'll be the first to know." Celeste could hardly believe she had the wherewithal to carry on with this banter, not to mention putting up a front of normalcy after what she'd been through that morning, but she didn't know what else to do. "Right now I don't think talking to you would be in my best interest. Do you, Gloria?"

"Based on this lawyer's advice, I'd say probably not. So you boys go back to your burgers and leave us alone. When we figure out who the killer is, I'll make sure you get the scoop."

"Promise?" asked Tony, flashing a bright-toothed smile.

Gloria nodded. "Now back to your own side, please."

Reggie and Tony slid down behind the barrier of their booth as two lunching ladies in pantsuits and jogging shoes passed by muttering, "It's terrible, unbelievable. In Riverton!" Celeste and Gloria picked up their coffee mugs and quickly grabbed the table the pantsuit duo had vacated, finally managing to get out of earshot from prying reporters.

Celeste looked down at her plate. Repulsed by the red tinge of burger juice soaking the bun, she sighed, "I don't know if I can eat this." She put her head in her hands and closed her eyes. "I thought I was hungry."

Behind her, a couple of gangly high school boys at the pool table set up a rack, and she listened to the clickety-clack of the balls as they were herded into the triangle, then the *smack and crack* as they broke.

"Don't think about it. Open your eyes. Eat. I need an active partner here, C, not some wimpy woman with low blood sugar. So buck up and chow down. You'll feel better. I promise."

At least Murphy's burgers weren't those dried-out grass-fed discs you got at most places, including the Broken Gate, in this locavore town.

"You can give me the gory details later, but right now all I want to know is where you found him," Gloria mumbled with her mouth full.

"Where I found him? In the cemetery, the one up by Dreamland. Why?" She squirted ketchup on her plate and dipped in a couple of fries.

"What the hell were you doing up there?" Gloria swallowed, then slapped her hands on the table. "I hope you weren't talking to those Dreamers."

Celeste wondered how she could explain herself. "I had to go, Glor. I wanted them to know I didn't do it." She sounded pathetic, her voice shrill and quavering.

"I said no more whining. If you want to get out of this mess, you have to stand up for yourself, not go groveling on your knees to those idiots."

"Okay, okay. Got the point. Here's to the new-and-improved old Celeste!" They clinked mugs of coffee over the table. Celeste picked at the fries on her plate, skinny and crisp, the way she liked them. "Now tell me what happened."

"What I'm going to say might freak you out," Gloria said. The boys at the pool table were setting up again, laughing, so normal. "How do I tell you this?" Gloria stirred her coffee and sighed. She pushed her half-eaten meal to the side and leaned forward, arms crossed on the table, voice low, almost a whisper. "Last night, in bed, I started to worry about you. I couldn't sleep. So I came back to make sure everything was okay. Your lights were out and I saw Jake's truck parked down the block. I have to say—now don't get mad!—but I had more than a few 'what the hell?' moments wondering what he was doing there."

"After all your damn suspicions last night, I was pretty wary myself." Celeste quickly told Gloria about Adam appearing outside in the rainy night on her porch, holding up his desperate little sign, and Jake.

Gloria reached over and took a few of Celeste's fries.

"Hey, you've got your own!"

"What time did Jake leave last night?"

"He didn't."

Gloria shot her a skeptical look.

"Don't worry. He slept on the couch. All night. Didn't even try to sneak into my room."

"Uh-huh. So he was still there this morning? And his truck was down the block?" Gloria put her elbows on the table and lowered her chin to her hands, still looking up at Celeste, her eyes scanning her friend's face.

"Nope. In the driveway." She shook her head, not wanting to think about what that might mean. "Anyway," she tried to steer the conversation in another direction, "things were going fine until breakfast. We had a few words. About Nicole. Then he left."

"You had breakfast together?"

"Do you want to know what we ate too?" Her irritation at Gloria's questions revived her hunger.

"I figured you were probably okay, and I didn't want to barge in on anything, so I started to head home. But when I got to the stoplight at the bottom of your hill, guess what I saw."

"Adam?"

"Out in the rain, like he was waiting for somebody. So I pulled over to see what he would do. After a few minutes, a car came by, stopped, and he hopped in. And guess what was on the license plate." She took a bite of her burger and chewed slowly.

"I don't know if I want to hear this." Celeste leaned back and folded her arms across her chest as if trying to fend off whatever Gloria might dish up next.

"D-R-E-A-M-Y."

"Nicole? Nicole picked up Adam? On my street? In the middle of the night?"

"You got it. So I decided to follow them and guess—"

"Just tell me, Glor, for God's sake!"

"I followed them to Dreamland."

"Wait, I don't get it. Nicole and Adam? That doesn't make any sense. Maybe she was picking up a hitchhiker?"

"Yeah. Exactly the kinda guy she'd let hop in her Beemer, play the chauffeur for, then deposit in her precious Sanctuary." Gloria rolled her eyes.

Celeste shrugged. "Guess not."

"So I followed them. Stayed way back cuz no other cars were out. They went straight to Dreamland. I parked a bit down the road where they wouldn't notice me. In the rain, in the dark, goddamn it. Then I snuck up to get a look-see in the window."

"And that's how you got that telltale mud on your shoes."

Gloria glanced down at her feet, shrugged, then continued with her report. "I figured they'd already gone inside, but I couldn't see any lights on, so I got to wondering. They were there all right. Sitting in the middle of the room. On the floor. With a candle burning." She nibbled on the last of her fries. "With that squawky bird."

"Pete?"

"He was shuffling around, bawling so loud I could barely hear them. I could see enough to tell they were both pretty freaked out, but it looked like Adam was trying to calm Nicole down, patting her shoulder, stuff like that. She was crying pretty hard." Gloria gulped the last dregs of her coffee. "Then I don't know what I saw. It was way too weird."

"What? Come on, Glor, you can't just leave me hanging here."

Gloria reached for the few remaining fries on Celeste's plate. "Adam got up and walked away. I couldn't see where he went. Off in a corner, out of sight. Suddenly the whole room was ablaze, lit up, weird colors swirling all around, like the Northern Lights or some stoned-out light show from the '60s. The lights sort of transformed into these pictures—beaches, jungles, all kinds of exotic places. Then, I don't know how, but I saw people, like cartoons but real, running around in the pictures and the lights, like some kind of movie or video game, only all over the room, on the walls, up on the ceiling, across the floor." Gloria was whispering, her voice so low Celeste could hardly hear her over the cracking of the pool balls. "And there was this eerie music, sort of Zen or Tibetan or something. Chimey stuff. The bird was going bananas."

"What do you mean?" Celeste tried to break in, but Gloria rushed right on.

"Nicole kept spinning around real slow, clapping her hands, applauding. Then it all just disappeared."

Celeste gripped the slightly sticky edge of the table, inhaled, held her breath for a second, then forced it out almost with a whistle. "Wow."

The two women leaned across the table toward each other. Behind them the pool players were whooping, thumping the fat ends of their cues on the wooden floor. The smell of onion rings wafted toward them as the waitress delivered a plateful to the booth where Reggie and Tony still sat.

"Larry was always messing around with holograms and hypnosis, even back when I was there. But what I saw was something else. Something completely different."

"Hypnosis?"

"Yeah, how do you think he hooked you into thinking he was bigger than life? You never figured that out?"

"No." Celeste looked down at her hands. Had she really been so duped by the guy? And holograms? That explained the mermaid in the box. Mechanics, not magic. "Then?"

"Nicole walked away, I guess to where Adam was. I couldn't see them anymore, so I ran for it. I didn't want them to find me. Plus I was completely freaked out."

Celeste reached across the table and grabbed Gloria's hand. "God, you're brave."

"Stupid, I'd say, plus I was soaking wet, and now," she blew her nose on her napkin, "I'm probably getting a cold. Thank you very much."

"Then you went home?"

"I was going to, but—" Gloria blew her nose again.

The waitress was back at the table, refilling their mugs. "Anything else?" she asked, ready to put the check on the table. She snapped her gum. Celeste jumped at the sound. "Want me to wrap that up for you?" She looked at Gloria's half-eaten burger.

"Sure," Gloria mumbled. Then to Celeste, "Zion will love it."

The waitress cleared their plates and empty water glasses, while Celeste and Gloria watched in silence, waiting for her to finish.

"Come on, Glor. Tell."

"You're not going to like what happened next."

"There's more? Can't get much weirder than that." Celeste thought for a second. "Sarabande and Arun showed up?"

"No. Why would you say that?"

"I don't know. The movies on the walls. They were always shooting videos of everything happening in Dreamland. Constantly hovering around it, fiddling with things."

"No, not them." She blew her nose again. "I was walking back down the road, and I saw headlights coming at me, so I stepped back into the trees." She paused, stalling.

"And? Who was it?"

"Jake."

CHAPTER EIGHTEEN

ASTRAL PROJECTION

Celeste shrank back against the cool leather of the booth. "You're sure? In his truck?"

Gloria nodded.

Swirling cream into her coffee, Celeste wondered if she might need something stronger. She turned to watch the kids' pool game, glanced at the candy-colored cars still roaring across the TV screen above their heads. She wished she were in some fast car, racing away from all this.

"But he was asleep on the couch." Detective Pearl's questions shuttled around Celeste's mind. She sipped the coffee, swallowing hard.

"Yeah, it was him. I was close enough to see his face."

Celeste shook her head. This couldn't be true. "Did you go back up to the house?"

"Nope. Heard the truck door slam, then waited a bit, but didn't hear anything else. I wasn't about to go back if he was outside. Besides, I was really cold and I think my adrenaline had finally given out."

Celeste flashed on the mud on Jake's boots, slowly realizing it probably hadn't come from chasing Adam off the porch as she'd thought. The two sets of tracks in the forest, one large, like Jake's, one smaller, like Adam's. The truck not down the block, but in her driveway. She lowered her forehead to her hands on the table, breathing in the stale odor of beer and hamburger and grease. There had to be a way to make sense out of all this. She tried not to think about the rifle she figured was in the rack of Jake's truck. It was hunting season. Almost every pickup had a gun in it for those three weeks through Thanksgiving.

"Gloria, do you think a hunter could have gotten Adam, a stray shot?"

"I don't know, C." She came over to Celeste's side of the booth and slid in. "I know this is hard. When I left, Adam was still alive, and Jake was heading to Dreamland. Maybe someone else came after I left. Or maybe you're right, a stray shot. Lots of big questions. What did Adam have to do with all this in the first place? And how did he end up in the cemetery? And why was Jake at Dreamland in the middle of the night?" Gloria sighed. "But after yesterday—"

"I don't want to hear it." Celeste squeezed to the far end of the bench, pulling away from Gloria. They sat in silence as the bar hummed around them. A commercial for Nokia tires blared from all three televisions, mixing with the buzz of conversation at the bar. The topic had switched from Larry to deer and antler points, who'd gotten his buck, who was still waiting.

Apprehension scrambled Celeste's thoughts. She wanted to tell Gloria about the ring. About the boot-prints. But what could she say without making things look worse for Jake? Jean Pearl's observation was pricking at her now. Maybe Jake hadn't scooped the ring up from the porch. Maybe he *had* found it in Larry's office.

"Glor, I have to tell you something." She forced the words out of her constricted throat.

"Okaaaay." Gloria drew the word out as she turned sideways on the bench, one leg drawn under her to face Celeste. "Shoot."

"Not funny." Celeste looked at the half-empty mug in front of her, wondering if she could even force down the rest of her cooling coffee. "This morning I found some things in Jake's jacket. While he was still asleep."

Now Gloria nodded, encouraging her to continue.

She breathed in and then exhaled hard through her nose. "But, and now don't take this wrong, I had a feeling he wasn't telling me the truth, so I," she charged on, blurting out the rest before she chickened out, "I went through his pockets and found my ring. The one Larry took. And this business card. Some guy named McNeil."

Gloria narrowed her eyes, glanced up at the TV over the bar, and, after a few seconds that seemed like minutes, finally said, "Rowan McNeil?"

The question surprised Celeste. She'd been all set to defend Jake, but the jolt of Gloria's question knocked something loose, and suddenly the memory she'd been searching for that morning was right there, as if she had held it in her mind all along. She knew where she'd seen that name. At Jake's cabin on the river.

They'd spent the night on his bed, holding tight to each other, laughing on the lumpy mattress. Everything was still new then. The feel of his calloused fingers as they moved slowly down her spine, dissolving the tension and anxiety. December. The night was so long. They'd made love how many times? And Jake had played his guitar, sitting up naked, leaning back against the headboard, the black hair on his bare chest glinting in the firelight of the woodstove, while she curled up, wrapped warmly in the quilt his grandmother had made, lying against his long, tightly muscled legs, listening to the strumming and the sound of the river.

By morning, the wood had burned down to coals in the stove, and while Jake rebuilt the fire, she stumbled, freezing, into the mudroom, looking for her down coat. She finally found it, fallen behind a cardboard box overflowing with black rubber gas masks. At least that's what they looked like. Curious, Celeste had held one up to her face and strapped it on. She could barely see anything through the black, mirrored lenses, just an outline of Jake, squatting by the woodstove, blowing on the little licks of fire. The smell of rubber filled her nostrils; the mask was too tight. She ripped it off and sucked in air. As she tossed the mask back into the box, a glint of gold caught her eye. Pushing aside the tangle of rubber, she reached in and gingerly lifted out a gilt-framed painting, not much bigger than a sheet of typing paper. An oil painting of Dreamland gleaming beneath a marigold sun. Though she wasn't a Dreamer yet, she'd been to the retreat house for the annual gatherings of Larry's clients, long days of listening to the Dreamers bare their souls to a bunch of relative strangers. Even in the darkness of the mudroom, she could see how someone had managed to paint an exact miniature replica of the building.

"Who did this?" she'd asked, holding the painting up as she walked toward Jake, who was still fiddling with the fire.

"Put it back," he said, after a quick glance at what she held in her hands.

"Look, the rose window, the fairy-tale stepping stones . . . even the stained-glass borders on the windows!" She squinted, wondering how anyone could paint such perfect, tiny details. "The dragons and griffins and . . . a mermaid? Don't remember seeing that there."

Then she noticed something else. In the third window, seated on their thrones, Larry and Nicole, dressed in ermine robes so finely depicted she could almost feel the softness of the fur. The tiny jewels in their crowns glinted in the woodstove's flickering firelight. "'RGB', it says. That's the signature."

"Rachel painted that." Jake poked at the logs, then under his breath added, "Larry's wife."

"Larry's wife? Why do you have it?"

"She gave it to Nicole. They were best friends. Until Larry got a hold of them." He stood and went over to the counter that served as a kitchen and began to measure out ingredients for pancakes, his back to Celeste. "Doesn't matter. Been gone for nine, maybe ten years. Haven't kept up with her." Butter sizzled in the cast-iron pan that Jake had set on the woodstove. He poured perfect circles of batter into the pan as Celeste came over. Silent again, they stood side by side, watching the edges begin to bubble up.

Celeste looked at the painting in her hands again. "Couldn't have been that long if she painted Dreamland. Didn't they build it, like, six or seven years ago?"

"Could be." He shrugged. "Now, please, put it back."

Clearly this was a conversation Jake did not want to have. Celeste pushed aside her questions, not wanting to spoil their morning together. She'd returned to the mudroom, pulled on her coat, then gently placed the painting back in the bottom of the box. As she'd closed the cardboard flaps, a return address had caught her eye. Rowan McNeil, Nagano, Japan.

"*Rowan* McNeil?" Gloria repeated.

"That's the name! How did—"

That was as far as Celeste got. Suddenly the low lights in the bar started to flicker, then went out. On the televisions around the barroom, crackling static overtook the roar of the whizzing race cars. The track dissolved into digital snow.

"What the hell?" the bartender yelled.

Then, as if someone had changed the channel, the snow disappeared, revealing some kind of animated Technicolor tropical ocean, waves rising against a wash of blue sky on the horizon, spilling over the edges of the televisions, plunging everything and everyone to the bottom of a phantom sea that engulfed the entire pub.

Celeste reached for Gloria's hand on the table. Above them, where the ceiling had been just moments before, the surging sea gathered itself into a raging wave, gaining height and power, rearing up like a hundred angry stallions, heading straight for a sparkling cube of glass, no, a house, perched high up on a cliff where the bar had been seconds before. Inside, a tall, thin woman with a wild halo of hair stood looking out, her mouth a wide O of horror and wonder. The furious wave crashed over the heads of the noontime drinkers, smashing against the house. The walls shattered. The glass shards exploded into hundreds of shimmering stars that flashed around the woman as she rode the crest of the wave, propelled by an emerald-green mermaid's tail.

As it retreated, the wave sucked all the air from the room. Men clutched at the edge of the bar, swearing. Some struggled to stand, stumbled unsteadily from the stools, teetered on their feet. Pool cues clattered to the floor and the balls bounced off the table, rolling every which way. Then, as abruptly as it began, whatever it was, it ended. The water seemed to be sucked back into the television, the ocean views reassembling on the screen, then all of it dissolving back into snowy static.

"Shit!"

A familiar voice entered the room. Celeste looked around. Her eyes landed on a small, black plastic box clipped to the television over the pool table. The voice seemed to come from whatever that thing was. A speaker? A projector? She tried to focus, but Celeste couldn't think whose voice it was.

"Turn it off!" The voice sizzled and crackled, overtaken by the buzz of TV static.

Mike the bartender tried banging on the bottom of the screen while the men at the bar and the kids at the pool table just stared, eyes wide, utterly silent. Then, as if nothing had happened, the usual Murphy's lights flickered back on, and the racing cars were back, revving engines cutting through the silence, the garish swirl of the race heading round a tight curve.

The bar erupted into a chorus of "What the fucks?"

"I almost shit myself!"

"What the hell was that?"

As men in hunter camouflage stampeded toward the door, one teenaged pool player's hysterical, high-pitched laugh pierced the room.

Growing dizzy, Celeste hoped she wouldn't faint. The room swirled around her. "Gloria," she managed to whisper, "that was my dream!"

Moments later, out on the sidewalk, having escaped the mayhem in Murphy's, Gloria held tight to Celeste's arm, propping up her much taller friend so her wobbly legs wouldn't crumple beneath her. Celeste shook her head as if trying to come to from a knockout blow.

"What was that?" She was surprised to hear her own words.

"Hey, guys, I need you to pay up!" the bartender shouted from the door as the jumble of men kept fleeing Murphy's, some with hands over their ears, others blinking hard in the sudden daylight. The swarm separated around Gloria and Celeste like a river parting around a boulder. A few glanced at Celeste as they passed by and she heard panicked voices asking, "Is that her?"

"Excuse us, excuse us," Reggie's bumbling baritone preceded him and Tony as they squeezed through the crowd.

"Jeez, you guys," Tony said. The two reporters jostled into the two stunned women, almost knocking them to the ground. "How'd you do that?"

"Us?" Gloria said. "We didn't do anything. We were just sitting there!"

"But," Tony was practically panting for a story, "that woman, that was you, Celeste!"

"Don't be ridiculous," Gloria scoffed, "that was just some weird cartoon, some channel interference. Nickelodeon mixed up with ESPN."

Celeste looked at Gloria. What was she saying? Hadn't she felt that?

"It was clearly Celeste, whether you want to admit it or not," Reggie said. "How did you do that to the room? How'd you get that room to feel like the ocean? I swear, I mean, no kidding, I was transported."

"Beam me up, Scotty!" Tony chimed in, cracking his knuckles and bouncing nervously from foot to foot.

But Gloria wasn't laughing.

"Really, we don't know anything more than you!" Celeste's voice came out high and stringy.

"Maybe you don't," said Reggie, "but I'll bet my reporter's nose that your little lawyer friend here knows more than she's saying. I can smell a cover-up a mile away, and she's hiding something. Aren't you?"

Celeste looked at Gloria, now seeing what Reggie had already discerned. Her hands-on-hips, I-dare-you stance was a shade too defiant, even for Gloria. Don't go there, her body said, like she was defending the secret with bared teeth.

Gloria wasn't about to divulge anything in front of these two snoopy men, but Celeste was determined to get the truth out of her as soon as they were alone. "Listen, Reggie," she finally managed to say, "as soon as we find out anything, you'll be the first to know."

"Why don't we just go round up some of those guys," Tony pointed to the hunters waiting anxiously at the stoplight, "and get an eyewitness report? If we get it up online ASAP, maybe it'll go viral!"

Celeste and Gloria watched the two of them as they strode off down Hughes Street, sniffing around for the story from the characters who'd fled the bar.

"Gloria." Celeste looked down at her friend. "I don't know what you're hiding, but he's right. You're not telling me something." Rage flashed through her. She wanted to grab Gloria by the shoulders and shake her. "You need to tell me what's going on. What was that in there? Who's this McNeil guy? And while we're at it, what's a Doubter? I know you know!"

"Okay, calm down." Gloria paused. "I truly have no idea what happened in there. Believe me. But I think I know who might."

"You think? What the hell, Gloria! How much have you been hiding from me?"

"Calm down. If you can trust me a little longer, I know where we might get some answers, or at least get pointed in the right direction. Because whatever that was in there, dollars to donuts, I can guarantee it had something to do with the murders."

"Why don't you just tell me what's going on? I'm sick of being left in the dark." Celeste was fuming. Jake. Gloria. Everyone it seemed. They were all keeping things from her. But she wasn't going to let them get away with it anymore!

"Hey hey! Now that's the old Celeste!" said Gloria, giving her two thumbs up. Then she reached into her coat pocket and pulled out her phone.

Celeste could hear a woman's voice on the other end but couldn't make out what she was saying.

"I know. It's hard to believe. And there's more. I'll tell you when we get there." Gloria nodded while the woman responded. "I was thinking that too. Is it okay if I bring her?" Another pause. "All right, if it works. See you in an hour."

She tapped the phone and stuffed it back into her purple coat. "What time do you need to be at work?"

"Seven."

"That gives us," Gloria pulled the phone out once again to check the time, "a couple of hours out there."

"Out where?"

"You'll see. Too much to explain, but it'll make sense once you meet them."

"Meet whom? I'm not going unless you tell me." Celeste put her hands on her hips and struck her own power pose.

"I'll tell you in the car. 'Whom'—sheesh!"

CHAPTER NINETEEN

RENAISSANCE

Half an hour later, after dropping Celeste's car off at her apartment and swinging by Gloria's to pick up Zion, they were on the road, heading north. Gloria drove while Celeste sat beside her, clenching her hands together in her lap. She was still fuming that Gloria had kept her in the dark about so many things like where they were headed now. They traveled in silence punctuated by the shaggy malamute's loud, pink-tongued panting. He thrust his black-and-white head between the two front seats, his mossy dog breath damp on Celeste's cheek.

"Back," she snapped, as she pushed him away, her hand sinking through the dog's soft bristled fur to the hard wall of his chest.

"Hey, don't take it out on him. He only wants to make sure we don't forget he's here," said Gloria, reaching behind to scratch Zion between the ears.

The dog licked Gloria's hand and rattled his tags.

Celeste gave up her effort to dislodge him. With her forehead pressed against the window, she looked out as they drove past stubbled fields dotted with round hay bales encased in white plastic looking like giant marshmallows. The river running along and below the road was high and muddy with November rain. The colors had been leached from the land-scape, leaving only tones of gray with occasional splashes of red and rust in the soft bursts of sumac, as bushy as squirrel tails. Along the riverbank, knotweed leaves, like oversized leather gloves, waved in the wind.

Beyond the fields, across the river, forested hills cradled the valley. "Stick Season," most folks called this time of year—time for Vermont's snowbirds to head south. But Jake had taught her to see the beauty in the subtle colors, to observe the lengthening shadows across the hills, and to appreciate any rare breaks of sun slipping through the near-constant cloud cover.

Now Celeste focused on the smoke-colored, late fall skies, hoping the comfort of the hills around her would ease the horror and fear of the last two days. Nothing out of the ordinary could happen in this bucolic landscape. No murders, no tsunamis, no babbling in tongues. She lowered her head to her hands.

Pull yourself together, her father whispered in her head.

Don't embarrass yourself, her mother sniffled.

Dive into the waves, feel what you feel, said Larry. He was right on this one, but she was done listening to Larry. And her parents.

Shut up, all of you! I'm trying to listen to my own voice, she thought, looking up.

"Gloria, you need to tell me right now what's going on. I'm so sick of this game you're playing, I could k—!" She slammed her fists on her thighs, biting off the last words. "We're sup-posed to be partners in this."

"Cool it, sister!" Gloria stepped on the gas and pulled out to pass a truck loaded with logs. "I'm trying to bring you up to speed here."

Celeste turned back to the window. She caught a quick glimpse of her own disheveled reflection and hoped there would be time to get home and clean up before she had to face the Broken Gate crowd. No way was Allegra going to let her skip out on another night.

"We're on our way to get some answers. Trust me." Gloria patted Celeste's thigh.

"Trust you?" Celeste said, flinching at Gloria's touch. "I feel like I've been kidnapped." Celeste leaned back against the headrest, completely frustrated, trying to ignore Zion's panting. "Don't you think I've been through enough today? Another murder, the crazy scene at Murphy's, whatever that was. Tell me where we're going, or I swear I'm going to jump out of this car."

"I hear you." Gloria chewed on her lip, thinking. "Okay. What's Jake told you about California?"

"California? That he went out there for college, met Nicole, worked in some start-up in Silicon Valley, making video games and doing other techy stuff I didn't understand. The dot-com bubble burst, he missed home, so he and Nicole came back. Why?"

"Did he ever tell you about any of the people he worked with?"

"Nicole."

"He never told you that they worked for Larry?" Gloria swerved, avoiding a big piece of bloody roadkill.

"What are you talking about? No!"

"Well, they did. And it didn't turn out too great."

"Because of Nicole. That's why he and Larry hated each other."

"And some other stuff. Mostly some other stuff."

"Why didn't you tell me any of this before?"

"We haven't exactly been on speaking terms. Besides, I wasn't allowed to."

"Not allowed? Who said?"

"That's why we're going where we're going. Almost there," Gloria said as they whizzed through one of those quintessential New England villages with a white steepled church overlooking a village green. Zion, who had finally fallen asleep in the backseat, now sat up, wagging his tail, whining in anticipation. Unlike Celeste, he clearly knew their destination. Gloria turned left and bumped onto a dirt track so steep Celeste wondered if the straining Saab could make it to the top. Rocks scraped against the bottom of the car as Gloria urged it forward. At the top of the rise, a handwritten sign peeked through the last copper leaves of a giant beech tree. "Renaissance," Celeste read out loud. "We're there?"

"This is it." Gloria pulled the car into a gravel lot where several other cars were already parked. In front of them, at the top of a gently sloping lawn, stood a two-story gray stucco house, its roof shingled with terra-cotta tiles. Here and there the plaster seemed to have worn away, revealing pale, uneven patches of stone, as if the house had been sitting on the windswept hill for centuries. Cerulean blue shutters flanked windows wreathed with leafless vines.

"What the hell?" Celeste rolled down her window and stuck her head out to get a better look. "What'd they do, haul it over here from France?"

"You should see it in the spring," said Gloria.

"I'll bet." The house was surrounded by the autumnal remains of several large perennial beds now covered in dried leaves and straw, dotted with empty blue ceramic pots that probably brimmed with roses in the summer.

"You know these people?" Celeste breathed, her question

barely audible over Zion's eager scratching on the backseat window.

"Allies," said Gloria, getting out of the car to open the rear door for the excited dog. Zion jumped out and raced, barking, up the hill and through a grove of gnarled apple trees, the last stubborn fruit decorating the branches like wizened Christmas tree balls.

Gloria ran after her dog. Celeste trailed behind, then stopped short in front of a circle of towering granite blocks, each over ten feet tall. "Stonehenge" was the first thing that popped into her mind.

"Goody gumdrops. Look what the dog dragged in." A deep, gravelly voice seemed to come from inside the towering stone around which Zion pranced, tail wagging, tongue hanging from his smiling black lips. "Took you long enough."

"Came as fast as we could," Gloria called back, pulling Celeste by the hand to the center of the ring of stones. Gloria pointed up to a pair of leather work boots on the upper rungs of a wooden ladder that leaned against the tallest of the monoliths. Balanced at the top, practically camouflaged against the granite in gray overalls and a baggy sweater, stood someone Celeste couldn't quite make out.

"You know what I mean," the voice grumbled, as the gray denim legs began to descend. "Getting harder in the cold to climb up and down this damn ladder."

"Want me to hold it?" asked Gloria, looking up.

"No, I do not." The person descending the ladder turned and stepped off, boots hitting the ground. In front of Gloria and Celeste stood a lean, handsome woman with short gray hair spiked like a punk rocker's. Zion leapt up, thumping his big paws on her shoulders, his long sloppy tongue lapping at her ear.

"Get this monster off me!" The woman stumbled back a bit, dropping the chisel she had clutched in her left hand. "Bad dog," she reprimanded, grabbing the offending paws. Then she laughed, a surprisingly bright high-pitched laugh, as she pushed Zion away. The panting dog danced on his hind legs for a second, then toppled forward out of control, his forepaws landing on the woman's shoulders again.

"See right through me, don't you, boy!" Now she gently lowered Zion to the ground, rubbed his head, and bent down to whisper in his ear. Straightening up, she narrowed her steel blue eyes at Celeste, eyeing her up and down.

"Don't look so worried," the woman said to Celeste. "The natives are friendly. Or at least we won't eat you." She stuck out her hand. "Elinor Garrison."

When Celeste extended her own hand, Elinor enclosed it in both of hers. They were cold and rough, but gentle.

"This is not how I imagined we'd finally meet," Elinor continued, squeezing Celeste's hand tighter. "I've heard a lot about you from Gloria and Jake."

"Me?" Celeste couldn't remember hearing anything from Gloria or Jake about anyone named Elinor. And how did Gloria's and Jake's names end up in one sentence?

"Such an awful thing you've been through. But I have to say, I'm glad someone finally got him. What a deservedly gruesome death."

"You don't think I—"

"Gruesome, gruesome." Elinor dropped Celeste's hand and bent down to pick up the chisel that lay on the ground under the ladder. "Don't really care who did it, long as the deed is done," she said in her rough, ragged voice. "Such an evil man."

Celeste had never heard anyone talk about Larry with such vehemence. Except Jake.

"Working on a new one?" Gloria pointed to the leather apron tied around Elinor's waist, several chisels and a hammer protruding from its pockets.

"Getting started. Come on around." Elinor pulled a lighter and a pack of cigarettes from her tool belt and lit one up. She blew out smoke, then sucked the plume back into her nostrils. Celeste hadn't seen anyone do that trick in years.

Celeste and Gloria followed her to the center of the circle. Surrounding them, carved into three of the huge stones, were outlines of women in various poses, their faces defined by grief. One reached to the sky on bended knees, shouting, it seemed, at the heavens. Another lay crumpled at the bottom of the stone, despairing eyes peeking through long fingers that seemed to tear at her face. The last stood upright, stiff and resolute, anger in her balled fists and narrowed eyes. While Elinor smoked and watched, Celeste walked round the circle, running her fingers over the carvings, captivated by the raw emotion this woman had found deep inside the granite. Circling around again, Celeste looked closer, realizing that these carvings were self-portraits, that the faces were Elinor's; she had perfectly captured her own aquiline nose and angled cheek bones.

"What's this one?" Gloria asked, pointing up to the lightly chiseled outline of a face peeking over the ladder.

"Not sure yet. Either denial or bargaining. We'll see what she wants to be." Elinor rubbed her hands together. "Freezing out here. Let's go in. Tea time, in my book." She paused to drop her cigarette stub, then crushed it under her boot and took off in long strides toward the house. Zion galloped beside Elinor, while Gloria and Celeste trailed behind.

"This explains exactly nothing," Celeste hissed at Gloria. "What's that woman got to do with Larry? And how does she know who I am?"

"Keep your panties on. All will be explained," Gloria said. "Maybe not all. But some, at least."

Celeste and Gloria followed Elinor through the front door into a spacious entryway. They hung their outerwear near the door on a coatrack already loaded down with several down jackets. Then they pulled off their shoes and shoved them among the boots and clogs jumbled around the rack.

Celeste looked around, wondering where the other people were. To the left of the entry hall she could see a dining room with a long, gleaming cherry-wood table surrounded by a dozen high-backed chairs beneath a chandelier of enameled metal wildflowers in cheerful colors. The tall, wide windows let in as much light as possible on this dreary afternoon.

In the large room to the right, a gray-bearded man and a slim young woman, both dressed in flowing linen, practiced Tai Chi on the polished wooden floor. Against the far wall, among the pile of rolled-up yoga mats, Celeste noticed another woman, apparently meditating in a rattan chair in the otherwise basically unfurnished room. The woman looked up for a moment and smiled quickly before dropping her turbaned head: Juniper, the woman from Arts and Herbs.

A low fire burned in the wide brick hearth that dominated the room. Standing near the door, Celeste caught the faint smell of smoke and ash hanging in the air. Above the polished wooden mantel hung a gold-framed oil painting that reached almost to the high ceiling. The painting tugged at Celeste, like Zion on his leash. She tiptoed into the room, trying not to disturb the flowing movement of the Tai Chi pair, whose eyes followed her as she crossed the floor.

She didn't notice. All she could see was the royal blue sky, spangled with yellow stars—no, goldfinches, tiny, perfect birds as bright as stars. Painted below the birds, and hovering in mid-air, Celeste recognized this very house, the one she stood inside. It floated above a rolling green lawn, composed of distinct blades of grass, each one a singular, tiny dab of paint, melding together a dozen different shades of green. And flashing—yes, she was sure—*flashing* among them, little white lights of fireflies on a June evening. Shining above it all, a full silver moon beamed down on the gardens below. White blossoms danced on stems, waving in the moonlight. The blue ceramic pots brimmed with the roses she'd earlier imagined. And in the lower right-hand corner, unmistakable among the apple trees, stood the circle of giant Elinor stones, smooth-faced, not yet carved, their shadows stretching out long behind them.

As Celeste stared at the painting, the starry birds fluttered in her chest and the fireflies fizzed like champagne bubbles up and down her arms and legs. The tranquil moonlight flooded over her, like a soothing balm, washing away the fear, anxiety, and despair of the last horrible days along with the self-hate and doubt that had plagued her for as long as she could remember. She was transfixed, lost in the scene in front of her.

A soft cough from Juniper drew Celeste back into the room. The magic of the painting ebbed within Celeste, leaving behind a subtle residue of peace, and she blinked hard. Smiling, she turned to the couple, who smiled back, as if they understood exactly where she'd been.

Juniper unfolded from her meditation chair, rolled herself up to standing, then stretched her arms high overhead. "'Bout time you got here," she said through a yawn.

"Drove as fast as we could!" Celeste answered, repeating Gloria's line.

Juniper and the Tai Chi couple looked at each other and shook their heads, grinning.

Some kind of inside joke, Celeste thought as she backed out of the room, eyes still on the mesmerizing painting.

Following the scent of rosemary, garlic, and wine-simmered beef that wafted from the kitchen down a long hallway, she caught up with Elinor and Gloria, heads bent toward each other, talking softly at the bottom of a flight of stairs. Beyond them sat Zion in the kitchen, his tail beating on the stone floor while a skinny, pony-tailed man tempted him with a big chunk of stew meat. The dog licked his chops.

Wisps of the women's murmured conversation reached Celeste as she walked toward them. "Murder . . . no sign . . . weird wave." Engrossed, they didn't seem to notice her. Slowing down, Celeste couldn't help but notice a small painting hung at eye level on the hallway's cream-yellow wall. She sidled over to the painting.

"No way," she breathed, studying the perfect rendering of Dreamland, shimmering beneath a marigold sun. The same painting she'd seen at Jake's. "Where did you get this?" she asked Elinor who had come up behind her and was looking over her shoulder.

"Jake gave it to us. When he moved in with you. Didn't want to leave it just sitting in his cabin," said Elinor in her gravelly smoker's voice.

So Jake *had* been here! "Why did he bring it to you?"

"It's one of my daughter's . . . Dreamscapes."

Celeste said, "Your daughter was Larry's wife?"

"My daughter, Rachel," Elinor said, "*is* Larry's wife."

CHAPTER TWENTY

RACHEL

"I didn't mean . . ." Celeste grasped for words. "I thought they were divor—"

"Celeste! Meet my man, Randy!" called Gloria from the kitchen.

"We'll talk," said Elinor, stuffing a crumpled pack of cigarettes into her pocket as she headed up the stairs. Without looking back, she barked, "Randy, bring up that tea. Don't forget the scones."

"Yes, sir!" Randy snapped a salute. As Celeste stepped into the kitchen, he flashed a lopsided grin. The left half of his mouth seemed frozen. Burn scars ran down his neck, disappearing into his black Steve Earle T-shirt. "'Bout time you got here!"

"Why does everyone keep saying that?"

"Because we've been waiting months for you! Waiting months!" He turned back to the stove, his foot tapping an erratic rhythm as he stirred and hummed.

"Months?"

Totally confused, Celeste turned to Gloria, but she was already bounding up the stairs after Elinor.

"Don't you run away from me, Gloria Cross!" Celeste took the stairs two at a time. She caught Gloria at the landing, grabbed her arm, and spun her around so fast Gloria's red hair flew out like a flag. "You better damn well tell me what's going on here! Enough with this mystery—*sheesh!*"

"That's what I'm trying to do. God, Celeste! Really. I promise I didn't drag you out here for nothing." Gloria shook off Celeste's grip. "Calm down!"

"Calm down? Are you kidding?" Celeste said, following Gloria through the door into a large, gray-beamed living room where Elinor already sat waiting in front of a roaring fire.

"You two!" Elinor reprimanded them, an unlit cigarette dangling from her lips. "Enough! Come sit by me!" She slapped the space beside her on the shabby-chic floral couch, her eyes fixed on Celeste.

Just like Randy, Gloria snapped to Elinor's command. She landed on a second couch across from Elinor, her wiry little body sinking into the down cushions. Still pissed off, Celeste took her time crossing the bare wood floor to the far side of the room. She perused the floor-to-ceiling bookshelves lining the walls, hoping to find some clue as to who this Elinor person was. Expensive coffee-table art books, tattered paperback murder mysteries, bestseller hardbacks, and dozens of leather-bound classics crammed the shelves. Elinor's collection revealed an eclectic taste in literature and art. What told Celeste more than any of the book titles were all the small alabaster sculptures, the size of her fist, squeezed in here and there along the shelves, half-hidden among the books. Children's faces—or maybe one child's face repeated over and over—laughing, crying, smiling, sleeping. And in the middle of the marble-topped table against the windows, a single pink alabaster angel, reading a book. Her translucent wings rose from her back, luminous in the fading daylight.

Celeste walked over to get a better look. Randy clattered up the stairs, balancing a tray with a platter of scones and a flowered porcelain teapot with matching cups and saucers. Zion trotted behind, nose quivering.

"Rachel," said Elinor, placing her unlit cigarette in an ashtray on the table. "That's what you're looking at. Never trusted the camera to capture her like I could." She paused and stared at the fire, then turned to Randy. "Set it down here, please, young man," she instructed, pointing to the coffee table between the two couches.

"Rachel, our own angel," boomed a deep voice.

Celeste looked over her shoulder, turning her gaze from the statue to find a big bear of a man emerging through a door that interrupted the long row of bookshelves across the room from where Celeste stood. As he picked at spots of paint on his blue smock, she looked beyond him into a studio cluttered with large abstract canvases leaning against the walls.

"Hey," said Gloria, half rising from the couch to greet him as he walked up behind Elinor, briefly placing his hand on her shoulder as he passed by.

"No, no, don't get up," he said, flopping down next to Gloria. The couch shivered under his bulk. He turned toward Celeste, his paint-spattered arm draped across the back of the couch.

"Charlie, Elinor's better half," he chuckled, waving at Celeste. "I'm guessing you're Jake's Celeste?"

Celeste blushed as she nodded and finally walked over and perched, still wary, on the armrest next to Gloria. Something about the angel had smoothed the rough edge of her raging turmoil, but she still wasn't going to pretend this was a nice little tea party. She wanted answers, not scones, for God's sake!

"I'm waiting for an explanation." She cleared her throat, trying to control her voice. "You all know everything about me. You've even been waiting months for me, according to Randy." The skinny man now setting out tea cups on the coffee table between the couches looked up at the sound of his name. "But I've never heard a word about you two. I have no idea what this is, who those people downstairs are. And you say you're Larry's in-laws? Don't you think I've been through enough in the last two days, Gloria, to not leave me in the dark?"

"Hold your horses," Elinor said. "Now that the gang's all here, Charlie can explain."

Celeste leaned toward the fire. She rubbed her still-cold hands together, trying to bring feeling back into her numb fingers.

"Easy does it, buddy," Elinor grumbled, gently pushing the dog away from the platter of scones. "Randy, why don't you take Zion out for a bit?"

Randy whistled for the dog, and then he and Zion bounded back down the stairs. Elinor poured the tea. She handed around the cups, a whiff of chai spices wafting from each. Finally, she settled back and pulled her stockinged feet up under her on the cushions. "Charlie, tell her."

Charlie turned away, gathering his thoughts as he looked over his shoulder at the angel. A moment later, he shifted to look directly at Celeste and then began to tell a story that sounded like a fairy tale.

"Rachel was an angel all right. Flew into our lives long after we'd quit hoping for a child. Never truly landed on Earth, always somewhere out in the ether. Not all that unusual in California, I guess. She loved to paint. Fantastical things she said came from her dreams."

"Dreamscapes. That's what she called them," Elinor

added. "They were all that mattered to Rachel. Like she lived inside the paintings, not in our world."

Charlie scratched at a green streak of paint that crossed his prominent forehead disappearing into his tangle of wavy white hair. "When she was, what? Fifteen? She shut herself up in her bedroom early one morning. Locked us out all day. Wouldn't even come out to eat. Finally, round midnight, when she finally let us in, well, it was astonishing!" Charlie's voice rose and cracked. "The room we'd always known as hers had disappeared. We stood in the middle of the universe, midnight blue, stars, planets, suns, all around us, under our feet, over our heads. We were floating in space. Here and there among the stars, like constellations, were characters from the stories Rachel loved—'The Knight in Shining Armor,' 'The Beautiful Princess,' 'The Monk,' 'The Magician.'"

Goose bumps ran down Celeste's spine as she flashed on Adam's tarot cards.

"And in the middle of it all, a perfect self-portrait of our Rachel, shimmering, translucent, like Elinor's angel, holding hands with The Fool. I don't know how long we stood there. Felt like forever. We couldn't even begin to pull ourselves back out through the door."

Celeste nodded, remembering how she'd been hauled right into the frame of Rachel's painting of the house downstairs.

"We didn't know what to make of it. What to make of Rachel." Charlie shrugged and sighed. "Wasn't 'til a few years later when I started coding digital graphics at Blue Wave that I realized—"

"Blue Wave?" Celeste asked, remembering first how Larry had quizzed her about the color of the wave in her tsunami dream—and, it suddenly struck her, the name of the website on that Rowan guy's card! Celeste glanced at Gloria. "Is that the place you mentioned in the car? Where Jake worked?"

Charlie looked perplexed. Elinor shot a disapproving look at Gloria.

"I know! I'm not supposed to talk about this stuff outside of Renaissance," Gloria put up her hands defensively, "but I had to tell her something to get her here!"

Charlie nodded. "It's okay, Gloria. Now that Larry's gone, everything's going to change." He sipped his cooling chai. "Anyway, Blue Wave Technology. Larry's starter cult, where we all fell under his spell. Even back then, twenty years ago, he had some power, something about him that we couldn't escape. He was intelligent, innovative. So were a lot of those start-up guys. But Larry—he knew how to make you feel like you were part of something special, like you had an inside track."

"I know what you mean," said Celeste, almost to herself. That's how Larry had kept her enthralled for way too long.

"We weren't making video games, we were making *magic*, he told us. We were changing lives! And we all bought it, even though we weren't really doing anything you could call revolutionary. Until I got Larry to hire Rachel as a designer." Charlie took a bite of a scone. Celeste watched sideways as the crumbs tumbled onto his broad lap.

"Rachel's drawings *were* revolutionary—mesmerizing, way better than anything else out there. Everyone wanted to get lost in her Dreamscapes. Nicole—she was sales—created big buzz for Blue Wave." Charlie paused and sighed. "Nicole was such a sweet girl back then. Big glasses, bad hair, but smart as a whip.

"Our product flew off the shelves, money was rolling in. So when Nintendo tried to hire Rachel away, Larry freaked. Convinced her to run off to Vegas and marry him before she got away. She'd fallen under his spell like the rest of us."

Elinor sighed. "That's when we got our first glimpse of the real Larry. He barely let Rachel out of the house except to go to work. Convinced her that she needed to separate herself from us, that she needed solitude to be creative. To find the Dreamscapes inside herself," said Elinor, looking into the flames. "She hardly ate. Her dreams dried up. She couldn't paint."

Something prickled in Celeste's memory. Jake had warned her. Told her he'd seen Larry destroy people.

Charlie shrugged and continued, holding his hands palm to palm between his knees, leaning over and looking at the floor. "Nicole and Jake tried to help, watching over her, trying to pull her out of the hole she'd fallen into. Pissed Larry off, but Rachel was too far gone. Until Rowan came along."

"Rowan McNeil?" Celeste was trying hard to keep up, putting the pieces of the puzzle together.

Charlie looked surprised. "You know Rowan?"

Gloria jumped in and told Charlie about Adam, how he'd been killed, and the business card Celeste thought he'd dropped on her porch the night before. The one she'd found while snooping in Jake's pocket.

"Some tramp had Rowan's card? I don't understand." He shook his big head, then scratched again at the green paint on his forehead.

"*You* don't understand? You knew all this, Gloria, about Jake and Larry and this guy Rowan, but you never said anything?"

Gloria shrugged. "Not all of it."

"Rowan," Charlie continued. "He's a visionary. Like Rachel."

"A bit cracked, though," said Elinor. She picked up her still-unlit cigarette and pretended to smoke it. "He was one of the first people to work on what he called 'virtual reality,' back in the eighties. But the technology back then couldn't keep up. Huge headsets and gloves like gorilla paws, Rowan told me. Crashed before it got off the ground, so he spent the next few years traveling around. Until one day, somewhere in Japan, he saw one of our Dreamscape games. He got on the next plane back to California, came straight to Blue Wave looking for Rachel. They took one look at each other and head over heels, love at first sight and all that other stuff," Elinor said, getting up to put another log on the fire.

"Only it wasn't actually love at first sight," Charlie said. "One day, we invited Rowan over for dinner. Rachel came on her own, after pleading with Larry for days to let her come. It was the first time she'd been back to our house since their marriage."

"Kept her on a short leash, even though he hardly seemed to care about her. She was nothing but a cash cow to Larry." Elinor's voice caught in her throat and she coughed.

"After dinner, Rachel took Rowan into her childhood bedroom, into the cosmic painting." Charlie smiled, remembering. "That's how we discovered that Rachel, sometimes, dreamed ahead."

"Like déjà vu?" asked Celeste. This was getting crazy.

"Turned out Rowan was The Fool holding our angel's hand. In her Dreamscape room. She'd painted him ten years before they met! We hadn't recognized him, but Rachel had."

Celeste was beginning to think she'd fallen down Alice's rabbit hole.

"By the time they came out of the room, they'd come up with this whole idea of creating dream worlds anyone could walk into. Beyond virtual reality. No glasses or headsets needed."

"Like that Holodeck on Star Trek?" Gloria asked.

"Turns out *that* was one of Rowan's early ideas, back in the eighties. Anyway, the two of them stayed up all night, like little kids, drawing, giggling. The next morning they had a plan for the Light House, a virtual reality space you could actually walk into. Took the idea straight to Larry. Larry jumped on it, and he knew this was going to be the biggest thing to hit the market in years. Maybe ever!"

Celeste looked at Gloria. "Sounds like that box at Dreamland, the one where I saw the mermaid."

Charlie and Elinor nodded, then Charlie went on. "Something like that. They worked on it for three years, Rachel doing the drawing, Rowan teaching me how to code her designs, make them 3-D, and create holograms too. Jake designed the structures. They built a prototype, were planning a huge roll-out. But on the day before their press conference, Larry gave us the big news. He'd sold the company lock, stock, and barrel to this German guy, Wolfhard Hermann," Charlie said.

"Right out from under them," Elinor added.

"The next day," Charlie continued, "Rowan was gone again, but only after he'd destroyed the Light House and all the software. He took most of Rachel's dream drawings with him. Left a note for Rachel saying he'd be back to get her."

"Broke her heart. Put her right back where she was before they met." Elinor stared into the fire. "Larry hardly noticed. More interested in Nicole by then—was busy turning her head. Convinced her she was the key to success. She bought it all. Started dressing up, becoming the stunner she is now. Thought she was better than the rest of us. Even Jake. That's when they drifted apart."

Charlie jumped back in. "After losing Rowan, the deal almost fell through, but Larry convinced Wolfhard, the new boss, that we could re-create the Light House. He still had Jake and Rachel after all. Rachel didn't have much choice with Larry still controlling her. But Jake refused, wasn't about to help Larry, especially since Larry kept most of the buy-out money for himself. Jake spent months trying to convince Nicole to go back East with him. Larry was working even harder to keep her in California. Even offered her a big stake in the new company."

"Nicole was torn, still enthralled with Larry," Elinor said. "But she was one smart cookie. She knew the project was dead in the water. She could also see the tech crash coming. Sold all the investments she'd made in the dot-coms and finally came back out here with Jake."

Elinor and Gloria both looked at Celeste.

"I don't get it. Why didn't Nicole stay? If she'd changed so much?" Celeste asked.

Elinor reached over and patted Celeste's leg. "We're not sure. Their marriage was falling apart. Maybe she hoped she and Jake could put it back together. Start over. Didn't work, if that was the plan. Larry had bewitched her."

"Brainwashed her is more like it. Anyway, a few months later," Charlie continued, "the whole dot-com bubble burst. Like Nicole had predicted. Wolf and Larry managed to keep Blue Wave afloat, no pun intended, and Larry used his powers to keep Rachel creating the graphics. You know how he could manipulate anyone who relied on him."

Celeste hugged herself, remembering her ring dropping into Larry's outstretched hand. "I know how he makes people do things they don't want to. He's done it, did it plenty of times to me." She stood up from the armrest and went to sit next to Elinor.

Now Charlie patted her leg. "You're not alone," he said. "That was always how Larry got his way. He convinced Rachel that only he knew what was best for her."

"She was just the first of his victims," Elinor added.

Charlie nodded, then continued. "But Rachel's heart wasn't in it. Especially because they were ordering her to use her gift—her amazing gift!—to create images for flight training and war prep for the Pentagon. Wolf's idea. They told Rachel they'd fire both of us if she didn't fulfill the contracts they had. She kept going, afraid I'd lose my job, though, truth be told, I was only staying on to protect her. But even I couldn't help her. Larry had completely cowed her—"

"Ripped the very heart out of her," added Elinor, her voice quavering with anger and grief.

"That guy could even make me do things I never thought I would," Gloria said, leaning toward the fire. "And you know what a headstrong bitch I am. Poor Rachel. He must have wiped out her self-confidence, just like he did to you, Celeste."

"If Rowan had come back for her, then maybe . . ." Charlie's voice trailed off and he looked over at Elinor. They stared into each other's eyes for several seconds, grief on their faces, before he continued.

"Finally, one day, out of the blue, Larry packed up their things, got them both on a plane to New York, and like that they were gone. We never even got to say good-bye to her."

"Kidnapped her, is more like it," Gloria pitched in. "Still sniffing after Nicole."

"Rachel didn't want to go, afraid Rowan wouldn't find her," added Elinor. "But like Gloria said, she didn't have much will of her own anymore."

"We didn't hear from her for months," Charlie continued. "We had no idea where Rachel was. In the meantime, Wolf-hard closed up shop. Went back to Germany, I guess.

"Rachel finally managed to get a letter to us through Nicole. She begged us to stay away, said she was working things out, said she'd be in touch. That was the last we heard from her directly. Jake and Nicole checked in every couple of months, enough so we didn't lose our minds with worry. By then Blue Wave was dead, and I was out of a job. Wolf had already run off with whatever was left."

Charlie struggled to his feet, heaving his big body from the couch. He shuffled to the long table by the window and ran his hands along the wings of the angel. "I'm sorry. It's hard, you understand, to talk about Rachel." He was silent for a few seconds, then took a deep breath and went on.

"Then, about nine years ago, we got a call from Larry, from Riverton Falls, saying Rachel had run off with Rowan. But since then no one's heard from her. Either of them, in fact. This card you found is the first glimmer of hope we've had that she and Rowan are even alive."

"But what about the painting, of *this* house, downstairs? She must have been here, seen it."

"Except she painted it out in California," said Elinor. "It was the only thing she left behind for us when Larry brought her here. After a couple of years, we finally gave up hoping she would ever come home, so we flew out here, to see where she'd lived, to see Jake and Nicole. We even tried to get some answers out of Larry, but he refused to even show us the letter he claimed she left behind when she went with Rowan. Now, of course, I wonder every day if there even was such a letter. That snake."

"That snake," Charlie repeated. "We could tell he knew more than he was letting on, but what could we do? We felt completely powerless. Then one day, in the food co-op in Riverton, we saw this house, on a poster. Being sold by a community of Druids, with its own Stonehenge, exactly like Rachel's painting! We figured it was a sign, so we bought it— this house. And we've been waiting here ever since," he said, still looking out the window, his own reflection ghostly against the cobalt-blue backdrop of early evening.

From the driveway below came the sounds of arriving cars, slamming doors, and people greeting each other.

"They're coming! Everyone's coming!" called Randy as he and Zion ran back up the stairs.

"Everyone?" asked Celeste.

"Okay, Randy. We know. Take the tea tray back down-stairs and let them all know we'll be down in a few," said Elinor, leaving Celeste's question hanging in the air.

Randy picked up the plates and cups, mumbling to himself as he counted the almost full plate of scones. He handed one to Zion, who gobbled it down in one bite.

"Please stay, you two! You have to! Won't you?" asked Charlie. "They're all dying to meet you, Celeste."

"Me? Who wants to meet me?"

"The Doubters! The Doubters!" said Randy.

CHAPTER TWENTY-ONE

RECLAMATION

"The Doubters? I never even heard the name until yester-day!" said Celeste, looking around at Gloria, Charlie, and Elinor. "I'm not sure if I should be pissed because no one ever told me about them," she glared at Gloria, "or excited that I'm not crazy and alone."

"I'd say the latter," answered Elinor. "Got to get over that anger before you can heal."

"But if anyone had explained . . ." Was this what Gloria had hinted at in her office over the Scotch? "If I'd only known . . ." Now she scowled at Gloria.

"Don't blame me! You had to get yourself out of there on your own," Gloria said. "I wasn't allowed to say a word."

"Not allowed? What is this? Some kind of rival cult to the Dreamscape?" Celeste pulled herself forward to the edge of the couch, getting her feet under her, in case she needed to get out of this place. No wonder it was so seductive. They wanted to suck her into something else right after she'd escaped from Larry.

"Not a cult. More like an antidote," Elinor said.

"Don't be mad at Gloria," said Charlie as he wandered back to the couch from the window and helped Elinor to her feet. "Or Jake. Everyone who comes to us takes a vow of silence."

"The Cone of Silence," added Elinor.

"Jake? He knew too?" Celeste asked, linking Jake and Gloria and the Dreamland painting on the wall downstairs. "I don't get it. He's never said anything about this place. He could have hinted, he could have at least . . ." A storm cloud gathered in her chest. Why hadn't he said something? They'd wasted so much time!

"Why do you think Jake was pushing you so hard to get out of the Dreamscape? That's why he left you. He couldn't think of any other way to get through to you!" Gloria's face reddened.

"He said it was because I lied. About being a Dreamer."

"You don't really believe he bought all that about working late at the bar? Come on!" Gloria said.

Celeste thought of Jake, of the night he took his things, of what that must have felt like for him. He was trying to help her and she was too stubborn, or too trapped, to listen.

"You'll understand when you meet everyone," said Elinor as she led the way downstairs.

In the large room where Rachel's painting of the house hung, a dozen people had gathered, chatting in small groups, hugging as they greeted each other. Celeste peeked into the room and had the strange feeling that she already knew the people assembled there. They were strangers to her and yet they seemed so familiar. These were Larry's people, all right. Middle-aged hippies, some, like the Tai Chi couple, still dressed in the flowing tunics and loose pants the Dreamers wore, others in skinny jeans and bulky sweaters. She recognized some of them from town. She'd seen them on the street, in the laundromat, out walking their dogs, but never at the Broken Gate.

"Hi Cel, do you remember me?" came a voice from the dining room. "Betsy?"

At the sound of her truncated name, Celeste flinched. She spun around and saw a freckle-faced redhead methodically setting the long table in the dining room.

"I think so," Celeste hesitated, trying to place her. Oh yes. She'd seen this woman on the day she was initiated into Dreamland. Now she remembered! Betsy arguing with Larry, telling him he had her dream all wrong, that he was leading her down the wrong path. Celeste had been so new to the Dreamers that she hadn't paid much attention then. Now, she realized, she'd never seen Betsy after that session. She'd never even heard her name mentioned again. "You look a lot happier than the last time I saw you," Celeste said.

"Hallelujah!" Betsy sang out as she placed cloth napkins under silver forks.

It was true. Though they still resembled Dreamers somehow, all the Doubters seemed loose, relaxed, not like their grim-faced counterparts at Dreamland.

Gloria took Celeste's hand and pulled her into the crowd, overlapping conversations abuzz with Larry's name.

"Everyone," called Elinor, "this is Celeste Fortune."

"'Bout—"

"—time I got here, I know." Celeste finished the sentence for the statuesque woman with flowing white hair who stood in the back.

"That's Audrey," whispered Gloria through the laughter in the room. "She used to be one of Larry's top Dreamers."

Celeste stared at the group staring back at her. "But how did you all find this place?"

"Jake brought most of us," came an answer from the Tai

Chi man. "He always has his ear to the ground, waiting for a rumble of disaffection. He would seek us out."

"Now I bring them too. Like I brought you," Gloria added. "It's kinda like a recovery program."

"We realized when we got the house that we couldn't do anything to help Rachel, but we could reach out to others Larry had damaged," Charlie explained. "We saw what a state they were in—quite a mess when they first get to us. Like this one," said Charlie, jerking his chin toward Gloria. "Confused, angry."

"Mad as hornets." Elinor looked at Celeste. "Unmoored, not able to find their footing. You know what we mean."

Celeste swallowed hard and nodded. "Like me."

"Damn right," said Gloria. "Took me months to find solid ground again. Felt like a complete failure. So angry at myself, at Larry, at the Dreamscape. I wanted to tear the head off anyone who came near me. Being here, finding out I wasn't alone—that's what brought me back to myself."

"After all the years with Larry, we'd forgotten how to trust our own feelings. Afraid anyone offering kindness was out to dupe us. Can't blame us though," Audrey with the long white hair said.

"We offer them time and space to reconnect with themselves, to remember who they used to be before Larry ground them down. They each need to find their own way back," explained Charlie.

"We're in the business of healing hearts," said Elinor, running her hand through her spiky hair. "Tom over there—he gardens." She pointed to a burly guy in the corner. "Randy cooks. Others, they paint, they dance, make music. Reconnecting with themselves through whatever passions Larry stole from them."

"Like my writing," said Celeste, remembering how Larry had, over the years, convinced her that her identity as a writer was simply an illusion of her Demon Mind.

"Like your writing. Our method seems to work. Slowly sometimes, but we see them come around. Right, Gloria?" Elinor put her arm around Gloria's shoulders.

"What did he take from you?" Randy asked, bouncing around Celeste on his tiptoes.

"Take?"

"Yeah, no one's ever gotten out without leaving something—"

"Something special," Betsy added.

"—something special behind," Randy said. "Something special! Like my dog tags."

"And the bracelet you gave me," said Gloria, holding up a bare arm.

"Our wedding rings," said the Tai Chi pair.

Celeste thought about the contents of the wooden box she'd found scattered under Larry's desk. "He took my engagement ring."

"Oh, not that lovely sapphire!" someone from the back of the room groaned. "The one Jake showed us?"

"That's the one. But why? Why would he take things?" Celeste asked the group.

"His way of keeping you on a leash," Charlie threw in.

"To keep you connected, always wanting to get it back," Randy said as he headed to the kitchen, Zion again at his heels.

Celeste looked around the room once more. So she wasn't the only one. She wasn't alone. She'd crossed over from Dreamer to Doubter, just like all the others who surrounded her now, and she wished she could put her arms around them all. Could Renaissance be where she finally belonged?

"But why does this have to be so secret? If I'd known—"

"Because," answered Gloria, "we all had to find our way in our own time. You wouldn't have listened, like you didn't listen to Jake."

Gloria was right, of course.

Randy, carrying a big earthenware bowl of his stew, came down the hall headed for the dining room. The smell made Celeste realize how hungry she was.

"Maybe, I mean, could we stay for dinner, Glor?"

Gloria grabbed Celeste's arm to check her watch.

"Yikes," said Gloria, "no way! I've got to get you back to town! It's already after six."

"Too bad," said Audrey, "We're having our own memorial for Larry tonight. Lots of complicated emotions to deal with. Even though he tried to control us, Larry did give us all something precious—a deeper understanding of ourselves, I guess I'd say."

Others in the room nodded, their eyes cast down.

"Sure you can't stay?" asked Juniper.

But Gloria was already in the hall, rooting around the loaded coatrack, trying to find her purple coat. Celeste backed out of the living room, waving to the Doubters. "I'll be back," she said. "I'll be back soon."

As Celeste dug among the coats looking for her vest, she saw it. On the wall by the front door, a watercolor she'd missed on the way in. She stared at the image; a four-paned window, looking out on a hedge of purple lilacs. Below it, on a wooden counter, a woman's hands pressing into a knob of dough. As Celeste moved in to look more closely, she felt something all too familiar tightening around her throat. She gasped, but couldn't breathe. Blackness swallowed her as somewhere far away a strangled voice cried, "Help me!" She stumbled. Charlie caught her elbow.

"My dream," she managed to mumble while leaning against Charlie for support, "the one that scared Larry. I dreamed this painting."

"It's Rachel's last painting," he said. "She gave it to Nicole, along with the Dreamland painting, a few days before she disappeared."

"You dreamed Rachel's dream," said Elinor. "She sent it to you so you can help her."

Celeste didn't know how to answer. She put her arms around Elinor, and the two of them stood in a stiff embrace. They pulled apart and looked into each other's eyes. Two women who found it difficult to accept solace had found each other. Rachel had brought them together.

"I do wish you'd stay," Charlie said, placing his warm, heavy arm around Celeste's shoulders.

But Gloria had already opened the door and stepped out into the blue-black night. She turned to look back into the warm light of the house where the Doubters were now gathered around Celeste in the hall. "Sorry. We gotta go. Looking kind of nasty out here!"

CHAPTER TWENTY-TWO

NIGHT RIDE HOME

Gloria inched the wheezy old Saab back down the driveway, slowly steering her way around the major boulders. Randy, who'd begged a ride to town, sat in back and sighed with relief as Gloria pulled the car out onto the rural highway. The dim headlights barely lit up the road, and she relied on the added shine of the half moon, pushing through the cloud cover, to see what lay ahead. The car's heater only worked on high. A blast of hot air filled the small space, intensifying Zion's wet musky smell mixed with the heavy aroma of the stew Randy had brought along in a Tupperware container.

"Wish we'd gotten an earlier start," said Gloria. "We need to get you to work. But I'm afraid this road could turn to black ice, and I can't see three feet in front of me now that the moon's gone again." She arched over the steering wheel and rubbed her arm across the windshield, trying to clear the steamy glass.

"Don't worry. Just give me your phone."

"Not out here, you can't," said Randy, his head resting on Zion's as the two of them peered between the front seats. "No reception for miles."

This patch of northern New England countryside has to be the last place on Earth where cell phones aren't in constant use, Celeste thought. She flashed on a memory of an Indian man dressed in nothing but a dhoti, goading his camel with one hand while holding a cell phone to his ear with the other. She wrinkled her nose at Zion's breath, then reached back to push him away from her face. She cracked her window for air.

"Maybe this will help clear the window," she said, not wanting to admit that her claustrophobia was getting the better of her. "Any tunes, Glor?"

Gloria reached into the center console and pulled out a cassette. "Try this."

"Joni Mixall," Celeste read by the faint light of the dash. "You still have this? I remember making it for you in college!" She pushed the cassette into the stereo. "This is probably the last car on the road with a cassette player," she said, as Joni's sultry smoker's voice began to purr "Night Ride Home" from the speaker.

"How perfect is that?" she said, shifting slightly to lean her back against the door, drawing her left foot up and tucking it beneath her right thigh.

"Man, I hate that chick music," said Randy. "Got anything else?"

"Nope," Gloria shot back. "Sit back and put on your seat belt if you know what's good for you."

"Yes, sir!" Randy flipped her a salute. He sat back, pulling Zion with him, and clicked his belt.

Celeste was surprised that this young guy was so obedient. "You were in the army?"

"Marines. Three tours. Two Iraq, last one in Afghanistan. But I don't like to talk about it, okay?"

Celeste could no longer see his face in the shadows of the backseat, but she could hear a catch in his voice.

"Sorry. I don't mean to be nosey."

"Let's talk about when Gloria left—*left Larry!*" Randy said, his hands nervously shaking the back of Gloria's headrest, his wiry body like a taut spring. Even his tired old black ponytail seemed to quiver with pent-up excitement. "You shoulda seen her! Seen her! There was this dream, Bill's, I think? Yeah, yeah, Bill's. 'Bout the stadium, where we were all cheering for Larry, who's standing there like Caesar, leaves, toga, the whole getup. Larry had all of us, all the Dreamers, acting it out, right?" he asked Gloria, who stared straight at the road, jaw tensed. "Everyone's standing around Larry yelling and cheering for him. Then we hear it, this voice, 'The Emperor has no clothes! Down with the Emperor!'"

Gloria snorted, "Like some scales fell off my eyes. I got that Larry was completely bogus. All hypnosis and holograms, fake. It was all fake."

"One by one, we quit cheering." His voice flattened, and he let go of the headrest. "We couldn't believe what Gloria was saying. Next thing you knew, Nicole had her by the arm and was pulling her out of the Sanctuary. Gloria kept yelling all the way to the door. Never saw her again 'til Jake brought me out to Renaissance myself."

"Okay, Randy, now that you've got that off your chest, I need you to listen." Gloria addressed him as if he were an overexcited kid. "We're trying to figure out who killed Larry and maybe that other guy, Adam. I think you know something, don't you? I've heard you talking to Charlie. About weird things Larry did to you after I left." Gloria was putting on her lawyer voice and again Randy responded to her authority.

"I'll tell you if you turn off the chick music."

Celeste hit the power button and the car was silent.

"I was having dreams, bad nightmares, couldn't sleep more than ten minutes at a time. Tried to get into the VA, but they had a long wait list, and besides, I didn't want much to do with those military people. I'd heard about this guy Larry from some contractor dude I worked for. Said he might be able to help with the nightmares. Plus I kept hearing about him around Riverton."

Celeste nodded, though she figured he couldn't see her. "I know what you mean. Hard to walk down the street without hearing talk about Larry."

"So I went, and right off the bat, he got all excited when I told him about the dreams. Said I was his first vet and he had something super special for me. And he put me straight into the Dreamers, after only a few sessions."

"Some kind of PTSD therapy?" Celeste asked, feeling that competitive tug that always came when people told her they'd been sent to Dreamland after only a couple months with Larry.

"I don't know if you'd call it therapy. I don't know what the hell it was. The hell it was! All I know is it messed me up way worse. Messed me up."

"What do you mean?" Celeste asked.

"He had everyone act out this recurring nightmare I was having, about the kid and the goat with the bomb." He grabbed Gloria's seat so hard her head bounced against the headrest.

"Okay, okay," said Celeste, putting her hand on his. "We're in the car now."

Randy shook his head and his eyes refocused. "Oh man, see, he did a number on me! It was like torture. Torture! He said it was to desensitize me. But I just got more and more freaked. One night, I woke up and found myself out on the street with a loaded gun in my hand, hiding behind a dumpster. Lucky no one walked by." He flopped back and pulled Zion to him. "Told Larry about it. That's when he made me give him my dog tags. He thought it was a big breakthrough."

"Jesus fucking Christ, I knew the guy was a nutcase, but that takes the cake," Gloria said. "How'd you finally do it? Get away, I mean? I don't think you've ever told me."

"It was freaky. The next night, Larry took me out to Dreamland, alone. In the middle of the room was this big box. I'd never seen it there before. Taller than me. He called it a lighthouse. He told me to get in, so I did, onto this kind of bouncy mat on the floor. He locked me in there and then turned out all the lights. Then the walls of the box, the top and the bottom, lit up." Randy paused, then let out a whimper and covered his eyes with his hands. "I was surrounded. Guns, explosions, bloody body parts flying everywhere. Worse than my nightmares. I was right back in the middle of it all. Somehow I broke outta that box and started running. I got all the way down the road before he caught up with me in his car. I thought he was going to make me get in. But he stopped and started yelling at me. 'Don't come back!' That's what he said! Like I was ever going back up there. No way! No way, man!" Now Randy was panting, and Celeste could hear Zion licking his hand. "Is that what you wanted, Gloria? Heard enough?" He sank back into his seat, crossed his arms over his chest, and looked out the window into the night. Celeste could see his shoulders still quivering.

His next words disappeared into the ragged, raging rumble of a car racing up fast on their tail. The roar of the engine drew closer. Now it was right behind them, riding tight on the bumper. Celeste and Randy traded anxious glances. They both turned to look out the back window but could see nothing but darkness behind them. Where was the car? All they could see was the flash of Gloria's taillights glinting sporadically off a high metal fender.

"What the hell? Is that guy crazy?" Gloria kept her eyes on the road and pressed down hard on the gas. "What's he trying to do?"

The rumble of the car they could barely see filled the Saab. With a loud crash, the car hit Gloria's bumper, jolting all three of them forward then whipping them back hard. Celeste's head slammed against her headrest. Her seat belt bit into her shoulder.

"He's trying to run us off the road!" she said, grabbing the sides of her seat, fingers buzzing with the vibration of the engine.

Gloria pressed even harder on the gas. The Saab surged forward. Then they hit a patch of ice on the road. The speeding tires spun. Flung against the door, Celeste tried to brace herself as the car fishtailed, just barely missing the guardrail. The brake lights reflected off the hood of the car behind them, red flashes, sliding wildly from side to side. The chasing car crashed against them again. The screech of metal tore through the darkness, sending the Saab into a spin. Gloria steered in the direction of the swerve. "Hang on!" she yelled and jerked the wheel hard. The Saab bumped across the road onto the opposite shoulder. Gravel shot against the windows. The Saab shuddered to a stop. Zion, thrown hard against Celeste's seat, let out a high-pitched yelp. A horn blasted through the night as the other car, a black SUV they could see now, raced past them.

In the chaos, the back door popped open and without warning Zion leapt out and took off at a fast run, chasing after the fast-moving vehicle. Its headlights, now on high beam, blazed like torches as it zoomed down the road.

"Oh my God," said Gloria, holding her face in her hands. Blood trickled between her fingers.

"Glor, are you all right?" asked Celeste.

"Get the dog!" Gloria cried, her voice muffled in her hands.

Randy was already out of the Saab, screaming, "I'm going to get you fuckers! You're gonna die!"

But the SUV was almost gone. Red pinpricks of light disappeared into the distance. Randy stood in the middle of the road, cursing after the taillights. Finally, he turned back toward the Saab. In the headlights, his face, shiny with sweat, twisted in a rage Celeste knew she couldn't fathom. He headed back toward them now, his fists balled, arms flailing. She could tell by the wild look in his eyes that Randy was no longer on this road. Wherever he was now, bombs were falling.

"Glor, he's out of his head. We have to calm him down before he hurts us!" Celeste said, as she opened her door and struggled out of the tilted car. Behind Randy, she saw Zion running full bore toward him. The dog circled round in front of the crazed soldier, leaping at him, knocking him down on the stony shoulder of the road, barking wildly. Silhouetted in the pool of headlights, Zion pinned Randy with the full weight of his muscled body.

"Don't hurt him, Zion!" Gloria scrambled from the car as the dog's muzzle hovered above Randy's terrified face. Celeste closed her eyes but instead of a scream of pain, there was only silence. She opened her eyes and saw Zion, big forepaws still on Randy's heaving shoulders, his tongue licking Randy's cheeks.

"That tickles!" Randy giggled and gently pushed the dog off as he tried to sit up. Zion lay next to him, still licking his hand as Gloria walked up to them.

"I'm okay," Randy coughed. "I'm sorry, I'm sorry, I . . ." He kept muttering as Gloria helped him up and they made their way back to the severely tilted car.

"I'm okay, too," said Gloria, wiping her bloody hands on the back of her jeans. "Banged my nose on the wheel, that's all. Celeste?"

Celeste's body buzzed with adrenaline, but everything seemed intact. She greedily breathed in the cold November night air. "What the hell was that?"

"Crazy fuckers," Randy said, still short of breath but his voice now low and calm. "We gotta call the cops. They could have killed us." Zion leaned against his legs and Randy rhythmically stroked the dog's head.

Gloria pulled her phone from her jacket pocket and looked at it. The face of the phone and the Saab's dim headlights were the only light in the dark, the moon now completely hidden by clouds. "Need to be closer to town. Still no bars."

"Bars?" asked Celeste. "Out here?"

"I mean on the phone. And you're going to be late, by the way."

"Better late than never, right?" The three laughed, feeling tension seeping from them, floating across the black open fields into the barely visible forest beyond.

"Why would someone do that?" Celeste asked as the laughter died away. She reached out and grabbed both Gloria and Randy by their forearms.

"I don't know, but right now I want to get out of here, back to civilization, before they decide to finish the job," said Gloria. "Could have just been some crazy kids out on a murderous joyride, but I kinda doubt that. Whoever it was, I think they were waiting for us back at Renaissance."

Gloria clambered back into the driver's seat. Short clicks came from under the hood. "Let's hope this baby starts or we're screwed." Besides their attacker, they hadn't seen another car on the road since leaving Elinor and Charlie's.

Gloria reached over and rooted through the glove compartment, pulled out a rumpled tissue, held it against her bleeding nose with her left hand, and turned the key with her right. The engine coughed, then died. "Hang on." She tried again, and this time the engine caught. Randy and Celeste sighed with relief.

"Thank God!" Celeste said. "Here, Zion!"

The dog backed away at first, whimpering, until Randy took over, calling, "Come on, ya big baby! Hop in here! In here!" At the sound of Randy's voice, Zion leapt into the car, circled a couple of times, then lay down, a tight ball of black-and-white fur, sliding down against the far door.

"We're going to have to push to get you out of here," Randy said, shutting the door and motioning Celeste to move to the rear of the car. The right rear wheel had gone off the shoulder into a deep rut. The fender was crumpled, and Celeste bent down to inspect a six-inch gash under the taillight.

"At least it's still attached," she said. She and Randy leaned into the tail of the hatchback and pushed. And again. On the third lunge, it moved forward as the rear wheel found purchase on the shoulder. Gloria maneuvered the Saab onto the pavement. With a weary sigh, Celeste climbed back into her seat, clicking the seat belt. "Good thing this car is so old it doesn't have airbags, or we'd be going nowhere."

"Yeah, they don't make 'em like they used to." Gloria tried to laugh as she drove off, cautiously now, remembering to look for the glare of more black ice ahead, keeping both of her white-knuckled hands on the wheel.

They drove in silence, each of them trying to calm down and breathe normally. Finally, they saw the lights of Riverton Falls in the distance.

"Almost home," said Gloria. "I've never been so happy to see the place."

CHAPTER TWENTY-THREE

BACK AT THE BAR

"I know, I know. I'm really late." Celeste called to Allegra as she clambered up the steep flight of stairs leading to the Broken Gate. "Don't even ask." As she reached the top she realized there was no way Allegra had heard her. The place was packed. Customers stood three deep at the bar, calling out orders, waving empty glasses. The noise level rose. A thirsty horde jostled for space and attention. Celeste had forgotten it was Green Drinks night, drawing every crunchy granola activist from miles around. The air was hot and muggy with breath and liquored-up body heat. Drops of sweat immediately collected along her hairline as she shoved her way through the young, flannel-shirted crowd and opened a window to let in a thin stream of fresh air that smelled of wet snow. Grabbing up empty glasses, she wove her way to the bar.

"Cool your jets," Allegra yelled into the fray, though no one seemed to hear her either. "Glad you finally found time in your busy schedule to get here," she hissed at Celeste. "Though maybe you should've taken some time to change." Allegra sidled by her, pushing a Dark and Stormy toward a young woman with a blue-streaked Mohawk and thick black eyeliner.

Celeste did a quick survey of her attire. *You're wearing that?* her mother hissed in her head. Celeste knew she was just barely presentable. The sweatshirt and patched jeans she'd pulled on that morning before heading off to Dreamland were flecked with mud from her fall in the cemetery. On top of that, she smelled faintly of exhaust after pushing the Saab out of the ditch.

"I could run home now," she said, feeling embarrassed standing next to Allegra in her way-beyond-skinny jeans and white T-shirt tight enough to match.

"No way, José, I've been holding down the fort on my own for two nights now, and I'm done." Allegra sighed loudly then blew upward at a loose lock of sweaty hair to get it out of her eyes. She looked back at Celeste and tossed a scarlet Broken Gate apron her way. "Throw this on."

Celeste turned to study the swarm again. Impatience began to creep in. She wished she could ask Allegra to stick around, bribe her with tips if necessary, but she knew she'd already used up all the goodwill her bar partner was going to expend.

Allegra pulled the draft beer tap and expertly filled a pint with Guinness, angling the glass exactly right on the first pour. While she waited for it to settle, she started whipping up a chocotini.

"This is my last order, then I'm outta here," she said, pulling the Guinness tap handle toward her for the second pour. "Goes over there." She nodded toward a table far in the back, mostly hidden behind the mob. "Like I said, all yours."

Celeste balanced the 'tini and Guinness on a damp tray and looked out over the crowd for the target. Seated there at the round table up against the back windows, clutching each other's hands, sat Bill, Ingrid, Andrew, and Karin, still dressed in flowing black tunics, looking mournful.

"Thanks a lot," Celeste said over her shoulder to Allegra. "Were there any other Dreamers in here?"

"Lots. Still sniveling away," Allegra answered, pulling on her bomber jacket. "Seemed like they were planning the funeral. Tomorrow already. Maybe I'll even go. Sounds like quite the extravaganza."

"Nicole?"

"Yeah, she was here too. Left right before you came in. Meeting someone, I think I heard her say."

"Someone?"

"I'm not here to keep tabs on your boyfriend, if that's what you're asking." Allegra tugged on the furry earflaps of her bomber hat. She looked just like Amelia Earhart taking off for the Arctic Circle.

"No, that's not what I meant," Celeste lied.

"Yeah, sure," Allegra said. "I'll wait 'til you get back from the delivery."

Celeste ducked under the bar leaf, the beer and the spindly martini glass wobbling slightly on the tray, then pushed through the crowd.

"'Scuse me, 'scuse me," she said as she held the glasses above her head, weaving through, trying not to spill. Emerging from the huddle around the bar, she inched reluctantly toward the Dreamer table, hoping she could dump the drinks and run. As she got closer, she heard singing. Could it actually be "All I Have to Do Is Dream"?

"Hi! Guinness?"

"Mine," said Karin, tightening her black pashmina around her shoulders as if trying to protect herself from Celeste.

"They haven't locked you up yet?" asked Andrew.

Celeste tried to laugh him off, but he wasn't smiling. Under his tangle of carrot-colored curls, his face was pale except for violet pouches of flesh beneath his bloodshot eyes. She looked at Bill and Ingrid. They too looked exhausted, their faces suffused with grief.

"Chocotini for me," said Ingrid as she looked Celeste up and down. "You look like you've been through the wringer."

"The funeral's tomorrow?" Celeste asked, ignoring the barb as she set the glass down.

"Memorial. We can't get the body from the cops, so it's a memorial. Technically." Andrew was always precise. "Sarabande insisted on tomorrow."

"Sarabande?" Since when is Sarabande in charge? Celeste wondered. "Okay. I'm wondering when I should be there." Celeste leaned over to place the check in the middle of the table.

"You think that's a good idea?" asked Ingrid, clearly suggesting it wasn't.

"Hey, Celeste—Brandy Alexander, over here!" Allegra called, trying to rescue her. She had already zipped up her leather jacket, impatient to get out of the bar before another crowd appeared.

"Gotta go!" Celeste said. Ingrid gave her an acid smile before she rushed back to the protection of the bar. Behind her, the Dreamers picked up the song again. She was not venturing back into their territory. She'd have to get a busboy from the restaurant on the ground floor to help out the rest of the evening now that Allegra was making her escape.

Celeste waved to Allegra as her coworker headed down the steep flight of stairs to the street.

"Send Phil up to help, please?" she pleaded as Allegra's coppery topknot disappeared down the stairwell. "Okay, one Brandy Alexander, coming right up!" she said to Mike as she squatted down to slide back under the counter, too tired to raise the leaf. That guy could be a real winner if he'd just lay off the dessert drinks and drop a few pounds, she thought.

Even with the Dreamers there, the bar was her haven, the only place busy enough to take her mind off the insanity of the last two days. This red-lined candy box of a place, with its fake flickering gas-lights and its genuine, funky, overheated body odors, was exactly where she needed to be. Here she was the bartender, purveyor of classic cocktails—not a traitor, not a suspected murderer, just the gal behind the bar. She poured brandy and cream into a balloon glass as the post-movie crowd puffed up the stairs. They blew on their cold hands and stamped their feet as they entered, a rush of welcome air following them.

The newcomers wanted hot toddies, and it was all she could do to get the steaming drinks to the right customers before they went cold. She poured the Jack Daniels, mixed in the lemon juice Allegra had prepared ahead of time, added a spoonful of sugar and a splash of hot water from the coffee machine, and stirred it all up with a cinnamon stick. This was her signature drink, and she could make a trayful on automatic pilot, barely registering now the weariness she'd felt when Gloria dropped her off.

Slowly, however, as the place began to empty and the noise level fell, dread and exhaustion crept back in. Celeste sat down on the stool behind the bar and wiped her hands on her apron, pushing away the dream image that swam up as the apron strings tugged against the back of her neck. She glanced over to where the Dreamers had been sitting and saw that they'd been replaced by a tall, skinny, white-haired man in black jeans and a down jacket who sat bent over the Sazerac busboy Phil must have served him in the midst of the rush. She remembered swirling the absinthe wash around the glass, pouring the WhistlePig rye, but she couldn't remember ever seeing the man at the Broken Gate before. Still, he looked familiar. She stared at him for a few seconds. She'd seen him before. Coming out of Larry's, that was it. The guy she'd thought was the pharmacist. A pile of bills lay on the table in front of him. At least he hadn't pocketed the Dreamers' payment—at least not all of it.

She put Phil behind the bar, yelled out "Last call," and went over to collect the cash. "Anything else I can get you?" she asked as she shoved the bills into the pocket of her apron. The man shook his head without looking up. He was tense, agitated, his hands balled into tight fists on either side of his drink. His foot jiggled the table.

"Hey, Celeste, two more toddies over here!" one of the last stragglers ordered from the other side of the room, his words unsteady and slurred, as she made her way back to the bar.

"Sorry," she called over her shoulder, glad she had an excuse to shut him off. "Done for the night. Time for everyone to drink up. Gettin' on time to close." She pretended she sounded like Joni Mitchell on one of those albums. *Court and Spark*? Her body ached, and she wondered if she had the strength to make it home. Almost midnight. Leaning on the bar, head in hands, she watched the man from Larry's down the last of his Sazerac in one long gulp, stand up, stretch his arms high over his head, then stick some cash in the server book. Hands shoved into his jacket pockets, he galloped down the stairs, looking back at her as he began to descend. The last few stragglers followed him down. Celeste gave a weary sigh and gathered in the stray glasses left on the bar, then swabbed it down with a damp towel. Phil piled the glasses into the dish tray.

"'Night," he called as he carried the last load down to the restaurant for washing. The glasses chattered against the tray's plastic dividers on each step.

"Night," she called. From the window she watched a few cars pass below, spraying little fountains of water as they drove through the slushy street. She went back behind the bar and poured herself the last of a bottle of Cabernet Sauvignon.

"Jake, where are you?" she asked the empty barroom. Even if he hadn't shot Adam or had anything to do with Larry's murder, something she wished she could still feel certain he hadn't, why had he never brought up the Light House project, mentioned Charlie and Elinor, or said anything about his past connection to Larry? Maybe, like Gloria, he was stuck in the Cone of Silence.

As Celeste closed out the register, she sipped the wine and hoped it would give her the courage to walk home. She'd done it hundreds of times, but now everything about late-night Riverton had changed for her. There was danger out there, something she'd never felt before. She swabbed the tables, stacked the chairs on top, and heaved the stools upside-down onto the bar. As she bagged up the recycling, she kept hearing the sound of that black SUV's engine raging behind them as it chased them down the icy road.

At the window again, she looked up and down the street, not sure what she was even watching for. She flipped off the lights, slowly descended the steep stairs, and set the security alarm. Zipping up her vest, she stepped out into the cold, glad the day was finally over.

CHAPTER TWENTY-FOUR

ACHY BREAKY

O utside, a few stray flakes of snow danced in the streetlights. Celeste hugged herself. She wished she'd brought a real coat instead of her vest, but it hadn't occurred to her when she'd headed out in the morning that she wouldn't make it home again that day except to drop off her car. She checked the few vehicles still parked on the street, the usual assortment of pickup trucks and Subarus tucked up along the curb and illuminated by the backlit marquis of the Paradise Movie House and the spotlight over the China Moon restaurant across the street. No dark-colored SUVs in sight. She shivered, wondering why the car had chased them in the first place. Had it been after her? Gloria? Or had it been after Randy? What a nutcase he was! Nuts enough to whack Larry in one of his rages?

"Calm down, you're being paranoid," Celeste chided herself out loud, wanting to hear a familiar voice in the dark. She longed to call Jake, ask him to come for her, take her home, cradle her in his arms. But, as usual, she didn't have a phone on her, and of course Riverton Falls no longer had any pay phones. No, she'd wait for the late-night Jackie-O's crowd to stumble out onto Main Street. She'd probably feel less vulnerable if there were others heading home, preferably on foot like she was and not drunkenly driving, at this late hour. Pack slung over her shoulder, she marched toward the other bar, head up, whistling "I Whistle a Happy Tune" from *The King and I.* She'd been a stranger in enough cities around the world to know you had to move with confidence to keep away unwanted attention and show tunes always made her feel better.

She stopped under Jackie-O's faded striped awning and turned to look in the window lit with a neon guitar that advertised Budweiser in its fire-colored frets. Figuring she'd look like she'd stepped out for a smoke, she rooted around in her backpack for the kretek Adam had left her, hoping Wally hadn't requisitioned it. As she dug around, the door to Jackie-O's opened. She pulled back quickly into the shadows just as Jake, his arm around a weeping Nicole, walked out.

Celeste held her breath and forced herself to stay still, her back pressed against the cold window of the bar.

Told ya. Missed your chance to get him back. Larry's voice coiled around her thoughts. She wanted to run after them, grab Jake's other arm and demand he go home with her. Instead she stood in the shadows, pain tightening her chest, her throat, her jaw, watching them walk away.

What a match, those two—Nicole in her fur-collared coat and high-heeled black leather boots, leaning in to listen; Jake in his well-worn Carhartt jacket and paint-spattered work pants, talking low, saying something to her, ". . . get through tomorrow . . . Promise not to let you down this time."

Nicole leaned her head against his shoulder, her answer drowned out as the bar door opened again. The twangy guitar riffs of "Achy Breaky Heart" spilled out onto the street. That was Fritzi's famous closing call, and right on cue, several more couples piled out, the happy drunks stumbling farther away, out of Celeste's earshot. Achy breaky heart was right. Melding into the crowd of chattering women in skinny jeans and inattentive men in work pants and flannels, Celeste followed them. She hummed along with the song still blasting from the bar, willing herself not to break down. From the shadows of the Jolly Jewels bead shop, half a block away, she watched Jake boost Nicole into the passenger seat of his truck, her fur-trimmed coat so incongruous in his beat-up vehicle. Celeste could still run over. She could ask for a lift. Three could squeeze into the cab. But what if Jake said no? Stepping into the yellow platter of light on the sidewalk under the street lamp, Celeste examined the thin white circle around her left ring finger.

Was I right or what? Back together. Larry sounded triumphant.

We knew you weren't good enough for him, her parents added, speaking together. Celeste's hands flew up to cover her ears. Why couldn't they all shut up?

The now-too-familiar sound of a revving car engine ripped through her thoughts. She jumped, spun around, and looked back toward Pelletier Bridge. A pair of high-beam white headlights raced down Main Street. The black SUV zoomed past the movie house and the Chinese restaurant, then swerved across the center line, heading straight for her, right there on the sidewalk corner, vulnerable and conspicuous under the streetlight. Celeste froze, watching the monstrous vehicle barreling toward her. Its toothy silver grille grew larger, its license plate suddenly lit up by streetlights. PC2U! The same car that had almost hit her in front of Larry's! She raised her hand to shield her eyes and stumbled backward, afraid of the coming impact.

At the last second, brakes screamed. The big black car swung a hard left. Its tires screeched against the pavement as it veered toward Jake's Tundra. Celeste braced herself for the horrific sound of metal on metal. Right in time, Jake jammed on the gas. As the Tundra blew past Celeste, heading toward the bridge at the end of Main, Jake's and Nicole's faces whizzed by, white blurs under the streetlights.

The SUV threw a hard one-eighty and closed in tight on the Tundra's tail. As Celeste struggled to focus her eyes, a gunshot shocked her ears, ripped through the night, shattered glass. The rear window of the truck collapsed into a web of cracks. Nicole's scream echoed down Main Street as the truck careened past the China Star. It spun through the round-about, listing on its two right tires, about to flip, but in a heartbeat it somehow righted itself and sped back down Main, with the SUV a few yards behind.

Celeste ran up the street toward the truck. "Jake, Jake!" she called, but no sound emerged.

Behind her, people screamed and darted back into Jackie-O's for cover. Celeste ducked behind a FedEx deposit box, too shocked to follow them inside, to even move.

Both vehicles raced past her again, side by side now, heading for the highway. Nicole leaned out the passenger side window, holding something long and black . . . Jake's rifle!? Celeste froze as she heard the shot. The bullet zipped past her. It hit the pavement and ricocheted, ripping through the FedEx box on the sidewalk. Celeste's cheek stung as if it had been sliced by a sharp knife. She pressed her hand against her face where it hurt the most, then pulled it away to see a thin line of blood across her palm. She'd been hit! The bullet had grazed her cheek.

More shots, louder than the engines now, echoed down Main Street. The wildly zigzagging SUV sideswiped the truck, and another piercing scream came through Jake's shattered rear window. Jake gunned the engine. The Tundra skidded on wet leaves, sending out a rooster tail of water in its wake, spewing spray across the windshield of the SUV. The big black car spun out of control, careening across the lanes, then smashed into the traffic light on the corner. It stalled there long enough for Jake to pull ahead, but then the SUV backed up and sped after him again. The damaged traffic light blinked repeatedly. Red, yellow, green, red, yellow, green flashed over and over again like fireworks on the wet street below.

Sirens blaring, blue lights spinning, two squad cars pulled out of the police station across from the Broken Gate. All four speeding vehicles now raced down Main. The Tundra held the lead, the SUV hard on its fender. The blue lights trailed behind as all four vehicles raced out of sight, leaving only the wail of the sirens over downtown Riverton.

Celeste sat up and tried to breathe. Blood trickled down her cheek. From behind her, footsteps pounded on the sidewalk; all at once, hands grabbed her shoulders. She struggled against them, clawing at them with her fingers.

"Celeste, it's okay. It's me. You're all right."

Still fighting, Celeste turned toward the voice and looked straight into Jean Pearl's green eyes. She focused in on the freckles lightly scattered across the bridge of Pearl's nose.

"Are you hurt?"

Celeste tried to breathe.

"Take it slow. That's it, long and slow."

Finally, Celeste wheezed and felt a rush of air fill her lungs.

With a tissue, Pearl dabbed at the blood that trickled down Celeste's chin. Pearl's warm breath smelled of toothpaste and whiskey. Kneeling on the sidewalk, in her black track suit, she looked so much younger, more girlish than she did in her green cop clothes.

"That was him, wasn't it? The guy who tried to run you off the road?"

Celeste could only nod, trying to push herself up to a standing position with her hands, palms still stinging from the fall. "How?" was all she could manage.

"Gloria," said Pearl. "She told me what happened. The car chasing you? Terrifying." Pearl stood and leaned down to offer Celeste a hand up. "She was worried about you going home alone. Knew you wouldn't ask for a ride. I got here as all hell broke loose."

"Gloria . . . called you?" Celeste, now standing, wrapped her arms around herself and took tiny shivering breaths between each word.

"Mmm, not exactly, but ah, we were . . . I was off duty."

"What . . . you were . . . on a date?"

"Not a date." Pearl looked down shyly and shuffled her tennis shoes. "She needed some company after all that happened."

"And she called you." Celeste felt a little twinge of jealousy, not quite sure who she was jealous of. She certainly wasn't interested in Jean Pearl, not that way, but she wanted both Gloria and Pearl to like her best. She snorted a small laugh at herself, realizing this woman had raced into danger for her. And she wanted more?

She swayed on her feet, then grabbed onto the lamppost for support while Pearl pulled out her cell phone and began to dictate details of the chase to someone on the other end. "Yep, I got a look at it." She paused. "Same one. Heading toward Middlesex." She paused again. "Nope, no idea." She nodded, listening. "Okay. I'll go with her." Pearl punched off the phone.

"You're taking me home?" Celeste whispered, suddenly crying, heaving big, gulping sobs of relief and fear all balled up together, unsure what exactly she should be feeling. Celeste grabbed Pearl's outstretched hand with her free hand and let go of the cold metal lamppost, steadying herself as she did.

"Come on, my car's over there." Pearl pointed to a silver Impreza in the lot by the police station. "After those two incidents, I'm not leaving you alone. You may not have killed Larry—"

"I *didn't* kill Larry," Celeste objected.

"But in any case, you're involved in this somehow. And I don't think you're safe. I could stay with you. How's that sound?"

"Thanks!" She stopped, surprised at herself. Her mind flashed back to the night before, how she'd brushed off the same offer from Gloria, and later her terror, even asking Jake to spend the night. But her all-too-real fear had taken a sledge hammer to that false independence Larry had always harped on. Right now, accepting help felt easy.

Jean Pearl put her arm around Celeste's waist. "You can lean on me," she said holding the much taller Celeste upright as they wobbled down the sidewalk toward Pearl's car.

CHAPTER TWENTY-FIVE

PEARLY GIRLY NIGHT

Celeste's apartment building seemed less foreboding than it had the night before. Winnie, her upstairs neighbor, must have left the porch lights on after last night's commotion. Having Detective Jean Pearl at her side helped, too. Celeste pulled the key from her pack and wiggled it into the lock, unsure if it would work since she'd never locked her door before that morning when she set off for Dreamland.

"Wait here, I'm going to check around outside real quick," Pearl said, before disappearing into the moonless night. Opening the door, Celeste was surprised by how grateful she felt with Jean Pearl watching out for her, even if she was a cop and it was her job.

Celeste fidgeted in the hallway, waiting for Pearl, wondering if she could go any further without the other woman at her side. She fumbled in her pack again, finally locating the kretek down in a side pocket. On the table by the door, she found the lighter she'd used to light the jack-o-lanterns a couple of weeks earlier. Another lifetime ago. She lit up the kretek and sucked in, taking a deep drag of the spicy smoke, coughing at the sudden assault on her lungs. She hadn't had a cigarette in over a decade. She walked back outside to the porch steps, woozy and light-headed, and took a smaller puff.

"All clear out here," Pearl said, reemerging from the shadows. She sat down on the steps next to Celeste and watched her inhale then blow out the smoke in practiced rings.

Smoking was like riding a bike, Celeste thought. Something you never lose the hang of, no matter how long it's been. She drew on the kretek again, little shreds of the clove-infused tobacco sticking to her tongue with a spicy, pleasant heat. Around her, the wreath of smoke reminded her of the undertone of Adam's body odor.

"That actually smells good. What is it?" Pearl asked.

Celeste tapped a shard of ash onto the frosted spears of grass at her feet. "Indonesian cigarette," she answered.

"Can I try?"

They passed the thick, crackling cigarette back and forth, smoking in silence, watching the dark clouds skate across the sky, hiding the stars.

"I don't usually smoke, but there's nothing usual about today," Celeste said, crushing the butt out on the stair. She stood up, opened the door, flicked on the lights, and headed toward the living room.

"Sometimes we all need a cigarette," Pearl said, following her in. She sat down on the couch, where Jake had sat the night before. Celeste fell into the cushions next to her.

"Nice place you've got here."

"Yeah, sure." Celeste sniffed. Who was she trying to kid? Celeste knew her place was way closer to Salvation Army functional than nice, but then there's no accounting for some people's taste. "Want a drink?"

"No thanks. Need to keep my head clear, but go ahead. After what you've been through. But first you should wash out that wound, where the bullet grazed you."

Celeste put her hand to her cheek. The area around the wound had begun to throb and she touched it gingerly, letting her finger follow along the thin line of crusty blood that ran from under her eye to her ear. In the bathroom, she gazed at herself in the mirror. Her hair was wild, her eyes bloodshot, the fine line of dried crimson the only color on her pale skin. She dabbed at the blood with a threadbare washcloth and hoped that was enough. Do wounds like this get infected? she wondered as she made her way unsteadily into the kitchen. She poured herself a tumbler of Jameson's, holding the glass and the bottle over the kitchen sink. Her hand was still so unsteady, half of what she poured went straight down the drain.

In the living room, settled on the couch, Pearl was on her phone, but she hung up as soon as Celeste sat down next to her. "Did I hear you say something 'bout the license plate?"

"It's an all-car alert. Cops from three towns are out there looking for the guy. And for Jake and Nicole."

"Jake? Did they say what happened to him?" Celeste's voice was so high and squeaky she sounded close to hysteria. She slugged down half the whiskey to steady herself.

"And Nicole," Pearl said. "Still waiting to hear."

"Okay, and Nicole," she added, feeling slightly ashamed of herself. "The license plate?"

"Supposedly it belongs to a computer repair company, the one that may have picked up Larry's computer yesterday? Dreamscape Computers, I think." Pearl leaned down and pulled off her boots. "Mind if I put my feet up?" she asked, stretching her legs out to rest on the coffee table.

"Larry's old company? The one he sold to those kids, Sarabande and Arun, last year?"

"Who? From the records we found in our search, he sold it to some guy named Wolfhard Hermann."

Celeste sat up so fast her whiskey sloshed out of her glass and down the front of her sweater.

"So you know who that is?" Pearl sat up too.

Pinpricks of sweat gathered on Celeste's scalp, and her entire body flushed hot, then cold.

"Do you?" Pearl narrowed her eyes.

"The guy who bought the company Jake and Nicole and Larry all worked for in California!" She staggered up from the couch and began to pace.

"Can you slow down and fill me in here? Who is this guy Hermann and how do you know about him?"

"They said he'd disappeared." Celeste stopped walking and leaned against the French doors, letting the cool of the glass calm her.

"Who said?" Now Pearl was on full alert, sitting up straight, eyes on Celeste.

Celeste started pacing again, telling Pearl about her visit to Renaissance and the little she knew about Blue Wave Technology. She walked back and forth across the living room floor, its center floorboards creaking at each pass.

"Well, that's quite a piece of information. Larry's in-laws? Don't you think you should have told us about them? Sheltering all those, what? Doubters? Who could be suspects?"

"Gloria was the one who knew, not me. She didn't mention it tonight? On your non-date?" Again, Elinor's Cone of Silence. But no one had ordered Celeste not to talk.

Pearl shook her head. "Only told me you were out in the Kingdom when someone rammed her car. So I guess this Hermann guy—Hermann the German, I suppose?—bought Larry's computer repair company with a couple of kids?" Pearl quickly got back to business.

"Sara and Arun. Right. And that SUV—I saw it, yesterday, right in front of Larry's! I'd forgotten about it, didn't seem important, but it must be the same one that chased us tonight and then went after Jake. It had to have been that Wolfhard guy. Or maybe Sarabande or Arun. But they're barely old enough to drive. I wish I could have seen who was behind the wheel, but everything keeps going too fast." Celeste stopped in the middle of the room, then pirouetted on her stockinged toes and went back into the kitchen for another glass of whiskey.

"Sure you don't want any?" she called to Pearl.

"No, I want to figure this out. Come back here and talk to me. You drink way too fast."

Celeste came back, her glass filled nearly to the brim, and perched on the edge of the couch next to Pearl.

"They, he, must have killed Larry and then taken the computer! It has to be. Then they went after Adam because he was a witness! It's the only thing that makes sense!"

"So you don't think they just picked it up for repairs?"

"Larry didn't need someone else to fix his damn computer. He could do that himself. Something was on that computer, and someone killed him to get it! Why didn't you go to this computer company's office and pick it up? Evidence, right?"

"To tell you the truth, we tried. But the address that's listed for them doesn't seem to exist. Ever heard of Crow's Nest Lane?"

Celeste shrugged. "No, but couldn't you find it on one of those map thingies on your phone?"

"Nope, says 'no results.' Believe me, we've had someone on this all day." Pearl leaned over and took the glass of whiskey from Celeste's hands, then delicately sipped. "So maybe you're right, they—or he—killed Larry and then Adam." She sipped again and handed back the glass. "Maybe, thinking about what you told me tonight, about California, Blue Wave?

Maybe this guy has some old grudge against Larry, Nicole, and Jake?"

"I have no idea. That whole California connection freaks me out. But why would this Wolf person be after me and Gloria?" Celeste put her glass down on the coffee table.

"Maybe he was after Randy? The vet Gloria said was with you?" Pearl mused.

"Randy did say Larry had threatened him after torturing him in that box up at Dreamland. Maybe he saw something he shouldn't have? Or maybe Randy killed Larry and these guys are after him now?" Celeste's thoughts whirled through her brain, spinning around, crashing into each other like some cranial Tilt-A-Whirl lubricated by adrenaline and alcohol. "Or maybe—"

"Whoa, calm down. I think you need to get to bed. And I need to phone all this in." Pearl placed her hand on Celeste's shoulder.

"But you're not going to leave me, are you?" Celeste sank back on the couch. The old thing creaked and she could feel a spring poking up from the cushion she sat on.

"No, no." Jean Pearl reached out and placed her hand on Celeste's arm. She bent toward Celeste so their faces were almost touching. "Why don't we breathe together to help you calm down a bit. You're spinning into outer space."

Celeste could see the brown and amber flecks in Pearl's green eyes as the two of them breathed in and out together until Celeste's shoulders relaxed and the fist of fear in her stomach unclenched. "I'm just so scared, and so worried about Jake." Celeste turned her gaze away from Pearl's. This was getting a little too intimate for her.

"I promise, I'll let you know as soon as I have any word about him. Now you need to get some sleep."

"How am I supposed to do that? I feel like I'm flying to pieces."

"Here's something else I've learned along the way, something that helps when it feels like *I'm* flying to pieces."

"Okay." Celeste nodded.

"Wherever you go, whatever you do, you're supported. You're supported by your feet when you're standing. You're supported by your chair when you're sitting, by the bed when you're lying down. There's always something holding you up. You don't need to look further than that. Think about it. It helps."

Celeste nodded again. It sounded way too simple after all the knots she'd tied herself into trying to find support from Larry's dream images. But Pearl was right. Celeste felt the solidity of the floor under her feet, the strength of her own body, holding her up, not letting her down.

"Thanks," she said as she got up, stretched, and headed into the bathroom before Pearl, already on her phone, could catch the tears of relief streaming down her face. When was she ever going to quit crying?

CHAPTER TWENTY-SIX

DREAMS TO REMEMBER

"Celeste! Stop!"

Celeste swam up toward the muffled voice, propelling herself out of the dream, trying to find a way to reach it. Her eyelids were heavy, so hard to open.

"Let go!"

Pain shot through her shoulder. She broke the surface and stark light blinded her. She shook her head, gasping for air.

"Wake up! You're hurting me!" The words sounded like chunks of ice.

She turned toward the voice and Jean Pearl's frightened face came slowly into focus. Then Celeste saw her own hands, tight around Pearl's neck, Pearl's own hands on top of hers, trying to loosen their grip.

"Let go! Now!" Pearl pulled hard and Celeste opened her fingers then brought her hands in tight against her chest. She was in her own bed, in her own room, but everything looked distorted, as if she were looking at a fun house mirror. Pearl sat down on the edge of the mattress, trying to catch her breath. Around her neck were the reddened marks left by Celeste's fingers.

"Oh my God! What was I . . . ? What?"

"You were having a nightmare. At least, you were screaming, so I came in and then you grabbed me. Girl, you are strong!" Pearl rubbed her neck with both hands, bringing back the circulation, erasing the marks left by Celeste's fingers. "You could have killed me!"

"I'm so sorry." Celeste pulled back. She shut her eyes and tried to find the dream before it completely disappeared again. That feeling was still there—not horror or fear this time but a sense of power, strength, triumph.

"Rachel's painting."

"What are you talking about? Celeste, come back to me." Pearl shook her lightly. "What's going on? Were you dreaming about yesterday?"

"It's not my dream."

"Your nightmare then." Pearl straightened up and pulled away.

Celeste knew she was putting Pearl's Buddhist compassion training to the test.

"No, I mean I'm dreaming Rachel's dream. Her last Dreamscape." Celeste struggled to sit upright. She leaned back, exhausted, against the wooden headrest of her bed.

"Rachel?"

"Larry's wife. Charlie and Elinor's lost daughter." She gulped the coffee Pearl had put on the bedside table. "I told you about her last night?"

Pearl nodded.

"The dream I told Larry. The one that got me fired? I know you won't believe this. I can hardly believe it myself.

Apparently, Rachel dreamed about the future, then painted it." Celeste shrugged. "Or something like that."

Celeste pulled up her knees along with the bedcovers then dropped her head into the downy nest of the comforter. She closed her eyes and there was the woman with the braid—Rachel, she now knew—kneading dough on the table in front of her, her bare elbows moving forward and back. The apron strings tied around the woman's neck and waist jiggled slightly with the movement. Then the sudden flash of lilacs blowing in the breeze outside the window. The rest of the dream flooded in. The woman gagged, struggling against something tightening around her neck, strangling her. Celeste opened her eyes to escape.

"I think that guy Rowan may have done something awful to her. Or maybe that Wolfhard guy? Someone."

"It was just a dream," said Pearl, sounding less sympathetic as she again massaged her still-searing neck.

Celeste looked over the blanketed hill of her knees. "I know. But the painting," she said, the confusion and anxiety in her voice muffled in the thick duvet.

"I don't have a clue what you're talking about." Pearl stood up and stretched. Even after a night on the couch, Jean Pearl still looked all put together. Every glossy hair in place, tracksuit without a wrinkle.

"Did I say anything? When I was dreaming?" Celeste asked. Maybe Pearl could give her a clue.

"I couldn't really understand you. You were grunting, said something . . . stopping, stomping? I'm not sure, except your voice was deep, low, like a man's voice almost."

"Yikes. Sounds like *The Exorcist*. Listen," Celeste looked up at Pearl, "I am so sorry. I didn't—"

"Never mind. Drink." Pearl pointed to the mug she'd placed on the nightstand. "Cute mermaid," she added, pointing to the tiny statue on the nightstand next to the coffee.

Celeste picked up the mug, breathing in the hot steam and the scent of cinnamon Pearl must have added. Too bad Celeste didn't go for girls; this woman would be great to have around the house. But then maybe Gloria would be the lucky one there.

"You might like to take a look at this," Pearl said, picking up the newspaper she'd dropped on the bed before Celeste assaulted her.

Celeste zeroed in on the frontpage headline: "Riverton Falls Rocked by Second Killing." Quickly, she skimmed the report on Adam, noting that the police were still labeling it "a presumed hunting accident." How could they possibly believe that? Maybe it was an official line prepared to flush out the real murderer. She was relieved to see no mention of her or Bruce beyond, "Witnesses said."

She scanned down the front page, her eye catching on "high-speed chase" in a sidebar of last-minute news. "Jake! Where is he?" The sound of the guns and the roaring engines rushed into her memory. "Is he okay?"

"Haven't gotten the full report yet."

"But Jake's okay?" She gripped Pearl's arm almost as hard as she'd grabbed her neck earlier.

"Far as I know. The other guy shot out their rear tires. Flipped the truck. Mackey and Jones found Jake and Nicole in a ditch on the side of the road. They climbed out on their own, so I'm guessing they're all right. That other car, the black one, seems to have disappeared into thin air."

"Where is Jake? I need to find him!"

"They had him, them, up at the hospital for observation, but they must have been released by now. It's after 10:00. Maybe he's still asleep too."

"But he's all right?"

"Like I said, I don't have the full story yet. You don't need to worry right now. You should stay here, try to relax. You've been through enough. How's your cheek, by the way?"

Celeste put her hand up to her face. The wound felt like a tiny zipper, bumpy with newly formed scabs. Maybe she *should* just stay in bed, behind locked doors, close out the danger.

"I have to run to work," said Pearl. "I'm on duty in half an hour."

"You're leaving me?" Celeste sat up.

"Gotta go. There's a couple of murders I need to work on today."

"Ha ha. And a funeral," Celeste called after Pearl as she headed for the front door.

"Right. And a funeral," Pearl called back. "You'll be okay? I could send someone else over. Not DeTouche, I promise." Celeste heard the door open, felt a rush of cold air seep in, pictured Pearl pausing in the doorway.

"No, but if you gotta go, you gotta go," she called from the bedroom. "I get it. I have stuff to do too."

As she left the entryway, Pearl said something Celeste couldn't hear over the sound of the door blowing closed behind her.

Celeste was alone again. The seductive smell of more coffee wafted from the kitchen, but instead of getting up, she leaned back against the pillows and flipped to the obituaries. There he was, that same pose, that same picture that had always hung on the wall in Dreamland, smiling like a kindly father, hands resting on his bulging belly. Celeste ran her eyes down the narrow Obit column, surprised the whole thing was only a couple of paragraphs. Nothing about where he'd come from, who his parents were, the usual stuff she'd read on this page. "Gifted . . ." "Loved by his many clients . . ." Who wrote this? Then: "Survived by his wife Rachel and the members of Dreamland." Really, who wrote this? "Memorial in celebration of his life today at 2:00 p.m. at the Riverton Falls Unitarian Universalist Church."

Celeste threw back the bedcovers and tossed *The Spectator* on the floor on top of the *New York Times* pile. She was hoping there would have been more, something about this Blue Wave group, Larry's life before Vermont. "Blue Wave," she repeated to herself in the shower and again as she rifled through her dresser drawers, trying to decide what to put on for the memorial. In the back of her bottom drawer, she discovered an old, favorite black sweater and a pair of black wool pants bunched up and, it seemed, long forgotten. They were quite wrinkled, but they'd look better after a couple of hours of wear. She shook them out and started getting dressed in a hurry, anxious to get to the library computer before the funeral started. She needed to find out what she could about Blue Wave Technology and perhaps this Light House project of Rachel and Rowan's.

Light House, she thought again, zipping up the pants. House of Light. The box of flashing lights at Dreamland, where she'd encountered her mermaid, the one that was on the television at Murphy's. After everything else that had happened, she'd almost forgotten about that unnerving experience. What was that? And whose voice had she heard in the background?

"Shit!" Celeste said, as she kept trying to re-create the voice she heard as the wave dissolved. It was so familiar, but she couldn't place it. There had to be a connection, some key to figuring out who killed Larry and Adam. She drank the last of the coffee in the carafe, buttoned her wool jacket over her vest, and headed out, locking the door behind her. This time she'd be prepared for whatever came at her next.

CHAPTER TWENTY-SEVEN

THE LIBRARY

Fifteen minutes later, Celeste trudged up the broad granite steps of the Riverton Falls public library and opened the heavy oak door. Warm air and the smell of leather, furniture polish, and musty old books enveloped her as she walked from the white marble foyer into the oak-paneled reading room. She loved this place. So civilized and staid; its heavy velvet curtains, brass-studded club car chairs, and long wooden reading tables seemed to have been there since the grand building was constructed over a hundred years earlier.

Today the library was a welcome oasis, a place of calm in the midst of the craziness that seemed to have overtaken the town since Larry's murder. Celeste headed to the front desk to get her name on the computer sign-up list, hoping she wouldn't have to wait too long to use one.

This might be the last time anyway. She'd no longer be part of the Dreamer e-mail threads, and she'd lost touch with her other friends still out there traveling the world. Larry had convinced her she didn't need them anymore.

"Good morning!" chirped Joanie, her favorite librarian who seemed both chipper and harried, as usual. "What happened to your face? Are you okay?"

"Lucky shot. At least for me," answered Celeste, running her fingers over her cheek again.

"And Victor told us he saw you in the police car!"

Celeste remembered the surprised gasp of the other librarian, Victor, at the stoplight while she sat trapped in the back of Wally's car. "I didn't do it. Didn't kill either one of them."

"Oh, we knew that!" Joanie smiled, her round blue eyes open wide. "We have our own theories."

Joanie and Victor read more mysteries in a week than Celeste read in a year, and now here was a real live one, right on their doorstep. Joanie leaned across the desk and whispered, "We think it might be *two* murderers! Victor and I are almost sure of it!" She leaned further forward and whispered in Celeste's ear. "I don't think it was Adam. He was weird, but a murderer? He seemed so gentle."

"Did you know him?"

"He was here almost every evening, a real whiz on the computers! Not like most of those . . . less fortunate folks we have. Says in the paper a 'hunting accident,' but we can't help but wonder if it wasn't one of those cult people?" She glanced over her shoulder at Victor, who was picking white hairs off his "Curiosity Killed the Cat" sweatshirt.

He looked up through his thick-lensed, round glasses and nodded. "Maybe one of them thought Adam killed Larry and was out for revenge?" Victor said, an edge of glee in his voice. "Crimes of passion! Lots of passion!" He rubbed his hands together, a smile lighting up his round, impish face.

Celeste frowned. "I don't get it. You think Larry's was a crime of passion, and Adam's was what? Wrongful revenge?"

"Exactly!" They both nodded vigorously.

"I mean, who kills someone with a crystal? Doesn't sound premeditated to me!" said Victor.

"Okay. Hadn't thought of that."

Joanie pushed the computer sign-up sheet across the broad circulation desk toward Celeste. "A computer should be free in a few minutes." She nodded toward the two long tables, four terminals on each, in the midst of the tall, polished wooden shelves of books and DVDs. Every seat at the tables was occupied. A couple of greasy-haired teens, a young mom nursing her baby, and several of Riverton's elders peered closely at the bright screens, reading whatever they'd brought up.

Celeste wandered into the brightly lit reading room to wait. The library seemed particularly crowded with Riverton's peculiar conglomeration of street people. Joanie had her hands full keeping down the scuffles over club chairs and outdated magazines as the regulars settled in to wait out the day in the library's comforting warmth.

Celeste sat down at a table and pulled the brass chain to turn on the green-shaded lamp. She rummaged through her pack and pulled out the long, skinny reporter's notebook she kept on hand in case Reggie or Tony actually asked her to write another article someday. She jotted down the thoughts that had been circling her mind, trying to make some sense of the last two days. Joanie and Victor might be right. Two killers. Adam and . . . the guy in the car? The Dreamers? Jake? She shook her head, trying to erase Gloria's description of Jake's truck heading up Beaver Pond Road toward Dreamland in the middle of the night.

Come on, Cel. Drowning in denial as usual, Larry scoffed somewhere inside her left ear. *All systems point to Jake. Am I right? Ring in his pocket, rifle in his truck?*

Celeste bit into the yellow pencil, tasting wood and paint. She had to stop circling back to Jake. He was probably still with Nicole, nursing her wounds. She shook her head again to clear it of her vision of them clinging to each other there in the overturned truck.

Frustrated, she drew a large circle on the page and colored it in, pushing the pencil so hard she almost ripped through the paper. What was the connection between Larry and Adam? Was it strong enough to incite a crime of passion, as Victor surmised? And what did Larry have to do with the guy in the SUV? A big black hole. That's what she was facing, a black hole sucking in everything, leaving her with nowhere to stand. Unmoored, unable to find their footing, she remembered Elinor saying about the Doubters.

The ancient radiators hissed and clanked, jerking Celeste out of her funk.

Joanie tapped her on the shoulder. "I've got a computer available for you."

She looked up from the notebook. "Joanie, did you notice, ever, what Adam was doing on the computer? What he was searching for?"

Joanie hesitated then shook her head. "Sorry, Celeste, I couldn't tell you even if I had."

Celeste understood. She didn't want to push Joanie into some illegal library territory. Still, Joanie seemed to know everything about everybody in town. She must have at least been curious about Adam, especially if he was in the library so often.

Celeste took her place at the one free terminal, next to a paunchy middle-aged man scrolling idly through Match.com. She signed in to her e-mail account and shot Gloria a quick message. "At library. Pick me up on way to funeral?" Then she clicked on the circle icon with the blue G on the screen. She knew how to get onto the web, but she still wasn't great at finding what she wanted. She typed in "Blue Wave." The rainbow-colored wheel spun around for a couple of seconds before delivering what looked like dozens of pages of hits. Blue Wave seemed to be a popular name, especially for pool products. Celeste scrolled through quickly. The memorial started in less than an hour and she'd have to leave soon if she hoped to get a seat. She figured the chapel would fill quickly with Larry's grieving clients.

"Joanie! I need you!" she called in a loud whisper.

Joanie knew exactly how to set up the search. In seconds she found what Celeste had been looking for—"Future Bright for Blue Wave Technology," *Wired*, June 1995.

There it was! She clicked on the article and read: "'With McNeil on board, we believe we're close to a major breakthrough in the presentation and applications of virtual reality, overcoming many of the technical problems that plagued the promising technology in the 1980s,' boasted President Lawrence Blatsky at a press conference. 'McNeil is a game changer for us.'"

Celeste scrolled down the page until she saw a small black-and-white photo. Zooming in, she looked hard at the grainy image of a group assembled in a line beneath a banner that read RIDE THE BLUE WAVE! In the middle of the row sat a woman, a girl really, in a pantsuit, big glasses, and a tight-curled perm that made her look like a brunette Lamb Chop. Yup: Nicole. And to her left: a smiling, deeply tanned, bleach-blond Larry, his rumpled, button-down shirt open halfway down to his navel, chest hair curling out the gap, head cocked toward Nicole. There was something unsettling about him even then, she thought, something hard and a little cruel in those eyes.

You're projecting! Larry's voice needled her again. Celeste tried to tune him out, just like she was trying to tune out the strange low hum of voices that penetrated the library from outside. She looked out the window above the clanking radiator and saw a crowd gathering in front of the church. Dozens of people clutched at their mufflers and hats in the wind.

She moved the cursor to the girl on Nicole's right. Hair pulled back from her face into a braid that hung over her shoulder: Rachel, it had to be. Celeste stared at her, recognizing Charlie's high forehead, Elinor's aquiline nose. She peered closer, pulled in by a frisson of recognition, a sense of connection to this girl, the artist whose dream kept invading her nights. She wanted to read Rachel's eyes, but there within the picture's frame they seemed focused on something far away from wherever this photo had been taken almost two decades earlier.

Celeste turned her attention to the man standing behind Nicole: Jake. Even given this thinner, unlined version of his face, Celeste recognized his eyes—the way they sloped down at the outer corners—the soft fullness of his lips, his dark hair falling to his shoulders. He looked like a kid. But then, he would've been barely twenty when this photo was taken. Next to Jake: a younger Charlie, his hand on Rachel's shoulder.

Finally, she moved the cursor down to study the man on the other side of Rachel. Short, like Larry, but thin and wiry, he wore a rumpled bowling shirt, the name "Don" embroidered on the pocket. She zoomed in on his large, dark eyes, staring at her as they had two days ago on the sidewalk in Riverton Falls.

"Oh my God!" she said out loud. The rest of the people sharing her same table looked up from their screens, puzzled.

"You okay?" asked the Match.com guy next to her, eyes still glued to his own screen.

"I think so," Celeste answered, moving the cursor to read the string of names listed in the caption below the photo. "*Front row, left to right:* Lawrence Blatsky, Nicole Tromblay Kelly, Rachel Blatsky, Rowan McNeil. *Standing:* Jacob Kelly, Charlie Garrison."

"Twenty more minutes," Joanie whispered behind her. "Sorry! Got a long waiting list today."

Celeste looked up, startled. "It's him!" She pointed to the picture on the screen. "Adam."

Joanie leaned over her shoulder and peered at the photo. "Could be. Hard to tell without the dreadlocks."

"But those eyes! It's him!"

"Cute," Joanie giggled, "but twenty more minutes!"

"I know." Celeste turned her focus again to the screen and clicked back to the search results, wondering what else would come up. There were several links leading to articles written by Rowan himself. "Light House: The Real Magical Mystery Tour," "The VR Promise of Peace: Standing in Each Other's Moccasins." Also links to various interviews, most proclaiming Rowan to be the mystical master of virtual reality.

She quickly skimmed a couple of the hits. Her breath caught as she read, "According to McNeil, with the invention of the Light House, we can walk in each other's dreams, share the beauty and magic of our inner lives. We will have the ability to re-create the intricacies of our minds, helping us see across generations, through cultural boundaries. Using visual imagery, we can share ourselves—in ways that transcend words—to overcome the shortfalls of spoken language. We will truly understand what is lodged in each other's hearts as well as in our own. But, warns McNeil, 'technology must be developed with tenderness, kindness, and love,'" words Celeste had never seen connected with computers before. "Technology will either trap us or free us. The struggle between these two outcomes will be the defining issue of the 21st century."

Then her eyes fell on a link that made her shiver. "Where in the World is Rowan McNeil? MacArthur Genius Award Winner Missing." She opened it. "Last seen in 2003, McNeil disappeared after publishing a final manifesto on his website.

Broken-hearted that virtual reality programs and the Light House technology he developed had been sold to the Pentagon for military training by German-based Hermann Industries, McNeil left behind these words before disappearing: 'Dreams crushed, I fly, far from you, Reality, with your bombs and your bluster. Above down under, spirited away, let me float on waves of music, dance with the puppets of skin.'"

Definitely Adam-speak, thought Celeste. Puppets of skin must be *wayang kulit* puppets, Javanese shadow puppets! So he did go to Indonesia. Above down under—of course. The kretek!

She scrolled further and found, at the bottom, a picture labeled "Last known photo of Rowan McNeil." Only it wasn't Rowan. It was Adam, his dreads still tight, little, slightly fuzzy cornrows, his clothes still neat, presentable. Somehow he seemed to be transitioning into the tarot reader even before he'd disappeared. But how and why had he sunk so low? She clicked back to the Blue Wave window, wondering if there was more about Rowan's departure, finding on the third page, "Blue Wave Crashes on Rocky Shore." Hurriedly, with only a few minutes remaining in her allotted computer time, she clicked it open and quickly skimmed the article that said in-fighting and internal tumult as much as the dot-com crash led to the demise of the company. Celeste scrolled down further and found a photo at the bottom of the page. *"Wolfhard Hermann, Blue Wave CEO."*

"Hey, Celeste!" a loud voice jerked Celeste's attention away from the screen. She spun around to see Gloria in her purple coat and explosive red hair flame into the room. Under her eyes, hints of blue bruises from her collision with the steering wheel the night before.

"Sssh!!! It's a library!" one of the teens said, barely glancing up from his video game.

"Whoops! Sorry!" Gloria lowered her voice to a loud library whisper.

"You won't believe this!" Celeste hissed back. "Look!"

Gloria peered over her shoulder at the picture of the tall, gaunt man wearing a white linen suit that hung on him as if there were no body underneath. Square black-rimmed glasses covered half his hollow-cheeked face. She leaned toward the screen, her eyes squinting to read. "Wolfhard Hermann."

"It's him! He was at Larry's office! I saw him! And last night at the bar! He's the guy in the car!"

"You're sure? This guy?"

Celeste nodded hard. "Wait. There's more. How do I get back to a couple of screens ago?"

"You really are pathetic," said Gloria as she clicked expertly back to the Blue Wave team picture, then moved her finger under the list, reading off the names. "Look at that perm! God. Jake was a hottie though." She moved the cursor over the name Rowan McNeil, her eyes tracking from the words to the photo.

"Look closer! It's Adam! Adam was Rowan McNeil!" Celeste was frantic.

"And the Wolfman followed him here?"

"I don't know! Something brought them both here. Something that has to do with Larry."

"And Jake and Nicole. Can you make a copy of that?" asked Gloria, bouncing on her feet, anxious to get out the door. "We've got to give it to Pearl. But hurry! All hell's breaking loose outside. If we want to get into that church, we need to get moving. If you're right about this Wolfman, then there's a good chance he'll be there. I don't think he's giving up his hunt yet."

"Last guy I want to run into. First guy being Jake."

"Okay, so get a move on!"

Dragged from the world of the search engine, Celeste clicked "log out" and ran to the printer. She grabbed the pages as they emerged, paid Victor for them, then followed Gloria to the door, shoving her arms into the sleeves of her coat as she went.

Across the street, it looked like the entire town had amassed on the steps and lawn of the white-steepled church. The low background noise Celeste had been trying to ignore while she read the articles had turned to a roar. Men and women jostled each other as they shoved their way to the front of the crowd to get into the church.

"What's going on, Glor? Has everyone gone crazy?"

"Looks like. Follow me!" she said, charging headlong into the crowd, dragging Celeste behind her.

CHAPTER TWENTY-EIGHT

THE FUNERAL

"This is a mob scene!" Celeste yelled so Gloria could hear her over the rumble of the crowd now shoving its collective way toward the tall white double doors of the church. "No way everyone's going to squeeze inside! We could just skip this, right?" Even though they were still on the far edge of the mob, Celeste's chest tightened. She wasn't going to be able to breathe. There wouldn't be a way out of the church. She'd be trapped inside, trapped in the crushing crowd.

"I can do this," she said to herself, linking arms with Gloria. Together, they tried to squeeze through the roiling mass of mourners toward the broad flight of stairs leading up to the closed doors. An elbow jabbed Celeste in the ribs. A heavy boot landed on her toes. She took a deep breath, inhaling the smell of wet wool, patchouli, and body odor as they inched forward.

Who were these people? Larry couldn't possibly have had this many clients. They all looked vaguely familiar though, people she passed on the street every day. To distract herself from the panic rising in her chest, she sought faces she knew. To her right she could see Allegra's hennaed topknot bobbing as she struggled to hold her place in the surge, and in front of her, the Thai woman who owned the Buddhist laundry. The bucktoothed, pot-bellied chiropractor sporting a fresh crew cut pushed at her from behind. The whole town seemed to be here.

Celeste tipped her head back, concentrating on the wide pewter bowl of November sky surrounding the church spire instead of on the gray-faced crowd bunching and jostling around her. She opened her mouth and let the cold air filter in. "It's okay," she said out loud to herself, gathering her courage. She shoved Gloria past a long-haired earth mother with her baby strapped to her chest.

"Hey!" Gloria looked up, a scowl on her face. "Watch it!"

They'd reached the bottom of the flight of stairs in front, close enough to see Karin peeking from the inside out through the gap in the church doors to survey the crowd.

"I wonder if she'll let us in. Those Dreamers still want to believe I killed him!" Celeste bent down and yelled in Gloria's ear.

"The only way to change their minds is to get in there and find the person who actually did," Gloria yelled back. "That Wolfman, if you ask me!"

"And you think he'll show up?"

Gloria stood on tiptoes to yell in Celeste's ear. "Why not? Looks like everyone else in Riverton is here! You know, returning to the scene of the crime and all that jazz. Probably still out to get us, so keep your eyes open! I'm sure he's here somewhere!"

"The only person I want to find is Jake," Celeste yelled back.

By now the two women had almost reached the door where Karin in her long green Dreamer robe stood, trying to stem the tide of mourners, allowing in only two at a time through the narrow opening she guarded between the immense front doors.

As Celeste and Gloria reached the top step, finally in position to breach the barricade, Karin gave them a sour smile.

"I wouldn't let you in if I hadn't been given explicit instructions to make sure you were here before we start. God knows why, but hurry!"

"Nicole told you to let us in?" Celeste asked.

"Nicole? No, Sarabande. What does it matter? Get in here!" Karin pushed them inside, then called out over the heads of the crowd, "That's it! No more room!" in a voice deeper and louder than Celeste imagined she could muster. "People, people! We've got speakers and video screens set up around the building and in the parking lot."

Celeste followed behind Gloria as they each squeezed through the doors, just before Karin slammed them closed behind her with a harsh clang, muffling the moans and protests from the crowd. Karin turned the bolt to shut the rest of the mob out. Their feet thundered back down the staircase, and the throng rushed on to the next-best viewing opportunity, leaving only the familiar voices of *Rag* reporters Reggie and Tony yelling as they pounded vigorously on the doors.

"Celeste!" Reggie's baritone called. "We're counting on you to get the story!"

Right, she thought, exactly what I had in mind, taking notes while I search for a murderer.

Inside the packed chapel, mourners with long faces sat, jammed hip to hip, shoulder to shoulder, in the polished pews, and dozens more leaned against the walls, while the overflow squeezed into the narrow vestibule in the rear, overheating now, their coats hanging open, knitted caps in their hands. The air had quickly grown humid and warm with the combination of body heat, concentrated breathing, and damp wraps, which everyone seemed to have left on having no room to remove them. Celeste scanned the room for the skeletal Wolfman. No luck. No sign of Jake either.

"Look, there's Wally and Pearl over there." Gloria gestured with her chin toward the right wall. The two cops sat on the deep ledge beneath the stained-glass window depicting Jesus surrounded by an adoring crowd of children.

Celeste squared her shoulders and took a deep breath, still fighting the sense of suffocation in the stuffy chapel. She looked up again, this time at the white vaulted ceiling, trying to gain a false sense of airy spaciousness. She counted the recessed lights. Eleven, twelve, fourteen. And the arms of the forged iron chandeliers. Five, six, seven, eight. Then the small black boxes—like she'd noticed at Murphy's—mounted in each of the ceiling's four corners.

"What are you doing?" asked Gloria following her gaze.

"Those things up there," she whispered to Gloria, pointing up to each corner.

"Speakers?"

"Maybe." Music was certainly coming from somewhere. She looked down the center aisle to the raised stage in the front of the chapel where golden organ pipes gleamed, reaching toward heaven from their peach-colored alcove. It took her a moment to recognize Sarabande sitting there at the keyboard, playing along to a piped-in recording of the Everly Brothers crooning "All I Have to Do Is Dream." Sara seemed so tiny, swallowed in her purple robe, but there was something commanding about the way she sat, ramrod straight, her elbows pumping vigorously up and down. In the pews, people hummed and softly sang along, swaying ever so slightly on the overfilled benches that seemed to creak in rhythm with the disconcerting organ music.

"How are we going to find a seat?" Celeste asked Gloria as they moved forward.

"Don't worry, I've got some saved," Gloria said, grabbing Celeste by the wrist and pulling her down the aisle to the front. As they made their way forward, a wave of whispered *Celeste*s washed through the pews. She blushed and put her hand up to cover the scabby wound on her cheek, unable to keep from looking ashamed or guilty. How appropriate: the two emotions Larry loved to stir up in her. The three front pews to the right, still empty, had been roped off with a golden chord from which hung a hand-printed sign that read RESERVED FOR DREAMERS.

"Wait, we're not sitting with them!" Celeste pulled back, but Gloria kept tugging, dragging her forward through the whispers, the stares, and now the peppy strains of "Daydream Believer" groaning from the organ pipes.

"They're over there."

Celeste followed the line of Gloria's finger pointing across the aisle to the front pew, marked with another printed sign: RESERVED FOR FAMILY. Charlie and Elinor, bundled in their puffy down coats, caps askew on their heads, turned and urgently beckoned toward the two women as they scooted over to make room.

"Family? We're going to be Larry's family?" This was more alarming than sitting with the Dreamers.

"Best seats in the house," Gloria said, sliding onto the polished pine bench. She kissed Elinor on the cheek then reached across to shake hands with Charlie.

As Gloria leaned forward, Elinor leaned back and said to Celeste, "We're hoping Rachel might turn up today." She stretched her arm along the pew, and Celeste grasped her hand. "That's why we came. Hoping she felt safe enough to return now. But I don't see her anywhere." She shook her head and sighed.

"Greetings, Celeste." Charlie nodded in her direction. "I told her it was a long shot. Then again, you never know, do you?"

"Maybe she came late. Maybe she's still outside? There are a lot of people out there," Celeste said.

Charlie nodded again, but she could tell he had given up what little hope he'd come in with.

"Why the black eyes?" he asked Gloria.

"Your man Wolfhard, or Wolfman, as Gloria calls him," Celeste answered for her friend. "After we left your place last night, he tried to run us off the road. He must have been staked out there, waiting for us."

Charlie's ragged eyebrows shot up. "Wolfhard, here?"

"Then he went on a rampage in the middle of town," Gloria added. "He tried to shoot Jake and Nicole."

"What are you talking about? Wolfhard? In Riverton Falls?" asked Elinor.

Gloria only had time to nod before the lights in the chapel dimmed, and both the music and the buzz of voices around them died away.

From the wings on either side of the organ, the Dreamers trooped in, their flowing jewel-toned robes like a rainbow in the church filled with mourners in more somber colors. The two groups converged in the center of the dais, arranging themselves in front of the organ, and began to sing the Cranberries "Dreams." To Celeste, the words made perfect sense. Larry had changed her life in every possible way. And all around her nothing was quite as it seemed. Not today. And maybe not ever again.

The song finished and the choir walked silently down the broad steps to the empty pews reserved for them across from Celeste and Gloria. The crowd stirred, rustling in their seats as the Romano sisters went around the chapel pulling the heavy velvet curtains closed across the windows. The lights lowered until the chapel was completely dark.

A spotlight above the stage lit the center aisle as the

opening riff of Aerosmith's "Dream On" filled the room. Steven Tyler's searing voice rose as all heads turned to the rear of the chapel. Bill, Andrew, Bruce, and Sequoia, draped in floor-length red velvet capes, glided effortlessly toward the dais. They joined hands in a circle then sank slowly to their knees, humming and moaning in discordant, primeval voices, as if all the pain of a thousand years was flowing through them into the church. As they swayed back and forth, their capes loosened from their shoulders and fell, puddling on the floor around them like pools of blood. The four men rose, completely naked now, and holding hands they began to circle, faster and faster to the beat of the music, their floppy bellies and flaccid penises flapping as they turned. Then, just as Celeste thought they might lift off into the stratosphere, they gave a collective sob and collapsed on the floor together in a shuddering heap.

Celeste tried hard not to giggle, but she couldn't stop the hiccups and gasps from escaping her. From across the aisle, Ingrid shot her a dirty look. It only made her laugh harder. Celeste bit down on her tongue. Behind her a few other nervous titters spiked through the trance the mourners seemed to be entering.

From the hidden entry by the organ, Nicole appeared. Even in the low light, Celeste could see the toll the last few days had taken. Her peachy skin looked blotchy. Her eyes were swollen from crying. Dark bruises surrounded them and a bandage bridged her nose. She must have hit her face in the crash.

Nicole walked over to the lump of naked men and pulled their robes over their shoulders like a mother covering her shivering children. The last strains of the song faded away. As if on cue, the men rose and stepped down to join the other Dreamers in the front rows. Nicole now stood alone on the stage, her dark hair and long white gown glowing in the spotlight. The chapel was silent, everyone waiting for her to speak.

Instead of stepping up behind the altar, as Celeste expected, Nicole threw back her arms and head, opening her chest to the ceiling as if offering her heart as a sacrifice. Then she began to sing, her voice like a cracked bell, "Dreamweaver." As she reached the final chorus, the Dreamers in the front three rows rose and picked up the tune. Their voices, filled with grief and longing, resounded through the chapel as they pleaded to be helped through the night. Celeste's throat closed, her giggles overcome by a stab of pain. From behind her came dozens of deep, wrenching sobs.

As the song's final chords echoed to silence, Nicole turned. Instead of stepping down to join the Dreamers in their pews, she disappeared back through the exit next to the organ.

Sarabande now stood up from the organ bench and turned to survey the chapel. She stared at all the people squeezed together in the pews, crowded along the walls, spilling into the vestibule. For a moment, she let the tension build. Then she lifted the hem of her purple robe and strode purposefully to the altar at the left corner of the dais. The lights in the chapel came up, just enough so she could be seen in the twilit room.

"What's she doing up there? Shouldn't this be Nicole's show?" Gloria whispered to Celeste.

"Larry has left us." Sarabande shook her head. Her black ringlets danced around her face. Her high, clear voice caressed the crowd. "We are fumbling, naked children, orphaned by evil. Larry loved us all. Every single one of us. We were the reason for Larry's life, and he was the director of ours."

The sounds of sobs and noses being blown rippled through the chapel.

"Larry left each of us some powerful lessons and insights. He also left us a dream of his own—that someday we would reach beyond ourselves into a new realm of possibility, guided by the archetypes through the poison of our Demon Minds into the healing light of the Spirit. You may wonder now how you will ever reach that state of joy and perfection so beautifully mirrored for each of us by Larry."

Joy and perfection? Celeste thought. Larry?

"How will we continue on our own, you wonder."

Now the sobs grew deeper, the pews trembled beneath the shaking mourners, and someone behind Celeste began to wail like an abandoned baby. "Don't despair!" Sarabande raised her arms. "Larry lives on!"

"Oh, dear God, no!" Elinor whimpered.

"Though he may not be here in body, Larry has left us a legacy, a magnificent gift he was about to unveil just before he was . . ." Sarabande gulped hard, looked down at the altar, and then raised her eyes to the multitude before her. In an even stronger voice, she continued: "And though Larry is no longer physically with us to share in the joy of its release, his power is still available to each of us through the wonders of technology."

"Oh my God, this can't be happening," Charlie mumbled under his breath, shaking his head back and forth, squeezing his hands into tight fists.

"Quiet!" Elinor reached out and grabbed his arm. "We need to hear what she's saying. We need to know what he's done with—"

Done with what? thought Celeste, glancing at Gloria, who looked as puzzled as she felt.

"Close your eyes, all of you," Sarabande said. "I want you to reach back into your dreams."

Celeste dutifully closed her eyes as the lights dimmed to darkness again. She tried to conjure up a dream that wasn't *that* dream. Instead of apron strings, she forced herself to remember another dream—a dream of standing inside an Indian palace of yellowed ivory, its openwork walls carved fine as lace, sunlight streaming through them. Next to her stood Jake . . .

"What are you doing?" Gloria shoved her. "Now's the time to look around the room and see if Wolfman is here!"

"Whoops!" said Celeste. She turned to look behind her, her eyes adjusting to the semi-darkness, straining to comb the pews as fast as she could.

"Jake," said Gloria, pointing to the rear of the chapel, where he sat, looking around the room just like they were.

Celeste tried to catch his eye, noticing the long row of stitches that ran down the side of his cheek, almost a match for her own wound. At last, his wandering gaze met Celeste's, and for a long moment, he looked straight into her eyes as if the crowd in the pews between them didn't exist. A shock of deep connection surged through her body, a reverberation she'd been missing since the day he'd walked out. She'd been so afraid they'd lost it. But here it was ringing through every fiber of her body, like the chime of a giant Japanese temple bell, pure and true. She stared back at him. She wanted him to know how much she wished she could reach for him, how much the last three days had scared her and made her need him more than she ever believed she could.

As she stared at Jake, she gradually became aware of another pair of eyes staring at her over Jake's shoulder. Blue and cold as glaciers, they peered out from the shadow of a brown hood. Celeste's hand shot up to cover her wounded cheek. She opened her mouth and yelled "Jake! Behind you!"

But her words were drowned out as Larry's voice filled the chapel.

CHAPTER TWENTY-NINE

THE LAST OF LARRY

"*Hi, my name's Larry Blatsky, and I'm here to change your life.*" A wave of surprise and shock washed over the faces behind her as hundreds of eyes flew open. Celeste spun around to the front. There he was—a larger-than-life Larry—sitting behind his desk, hands folded over his belly. He wore a white linen sports coat and a tightly knotted string tie, something she'd never imagined him in. Pete perched on his shoulder, nodding and bobbing his blue head.

Larry leaned forward, placing his folded arms on the desk, and Pete pecked at his back-combed thatch of blond hair. Larry looked out as if to survey the audience, and for a second Celeste felt he was looking right at her. Then, with an all-too-familiar creak from his chair, he stood up, strode out from behind his desk, and opened his arms to embrace his own mourners.

"What?" "How?" Question after question, punctuated with gasps of awe and disbelief, buzzed through the church. Elinor began to sob.

"It's a hologram!" hissed Charlie, as he tried to console Elinor, patting her gently on the back. "See how the edges shimmer? Must be projecting from somewhere in here."

With all eyes now glued on the front of the chapel, the Dreamers and the skeptics and the simply curious of Riverton Falls waited to see what this shining version of Larry would do next. As Celeste turned and looked toward the back of the room, she noticed Arun, atop a ladder, fiddling with the projector. With her eyes she traced the path of the single beam of light it emitted to the spot where it landed: a small spinning mirror Sarabande must have surreptitiously placed in front of the dais while most of the audience had closed their eyes.

In the pews across the aisle, the Dreamers' facial expressions morphed from mournful to confused and puzzled. Ingrid whispered to Bill, who nodded in agreement so fast and hard it looked like his neck would snap. Bruce shot abruptly to his feet, jostling his eyeglasses, and Karin tugged insistently on his arm to get him to sit down. Andrew's bony shoulders hunched almost to his carroty curls. Clearly, they had no idea what was going on either. Up on the stage, to the right of Larry, Sarabande stood pressed against the wall, hands behind her back, a triumphant smile across her froggy, freckled face.

Hologram Larry sat on the edge of his desk, waiting.

"*Happy day!*" Pete's familiar squawk filled the chapel.

"*Happy day is right, Pete!*" said Larry. His voice had the same shimmering edge as his holographic body. "*Hello to all of you out there! Today I'm here to tell you about an amazing invention that has been years in the making and is now available to each and every one of you.*" This wasn't the scruffy Larry she knew. He was a younger, thinner, smoother version of himself, and more like some kind of fake actor-doctor from an aspirin commercial or in one of those infomercials on TV. And as sincere and loving as this Larry kept trying to look, Celeste realized he wasn't speaking to her or to any of them. He must have been talking into a camera, probably reading from a teleprompter. And when he spoke, he used the formal voice she'd only heard him use inside the big box at Dreamland. Obviously, he had no idea that this video, or whatever it was, would eventually debut at his own funeral!

"What you are about to see might seem miraculous, beyond your imagination, but I assure you, it is real. I'm about to reveal an invention that will change not only your life, but possibly life as we know it."

Hologram Larry took a step forward to the front of the stage. The power of Larry pulsed through the chapel, eliciting more gasps and longing sighs from the packed church. Looking up from her seat in the front pew, Celeste felt like she was back in that little folding chair in front of his desk, waiting for judgment. Her limbs went loose with fear as he seemed to look directly into her eyes.

"It's not real," said Gloria quietly as Celeste stiffened next to her. She linked her fingers through Celeste's.

"What's going on?" Elinor whispered to Charlie.

Behind them someone hissed, "SHHHH!"

"For over twenty years, I have been working on a way to combine the power of dreams with the wonders of technology. I imagined a way to revolutionize the way we human beings understand and communicate with each other, a way for us to walk, so to speak, in each other's moccasins."

Rowan's words, Celeste realized.

"With the help of my colleagues, soon-to-be world-famous coders, Sarabande and Arun Roy"—Sarabande and Arun both waved at the audience—*"I have found a way for each of us to*

actually enter dreams, not only imagine them or remember them, but actually experience them in our waking life, to learn from them ourselves, and to reach out and share them with others through the wonders of virtual reality."

Larry strode back and forth across the stage as if he were a professor in front of a class.

"It's called Dreamscape Adventures, and it's going to change everything." He stopped and looked out at the awestruck crowd, or at least Hologram Larry appeared to look out at the crowd. He seemed so real, sounded so much like Larry on a good day that it was hard not to believe he had actually been resurrected.

"Now, friends, I'm not talking about some simple, isolating headset like that Oculus Rift. I'm talking about a full-on, whole body experience we can share together. No headsets needed. My Dreamscape projection system can transform almost any room into a magical mystery tour!" At this, Hologram Larry turned and flung his arms wide for emphasis. *"A technological trip that will, I guarantee, blow your mind. Think of it as the twenty-first-century hallucinogen that will bring you closer to the mysteries of the cosmos and help you understand the workings of your own soul."*

The church buzzed with whispers. The Dreamers still looked dumbstruck.

"Thief! That was Rachel and Rowan's idea," said Elinor, the knuckles on her tightly clasped hands white with her fury. "The Light House!"

"And the best part, my friends, is that over the past decade, I have captured hundreds of dreams on a new digital format with the help of Dreamscape Computing and an incredible group of believers. For years, I have nurtured a very special band of dreamers, guiding them along their sacred inner paths to find what I call the Big Dreams, the dreams that have helped them overcome major stumbling blocks in their own lives. I've seen men and women afflicted with crippling anxiety and fear fight their demons and

emerge victorious into the rainbow of joy. I've seen others who had closed their injured hearts against the world but who—through our work together in the Dreamscape—have now been healed through the power of dreams."

He means *me*, Celeste thought, squirming in her seat, tiring of the hard, uncomfortable pew.

Larry walked back behind his desk and sat down. *"Their effort has yielded a special copyrighted package to go along with your Dreamscape Adventure system.*

"Rather than spending years and thousands of dollars in therapy, now—for an introductory price of only $1,500—you can jump right into these Big Dreams, let them heal you as they have healed their originators."

"He's selling our dreams!" Celeste exclaimed out loud. That's why Larry had had her sign that release. To steal her dreams!

"If you can't be quiet, you should leave!" the shushing woman behind her whispered, spraying spittle on Celeste's neck.

". . . have transformed these Big Dreams into something the world has been waiting for. Today, right here and now, my friends, you will witness the release of Dreamscape Adventures!"

"Hit it, Arun!" Sarabande called to the back of the chapel. Instantly, with the flick of Arun's remote, the vision of Larry disappeared.

The buzz of anticipation only grew louder in the pews behind Celeste, but the Dreamers across the aisle simply sat there, transfixed, staring silently with wide, incredulous eyes, as if frozen in place. Echoes of Larry's words reverberated from the speakers outside on the church lawn.

Arun called back, "Ready!"

Celeste looked back and watched him aim the remote control at each of the little black boxes up high in the four corners of the chapel, the ones she'd noticed earlier. One after the other, they lit up. Suddenly the room filled with dazzling color and cosmic, New Age music. The walls, the floor, even the ceiling— the entire chapel seemed to be swallowed up in swirling blue light that gradually coalesced into one giant wave, towering above the awestruck mourners—like the blue wave that had engulfed Murphy's the day before! Celeste's wave! Beneath the curl of the wave's frothy crest, a string of words appeared in italic script: *Blue Wave Technology Presents Dreamscape Adventures! Produced by Hermann Industries. Directed and edited by Blatsky and Roy.*

Instantly, another image appeared, transforming the walls of the chapel into bleachers in a huge stadium. Crowds roared "Larry! Larry!" In the center stood a second holographic Larry wearing a toga, a crown of olive leaves around his head, his arms raised, huge smile splitting his face. A growling holographic lion in the distance bared its teeth and rushed toward Larry from behind, ready to attack. Screams flooded the chapel. But Larry turned, opened his arms, and the lion became a marmalade-orange kitten, purring, rubbing in circles around his ankles.

More dreams followed. On the rear wall, Celeste walked hand in hand with a tall black man draped in vibrant African robes on a grassy cliff overlooking the sea, a dream she had had right after joining the Dreamscape. Bill and Ingrid tangoed across the ceiling. Barb held tight to Angus as they rode a green dragon all around the chapel.

The scenes were all too familiar. These were the reenacted dreams Arun and Sarabande had videotaped at Dreamland! Somehow, they'd transformed those silly psychodramas into life-like, three-dimensional virtual reality. Celeste marveled at the scenes as they rolled along, one dream flowing into another, changing every couple of minutes. They seemed so real, it was almost impossible to believe they weren't. Just like dreams—or nightmares—when you're stuck in the middle of them.

Then the room went dark. Quiet returned. The crowd sat waiting as the projectors whirred then clunked. Seconds later, across the golden organ pipes appeared a translucent banner that read Larry's Private Back-up. The banner faded as several different images appeared around the room. These dreams were something else completely—the kind of ugly, horrifying dreams you hoped no one would ever knew you'd had.

"Something's wrong! Someone messed with our disc!" Arun called to Sarabande.

Celeste looked up and saw herself, chained to a post while a naked Bruce danced in a frenzy around her, a hungry grin across his face. A mortified screech from the real Bruce ripped through the room. On the right-hand wall, caged children wailed and wept as Karin waltzed in front of them, eating from a basket of giant strawberries, red juice running down her chin. Across from her, bigger than life, Bill and Ingrid threw crystal goblets at each other, bloody and wincing as shards of broken glass tore their skin to ribbons.

"Stop it!" Sarabande shrieked. "What's happening?!"

Wails filled the chapel, some emanating from the projected dreams themselves, others from the bewildered, frightened spectators. The Dreamers, the people actually in the horrific nightmares cascading through the chapel, clutched at each other, their faces contorted with confusion and anger. Ingrid clung to Bill. Andrew tore at his orange hair, repeating over and over, "He stole them. He stole our dreams!"

Over it all, Celeste could hear Sarabande yelling at Arun, "Turn it off!"

Hers was the voice Celeste had heard at Murphy's!

Arun called back, panicked, "I can't! Someone's sabotaged us!" He held the useless remote, pointing it at each of the projectors, punching buttons in vain.

Now another, single dream appeared, spreading across all four walls of the church. Celeste's dream. No, Rachel's dream. The room fell silent again. The woman in the apron, kneading bread on the counter in front of her, her long brown braid swinging with the motion. Outside the window a hedge of lilac blooms tossed in the wind.

"Rachel!" Elinor called out, her voice cracking.

On the church ceiling, a dark shadowy figure of a stocky man glided slowly, silently toward the woman, closer, closer, until he was right behind her. He raised his arms. Clutched in his fists, strung tautly from one to the other, a piece of twine. He swung his arms up high over the woman's head, then dropped them down onto her narrow shoulders and quickly, savagely wrapped the twine around her neck, pulling tight, then tighter, until the woman stopped her struggle and sank to the floor. Up on the ceiling, the shadow turned around. Now everyone below could see a face—Larry's face!—twisted into a demented grin. He stared straight into the crowd of mourners.

The church chandeliers blazed overhead, breaking through the darkness. The horrible image disappeared, leaving the room in stunned silence—until all hell broke loose. People clambered over each other, racing to flee the chapel, their faces horror stricken. The buck-toothed chiropractor vomited in the center aisle. The woman who had shushed them earlier sobbed uncontrollably, then stumbled and fell, shrieking as rushing feet pounded around her. People ran for any exit.

The Dreamers' cries resounded through the chaos. "He stole them! . . . betrayed . . . Nicole!"

Charlie wrapped his arms around a distraught Elinor. "It's not real. It's a dream. It doesn't mean anything," he tried to reassure his wife.

But Celeste knew it was more than that—the lilacs waving outside the window, the all-too-familiar hands tightening the twine, the sound of the woman, Rachel, fighting for her life. A recurring nightmare that may have actually happened.

"What the hell?" she yelled to Gloria over the noise.

"I don't know, but obviously that wasn't the plan!" Gloria yelled back, pulling her purple coat on and standing up.

Celeste stood, disoriented and wobbly. She wanted to run to Jake, but she couldn't find him as the crowd rushed the door.

"Wolfhard. He was here! I saw him in the back. Now he's gone!" Celeste was frantic.

"You saw him? Are you sure?"

"Yes, I'm sure! Come on! We can't let that Wolf guy get away!"

Gloria turned to Elinor and Charlie and said something Celeste couldn't hear, then kissed the top of Elinor's head.

"Hurry!" Celeste said.

"Where are we going?" Gloria called back.

"I don't know! I'm going out the way Nicole went! Maybe I can catch her. She knows something, I'm sure. Meet me out front and look for Jake! Please!"

As the crowd pushed and stumbled toward the two rear doors, Celeste charged up the stairs of the dais, where Sarabande still stood, stricken, mumbling to herself. Celeste rushed past her through the narrow opening by the organ, wondering if she'd find Nicole still there, hiding.

But the dark, narrow corridor was empty. A shaft of light illuminated the bottom of the stairs that led down to the kitchen. Grabbing the rickety banister, she clattered down two at a time, sliding on the slippery waxed linoleum as her feet hit the kitchen floor. No Nicole. Only the lingering scent of her jasmine perfume.

Outside, the pandemonium was startling. On the super-size screens hanging on the church's exterior, more horrendous dreams flashed: A pack of wild dogs chased down Burt from

Winzer's, tearing him to pieces. A shark flashed through blue waves, a pair of legs hanging from its jaws. Allegra, naked and gyrating up on the bar counter, while tiny men licked at her legs.

Outside, the clashing nightmarish projections overlapped on the giant screens, their horrible sounds still echoing through the streets of the usually tranquil Riverton Falls. Below them, on the lawn and on the sidewalks, people clung to each other. Others stood stupefied, unable to even close their mouths.

"Stolen dreams! Stolen dreams!" On the lawn, Bruce spun in frenzied circles yelling at the top of his lungs.

Celeste raced to the front of the building. She had to find Gloria. From the top of the stairs in front of the church, DeTouche and Pearl struggled to quell the craziness festering all around them, but they seemed as disoriented and confused as the rest of the horrified crowd. Multi-tasking even now, Pearl held her phone up to her ear with one hand and strained to direct people to calm down with the other. DeTouche blew his whistle, little lips pursed, cheeks bright pink with effort as he tried to make a dent amid the cries all around him. No one seemed to notice.

Suddenly, the screens froze. As if someone had hit a giant pause button, in one fell swoop the sounds, colors, and riotous motion all dissolved, leaving only one image—Larry's demonically smiling face, winking at them all.

CHAPTER THIRTY

CROW'S NEST

With frightened faces staring up at the leering Larry, the crowd now stood, stunned into silence, as still and mute as stone, as if an evil fairy had tapped each person with her wand. Celeste shook her head, trying to regain her own senses. She took a breath and began to walk among them all while keeping her eyes peeled for Jake, Wolfhard, and Nicole. Where had they gone?

Slowly, around her, the crowd began to stir and look around at each other, everyone drained and weak. Mourners from inside the church continued to stumble out the door, holding each other up as they came, as if they'd been through a hurricane. As she paused there taking it all in, Celeste picked out faces she knew: Charlie and Elinor, Bruce, Andrew, Ingrid, Bill, Karin, but no sign of the people she needed to find. She caught a quick glimpse of red hair. No, not Gloria. Allegra's hennaed topknot.

Celeste pushed her way through the mob and made it to the sidewalk in time to see the Saab nosing its way out of the parking lot next to the library onto Main. Swinging her arms in wide arcs, trying to make herself visible among the crush of hysterical funeral-goers rushing away from the church as fast as they could, Celeste signaled wildly to Gloria. Gloria angled quickly to the curb where Celeste stood, still flagging her down.

"Hurry up! Get in!"

"Oh my God, oh my God," said Celeste, flinging her pack in the backseat then jumping in next to Gloria. "That was my dream! Larry killed Rachel!"

"I just saw the Wolfman's car heading out of town with Nicole in the seat beside him! If we don't find out where he's taking her, she might be his next victim!"

"Taking her? You think he's kidnapped her?"

"After last night, I figure she's not going along willingly," Gloria said while Celeste buckled herself in for the ride. "What was going on in there, anyway?" asked Gloria, stepping on the gas and peeling away from the curb with a loud screech.

"God knows! But that was my dream! Or Rachel's dream. Or was it Larry's dream? I'm so confused!" Celeste bent over and put her head in her hands, shaking it from side to side.

"Something went really wrong in there, whatever it was. Did you see Sarabande's face?"

Celeste looked up, laughing now. "What about that brother of hers, Arun? Thought he was going to have a heart attack. Pearl said something about how those two had bought Larry's computer company, so they have to be in on it with the—what did you call him?—the Wolfman? And where does Jake fit into any of this?" Celeste looked at Gloria, waiting for an explanation.

"No idea, but right now, I need *you* to keep your eyes open for that car. I saw it heading up River Bend Road. That's our best bet right now. Hang on!" Gloria warned as she accelerated into the curve of the roundabout, tires squealing.

Celeste was thrown forward then back by the force of the spin. She shot a quick glance over at Gloria, noticing how hard her hands gripped the wheel. "Drive, sister, drive! We're going to get you, you bastard!"

Gloria shifted into high gear and sped up, roaring past the reservoir. "That's the Celeste I've been waiting to see! We can't let him get away! Hermann's the key to all this, has to be."

Then it hit Celeste like a hammer. Hermann. She pulled her pack onto her knees and rifled through it until she found what she was after, the card Adam had left on her porch. "The Hermit," she said. "*Hermann's* the Hermit! That's what Adam was trying to tell me."

"I thought Adam was the Hermit."

The two women fell silent, each trying in her own head to put the puzzle pieces together as they raced away from town. The road ahead was empty. No sign of the black SUV.

"How the hell are we ever going to find him? He could have gone anywhere," Celeste said, thinking of the dozen roads that led off River Bend as it headed out of town and turned to highway before hitting the uninhabited stretch of Leicester Woods.

"I have no idea. But keep your eyes open so I can drive. He's out here somewhere."

On the outskirts of town the road skimmed the West Branch River, running furiously now after a day of snow and freezing rain. Along its banks, bare trees pierced the gunmetal sky, and the familiar flock of crows perched like big black boots in the leafless branches above. The car zipped beneath them, stirring the air, and the crows flew up and off, their raucous caws stirring Celeste's thoughts. "Here! Turn right!" Celeste yelled.

The Saab swung sharply into the narrow, nearly invisible dirt drive, slowed to a crawl, and then stopped, idling there in what seemed like the middle of nowhere. As far as the two could see up the hill in front of them, boulders jutted like crooked teeth on the track ahead, a steep, rutted, dirt right-of-way flanked by a thick guard of tall red pines. "You're kidding. Here? Why here?" Gloria looked skeptical.

"Something Pearl said. Crow's Nest Lane, the address for Dreamscape Computing. A murder of crows. I don't know. I just have this feeling."

Gloria pulled over into a small clearing cut into the row of pines and turned off the engine. "There's no way this car is going to make it up there. Wish we had more than your 'feeling' to go on."

"Look." Celeste pointed at the fresh tire tracks swerving in and out among the boulders. Someone had gotten here right ahead of them, someone who knew how to navigate this treacherous drive.

"I don't know . . ." Gloria hesitated.

Celeste knew she should pay attention to the flurry of apprehension in her stomach, but her anger was stronger than her fear. "Chickening out just as things are getting good?"

"That's right! This guy has guns!" said Gloria.

"Yeah, but we don't even know if this is the right place. What if we sneak up the road, check out the scene to make sure?" Celeste was taking the lead now.

Gloria looked at her as if trying to figure out if her friend's bravado was just a way to shut down her own fear or if she actually believed that following this crazy gunman was a good idea. "Maybe we should wait until Pearl and DeTouche get here," she suggested.

"And what if they don't? At least if this *is* the place, we can call them."

Gloria pulled out her phone. "Nope. No service. Again. I'm not going up there unless I think they're behind us."

Celeste thought for moment. "I'm going to leave the cops a sign!"

She dashed back to the corner of the drive at the highway, zipped off her green vest, and hung it from a sturdy branch a few feet from the turn, hoping DeTouche and Pearl were out there looking for them. Maybe they had spotted Gloria's car racing away from the funeral and had remembered which way they'd gone. A long shot, she thought as she hurried back to Gloria. She hugged herself and rubbed her upper arms against the blast of cold wind. Damn! She'd forgotten her coat in the church.

Gloria was still standing by the car as Celeste ran back to her. Cautiously, they began picking their way around the boulders, heading deeper into the woods. No bullets came whizzing out of the forest in their direction. Side by side, hand in hand, the two women crept up the road, toward the bend a few yards ahead. Celeste's foot hit a loose rock and she stumbled, pulling them both to the ground. They sat for a few seconds, straining to hear the sound of any other cars, catching nothing but the intermittent cackling of the crows.

Back on their feet, they both breathed deeply and blew out streams of frozen air. They rounded the bend and stopped, hiding in the shadows of the trees. Up ahead, almost hidden, stood a cabin within a thick stand of evergreens. Orange pine needles lay in heaps around its foundation and covered the roof like thick shaggy shingles. A row of full-length picture windows faced the rocky path where they stood. The SUV was parked in front. This was the place all right.

"Can he see us?" Celeste whispered.

"Don't know."

The windows seemed to be covered completely by black curtains, shut tight against the light. They waited, watching for the slightest movement, a flick of the curtains, the sound of a door.

"I'm so scared I think I'm going to pee my pants," Gloria whispered in Celeste's ear.

Celeste looked at her, not sure which of them was more afraid. "I thought you were the brave one."

"Today it's your turn. But let's make a plan before we get any closer." Gloria's voice sounded tight as if she were forcing the words from her mouth.

"I figured you'd come looking for me." The voice behind them was as loud as a shot. They spun around and there he stood, a few feet away, the brown hoodie pulled tight around his cruel, skeletal face.

"Fell right into my trap, didn't you, ladies?" The slight rasp of his German accent rubbed against Celeste's nerves like sandpaper.

"Now move!" he commanded, shoving what felt distinctly like the barrel of a rifle into Celeste's lower back. "Into the house. Your friend is already waiting."

CHAPTER THIRTY-ONE

THE HERMIT

Wolfhard Hermann slammed the door behind his two captives. He pushed them roughly forward, plunging them into complete darkness. Terror rippled through Celeste. She grabbed Gloria's arm to steady herself, gripping a chunk of her felted sleeve to keep herself upright. Gloria tensed at her touch. The air was thick with stale cigarette smoke and spilt beer, like an early morning at Jackie-O's, back when you could still smoke in there.

Wolf flipped a switch. A table lamp blinked on but barely pierced the gloom. Celeste could see that they stood in a wood-paneled living room. On the opposite wall, black velvet drapes concealed the row of windows they'd seen from the outside, completely blocking out the daylight. Cobwebs clung to black iron curtain rods and had spread into the dark corners. In the center of the room, facing a fieldstone fireplace, a battered, pea-green couch and two lumpy-looking chairs hunkered around a dusty coffee table where a plastic ashtray overflowed with half-smoked butts.

"Have a seat," Wolf ordered, shoving Celeste and Gloria forward. Without daring to turn around, they marched obediently to the couch then sat side by side, clutching each other's hands. Silently, Wolf followed, his rifle pointing at them as he crossed the room. He leaned up against the fireplace piled high with cold ashes, left arm slung across the mantel, rifle tucked under his right. "Welcome to my humble abode. I think we're about to have some fun," he said, in his cruel, unctuous baritone.

"Yeah, right," said Celeste. "Some real fun." Gross as it seemed, she wished she could reach over and grab one of the butts. What she'd give for a cigarette! Instead she looked around the room, thinking that it did look like a hermit's house. Certainly not set up for entertaining guests. From under a door to the left of the fireplace, she noticed a faint sliver of light. From behind the door came a slight rustling and what sounded like mumbled groans.

She nudged Gloria and nodded toward the door. "Is that where you're hiding Nicole?" Celeste asked Wolf.

"Hmm, that's an interesting guess." Still holding the gun, Wolf crossed the room. "Let's just see what's behind door number one, shall we?" He turned the handle and pushed the door open a crack. Not Nicole. Pete, pacing the top rung of a chair, muttering and moaning in grief. Instead of emitting his familiar piercing squawks, he kept repeating, "Gone away, gone away," over and over.

"Where is she?" Celeste demanded, turning to the gaunt German. "I saw you drive away with her."

"Nicole? Ah, glad you asked." He pushed the door further. There she was, Nicole, in a far corner, on a rolling desk chair, hunched over, her sable hair cascading over her face, her long white gown now torn and stained with dirt, looking as if

Wolfhard had dragged her up the rocky path to this hidden cabin. On the desk behind Nicole was Larry's computer, the one Celeste had sat in front of every week for years. The Blue Wave logo, the one she'd seen floating in the wave, now floated around the monitor like a screen saver.

"Move!" Wolf ordered Nicole. "Get over there!" He pointed the rifle at the couch.

Nicole looked up. The bruises around her eyes were already darkening and traveling down to her high cheekbones. She pulled herself to her feet, slowly as if she were in pain, then shuffled toward the couch and sank down in the space Celeste and Gloria made between them.

"Ouch," she winced, reaching behind to rub her lower back. She must have taken a real beating when the truck flipped and probably more from Herr Hermann. Celeste surreptitiously squeezed Nicole's hand.

"Oh, quit your whining," said Wolf. "You should feel lucky you're still alive." He shifted the gun so that it pointed at the three of them huddled on the couch. "Now that you're here, you ladies are going to tell me why. Why you killed Larry."

Celeste stared at him. "*We* killed Larry? No, it was you! 'Her,' he said 'Her,' Hermann!"

Wolfhard glared at Celeste. "Stop with these games. Don't act so innocent. I saw you all there. In and out of Larry's house. First you, pretending to wait for your appointment. I go out back to Larry's workshop. I see you then, running away. I think, that girl's in a hurry. But I don't think much else. Until Larry calls me. He is scared. 'They know about Rachel,' he says."

"My dream," Celeste murmured.

Wolf didn't seem to hear her. "We needed to hide the computer. Twenty years of work on it. Our project ready to launch. Larry, he brings it into the workshop and I go to get my car. I come back maybe half an hour later and park behind the house. Then you," he pointed the barrel of the shotgun at Nicole, "I see with Jake. Jake puts you in his truck and I see you give him something. You take the truck. And Jake he is running away. I am then finding Larry on the floor, already bleeding. Then I know why Jake is going so fast away."

Now Celeste understood. Jake running down the street. Jake in the bar, trying to stop her from going back to Larry's. Cold sweat rolled down her back.

"I want to call the 911," Wolf went on, staring at Celeste's stricken face. "Larry, he tells me no, get away. But I cannot find the backup. What you," he pointed the barrel of the rifle at Nicole, "gave Jake, I then understand. And Larry, now I think he is not moving, he's dead. *Tot.*" Wolfhard's English was starting to disintegrate. He stepped back, into the shadows, his face strangely blank, all his rage contained in his voice and in the hands Celeste could see tighten on the gun. "And now you're going to pay."

"You're lying!" Celeste started to get to her feet, but Nicole pulled her back. "You're the one with Larry's computer, not us! Why do you think we had anything to do with this when it was you!"

"I am doing Larry's final wish. I am saving our project. I come out of Larry's house, someone calls my name. That dirty man. He says my name again and I know. That voice, even after so many years. Rowan. I think he knows about Rachel, what happened to her. He's part of your plan. I go fast to get away, then I see you," he glared at Celeste, "coming back and now I know. Four of you, four killers in this together!"

The front door crashed open. Chill air blasted through the room. Filling the doorframe in the late afternoon light, the black silhouette of a man, rifle aimed straight at Wolf. Celeste forced herself not to run to Jake.

"So, Herr Kelly, I am wondering when you are getting here. Come to save your girlfriend?" He inched the barrel of the rifle to the right so it pointed between Celeste's eyes. "Or your wife?" He swiveled slightly to the left to take aim at Nicole. "I doubt it was the dwarf over here, but you never know." He smirked as he pointed the gun at Gloria.

Gloria glared back. "Damn," she whispered, "now I did pee my pants."

"Let them go, Wolf. They didn't do anything to you." Jake stepped into the room and the door blew closed behind him with another bang.

"Let them go, Wolf," Hermann mimicked Jake in a crack ing falsetto. Then his voice shifted. "You ruined it all, didn't you? You killed Larry. You and your girlfriends. Didn't want to see him triumph. Couldn't bear that he is at last getting the rewards of all those years at Blue Wave. Leaving you and that crazy man out."

"Whadaya mean?" Gloria said shifting to the edge of the couch, ready to get up.

"Sit! Whoever you are. You," he lifted his chin toward Jake, his white forelock flopping back, "and your women and Rowan, you want to ruin us. You killed Larry, then sabotaged the Dreamscape. Twenty years we worked."

Celeste's stomach knotted. What was he saying? "But Larry said 'Her,'" Celeste croaked. "The Hermit, Hermann, you." If Wolfhard didn't do it . . .

Then in a flash, she understood. Not Wolfhard. Not Jake. Nicole. The scent of sweet perfume in Larry's waiting room. The woman's voice fighting with Larry. Her. Celeste turned to Nicole.

"It was you. *You* killed Larry."

Nicole nodded slowly, eyes downcast, not lifting her head.

"And Rowan, you killed him?" Celeste asked, looking at Jake. "Because he knew what Nicole had done?"

"No, that's . . ." Jake said, his eyes pleading with her to understand. He quietly took a step closer to Wolf.

"Jake didn't kill Rowan. If you love Jake, you know he couldn't kill anyone," Nicole said to Celeste, her voice hoarse and unsteady.

"That one, I did." Now all eyes turned to Wolfhard, backed up against the cold, empty fireplace. A dusty, desiccated Christmas cactus drooped on the mantel behind him. "I was there in Dreamland that night after Larry died. I heard your plans. I see the three of you, Nicole, Jake, Rowan, the dreams on the walls. But I never think you will destroy all the work, the work you did with Larry. It was yours too!" he looked from Jake to Nicole.

"No," Nicole said. "Our work died when you and Larry killed Rachel. I'd kept hoping, but now I know . . . the dream—"

"We—Larry and me—had to stop Rachel and Rowan. We knew they would build again their own Light House as soon as they got together. We could never match what those two could do. We had to keep them apart. For our Dreamscape Adventures!"

"Not for the Dreamscapes, not for anything but money." Nicole's face was twisted with grief and fury. "You, and those nasty Roy children, you never understood. Rachel and Rowan, they believed in the spirit."

Wolf took a step toward the couch.

"Not another step, Wolf," said Jake as he cocked his gun.

But Wolfhard kept moving forward, almost imperceptibly, as if daring Jake to shoot. "Now I'm finally going to get the rest of you. You won't stop me."

Letting go of Celeste's hand, Nicole staggered to her feet, her mud-spattered white gown tripping her slightly as she tried to step forward. They all watched as she regained her balance then stepped into the space between Wolf and Jake and their guns. Celeste held her breath and dug her fingers into the sofa cushion.

"Rowan knew what you were up to." Nicole stood stock still, looking straight at Wolf, forcing him to focus on her. "He'd hacked into Larry's computer years ago, trying to find out why Rachel had never come to meet him." Her voice was low and steady, her body rigid. "All these years, I believed Larry! That Rachel had run off to join Rowan. Until Rowan appeared in my living room a few weeks ago, out of his mind. Nothing like the brilliant man we knew in California. He told me what I hadn't wanted to see. About Larry's Dreamscape Adventures. He knew it was about to go live, and he knew he had to stop it. For Rachel. For all of us."

Tears ran down Nicole's bruised cheeks, and she winced as she wiped them away.

"Everything has been a lie and I've been part of it! I'd believed in Larry, in the Dreamscape, in our Dreamers. But when I talked to Rowan, I understood I'd been part of some scheme. Not magic. Not beauty, something ugly and dangerous. I was so entranced with being a queen, with my own power, I didn't see that I was his accomplice!" she said, her voice rising. "My heart had been torn into a million pieces. Grief for Rachel. For myself. For everyone I'd hurt." She turned away from Wolf toward Jake and swayed closer to the barrel of his gun. They looked into each other's eyes and Celeste could see the deep feeling that still connected them.

Tumbling down, Celeste thought.

A second gun was cocked.

"I didn't mean to hurt Larry. I only wanted to confront him, tell him I knew. But you know what he said?" Her voice surged with anger and her hands balled into tight fists at her side. "That he'd done it all for me! For me, he'd killed Rachel, so he and I could own her Dreamscapes. For me he'd stolen the dreams and Rowan's vision, so I would be impressed by his money. For me he'd taken your ring, Celeste! He didn't understand that Jake and I were done."

"All *scheisse*!" said Wolfhard. "You wanted to ruin it all. He leaves you out of his plans. That is why you murder him. You want his money." Wolf's voice was a poisonous hiss. "But you cannot stop our Dreamscape Adventures. We had Larry's computer full of dreams. And Rowan, he was nothing without Rachel." He looked straight at Nicole, a tic just below his left cheekbone starting to twitch.

"No! That's not it!" Nicole spun back to face him. "I didn't care about being part of the Dreamscape, making the money. Not anymore. No! I couldn't let him ruin any more lives! I had to stop him, but I didn't mean—"

The door crashed open. "Drop those guns—right now!" Pearl and DeTouche stepped into the room, pistols drawn. "Drop them and no one will get hurt."

"Feel the pain!" Pete flew straight at Wolf, pecking viciously at his white hair. At the first flurry of wings DeTouche reflexively dove forward and grabbed Wolf around the knees, knocking him to the floor. The bird flew about the room, screeching. Pearl karate-chopped Jake's outstretched arms, breaking his grasp. His rifle clattered to the floor. A shot ripped through the air. Nicole collapsed on the bare floor. A red stain spread down the front of her robe.

Jake lurched forward, almost stumbling over the bloodied Nicole. Then his arms were around Celeste, his face in her hair. "You're okay, you're okay," he whispered over and over as she pressed her face hard into his shoulder.

"Gloria!" Pearl called, her gun trained on Wolf.

"I'm good, don't worry!" she called reassuringly. "But Nicole! Help her!"

Slowly Nicole pushed herself up from the floor and leaned back against the couch. In her lap lay Pete, his feathers smeared with the blood that had soaked Nicole's robe. Pete's blood. Not hers.

"Pete!" she wailed, but the bird didn't stir.

CHAPTER THIRTY-TWO

UNDER RACHEL'S STARS

"Thank you all for being here," said Charlie, opening his arms to include the group gathered in the large downstairs room at Renaissance three days after the chaos of the funeral and shoot-out that followed. "I can't believe we're sitting here together this evening."

Celeste looked around at the two dozen or more people sitting in a circle on the floor, under Rachel's magical painting of the house. Most of the Doubters and Dreamers had known each other for years. They'd all been part of the Dreamscape at some point, like Celeste and Gloria. Larry's death had reunited them in shared grief and a sense of betrayal.

Bruce, Andrew, Angus and Barb, Wally DeTouche, and the other Dreamers sat in the circle on the floor, side by side with the Doubters, the very people they had ostracized, one by one, over the years at Dreamland. Celeste studied the group, glad that everyone was together. Like the happy ending to the scary fairy tale. Jake was by her side and Jean Pearl by Gloria's. Next to Charlie sat Elinor, her face a mask of grief, like those she'd carved into the standing stones outside. Across from her, Bill fidgeted, trying to balance on a meditation cushion.

"I told you, you should do yoga," Ingrid whispered loudly to her husband as he rubbed his aching knees.

The Dreamers had entered the house warily, but the Doubters had greeted their old friends with quiet smiles and long hugs, and the Dreamers had fallen into their arms like lost children who had finally found refuge. All they had known, everything they had believed in, was gone. They looked stunned, heartbroken, confused. Not only had they lost Larry, the preview of Dreamscape Adventures had forced them to face the fact that he'd duped them all. He'd stolen their dreams, the dreams they had entrusted to him over the years. For what? Money, power? All the things he'd told them did not matter if they lived fully in the dreams. The Doubters had been right about Larry and the Dreamscape all along. Yet none of the Doubters said "I told you so." None of them blamed the Dreamers for their blind obedience. They'd all been there themselves, and they knew better than anyone how hard it was to break away from Larry.

"The pain in this room is something we will carry forever," Charlie continued. "For better or worse, Larry has left his mark on each of us, and we will never be the same."

Charlie's guests looked at him, expectantly, waiting for words that would help them make sense of the last few days.

"I wish I could offer you solace or even an explanation for all that has happened. But Elinor and I can only offer this space and our wish that you will help each other as you search for your own answers."

"Your own truth," said Elinor. "And my truth is that I need to go to bed." She pushed herself to her feet and looked up at Rachel's painting of the house beneath the moon. Light from the flames in the fireplace flickered across her face. "Tomorrow the police begin the search for our daughter's body. Something I had hoped I'd never have to face." She walked slowly out of the room, head down, shuffling as if she'd aged overnight.

"I know you all have a lot to talk about, so I'll leave you too," said Charlie, awkwardly rising to his feet. "I want you all to know that as long as Elinor and I are here, you are welcome at Renaissance House."

He was silent for a moment, then added, "And there's something else. Tonight, I want us to think about Rowan and Rachel. What you saw in that church was stolen from them. A beautiful dream perverted into a monstrous money-making scheme." He looked around the room. "Tonight I want you to see what could have been if only Larry and Wolf hadn't let their greed get in the way. But love will always win. And because Rachel knew . . ." He looked down at the floor and paused. "Because she knew she wouldn't be here to give this gift to the world, she left us her most precious treasure. Jake and I," he looked over at Jake who sat on the floor with Celeste leaning back against his chest, "have preserved some of Rachel and Rowan's Light House images, and now I want to give them to you. A gift of peace, a gift left behind by two of the strongest hearts I have ever known. Please, lie back. Look up. I promise you comfort and hope."

Gloria, snuggled next to Jean Pearl, looked over at Jake and Celeste. "This is going to be good!" she said as the Dreamers and Doubters all followed Charlie's directions.

"No need to worry," said Charlie, responding to the murmurs of residual fear that crept around the room. "Randy, it's okay—you can lie down now too."

The lights went out. Around the circle, Doubters and Dreamers reached for each other's hands. Once again, images appeared on the walls and ceiling, as they had in the church three days earlier. This time, the entire room became the night sky.

Leaning back, looking up, Celeste surveyed the dark blue, star-studded heavens that suffused the room, reassured by the warmth of Jake's arm around her. Above them, like colorful constellations, floated the characters of Rachel's Dreamscape: Larry in his long red magician's robe, wand raised overhead in his left hand; Nicole, the Empress, stars twinkling in her golden crown; Rowan, the wandering Fool, smiling at his Angel. And there was Jake, the Knight in Shining Armor, and next to him she herself as a mermaid, her tail flashing silver and gold as cosmic waves flowed by. On the mermaid's left hand, Celeste noticed her sapphire engagement ring. It sparkled like moonlight on water.

"That's me!" Celeste sat up and gave Jake a gentle shove. "Rachel painted me into her Dreamscape? Twenty years ago? Even my ring?"

Jake pulled her back down and whispered in her ear, "How'd you think I recognized you when you fell into my arms at The Castaway?"

"You never told me that! I'd never have believed you anyway—it would've sounded like a really bad pick-up line," Celeste said. "I would have been out the door."

Jake squeezed her hand.

"So that's why Larry thought I looked familiar. Guess he finally put it together when you gave me that exact ring. Why he made the mermaid my totem." She curled up against Jake as all around them new images of mystical mountains, sparkling rivers, and soothing oceans came and went. These images, gifts left behind by Rachel and Rowan, acted like a balm to soothe wounds both old and new. Around Jake and Celeste, Doubters and Dreamers lay side by side, mesmerized. Wally DeTouche snored in the corner.

"Yup. Couldn't risk you turning me down from the get-go! But there's something I need to talk to you about. Outside. Under the real stars." Jake stood and helped Celeste to her feet. She grabbed her vest and followed him out onto the moonlit lawn.

"I still don't believe Nicole had no idea what Larry was up to. Do you?" Celeste asked, stamping her feet in the cold. She was nervous, not sure she wanted to hear what Jake had to say, so she led the conversation in her own direction.

"She didn't want to see. Like all those Dreamers. Like you," Jake answered.

Celeste waited for more.

"When Larry gave her your ring, he pushed her over the edge," he said.

"Drove her crazy." Joanie and Victor had been right about the crime of passion.

"Nicole's idea. The funeral sabotage, that private stash she found on the back-up she took. That's what we were doing at Dreamland that night. Didn't know Wolf was out there watching us. Wish we'd never left Rowan to finish up alone." Jake sighed and turned to face Celeste. "But it's over. For now. Out on bail, Nicole and I. Figured we weren't a flight risk, like Wolfhard. But there's something more important you and I have to do."

She brushed a lock of his hair off his forehead, then leaned in to kiss him. "What's more important than being right here, right now?"

"I know I might have to face some jail time for my role in this. I have no idea how long I'll be gone. But, Heavenly Celeste," Jake dropped to his knee, still holding her left hand, "will you wait for me? Not run away?"

"I'm not going anywhere," she answered. This time she meant it.

He reached into his shirt pocket, took out the ring, and slid it onto her finger, like he had on Hunger Mountain. The sapphire, the same deep blue of Rachel's cosmos, sparkled in the moonlight. "I love you. Please marry me."

Love at last! In her head, her parents cheered and clinked champagne flutes. *It's about time!* No words from Larry followed.

"Yes, yes, and always yes," Celeste answered, leaning into Jake's embrace. "There's nowhere else I'd rather be than under these stars with you, Jake Kelly."

THE END

Acknowledgments

Many thanks to all those who have encouraged and supported me through the many years it took to get this book from beginning to end. It was a long haul, and I couldn't have done it without you. Special gratitude goes to the stalwart members of my writing group: Shelagh Shapiro, Coleen Kearon, and Kathryn Guare who taught me how to write fiction; to Kathryn Davis and Eliza Thomas for understanding where I was headed and showing me how to get there; and to Tamar Cole and Janice Gary for coaching and cajoling me to the finish line. Thanks to the readers whose suggestions made this a better book than I could have written alone: Jeffrey Seeds, Tiffany Bluemle, Raymond Lowe, Mark Jacobs, Karen Gerdel, George Spaulding, and my mother, Topsy Simonson. Thanks to the Vermont Studio Center for the gift of time.

Copyeditor Mary Elder Jacobsen smoothed the rough edges with poetic sensibility. Officer Erica Schaller and Captain Neil Martel gave me insight into small-town police work. Phyllis Boltax and Bernie Lambek offered their lawyerly advice, and

Kevin Kerner of Three Penny Taproom taught me the vocabulary of bartending. Jack Donovan of Iris and the Burlington Virtual Reality Meet-Up were my patient tech teachers.

Thank you Brooke Warner, Caitlyn Levin, and everyone at She Writes Press for getting this book into the world and to my She Writes Press sisters, Rickey Gard Diamond and Mary Dingee Fillmore, for all their helpful wisdom. Kudos to Stephen McArthur and Danielle Hoffman of Rootstock Author Publicity and Promotion Services for their marketing expertise.

Thanks to my wonderful women's group, Carley Claghorn, Susan Darrah, Jo Romano, and Mary Beth Watt for sharing the journey with me for almost thirty years.

Finally, all my love and gratitude to my patient, loving husband Ethan Atkin for holding my hand through it all, and to our children: Daniel, Michelle, Theo, and Espen Otter; Nina Otter and Matthew Williams; Elisa Otter; Adley Atkin; and Kendra Atkin. You never stopped believing I could do it, so I did.

About the Author

Susan Z. Ritz grew up in Minnesota, but she left home to become a wandering scholar; she lived, studied, and worked as a social worker in Kenya, Japan, Singapore, and Indonesia in the 1970s. During the Carter Administration, she was a human rights lobbyist in Washington, DC, then moved to Dachau, Germany, the setting for her memoir in progress, *On the Edge of Dachau.*

For the past thirty years, she has lived with her husband and her three children in Montpelier, Vermont, where she has worked as a fundraiser, events coordinator, and philanthropic advisor for a wide range of nonprofit organizations, especially those promoting economic equality for women.

Writing, however, has always been her passion, and after receiving an MFA in creative nonfiction from Goucher College, she began writing for local publications, teaching creative writing to adults and high school students, and writing her first novel, *A Dream to Die For.*

Author photo © Chris Loomis

SELECTED TITLES FROM SHE WRITES PRESS

She Writes Press is an independent publishing company founded to serve women writers everywhere. Visit us at www.shewritespress.com.

The Lucidity Project by Abbey Campbell Cook. $16.95, 978-1-63152-032-7. After suffering from depression all her life, twenty-five-year-old Max Dorigan joins a mysterious research project on a Caribbean island, where she's introduced to the magical and healing world of lucid dreaming.

Provectus by M. L. Stover. $16.95, 978-1-63152-115-7. A science-based thriller that explores the potential effects of climate change on human evolution, *Provectus* asks a compelling question: What if human beings were on the endangered species list—were, in fact, living right alongside our replacements—but didn't know it yet?

The Tolling of Mercedes Bell by Jennifer Dwight. $18.95, 978-1-63152-070-9. When she meets a magnetic lawyer at her work, recently widowed Mercedes Bell unwittingly drinks a noxious cocktail of grief, legal intrigue, desire, and deception—but when she realizes that her life and her daughter's safety hang in the balance, she is jolted into action.

Last Seen by J. L. Doucette. $16.95, 978-1-63152-202-4. When a traumatized reporter goes missing in the Wyoming wilderness, the therapist who knows her secrets is drawn into the investigation—and she comes face-to-face with terrifying answers regarding her own difficult past.

Water On the Moon by Jean P. Moore. $16.95, 978-1-938314-61-2. When her home is destroyed in a freak accident, Lidia Raven, a divorced mother of two, is plunged into a mystery that involves her entire family.

The Great Bravura by Jill Dearman. $16.95, 978-1-63152-989-4. Who killed Susie—or did she actually disappear? *The Great Bravura*, a dashing lesbian magician living in a fantastical and noirish 1947 New York City, must solve this mystery—before she goes to the electric chair.